SONG FOR A BUTTERFLY

From a chrysalis to a butterfly...

When young paintress Megan Cresswell is left penniless in 1950, her choice is stark – struggle to pay the bills or find a husband. Choosing independence over a mother-in-law from hell, she takes an extra job with the wealthy Celia Bevington and discovers a different world to the one in the pottery factory, one of refinement and snobbery. The mystery of her inherited silver hairbrush reveals a shocking and tragic family secret – then Megan faces a heart-wrenching decision. She has found a deep love that could transform her life, but can she find the courage to follow her heart?

SONG FOR A BUTTERFLY

SONG FOR A BUTTERFLY

by

Margaret Kaine

Magna Large Print Books
Long Preston, North Yorkshire,
BD23 4ND, England.

British Library Cataloguing in Publication Data.

Kaine, Margaret
    Song for a butterfly.

    A catalogue record of this book is
    available from the British Library

    ISBN   978-0-7505-3642-4

Magna Large Print is an imprint of Library Magna Books Ltd.

Printed and bound in Great Britain by
T.J. (International) Ltd., Cornwall, PL28 8RW

Chapter One

A child screamed and hearing high pitched yelps, Megan began to run, until she saw just inside a side road two boys hurling stones at a tin can dragging down the tail of a petrified cowering puppy, its lead fastened to a lamp-post. A small girl was sobbing in terror as she clung to nearby brown wooden fencing. Incandescent with fury Megan dropped her shopping, and with a few long strides grabbed one of the boys roughly by the shoulder. 'What on earth do you think you're doing? Stop that this minute!' The other lad ignored her and lifted his arm to throw again so Megan reached out and caught him too. 'Don't you dare, you little ruffian! You ought to be ashamed of yourselves, the pair of you. Now clear off, or I'll fetch a policeman!'

Their knees grubby and scuffed beneath short trousers, they began to back off. Megan shouted, 'Go on, you heard me – scatter!' She wasn't sure which to comfort first, the frightened puppy or the devastated child. Tearful blue eyes won and she went over to the little girl. 'It's all right, sweetheart, they've gone now.' Megan drew her into a warm hug. 'There, it's all over. Come on, let's go and untie him.'

Gulping, the child nodded and seconds later the tin can removed and the quivering puppy free, Megan bent down and stroking the soft fur gazed down into its appealing velvety eyes. 'I don't think he's badly hurt. What's his name?'

'Laddie. I had him for my birthday.'

'Did you? You're very lucky – I wish I had a dog. And what's your name?'

'Julie. They snatched the lead from me,' her lip began to tremble. 'They're naughty boys, aren't they? I hate them.'

'They're very naughty boys, and you were a very brave girl!'

'Julie!' The shrill voice could have cracked a pane of glass. 'I told you to stay in front of the house!' Megan looked up to see a young woman hurrying towards them, her harassed face full of anger, but her expression soon changed to one of anxiety and concern as she saw her daughter's distressed and blotchy face. 'Whatever's happened?'

Julie ran to hide her face in her mother's apron. 'It wasn't my fault, they were bigger than me!'

Swiftly Megan related the scene.

'Of all the cruel things ... do you know who they were, Julie?'

She nodded.

'Right we'll see what your dad has to say about this. They want a damn good hiding!' She turned to Megan. 'It's a good thing you came along, I can't thank you enough. And what do you say, Julie?'

'Thank you!' Julie gave a wavering smile and before collecting her bulky string shopping bags Megan watched them go, the puppy now scampering along the pavement. After a morning's work in a potbank – then hurrying home to see to her mother, these shopping trips late on Saturday when the stallholders in Longton Market Hall had marked prices down, left little time for Megan to do anything else. What would she have done if she'd had a choice? On a sunny day like this it would have been wonderful to spend the afternoon in the park, strolling and perhaps reading beneath the shade of a tree, but her only hope of that was in a fantasy world.

'Is that you, Megan?' Ellen's voice drifted down the stairs as soon as the front door opened.

'Yes, Mum. I'll be up in a minute with your tea.' Beginning to unpack her shopping, Megan discovered that their eggs – still rationed in 1951 – were broken, their runny contents hopelessly mixed with bits of eggshell. 'Damn!' The expletive was muttered beneath her breath, even now her father's influence still lingered. Well, she couldn't blame anyone else, she should have been more careful instead of just dumping the bags on the pavement; her mother needed all the nourishment she could get. Megan tipped the mess into the rubbish bin and as she waited for the kettle to boil, began to sing, *'I dream of Jeannie with the light brown hair'*, knowing that lying in the silent room upstairs Ellen would hear the lilting tune. It had been her mother's one act of defiance against her strict husband's wishes, her love of singing popular songs instead of only hymns. As for Megan herself, how many times had she been on the brink of rebelling against him, of going against the teachings of the chapel? She'd longed to go dancing, to have a boyfriend like other girls of her age. But that would have

9

meant rows in the house and not only had her mother's health been poor, she had always found any sort of confrontation so distressing that Megan hadn't had the heart to upset her.

It was in the early hours of Sunday morning that Megan suddenly woke up. Drowsily she wondered what had disturbed her, and then she heard the faint and strange sound. With her heart hammering in her chest she leapt out of bed to find Ellen fighting for breath, a harsh rasping coming from her lungs and in that one moment Megan knew. And saw that same terrifying knowledge in her mother's desperate eyes.

'I'll fetch the doctor!' And then Megan was running again, down the stairs to grab her coat and purse; only now it was not to rescue a puppy but to rush fearful and despairing into the dark night and to the nearest 'phone box.

'Beautiful dreamer...' the poignant words rang out sweet and true and as she brushed Ellen's long greying hair and gently buttoned up the collar of her thin cotton nightdress, Megan had no qualms about singing at such a time; Stephen Foster had been her mother's favourite composer. Then going over to the dressing table where Ellen's treasured silver-backed hairbrush lay gleaming in the early morning light, Megan wondered yet again why her mother had never used the beautiful object, always saying, 'Your father gave it to me and it has sentimental value, not that I'm telling you why. And I've told you – once you come of age, it's yours.' Now Megan picked it up and hesitated, after all it was the only

10

item of value in the house. But grief and compassion won. Ellen had loved it, and going back to the bed with a last caring gesture Megan placed the hairbrush carefully between her mother's pale folded hands. Then she turned to the window where before finally leaving, the doctor had closed the cheap rayon curtains. In defiance Megan had flung them back wanting sunlight to flood into the room, to bathe in warmth for one last time the woman who had borne and nurtured her. But now with her task finished and knowing that Ellen would have hated to flout convention, Megan once again shut out the light

The woman waiting below looked up with relief as at last she heard Megan's footsteps on the steep stairs. The buxom, comfortable looking Clarice Bath seeing that her young neighbour was struggling to hold back tears said, 'The undertaker shouldn't be long, love. They're very good at the Co-op.'

'At least we've got a plot in the cemetery.' Megan's father had died only two years previously in 1949. 'I never thought I'd lose Mum as well – at least not so soon.'

Clarice gazed at Megan with sympathy. Ellen Cresswell had never been strong, the result of a childhood spent in a damp cottage in Goms Mill. But no matter how the doctor waffled on about pneumonia, it was a broken heart that had killed Megan's mother – Clarice would stake her life on it. Ellen had adored that solemn husband of hers, but between her parents' strict religious views and the dutiful care of her mother, Clarice had seen this girl's youth slowly strangled. And those

11

were years that could never be recovered. 'You are all right for money? I mean – you've got enough to bury her?'

Megan nodded. 'You've no need to worry, I'll manage fine.'

Clarice hauled herself to her feet. 'Well, I'd better be getting back.' She paused and said gently, 'Your Mum had a good life on the whole, love. Try and remember that.' But when she reached the door, Clarice wasn't sure that was true. She had rarely come into this house; the Cresswells hadn't welcomed visitors and had been fiercely protective of their privacy. And what a dreary place it was; there wasn't a splash of colour anywhere. Both armchairs had scratched and scuffed wooden arms and flattened brown velveteen cushions, the pegged rug that rested on faded beige linoleum before a pitted brass fender was almost threadbare. A square dining table with bulbous legs in the centre of the room was covered with a brown chenille cloth, while a dark wood sideboard displayed merely a couple of Staffordshire dogs and a heavy glass vase filled with faded paper flowers. The house mustn't have changed for years. Clarice hated to leave Megan alone there. But then she thought with a sigh, the girl would have to get used to it because she had no other choice.

It was much later and not until after the undertaker had left, that Megan eventually went into the kitchen. Cutting two rounds of bread she placed them beneath the heated grill and stared unseeingly at the fat-splashed wall behind the grey mottled stove. This small house was the only home she had ever known. And as she waited for her toast to brown, she could see the future stretching bleakly before her; one of a mere existence in this cramped kitchen with its chipped sink, wooden draining board and washing copper in one corner. And now in addition to her grief there was fear, because Megan was realistic enough to know that she could be in danger of losing even this.

It was not until a few weeks later that Megan at last told Clarice of her desperation. They were sitting by Clarice's cosy hearth, where because of the late summer chill, there was a warm fire. She always had a plentiful supply of coal because her husband was a miner at the nearby Florence Colliery. Tonight Tom had gone off to a darts match at the Dunrobin public house and they both knew that he wouldn't be home until after closing time.

'I don't know what I'm going to do,' Megan said in a voice tight with strain. 'Mum's pension made such a difference. My wages will cover the rent and bills, but food will be a constant struggle, and there'll be nothing left for anything else.'

'The pottery industry's very low paid, especially for women – everyone knows that,' Clarice said. She frowned. As the daughter of a sitting tenant at least the girl had a roof over her head, but that wouldn't last long if she fell behind with the rent. Suppose she was ill and couldn't work? There were no relatives, nobody she could turn to. 'I don't suppose there are any savings?' she said, 'I don't want to pry love, but...'

Megan shook her head. 'Dad had a bit in the Post Office, but after he died we had to use it. And I've only got a few pounds in.' She glanced across at Clarice and said, 'I did wonder if I could get a better-paid job, in an office or something?'

'I doubt it. You need qualifications for that.'

Megan thought with bitterness that if she'd been allowed to stay on at school, then that wouldn't have been a problem. She'd accepted having to leave at fourteen, knowing how sorely her wage was needed, although the prospect of working at the same hardware shop as her father – which he was insisting on – had appalled her. At least she'd stood up to him that time, although when she'd flatly refused to fall in with his wishes, saying that she'd arranged to go with her friend Audrey to 'work on the pots', he'd been furious. But as Audrey's mother who was a cup handler had already 'spoken' for the two girls, even Les Cresswell had to accept defeat.

'I've only ever worked in the decorating shop,' she said. 'Anyway, it was my own choice so I can't complain.'

'But you still like your work as a paintress?'

'Yes, I suppose I do really.' She laughed. 'Do you remember how I used paint on white doilies on a piece of newspaper on your table? Maybe I knew all along where I'd end up. I get on well with the girls as well. We have many a good laugh and a singsong. So at least I get plenty of company.'

Clarice was smiling. 'It's funny isn't it, how everyone refers to women on a potbank as 'girls', no matter how old they are.'

14

Megan smiled. 'And the term 'potbank', that's local as well. Anyone else would call them factories.'

'You know you're an enameller,' Clarice said, 'but I've never really understood what that entailed. There's a difference isn't there, between that and a freehand paintress.'

'A freehand paintress is paid more! No, what I do is to follow a design. I have a sample and then when the ware has been glazed, I apply some of the colours to the pattern. For example I might fill in the petals on a flower after the girl next to me had painted in the centre.'

'Oh, I see.' Clarice smiled at her and leaned forward to poke the fire. 'Well, at least you're looking better than when you came in. It always helps to talk to someone.'

'Thanks Clarice, I don't know what I'd do without you.'

There was a short silence then Megan said, 'Anyway, that's enough about my problems. Tell me how your Avril is.'

Clarice grimaced. 'Not so good. She's having a hard time with this pregnancy. I told her four kids was enough, but would she listen? Mind you, I blame that husband of hers.' Her tone sharpened, 'As she says, if it stands up he thinks he has to use it!' Clarice clasped a hand to her mouth in dismay. 'Sorry, love.'

Megan smiled. 'Don't worry, I've heard worse.'

I bet it wasn't at home, Clarice thought. There would have been no coarse talk or swearing in Les Cresswell's household. But now she felt worried as she gazed at his daughter. Perhaps the girl would be able to manage, but she doubted it. Even by scrimping and saving, she'd struggle.

Megan stared with despondence into the fire. How she wished she had some relatives to turn to, but Ellen had been an only child. Her father had died at the Battle of Mons, and four years later her mother in the Spanish flu epidemic of 1918. Les never talked of his family. Any questions from Megan as a child had been rebuffed. 'There's nobody for you to worry about.' His tone had been sharp and she'd known better than to ask him again.

'You know our family doesn't seem to have much luck,' Megan said eventually.

Clarice who was darning Tom's socks, snipped the end of her wool, and inserted the needle back into its pincushion. 'You make your own luck in this life. Oh, I know it all depends on the cards you're dealt. But with a bit of effort you can sometimes turn them into a winning hand.' Clarice put her mending down. 'For a start, you could make more of yourself.' There, she'd said the words she'd wanted to say for years. She rolled up the newly darned grey socks and put them to one side. 'Why do you always wear such dull colours? They just wash you out. And your hair! It's lovely and dark but the way you wear it...' Clarice decided that it wasn't the time for tact. 'It's more suitable for a schoolgirl than for a young woman of twenty. You should lose that parting in the middle for a start!'

'It's neat!' Megan said defensively. She didn't add that her father had held strong views about vanity.

'And so it is, for kids! Look at the young princesses – why don't you try your hair like theirs.' Clarice was growing impatient. 'You've got your whole life before you, love. Do something with it, for God's sake! Live it your own way, not the way your parents wanted you to. Go to the hairdressers, try a bit of make-up. If you'd been like all the other girls and gone out enjoying yourself, you would have done it long before this. Get yourself out there ... you never know who you might meet!'

Megan was again staring into the glowing embers of the fire, seeing before her an unwelcome image of a penny-pinching future and a lonely one. She knew what Clarice was hinting at, of course she did. But was she ready to face the obvious solution – one that might cause her to lose her new-found independence and freedom?

Chapter Two

A week later, Megan's expression was obstinate as she sat facing her other next-door neighbour, the tense but efficient Rita Forrester. It had been Clarice who had suggested including her in the master plan to find a new life for Megan. 'You'll need all the help you can get now you're on your own, so it's best to include her. Anyway, three heads are better than two.'

But now both women were staring at her with frustration. Eventually, Rita said, 'Well, nobody's

17

going to come knocking at the door.'

Megan said swiftly, 'I know Rita! But as for going dancing, much as I'd like to, I haven't got anyone to go with. And I can hardly go on my own, especially when I've never been before.'

And we all know who stopped you, Rita thought with irritation. Religion could be taken too far. There were plenty of chapel-goers who weren't nearly so strict; her late cousin Fred for one, even though he'd believed strongly in temperance. Her husband Jack had grumbled for days after Fred's funeral. 'I mean,' he said, 'expecting folk to stand in a cold, wet churchyard, and not even a glass of sherry to look forward to!' Rita herself was Church of England. She went twice a year, once to the Harvest Supper and then to see the crib at Christmas and always did her Christian duty, giving to charity when she could, even if it was only a few pennies in a collection box. And in her opinion, that was enough religion for anyone.

'Is there nobody at work you could go with?'

Megan shook her head. 'I'm good friends with the girls, but they're all older than me and mostly married. Audrey was the only one my age, and now she's moved to Wales...'

'What about the girls you knew at school?'

Megan thought about how she and Audrey had been such close friends. Too close she realised now, allowing their shared link with the chapel to isolate them from the others. She gave a shrug. 'Most of them are married, some even with babies.'

'Well, we'll have to think of something,' Rita said. 'But meantime there's no point in your going

18

anywhere wearing dowdy stuff like that.'

Clarice winced. Rita was known for her plain speaking but surely even she could have put it more kindly.

Stung, Megan looked down at the grey twin-set she was wearing. Hair and make-up was one thing, but she couldn't afford to buy a load of new clothes.

But Rita was in full flow. 'It's that drab it's more suited to an old woman than a young one. Listen – you know my niece Shirley?'

'Yes, of course.'

'Well, she's put a bit of weight on – a lot to be honest. I bet she's got quite a few things she can't get into any more.' Rita held up a hand. 'Don't look like that! I know she can dress a bit tarty ... her mother's told her so, but it's her life when all's said and done!'

Megan stared at her, remembering how she'd asked for a blue cardigan but instead Ellen had brought home the grey twinset from the market saying that it was more practical. Shirley had had the backbone to stand up to her parents, to dress how she chose – why hadn't she? But then, Megan thought grimly, Shirley hadn't lived in the Cresswell household.

'And our Alan's girl, Debra, has just started at that hairdressers in Chaplin Road,' Clarice was saying. 'They won't let her loose with a pair of scissors yet, but she's dying to have a go. How about if I ask her to come and see you? She might be able to do something with your hair, and I bet she'd cut it for nothing – just for the experience.'

Megan had always cut her own hair, peering in

19

the small mirror in her bedroom, trimming it with the kitchen scissors. But it did always seem to hang limply... 'Are you sure she wouldn't mind?'

'She'll be glad to.' Clarice breathed a sigh of relief. 'Well, at least we've made a start. Now I don't know about you two, but I could kill a cuppa.'

Obligingly, Megan got up and went into the kitchen. As she waited for the kettle to boil, she slumped back against the sink. Even after her mental struggle she couldn't believe what she was planning to do. Not that she'd let on to Clarice and Rita; they thought they were encouraging her simply to go out and enjoy herself, make new friends, maybe even find a boyfriend. Whereas Megan knew that her real intention was to blatantly search for someone to marry. Wanting a husband so that he could give her a more comfortable life could be interpreted as a respectable form of prostitution. But hadn't upper class girls always done it? Was it any less acceptable just because she was poor? But she wasn't going to marry anyone unless she loved them. She wasn't that desperate!

In the sitting room Clarice was looking at Rita for reassurance. 'You don't think we're being too hard on her? I mean, it's a bit soon after...'

Rita shook her head. 'No. It'll do her good to have something else to think about. Besides, you know as well as I do that she's going to be really struggling for money – and soon. She can't afford to mess about. You've never actually said to her have you, what we're really after?'

'For her to get married you mean?'

Rita nodded. 'I can't see any other way round it. We both know how little money there is coming in.'

'I think it best not to put it into words. We don't want it to look as if we're interfering.' She caught what she took as an 'old-fashioned' look from Rita and said, 'Well, we're not really, just...'

They both laughed, and then Rita said, 'How could Les and Ellen not have any life insurance – not a single penny?'

'I know – it beggars belief. Ellen wouldn't even pay into a Christmas club. I suppose a burial policy was different, at least Megan had a payout from that.'

Clarice nodded. 'Nobody wants a pauper's grave.' She paused. 'You know we'll have to turn this chapel business to our advantage.'

'How d'you mean?'

'Sssh!' Clarice turned as Megan came back into the room with a tray.

'Sorry,' she said, 'I've run out of biscuits.'

Rita and Clarice exchanged knowing glances, followed by silence as the serious business of pouring and drinking tea took place. Then, Clarice put her cup down on to the saucer with a clatter. 'Right,' she said. 'I've got something to say.'

Megan looked across at her, wariness in her eyes. 'No need to worry, girl,' Clarice said. 'It's just that where we've been going wrong, is in forgetting that you don't do the same things as other young people.'

'Perhaps you'd let us know what you're on about, Clarice!' Rita, who prided herself on her smart appearance and secretly bleached her hair, raised her finely plucked eyebrows.

'Well, it stands to reason, doesn't it? If Megan wants to go out and make new friends, and she won't go dancing – at least not until she's found someone to go with – then there's only one alternative.'

Two pairs of puzzled eyes stared at her.

'Church,' Clarice said.

'Church?' Two voices echoed.

'Yes, church or chapel or whatever you want to call it!'

'But I go all the time, I know everyone there,' Megan protested.

'There's more than one chapel, love. You always go to the same one, but there are lots of others. Go to them all. Have a look around the congregations. I'm sure you'll soon find a friend, someone to go out with.'

'Good Lord!' Rita said, 'You'll be asking her to become a Jehovah's Witness next!'

'There's nothing wrong with Jehovah's Witnesses,' Clarice retorted. 'I used to work with one – a very decent woman. Tom nearly always brings one of their Watch Tower magazines back on a Friday night. I can't see any harm in them myself.' Clarice hadn't got any religious allegiance, but considered herself a better Christian than some, who in her opinion only went to church to show off their best clothes. Fashion didn't interest her. She considered that she'd reached the age when to be a cosy mother and grandmother should be enough for any woman.

Megan was staring at them both. What if her father would have been against her attending any other chapel than their own? Why shouldn't she? After all what Clarice said did make sense.

Megan was discovering the heady fact that now she could do exactly what she wanted. Only the day before, remembering Clarice's advice, she'd gone into Woolworth's to stand before the cosmetics counter. The display of make-up was bewildering and eventually an assistant, young and blonde with a bright smile, had asked if she needed help.

'I thought perhaps a lipstick?' Megan said.

'This one's very popular at the moment,' the girl said encouragingly. She picked up a shiny gilt tube and expertly twisted it to show a tip of vivid red.

Megan stared at it. The term 'scarlet woman,' came into her mind. 'Perhaps a bit bright?' she said doubtfully.

The girl gazed at her for one long moment. 'Try this one,' she said, 'It would suit you, being dark.' She showed Megan a soft pink. 'Give me your hand,' she slaked a smudge on the inside of Megan's wrist. 'Go to the door if you like, so you can see it in daylight.'

Megan walked out to the pavement and held up her wrist. Deciding she liked the colour she went back into the shop, and after being reassured that Outdoor Girl was a good brand, handed over her money. But so far, apart from trying it on in her bedroom, she hadn't used it. Her father's words, 'Paint and powder have no place in a decent family', kept echoing in her mind. Ellen's own skin, carefully preserved with Pond's Cold Cream, had been one of pale modesty. At one

23

time Megan had experimented with pinching her cheeks and biting her lips to redden them, but the effect had been so transient, that it hardly seemed worth the effort. In any case, who had there been to see her? Visitors to the house were few, and at work there was nobody she cared to try and impress. The men on the pot bank liked girls who flirted and joked with them, gave them 'come hither' looks, then slapped them down if they overstepped the mark. Megan was fully aware that they considered her quiet attitude boring.

And suddenly as Clarice smiled at her with encouragement, Megan couldn't wait to begin, to discover just what fate had to offer. It *was* time that she changed and after all, didn't she now have the freedom to do so?

Chapter Three

If this, Megan thought, had been a story in a novel then the man who had arrived late and sat beside her in the back pew at the unfamiliar chapel, would have been young and handsome, rather than approaching seventy. Megan loved reading, at least the Cresswell household had believed in books and she was familiar with authors such as Charles Dickens, Jane Austen, the Brontës and other writers Les considered to portray a moral view of life. Reading, he told her, was a form of self-education, and he believed in that too. But while some of the girls at the pot bank borrowed books from the public library, Ellen had been firmly against it. Cleanliness was next to Godliness in her opinion, and as she pointed out, you never knew where the books had been. Just think of Snow White, she said. Snow White was Ellen's nickname for a woman who lived in the next street whose toddler waddled about wearing a dirty vest and no nappy. While her dingy net curtains scandalised the whole neighbourhood. And as a result although she passed it nearly every day, Megan had never been inside Longton Library.

Now, back home and after failing to make a tiny lamb chop, mashed potatoes and a tin of garden peas resemble in any way the Sunday roast she'd been used to, Megan was just finishing the washing up when Clarice came round. 'I can't stop long,' she said as she came in. 'But I'm dying to know how you got on this morning.'

'I did go to a different chapel,' Megan told her, 'but it was useless.'

'What, no possible friends at all?'

Megan shook her head. 'There were two girls of my age but they both had boyfriends with them.' And she thought, I didn't see a single possible husband ... she looked at the woman who always wore her hair in the same way; scraped into a bun, its brown only lightly streaked with grey, and suddenly found her eyes filling with tears. 'Just look at me – again!' she said. 'I sometimes wonder if it will ever stop.'

'It will love,' Clarice reassured her. 'Time's a great healer.'

Megan had been told that so many times over

the past few weeks that she could only hope that like so many others, the old saying was based on truth.

When the appointed evening arrived and the expected knock at the door came, Megan's stomach knotted with nerves. She had never been into a hairdressing salon although she'd often seen through their windows women sitting under hooded hairdryers, their tortured scalps covered by hairnets. Ellen had considered it vanity to pay someone to keep your hair neat. She'd worn her own long hair in a coronet of plaits and until Megan was old enough to tend to her own, had cut her daughter's hair herself.

Slim and perky, the fifteen year old girl smiled brightly at her through crimson lipstick. 'I'm Debra! Gran asked me to come.' Tottering on high heels, she followed Megan into the living room where in readiness sheets of newspaper were spread on the floor around one of the dining chairs.

'This is really kind of you,' Megan said, desperately hoping she knew what she was doing. She looked so *young!*

'I'm looking forward to it.' Debra grinned at her. 'I've only cut our Mary's hair so far, and she's just a kid. It'll be a real challenge to cut yours.' She opened her shopping bag and put on the table a spotless comb, hairbrush, scissors, pink plastic hair rollers and a bottle of setting lotion. 'Come on – let's have a good look at you, then.'

With an inward grin at her bossiness, Megan

obediently sat on the chair while Debra stood before her, her eyes full of incredulity. 'And you've always worn your hair like this – held back with two hair grips and with that centre parting?'

'Yes, ever since I can remember.' Megan was beginning to feel embarrassed.

'And what do you rinse it with?'

'Just warm water.'

'I rinse mine in vinegar – it gives it a lovely shine.'

Looking at Debra's swinging ponytail, Megan had to admit that was true.

'Have you got any magazines?' Debra looked disparagingly around the tidy room, 'You know, "Woman's Weekly" or anything?'

'I might have an old one. Mum used to like the knitting patterns. Hang on a minute.' Megan went to lift one of the seat cushions on the armchair. 'Yes, here's one.'

Debra took it from her and began to flick through the pages, glancing at the illustrations. 'What about this?' Her brown eyes narrowed in concentration.

Megan looked in astonishment at the image of a glamorous young woman. 'You mean you could make mine look like that?'

'I can have a go. I do watch the stylists a lot.' She was obviously itching to begin and Megan laughed.

'Go on, then.'

'I'll have to wash it first,' Debra told her. 'You get a better cut when it's wet. Have you got a towel?'

When they went into the kitchen Debra was so

horrified to find that Megan used a block of Sunlight soap to wash her hair that she insisted on going to ask Clarice if she could borrow some Amami shampoo. Minutes later Megan, enjoying the novelty of scented foam and her scalp being massaged couldn't believe how relaxing it was. But it was a shock when Debra tipped the pungent smelling jug of diluted malt vinegar over her head and she had visions of ending up smelling like a fish and chip shop.

The next thirty minutes were anxious ones as back in the sitting room, Debra worked in complete silence. She took a long time, hesitantly snipping away, walking in circles around her, asking Megan to bend her head as she trimmed the back. Then at last she stopped, combed through the result then after applying pungent setting lotion, wound the ends around the pink rollers.

'All right, that's it.'

'Thank you Debra.' Megan tried to hide her alarm at the amount of hair on the sheets of newspaper as she bundled them up to take out to the dustbin and came back carrying two glasses of Tizer.

Debra was sitting in one of the armchairs and staring around, 'Your house looks so different from my Gran's.'

'Yes, I know,' Megan said, and added awkwardly, 'it was my parent's taste, not mine.' She handed Debra a drink and sat opposite. She's such a pretty girl, she thought but Megan dreaded to think how Les would have reacted if *she'd* worn make-up at such a young age. Or even any age.

'Gran says you read books,' Debra said, giving her a curious glance. 'I've never read one myself.'

Megan stared at her in surprise. 'Didn't you have any as a child?'

Debra shook her head. 'I used to get the Girl's Crystal Annual at Christmas. But I've never read a proper book – not all the way through. I like magazines though. We have them at the salon, and I always read one in my break. I like the love stories.' Debra looked a bit sheepish. 'Do you mind my saying something?'

Megan laughed. She found she really liked this young girl. 'I've got a feeling you will anyway.'

Debra grinned. 'You catch on fast! No, it's just that when I first came in, when I first saw you, do you know what I thought?'

'I daren't think!'

'I wondered why you don't wear any make-up; apart from lipstick I mean, and if you don't mind my saying so you don't put enough on. I know you're religious and all that,' Debra went on, 'but a bit of Creme Puff wouldn't do any harm, surely? Look, let me try you with a bit of mine.'

As Megan submitted to having her cheeks dabbed, Debra regaled her with hilarious stories about some of the clients who attended the salon – mentioning no names – but with enough mimicry for Megan to recognise at least one. As their laughter filled the room, she even forgot to feel anxious about her hair, until eventually Debra tested one of Megan's rollers. 'Another twenty minutes then I think we can chance it. You wait, you won't believe the transformation!'

Chapter Four

The following morning at seven-thirty, Megan left the house and began to make her way to work, following others walking hurriedly along the pavement to avoid being late and losing their weekly bonus. She turned right to walk up a short street, and then through the small graveyard of St James's Church. She liked this part of her daily journey, it was so peaceful and she'd become familiar with many of the names on the old gravestones lining her path. Then she crossed over the main road to make her way to the china factory where she worked and going beneath the archway, breathed in the familiar smell of clay and glaze as she punched her card into the time-clock by the side of the lodge office. The gateman, taciturn with a drooping grey moustache answered her greeting, 'Morning, Eric,' with his usual absent nod. Megan walked further on into the yard and began to go up the outside wooden steps to the door which led into the decorating shop. When the wolf-whistle came, she simply carried on.

'Oh, I see – stuck-up are yer?' came the shout and with astonishment she swivelled to stare across to where a middle-aged man in brown overalls stood in the opening of the packing shed. 'Bloody 'ell, Megan – it's you!'

'Yes it is, Frank.' Megan tilted her head as she'd

seen the other girls do. 'What of it?'

'Good fer you, chuck, that's all. You look smashing.'

'Thank you!' Megan felt her colour rise as she opened the door and going inside silently began to walk towards her locker.

There was a sudden lull in the usual morning grumbles. Then Lizzie, a narrow-featured woman with frizzy grey hair called, 'Blow me down with a feather! If it isn't Cinderella! When did yer fairy godmother come, Megan?' She grinned. 'It's lovely duck, just lovely.'

One of the gilders said, 'Whoever did it, you can send her round to me any day!'

And that was how it continued; when Megan went to hang her coat in her locker she even saw the under-manager glance with astonishment over his shoulder.

Later, Clarice was glowing with triumph and pride. 'Our Debra's really come up trumps,' she said, 'don't you think so, Rita.'

Rita was still gazing at Megan. 'It's a blooming miracle!'

Megan went to the round bevelled mirror which hung on a chrome chain over the fireplace and looked yet again at her reflection. 'I would never have believed it could make such a difference.' Her hair, instead of hanging limply now looked thicker and curved softly in a bob. The school-girlish centre parting was disguised by a technique that Debra had shown her.

'When you do your hair, lift the front strands and gently comb down the back,' she said. 'It raises the roots you see. It's going to be all the

31

rage in the future, back-combing is – according to Marlene.' Marlene was the glamorous owner of the hairdressing salon and Debra's idol.

Rita held out a brown paper parcel. 'Shirley's sent this for you, but I haven't a clue what's in there.'

Megan took it from her, undid the string and set it aside to be used another time. Then she drew out a powder blue sweater and held it doubtfully before her. 'I think it might be a bit small.'

Clarice and Rita exchanged glances. 'It'll show off your figure then,' Rita said briskly.

'Look love,' Clarice said. 'God gave you a bust for a reason. I don't know about Rita, but I haven't a clue what you've got under all those baggy clothes you wear. Go on, at least try it on.'

'What else is there?' Rita leaned forward to explore the parcel. She took out a straight navy skirt with a split up the back. 'This is nice – I remember Shirley wearing this. It wouldn't go anywhere near her now. Look, there's a blouse as well.' She shook out a pink and white striped seersucker blouse.

Megan looked down at her black cardigan. She remembered Ellen knitting it, complaining that working with black wool gave her a headache. 'But isn't it a bit soon to...?'

Clarice shook her head. 'It's been nearly three months now, love. Hardly anyone stays in mourning these days – not for long anyway.'

Rita agreed. 'Those days have gone. I can remember my grandma wearing black for a year when she was widowed. I was only a kid and what with her long skirts and pale face, she used to frighten me to death.'

Megan looked at the clothes again. She would have preferred to be on her own when trying them on, but seeing the expectancy on the two faces before her, knew she had no alternative but to go upstairs to her bedroom.

Rita turned to Clarice and offered her a cigarette. She shook her head. 'No, thanks, I've given up – it's been two weeks now.'

'Well done. What's brought that on?'

'To be honest, Tom's got on to me. He was fed up with me coughing in the mornings. He says he hears enough of that at work. Mind you, he says that since nationalisation conditions are much better in the pits. They're making all sorts of improvements at Florence.'

'They needed to. But who'd have thought it?' Rita said, 'Megan I mean. It's amazing what a touch of lipstick can do. I was thinking – there's that chap in the next street, you know – the one who's got the bulldog. He isn't married...'

'I'm not surprised,' Clarice was horrified at the idea. 'He never looks clean to me! She can do better than that, Rita.'

'Yes, well moneywise time isn't on her side is it?'

They turned as Megan came back into the room. The blue sweater clung to reveal a swell of breasts that as Clarice told a fascinated Tom afterwards, were a damn shame to hide. Megan's waist, normally hidden beneath a loose cardigan was trim and the navy skirt fitted her perfectly.

'Glory,' Clarice exclaimed. 'What a transform-

ation! And doesn't blue suit you? It matches her
eyes, doesn't it Rita?' But then her glance went
down to Megan's sensible lace-up shoes and 30
denier stockings. 'Oh, those will never do. You
need a pair of court shoes and a decent pair of
nylons.'

Rita's stunned reaction was to say, 'Megan,
where have you been hiding yourself all these
years?'

'Isn't it all too tight?'

'Love, you look like a woman. And that's nothing to be ashamed of.' Clarice gazed fondly at the
girl she thought of as a second daughter. If only
she'd been able to speak plainly to Megan before,
this could have taken place years ago. But it
wouldn't have done – not where Les Cresswell
was concerned. Sometimes Clarice wondered
how such a slightly built man could have been, as
she'd often said to Tom, 'a right little Hitler in his
own home.'

'You look lovely, Megan,' Rita tapped the end
of her cigarette to release ash on to her saucer –
it was no good expecting an ashtray in *this* house.
'So now, what's next?'

'Well, Debra tried a bit of her Creme Puff on
me,' Megan said, 'so I'm going to get some. And
I'd better buy some new shoes.'

'Can you afford it?' The question came from
Clarice.

'I'm going to draw a bit out of the Post Office,'
Megan told her. 'After all, I suppose you could
call it an investment in my future.' She didn't tell
them how little there was left in her rapidly
dwindling account.

And so on Saturday afternoon, one of sunshine and a fresh breeze, Megan stood waiting in one of the stands on Longton Bus station. She was wearing the navy skirt so that she could see how it looked with court shoes, and also the blue sweater. She already felt 'different' – she'd done so ever since Debra cut her hair. It was only now, since she'd spent so many hours alone, that Megan was beginning to realise exactly how repressed her upbringing had been. Her father's narrow and religious views had been instilled in her throughout her childhood; she'd seen no reason to question them. Was it because her mother's temperament had been such a mild, submissive one, that Megan had simply followed that same pattern? I never really thought about it until now, she thought with increasing anger, and that's my own fault – I certainly can't blame anyone else.

But she put such thoughts behind her when she eventually arrived in Hanley, the main shopping centre. First of all, she went to Boots and bought a compact of Creme Puff, some pink rollers, Amami shampoo and a small bottle of setting lotion. Then she headed for the Co-operative Department Store, which Ellen had always favoured. 'Reasonable but decent quality,' she would say, '*and* you get your dividend.'

Megan went into the shoe department and sat on one of the chairs to wait for an assistant. 'Can I help?' The woman was middle-aged, her lined face tired but kindly.

'I'd like to try a pair of court shoes, please –

size 6.'

'What colour?'

'Navy.'

'And what height of heel?'

Megan hesitated. 'I'm not sure.'

'Not to worry, I'll bring you a selection.'

Megan glanced around at the shoes displayed on the shelves, beginning to enjoy herself and a few minutes later with an array of shoes before her, she removed her own right one. The first shoe was much too wide. She gazed with some trepidation at the three inch heel of the second and put it aside. She'd probably stumble and break an ankle, then how would she manage? However the third pair with a medium slender heel not only fitted, but when she tried both shoes on and tried walking in them she found to her astonishment that she could balance perfectly. She loved the extra height they gave her and going to look in a mirror propped against the shelves, stood admiring her elegant feet, her shapely legs – was this really her? Suddenly she didn't care that they cost more than she'd budgeted for; she had never felt so feminine or so confident. As she gazed down at them with delight she wondered – could it be 'new shoes, new life?' But Clarice was right – Megan was never going to wear 30 denier stockings again.

When later she left the store carrying the shoes and two pairs of sheer nylons it was to be met by the tantalising aroma from Derricott's Fish & Chip Cafe opposite. Megan hesitated. It would cost more to eat inside a cafe but surely just for once she could treat herself? Before she could change her mind she was crossing the road, opening the door and stepping into the steamy warmth.

And it was while she was enjoying the succulent batter, soft white fish and chips sprinkled with vinegar, that she saw him. Or rather she saw him watching her. He was sitting at a table opposite to her own, facing her as she glanced across. He was tall with brown hair. He winked. Megan looked away. Then surreptitiously she looked over again. He was still watching her. He smiled. She felt her cheeks grow pink. Keeping her head down, she tried as daintily as she could to finish her meal, and began to sip her tea. But Megan could still sense his gaze. Suddenly conscious of her opaque stockings and lace-up shoes she hurriedly tucked her legs out of sight. Then, as no-one else was sitting with her in the booth, she leaned back against the tall seat and impulsively lifting her head, met his eyes directly. Again he smiled. She smiled back and once more the colour rose to her face. He got up. Breathlessly, Megan waited as he crossed the aisle and sat opposite her.

'Hello.' His voice was light, humorous.

'Hello.'

'I haven't seen you in here before.'

'I've never been before. I don't come to Hanley that often. I live just outside Longton. And you?'

'I live not far away in Smallthorne and I can never resist popping in here when I come to Sherwin's.'

'I love Sherwin's,' Megan said, 'I sometimes go in just to look at the pianos. Not that I play or anything, but I'd love to be able to.'

He smiled. 'I do play – that's where I get my sheet music.'

They were both silent for a moment, then he said, 'I don't usually do this, you know. Foist myself on strange young women. I don't mean that you're strange,' he added hastily, 'but you're so attractive that I noticed you straightaway.' His tone was low, almost caressing.

She could hardly believe that this was happening. For the first time in her life she was having a conversation – no more than that, a sort of flirtation – with someone like this. He was *so* good-looking. If only the girls could see me she thought. But was it the tight sweater? Megan felt hot at the thought that he might have been staring at her breasts.

'My name's Ben,' he said.

'Benjamin? That means "Son of the right hand."'

'Fancy you knowing that! I'm impressed. And you are...?'

'Megan.'

He gazed into her eyes. 'What a lovely name, it suits you.'

'Thank you.' Then to Megan's utter dismay a bustling stout woman followed by a small and harassed looking man came into the crowded cafe and paused by their table.

'Mind if we sit here?' she said, and sat next to Megan before she could answer. The man put down their shopping bags next to Ben. 'I'll 'ave fish, chips and mushy peas,' the woman instructed her husband, and called after him, 'don't forget to ask for bread and butter.' She turned to Megan and Ben. 'I suppose it'll only be margarine. Still, beggars can't be choosers.'

Megan moved slightly in her seat to make more room but Ben, obviously irritated, got up saying, 'Actually, we were just leaving.'

'Oh, right!' The woman, her face now perspiring heaved herself out of the way to let Megan pass and Ben followed her out to the entrance and into the fresh air.

'A pity we were interrupted like that,' he said as they stood on the pavement. 'You didn't mind, did you? You were about to leave?'

She nodded.

Silence fell between them and she waited then with some hesitation began to move away. 'It was nice to meet you Ben.'

'And you too.' He gazed into her eyes and Megan felt her heart race. Was he going to ask to see her again? But after a long pause he looked down at his feet and said quietly, 'Bye, Megan.'

'Bye, Ben.' She watched him go until he was out of sight. Then with suddenly lowered spirits she began to make her way to Fountain Square to wait at the bus stop. Had it been the sensible shoes? Or was it that he hadn't liked her after all?

Chapter Five

Megan always sang when she got home from work; in a strange way they seemed to keep Ellen close to her. Her mother had always said that an 'apron around her waist and a song in her heart', should be every woman's aim and Megan found that for her too, singing helped to bring life into the house. And she always had the wireless on, it was company. After she'd lit the gas under a pan of potatoes, put some bacon rashers in a grill pan and opened a tin of broad beans to go with parsley sauce, she hugged the warmth of her cardigan and thought yet again of Ben. There had been a young man she'd liked once before – when she was eighteen. He'd been a new member of their small congregation and seated between her parents she'd watched and dreamed of him for weeks. But he'd never even looked her way, and when one day he'd brought with him a girl with blonde curls and sweeping eyelashes, Megan had seen him smile down at her and knew that her hopes had merely been foolish fantasies.

She still hadn't made any progress with her search, with many fruitless visits to local chapels. Maybe she was being too choosy, but surely she had to feel some attraction. Marriage was for life; it also involved the 'bedroom thing'. There was one of the girls at work for instance called Enid who as the girls said, had a 'gob' on her like a railway tunnel. She also had dark circles under un-happy eyes. 'There's no satisfying him,' she would complain with bitterness, 'he's at me all the time.'

As Megan listened to Enid moaning yet again, one of the other girls shouted, 'Yer should tell him to tie a knot in it and give us all some peace!'

'It must be awful,' Megan muttered to the paintress sitting next to her.

Jean, a quiet sensible woman devoted to her husband and two boys said, 'Marriage is a life sentence, love. If you do decide to take the plunge just make sure you pick the right man, that's all. It's the most important decision of your life.'

Her words echoed in Megan's mind as that evening she stared thoughtfully into the dying embers of her coal fire. She was at a loss where to try next. She'd exhausted all the small chapels within walking distance. Then suddenly the name Bethesda flashed into her mind; the largest and most prominent chapel in the city. It was however, a Methodist chapel; the Potteries had always had a strong Methodist following – Charles Wesley had been a frequent visitor to the area in the second half of the eighteenth century. She would never have dared to go against her father's narrow views when he was alive – he would certainly have been against it, but later as she climbed the stairs to bed her decision was made. After all what harm could it do.

After Megan had caught a bus to Hanley on Sun-day morning, she walked along Bethesda Street and towards its junction with Albion Street to where the large chapel, with its impressive facade

41

and row of classical pillars stood. She hesitated for a moment and then as a balding man and his plump well-dressed wife smiled at her, followed them inside. Megan stood to one side amazed at the sheer size of the interior, admiring the beautiful mahogany pulpit and handsome organ, and then glanced up at the encircling gallery which was rapidly filling up with worshippers. Deciding that would give her the best view Megan climbed the stairs and after sidling along one of the narrow pews near the front, pulled down the flap-seat.

Within seconds a low voice said, 'Excuse me, please.' Megan picked up her handbag and hurriedly stood up to lean backwards as a young woman took the seat beside her, and then as Megan continued to gaze around, she turned and smiled. 'Your first visit?' she whispered.

Megan nodded and then she suddenly froze as she stared down at a young man who was walking towards the front pew. Surely she was mistaken? Then he turned his head and she saw his profile. *Ben!*

The girl beside her must have heard Megan's intake of breath because she said in a low, tense voice, 'You know him?'

Megan was only able to give a swift nod; no other whispered conversation was possible because the minister swept in. A tall man, his vibrant personality became apparent from the first moment he spoke. Not that Megan listened to his opening words – her gaze was glued on Ben, dignified in a grey suit, white shirt and tie, sitting at the end of a pew on a side aisle with a

42

girl beside him in a jaunty red hat. Could they be together? Then seconds later she forced herself to concentrate as the organist began to play a familiar opening hymn, *'Tell me the stories of Jesus'*.

Megan decided that the service was only slightly different to what she was used to. The Bible was the word of God, so of course no-one would dare to change that, and the readings were ones she knew almost by heart. But the sermon was the most stimulating she had ever heard. And then when eventually the congregation began to file out, all she could think of was Ben. At first she lingered, hoping that he'd look up at the gallery. But he'd gone forward to speak to the organist and beginning to feel conspicuous she went to wait outside, only to find the girl who had been sitting next to her was standing by the cast iron railings. Of a similar age to Megan she was pretty, wore her fair hair in an Alice band and without any preamble said, 'How do you know Ben?' Her eyes were wary and Megan realised with a shock, almost hostile.

'I don't really,' she said, 'I only met him once. He sat opposite me in Derricott's.'

'Oh, I see.' The girl's expression cleared. 'My name's Eunice by the way, Eunice Goodwin.'

'I'm Megan Cresswell.'

'Well, I can see we have one thing in common. It's obvious that he made quite an impression on you!' Eunice still had an edge to her tone, and Megan felt the colour rise to her cheeks. 'Don't worry about it,' the other girl continued, 'you're in good company. But we're on a ticket to nowhere, I'm afraid. Come and stand up here a bit,

43

and you'll soon see why.'

Puzzled, Megan followed her further along the pavement. 'Trust me,' Eunice said, 'just wait and see.' She went on to explain that she usually attended the chapel with her parents but as her father had the 'flu, her mother had stayed home to look after him. 'He's got a raging temperature, poor thing.'

'I lost my mother a few months ago,' Megan said quietly, 'and my father two years before.'

'Oh, I am sorry.' Eunice looked at her with shock and sympathy. 'Who do you live with then?'

'No-one – I live on my own.' Megan met the other girl's eyes, trying to look as if she didn't care.

'Haven't you got anyone – no grandparents or aunts and uncles?'

Megan shook her head, and then suddenly Eunice gave her a sharp nudge. 'Look – now you'll see what I mean!'

Both girls watched Ben come out of the chapel. He was smiling down at the girl in the red hat and Megan stared as they made their way towards a sleek black Daimler. Already waiting at the side of the car was a tall impeccably dressed man and a woman whose smart tweed costume had a silver fox tippet slung around the shoulders. Megan saw Ben greet them both and then follow the girl into the back of the car.

'And she,' Eunice said bitterly, 'is why neither you nor I will ever get anywhere with Ben. *I* certainly can't compete with that...' Her gaze flickered appraisingly over Megan's shabby grey winter coat, 'and I shouldn't imagine you can either.'

'You like him, don't you?' Megan said.

'I have for years. I thought he liked me too, but then *she* came along...' Eunice's expression hardened and she began to move away, calling over her shoulder, 'Maybe I'll see you next week. By the way I work in British Home Stores. What do you do?'

'I'm a paintress on a potbank in Longton.' Megan watched her go and later, as she waited at the bus stop in Fountain Square thought of the hurt she'd seen in Eunice's eyes. So Ben was a bit of a heart-breaker? At least she knew why he hadn't asked to see her again, and who could blame him with prospects like that? But what was really making her angry was that she'd been so preoccupied in watching Ben that she'd missed her chance of finding anyone else. But next time...

It was the following Saturday afternoon, and they were standing outside her front door. One, a woman of erect bearing wearing a grey velour hat, at that same moment turned. Megan, a string bag in each hand, had no choice but to walk slowly along the pavement and to give a tentative smile.

'Good morning, Megan.' It was the woman who spoke. Her companion, a rotund pink-faced man remained silent, simply giving a curt nod.

'We've called before,' Barbara Eardley said.

'Oh, I'm sorry, I must have been out,' Megan felt her neck and face redden at the lie. 'How are you, Mrs Eardley? And you, Mr Dutton?'

'We're both well, thank you dear,' Barbara smiled and moved aside so that Megan could open the door, and they both followed her into the tiny hall and then into the sitting-room.

'I'll just take these through to the kitchen,' Megan muttered. On the previous occasion she'd managed to hide from them, standing with her back pressed against the wall, carefully out of sight of the front window. Now with resignation she popped her head into the room, where they were sitting stiffly on the two armchairs. 'Would you like a cup of tea?'

'Not unless you're making one,' Barbara said, and Megan had no choice but to join them. She sat on one of the dining chairs and waited.

Mr Dutton, an elder at the chapel, spoke for the first time. 'It's more of a formal visit really, Megan, rather than a social call.' He fixed his pale blue eyes on hers. 'Only we haven't seen you at the chapel lately, in fact not for quite a long time.'

'We only have your best interests at heart,' Barbara reassured, 'your parents were such staunch members...'

'And you have attended since a child,' Mr Dutton interrupted. 'I'm sure you can understand our fears, Megan. We wouldn't want you to stray from the Lord's path. It's a wicked world out there.'

Megan looked at them both. She could hardly tell them the truth – that she was scouring other chapels for a possible husband.

'You haven't lost your faith, have you, dear?'

Megan shook her head. 'No, Mrs Eardley, you

46

don't need to worry about that.'

'Then I'm at a loss to know why you haven't been joining us?'

'I have been going to chapel,' Megan said defensively, 'just not to ours.'

Mr Dutton frowned. 'But for what reason?'

Inspiration suddenly came to her. Megan confided, 'I've missed Audrey such a lot since her father died and she moved with her mum to Wales, and then of course my mother died. To be honest, Mr Dutton, it's been very lonely for me. As you know, the only girls of my age at our chapel are married, so I've been going to other ones in the area to try and find another suitable friend.' Megan emphasised the word 'suitable'.

Barbara glanced across at her companion. 'That sounds quite reasonable, don't you think?'

His eyes narrowed. 'I have to concede that. Which chapels have you been attending?'

Megan listed them, leaving out Bethesda. 'I've heard most of the lay preachers before,' she explained, 'so it hasn't seemed too strange.'

'And have you made a friend, Megan?' Barbara leaned forward and smiled encouragingly.

Megan hesitated then, 'I think so,' she said, smiling at them both. 'Her name's Eunice.'

Mr Dutton looked searchingly at her then gave a satisfied nod. 'Well I hope it won't be too long before you join us again.'

Barbara said quietly, 'You are still managing all right?'

'Yes, I'm fine. And thank you for coming; it was kind of you to think of me.'

Once they'd left, Megan felt not only relieved

but surprised at the way she'd handled what could have been a tricky scene. Not that she'd lied, not really – she just hadn't told the whole truth. They were good people, but as the weeks passed and her independence grew, she was becoming ever more determined; never again would she allow another person to control her life.

And as if to prove it, the same evening Megan went to the cinema. Les Cresswell had disapproved of what he called 'picture houses'. But Ellen and Megan had occasionally been allowed to see such classic films such as *Great Expectations*, and *A Tale of Two Cities*. And even he couldn't find anything to disapprove of in the *Lassie* films. The Alhambra, only a short walk away, was showing *Gone with the Wind*, and Megan had always longed to see it. After buying a ticket for one of the cheapest narrow plush seats in the stalls, she gazed spellbound at the flounced crinolines of the Southern belles, enthralled by Vivien Leigh's brilliant portrayal of Scarlett O'Hara and her obsessive love for Ashley Wilkes.

Transported into a world of drama, colour and romance, when she felt the warmth on her left leg, her first distracted thought was that it came from her coat which was draped over her lap. But then, just as she was wishing that someone like Clark Gable would come into *her* life, the slow warmth began to seep further up her thigh. At first Megan was stunned with disbelief, and then to her horror felt through the fabric of her skirt the sensation of fingers nudging, creeping, moving towards ... towards... Appalled, she swung

48

both of her legs violently aside and immediately the hand slid away. Incandescent with anger Megan turned to glare at the man on her left whose coat too was on his lap, but he was staring at the screen, apparently absorbed in the film. She glanced wildly around, unwilling to disturb the crowd of cinemagoers, to make a scene; which would definitely happen if she called the usherette. She should move – get away – but the cinema was crowded, the auditorium full – there were even people standing at the back. And why should I be forced out, she suddenly thought with rage – I've paid for my seat! So instead she remained where she was, tense and wary, edged away from him, but her enjoyment in the film was tarnished. As soon as the lights went up, even before the National Anthem finished, she turned towards him. He was middle-aged with a pale, pudgy face. The filthy pig! Lifting her foot and glad she was wearing a solid lace-up shoe, Megan kicked him forcefully in the shin exulting as she heard him gasp in agony.

Hurrying, intending to report him, she went to join the safety of the crowd in the centre aisle but when she glanced over her shoulder he'd disappeared, had taken his chance to get out via the other exit. It was only later, after buying a bag of chips to eat on the way home that she remembered Mr Dutton's warning. It wasn't the world that was wicked Megan thought, it was the people in it.

Chapter Six

Megan didn't often go round to Rita's house. Her husband Jack was considered by most people to be anti-social. A quiet, withdrawn man, he seemed to spend most of his time tending his pigeons, whose loft Rita found a constant source of irritation. 'I mean,' she often complained, 'who wants a monstrosity like that in their back yard. There's little enough room for the clothes line as it is!'

Jack had been taken prisoner in Burma towards the end of the war, and had come back Rita said, a far different man. 'It's the dreadful things he saw and experienced,' she once told Megan. 'They're there in his mind all the time. He's a terrible sleeper. But at least he came back, which is more than a lot of them did.'

The previous Thursday she had come round to see Megan, her face full of determination. 'Now you're to doll yourself up on Sunday afternoon. I want you to come round for your tea.' It was an order rather than an invitation. 'Only our John's coming, you know my nephew who lives in Fenton. He's just finished his National Service, and he's a nice lad, I'm sure you'll like him and it'll be nice for him to have some company his own age.'

Megan began to smile. 'So you're going to inflict *me* on the poor man. Honestly Rita, he'll wished he'd stayed in.'

'Don't be daft. You put yourself down too much, that's your trouble.'

And so at four o'clock Megan brushed her hair, applied fresh lipstick and wearing the navy skirt, blue sweater and court shoes, rather self-consciously presented herself at Rita's.

'This is Megan from next door,' Rita told the fresh-faced stocky young man who rose to greet her. 'And this Megan is John, our Margery's son.'

'Nice to meet you,' John held out his hand.

Megan shook it, liking his firm clasp. 'And you too. How are you finding Civvy Street?'

'Grand,' he said. 'Not that I don't miss the lads, but it's good to have my freedom back.'

Megan glanced around the room. It was amazing how houses could be exactly the same in design, yet each family made them unique. Clarice's was cluttered and cosy. Rita's was pristine yet full of ornaments. She loved her elegant Doulton figurines in crinoline dresses that adorned her sideboard; her hearth was decorated with Toby Jugs, her mantelpiece with blue Wedgwood trinket boxes and a Beswick china horse and foal. Rita worked as a flower maker but there were no small clusters of china flowers. 'I see enough of them at work,' was her opinion.

The square table in the middle of the room boasted a clean white cloth, a floral china tea service, and in the centre, two plates of sandwiches, one of thin boiled ham and one of egg. Towering above them was a matching cake stand displaying a home-made fruit cake. 'Jack'll be

51

down in a minute,' Rita said, 'he's just gone up to change.'

'How is he?' John turned to his aunt. 'You know,' he said quietly, 'I understand him more now. Not that I saw active service, but you hear a lot when you're in the army.'

'He's not so bad,' Rita said.

They all turned as Jack, his greying hair slicked back with Brylcreem, came into the room. 'John!' His normally serious face broke into a smile and the two men shook hands.

'Uncle Jack. Good to see you.'

'The army's made a man of him, hasn't it, Jack?' Rita said proudly.

'It will have done.' Jack nodded to Megan. 'Are you keeping well, love?'

'Yes thank you, Mr Forrester.'

'Right,' Rita said. 'Get yourselves to the table.' She went into the kitchen to make the tea, and Megan uncertainly took one of the chairs. John sat next to her and Jack opposite his nephew. When she returned Rita kept up a flow of reminiscences, and local news and then looked at her visitors and said, 'It's good to see you young people tucking in.'

Megan flushed, knowing that she'd eaten quite a lot, and John caught her eye and grinned. 'Mum always did say I'd got hollow legs. I'll have another slice of that cake Auntie Rita, if I may.' He turned to Jack. 'And how's work doing?'

Jack, who worked as a thrower but at a different pot bank than his wife, said, 'Not so bad. It keeps the wolf from the door. How about you – what are your plans now?'

'I've gone back to my old job. I'm in sales now, and hoping to go on the road soon, then they'll give me a car.'

Jack smiled at him. 'Aye, it's a good thing to have ambition.'

Then immediately everyone had finished eating, Rita said, 'John, could you do me a favour?'

'Of course I will.'

'I've run out of cigarettes. Could you pop along to the shop and fetch me twenty Park Drive? And then you and Jack can have a chat about the army while we women wash up. Megan will show you where it is, won't you love.'

Once they were outside and walking along the pavement, John said, 'I was very sorry to hear about your mother. It must be hard – being on your own.'

'It's not easy,' Megan admitted.

John turned to her. 'Am I right in thinking that there was a bit of matchmaking going on back there?'

Megan began to laugh. 'You noticed!'

'I just thought I ought to mention...' John hesitated, and then said in a rush, 'only I'm already courting. It's quite recent, so Auntie Rita wouldn't know.'

'Please,' Megan turned to him, 'I wouldn't want you to think...'

'Oh, I don't.' They'd reached the shop now and he paused before opening the door. 'You're a smashing girl, Megan. I'm sure someone will soon snap you up.'

And that remark, however kindly meant, made Megan feel totally humiliated. Did she really walk around with the words, *'husband wanted'* written on her forehead?

That evening, Megan grappled with her weekly budget. Only a miserly sum remained once she'd laid out her wages to cover rent, rates, gas, electricity and coal. And it was difficult to eke out her food; not only because of a tight budget, but because many staples such as tea, sugar, meat, eggs and cheese were still rationed. Megan's tiny savings in the Post Office had dwindled to nothing. Each week she tried to put a little aside but always found she had to use it for some household necessity; a new light-bulb, even the repair of the kettle when it began to leak. And then there were the household cleaning expenses; Jeyes fluid for the drain, bleach for the lavatory or Vim for the sink. The list was endless.

Megan glanced at the calendar which hung by the side of the fireplace; 1951 was passing so quickly, and the only difference in her life was that she'd thrown out the paper flowers that Ellen had liked. Late each Saturday afternoon, when Megan went down to the Market Hall a friendly stallholder would let her have a few remaining fresh blooms for a pittance. The scent of the flowers and their splash of colour in the room had become a symbol, her hope for a brighter future. But she was becoming impatient for it to begin. She was still annoyed that she'd allowed Ben to distract her at Bethesda. What a wasted opportunity! She rose from her armchair to prop the mesh guard around the dying fire, remembering that Ellen had always maintained that problems had a way of sorting themselves out. Never a day went by that Megan didn't think of her mother – she missed her so much. Still she thought, brightening as she switched off the light and began to go upstairs, it *is* Sunday tomorrow and who knows what that might bring?

Chapter Seven

This time, Megan was determined to be completely focused. Blessing the fact that the weather was dry, she arrived at Bethesda half an hour early and as if she was waiting for someone, stood outside to watch people going in. Several minutes later Eunice was walking towards her, accompanied by a middle aged couple who Megan guessed were her parents. The fair-haired girl turned to her mother, a woman with a gentle face and wearing a blue velour hat. 'This is Megan I was telling you about.'

Mrs Goodwin smiled. 'Good morning, Megan.'

Eunice's father, a thickset man with a greying moustache gave a nod. 'Come and sit with us,' Eunice encouraged, and as she led the way to one of the box pews, Megan followed her with some reluctance wondering whether from there she would have such a good view of the congregation. She had already seen three young men come into the chapel without a female companion, and now she could see another man on his own – sitting at the end of a pew that hadn't yet filled up. It was she thought, beginning to look rather hopeful.

'Who's that?' she whispered to Eunice as they settled into their seats.

She peered round. 'I've never seen him before.'

And I, Megan thought, haven't seen Ben. Nor was there any sign of the family he'd been with.

As later she listened to another thoughtful sermon, she wondered just why her father had been so against other denominations. So far, she'd heard nothing that anyone could possibly object to. And once the service had ended while Eunice's parents remained behind to talk to a frail and elderly woman, the two girls joined the throng of other people leaving. Once outside almost immediately Megan spotted the first of the three young men – brown haired with a cheerful face.

'Eunice,' she hissed, nodding in his direction. 'Is that someone you know?'

'Peter Talbot? Yes, he was in my class at junior school.' As they stood at the side of the gate, Eunice turned to Megan and began to laugh. 'Are you eyeing up the talent?'

'I suppose you could say that.' Megan laughed, trying to turn it into a joke.

'So that's why you were so interested in Ben? Well he's one that got away from both of us!' Again, there was bitterness in her voice.

Megan smiled. 'More from you than me, I would imagine. As I told you, I only met him once.'

'Well you're wasting your time with Peter! He's married – his wife's just had their first baby.' Eunice's eyes were glinting with amusement. 'Go on, who else have you seen?'

Just then the second young man emerged, and seeing Megan gaze at him, Eunice began to laugh. 'That's Graham Hughes. He's engaged to a girl he met at Butlins. She lives in Manchester.'

'Go on then, what about this one?' Megan said and drew back slightly, as he came towards them. He was a thin young man with dark hair. She'd liked his sweet expression as he'd passed her earlier. But as the clear winter sun shone on his face she could now see his pallor.

'I don't think so, Megan,' Eunice said quietly. 'Daniel's just come home after eighteen months in Loggerheads with TB.'

'Oh, what a shame,' Megan felt a rush of sympathy. 'Did they cure him?'

'His family hope so. But he still has to take it easy.'

And then Eunice's parents came out and her father said briskly, 'It's time we were getting home, Eunice. We don't want the beef overdone.'

'Honestly,' Eunice muttered, 'It's all he can think about once he comes out of chapel – his Sunday dinner.' And before Megan could mention going to the pictures together, Eunice obediently moved away to join them. 'Maybe I'll see you next week,' she said over her shoulder, and seconds later they had turned the corner and were out of sight.

Megan still hadn't seen the solitary young man who'd been sitting behind them so she waited for several minutes then with determination went back into the now almost empty chapel. He was strolling around, staring at the tall windows and turning to look up at the gallery. She began to loiter as if she was also studying the architecture, glancing discreetly at him, liking what she saw. He was now studying the organ, still standing with his back to her. Should she do what a Jane Austen heroine would do? Should she stroll past him and drop one of her gloves? Megan felt a frisson of excitement; after all she was only taking Jane's advice and trying to find herself a suitable husband. A woollen glove in her hand – what a pity it wasn't an elegant kid one – Megan began to slowly move near to him, but he must have heard her step because suddenly he turned round. Megan's heart gave a somersault.

His mouth creasing in a wide smile he said, 'Hi. Do you happen to be local by any chance?' Behind horn-rimmed spectacles, his eyes were brown and friendly, his skin lightly tanned.

'Yes, I am.'

'Tell me – is it true that this place has the capacity to hold 3,000 people?'

She suddenly realised what the drawl in his voice meant. 'You're American!'

'You guessed!' He smiled down at her and held out his hand, 'Nathan Brittles from Kansas, ma'am.'

Megan felt his firm handshake; she'd never met anyone from outside Staffordshire – let alone America! 'Yes, it does – hold 3,000 people, or so I believe,' she said. 'Are you over here for long?'

'I reckon about a month.' He began to move slowly towards the door, and she walked with him back down the aisle. 'I spent the first few days in London – it sure is a fascinating city with all that history.'

'What brought you to the Potteries?' They were now approaching the door and he held it open so that she could go through.

'I wanted to see more of England than its capital city. Besides I'm a great admirer of Arnold Bennett.'

Megan stared at him in astonishment. 'I never thought of people in America reading books like *Anna of the Five Towns*.'

'I majored in English Literature,' he explained.

She wasn't sure what 'majored' meant, but guessed it was something to do with university. 'My name's Megan, by the way. Megan Cresswell.'

'It's good to meet you, Megan.'

They were now standing on the pavement and she was at a loss what to do next. 'Well, I hope you enjoy your stay.'

But he was looking along the street, now empty except for a small black Ford parked further up. 'Do you live near here?'

Megan shook her head. 'No, I live in Longton.'

'Hey, that's another of the five towns. Didn't Bennett call it Longshaw? I'd real like to see it. So how do you get home?'

'I catch the bus.'

'Please – let me take you.' He waved a hand towards the Ford. 'I've hired that little car along there. I've got the hang of driving on the left, but your roundabouts – well, I'm darned if I can get used to them.'

'But where are you staying?'

'At the George Hotel – I wanted to see Arnold

Bennett's "Bursley", but then found out that its real name is Burslem.'

'But that's miles away – Longton's in the opposite direction!'

Nathan grinned. 'Back home some folk will travel fifty miles or more just to see a movie. Besides, a bit of local knowledge would be kinda useful.'

Megan wavered. She wanted to – but to get into a car with a complete stranger? Wouldn't that be stupid? However he *had* just been to chapel so surely... He must have taken her silence for agreement and when he began to walk along to where he was parked she had no choice but to follow and wait with a rapid heartbeat while he opened the passenger door. Megan tried to look nonchalant as she swung her legs inside.

'Megan,' he said as he drew away, 'how does everyone here cope with all the smoke in the atmosphere? I could smell it as soon as I arrived.'

'I suppose we're just used to it.' She was feeling acutely conscious of being so close to him. And his legs were so *long*...

'And as for those bottle ovens,' he waved a hand in the direction of one, 'or do you call them kilns?'

'Both.'

'They seem to dominate the whole skyline.'

'When they're fired, it's awful. I've known my mother have to take the washing in if the wind's in the wrong direction.' Megan turned to him. 'You can get postcards of them, you know, with all the smoke pouring out. They might make a good souvenir to take back with you.'

'Hey, I'll do that. Now, tell me about yourself.

For instance what do you do?'

Megan told him what her job was, and also explained the local term of pot bank. 'I'll show you Fenton when we pass through,' she said. 'Arnold Bennett left it out and that upset a lot of the local people. There are actually six Potteries towns, not five.' She pointed out different factories lining the route, telling him that Longton was known mainly for bone china. When he saw the Victorian frontage of its Town Hall, Nathan gave a low whistle of admiration. 'Now that's what I call a real interesting building.'

But Megan hardly glanced at the familiar landmark; she was too busy worrying that within minutes the journey would be over. What was the right thing to do in a situation like this? Would he expect her to ask him in – offer him a cup of tea or something? But with panic she realised that she hadn't lit the fire before she came out – the house would look terrible – cold and unwelcoming. And she was still in a frenzy of indecision when Nathan eventually turned into her street and drew up in front of the house.

'Hey, Mum...' Avril had been pulling the net curtain aside to gaze idly out of the window. 'Quick...' she called. 'Come and look at this! It's Megan from next door – in a car!'

Clarice, wiping her hands on a tea towel, came hurrying in. 'Never in this world...'

'Careful,' Avril hissed, 'she'll see you.'

They both stood to one side to watch. Megan was talking to a stranger, a tall, broad shouldered man. After a few moments, he got back in the car and she stood on the pavement to watch him drive away. Seconds later, she'd disappeared into the house.

'Blimey, who'd have thought it – Megan of all people, and doesn't she look different with her hair like that?' Avril, a younger version of her mother, went to sit in an armchair. She rubbed a hand reflectively over her rounded stomach beneath a flowered maternity smock. 'Still waters certainly run deep! Did you notice that overcoat he was wearing? He never got *that* from round here.'

'If it wasn't for the dinner, I'd pop round,' Clarice said with frustration. 'But the men will be back any minute.'

'It's all right for them, off down the pub while we do all the work.' Avril looked down at her four-year old twins who were lying on the hearth-rug and crayoning into a colouring book, then at her elder daughter who was curled up in an armchair trying to knit. 'For heaven's sake Sheila, bring it here – you're dropping more than you're knitting.'

Clarice gazed fondly at her grandchildren, and then at her daughter's weary face. This pregnancy was taking it out of her, and that husband of hers wasn't much help. But then she couldn't really blame him. Being a welder at Shelton Iron & Steel was heavy work; he was bound to be tired when he got home. With a sigh, she went into the kitchen to baste the weekly joint; with rationing still in force, it would only stretch to one slice each. Sometimes Tom, who liked his food, would grumble about having to share it, but Clarice

62

knew it was only a token moan. He was devoted to his family, just as she was. Once the meat tin was back in the oven, she called to the 10 year-old girl, 'Sheila? Will you set the table for me, love?' I know one thing, Clarice thought, smiling at the child as she began to rummage in the cutlery drawer; I'm itching to know what's going off with Megan. Once they've all gone home and Tom's snoozing over his paper, I'll be round next door like a shot!

Chapter Eight

At work on Monday morning Megan managed to contain herself until after the wireless had ended Workers' Playtime, but then she couldn't help saying to the older woman sitting next to her. 'Jean, have you ever met an American?'

She looked up from her work, leaned back and flexed her arms. 'I'm sure I'm getting arthritis in these elbows,' she complained. 'It comes of sitting in one position all the time. Me? Met an American?' Jean shook her head. 'Not really love. Of course there were some stationed round here during the war; you must have seen them.'

'I remember seeing one or two, but never to speak to.'

'Nor me. But I do know someone who married one – my niece, Pat.'

'You mean she was a GI bride?' Megan's eyes widened. This really was a tale of romance.

'That's right.'

'Gosh. How did she go on?'

Jean frowned. 'Apparently he came from one of the southern states – Carolina, I think it was. And it was all very different from what she expected.'

'How do you mean?'

'Well, the house was on stilts for one thing.'

Megan stared at her. 'Why on earth would they build a house on stilts?'

'It was in the middle of a swamp, that's why. She couldn't believe it when she got there.' Jean frowned. 'And as for the heat, it was unbearable; she said she was drenched in sweat most of the time. They had to live with his mother as well. From all accounts she was a right tartar and she made our Pat's life a misery. She managed to stick it out for a couple of years and then gave up and came back home.'

She put down the vase she'd just finished painting and looked at Megan. 'So what's all this about?'

'I met one yesterday,' Megan confided.

'You met an American?'

Unfortunately Jean raised her voice on the last words, and another of the enamellers sitting further along the bench called out, 'Hey, our Megan's gone and met a Yank!'

'Get off!' The cry of disbelief came from another of the girls and soon the comments were flying around.

'Grab him quick, Megan. Americans are all rich!'

'Are they heck as like! They've got poverty over there just like we have.'

'I thought they were all millionaires!'

'He's bound to be richer than us,' one of the gilders complained. 'Mind you, I think anybody's rich who can afford an inside lav. I have to get up in the night these days, and I'm blowed if I'm going up the yard in this cold weather. And using the po isn't easy with my creaky knees!'

'You should raise it up, Evelyn – put it on a stool or something then you wouldn't have to crouch down so far!' This suggestion came from the most experienced paintress who even at the age of seventy was still working three days a week.

'I never thought of that, Minnie. Thanks.'

'My old man uses a bucket on the landing,' Lizzie called. 'It doesn't bother me, 'cos he empties it – and it saves him splashing.'

'Trust you to lower the tone, Lizzie!'

'Where did you meet this Yank then, Megan?'

'At church,' Megan called.

There were shrieks of laughter and someone shouted, 'We might have known!'

'Don't knock it! If God's sent her a rich American, I might go meself next week.'

'Well, they welcome sinners Flo, so they'd greet you with open arms!'

Megan laughed and picking up her brush dipped it into turpentine to blend the colour on her tile to the desired consistency, then she took a fine pencil – the name the girls used for their brushes and bent her head to concentrate. This particular pattern was an intricate one and she was on piece-work, so was paid an agreed amount per dozen. But it was a novel sensation to be the centre of

65

attention, of affectionate teasing; usually she was more of a listener, an onlooker. She might be lonelier now, but she couldn't deny that her life was becoming more interesting.

The following Saturday afternoon Rita was in Longton, queuing at a fruit and vegetable stall in the Market Hall when she felt a touch on her shoulder. Turning round she found Clarice smiling at her.

'He's a bit slow this morning,' Rita said, nodding at the man serving. He was grinning at one of the customers as he scooped Brussels sprouts from the back of a piled up display. 'A bit less chat and a bit quicker service wouldn't go amiss.'

'Oh I don't know. I like a bit of cheery banter.'

'That was a turn up for the books, wasn't it?' Rita said, beginning to move up the queue. 'This American, I mean.'

'You could have knocked me down with a feather when our Avril called me to the window.' Clarice looked critically at the mound of potatoes displayed on the stall; with that much mud on them they were bound to weigh heavy, but she hadn't got the time to queue twice.

'What's he like?'

'I couldn't see much, except that he was tall and wore glasses; well-dressed though. I suppose you've spoken to her?'

Rita nodded. 'He's picking her up on Sunday morning to take her to Bethesda.'

'Yes, I know.' Clarice frowned. 'The trouble is Rita – he'll only see her in that old grey winter coat again and it doesn't do a thing for her.'

'She needs a scarf to brighten it up,' Rita said, 'I'll lend her my emerald green one.'

'I suppose it would be too cold in the chapel for her to take the coat off? You know – show him what she's got?'

Rita laughed. 'Well, she could pretend she's too hot! I'll suggest it!' She was now fishing in her capacious bag for her purse and clutching it, called, 'A pound of carrots and one of parsnips, Joe, and I'll have a small cauli – a nice tight one, mind.'

It was after Rita had brought round the scarf that Megan felt restless. She went over to the small bookcase, opened the glass doors and ran her finger idly along the spines. She'd read every volume, some more than once. This is ridiculous, she thought, I'm going to join the public library, she didn't believe that you could catch germs from paper, otherwise what about newspapers and magazines? The paper lads handled those, and who knew what sort of homes they came from? Mum, bless her, had been *too* cautious in some ways.

And thinking about her mother, Megan began to tidy up the room. Most of the girls at work had a strict routine for keeping up with their household chores, but Megan wasn't convinced that the world would come to an end if she missed a week dusting her bedroom or cleaning her windows. She was enough of her mother's daughter to be finicky about some things, such as the kitchen and lavatory. And she never forgot to bring the silver-backed hairbrush downstairs every week, where she would lovingly polish it with a silver cloth.

It had been the undertaker who had persuaded her to keep it. 'You're in shock, love, you're not thinking straight,' he'd said gently. 'It's no good to your mother where she's going. Come on now, I'm sure she would have wanted you to have it.'

But now, thinking that maybe – just maybe – there might be a possibility of Nathan seeing her home tomorrow, Megan made a special effort. But as she dusted and polished her apprehension increased. That old hearthrug for instance – would the room look better without it? She bent to lift it out of position, only to be dismayed by how the brighter patch of lino drew attention to how faded and shabby the remainder of the floor-covering had become. Swiftly she racked her brains. Was there anything better upstairs? She had left her parents' room undisturbed, apart from an occasional dusting, but now she remembered the carpet cut-off that lay at the side of the double bed where her mother had slept. With triumph she ran upstairs and moments later stood back to study the effect. Cream, with pink and green flowers, it gave a much-needed splash of colour, and unless you looked closely it was hardly noticeable that it was just a remnant. Her spirits lifting, as a final gesture Megan went out to give her doorstep a fresh coat of red Cardinal polish.

Chapter Nine

On Sunday morning Nathan turned into the quiet street, and began to drive slowly along. He was wishing he'd made a note of the number – these damned little houses all looked the same – when he saw a flash of bright green as Megan came out of one of the front doors with an emerald scarf knotted loosely on her collar. Simultaneously, the net curtains of the houses on either side moved slightly. So he'd caused a flicker of interest? He grinned, but he supposed it wasn't surprising; as an American he guessed he'd be something of a rarity in these parts. After all, it was peacetime now. While Megan carefully closed the gate behind her, Nathan got out of the driving seat. She was a sweet kid, a little restrained maybe, but he liked that. In any case, the English were famous for their reserve – although back home 'tight-assed' was the term more commonly used.

Megan felt full of apprehension as she walked to meet him. In the narrow street, Nathan seemed taller and broader than ever, and even his warm smile failed to calm her fluttering nerves.

'Sorry I'm a bit late,' he said, 'I took a wrong turning.'

'I still can't believe you've come all this way. I could easily have gone on the bus.'

'No, you couldn't.' With a flourish he ushered her into the passenger seat of what he thought of as a matchbox of a car. It had been an impulsive gesture to offer her the lift, but what man didn't enjoy spending time with an attractive girl? And she *was* attractive in a quiet sort of way. He liked the directness of her gaze, and glancing sideways at her thought how pretty her hair looked today. Her face wasn't plastered with make-up either, which was a look he detested. At first they drove along in silence, his gaze carefully on the road then Nathan said, 'How would you like to come and have lunch with me at the George? I'm getting a bit fed up with eating on my own.'

Megan felt her heart somersault. 'I'd love to, thank you.' What a relief! She'd been agonising over what to do when he brought her home. Because how could she invite him in so near to dinnertime and not offer him a meal? One of the girls said that Americans lived on beef steaks as big as a plate, a dinner plate at that! But now she was in another panic; would everyone at the George be more smartly dressed than she was? And she was sure the blue sweater clung even more closely since its second wash...

As soon as they arrived the first person she saw was Eunice, walking along the pavement with her parents. They merely smiled and went straight on to the chapel but Eunice lingered, staring with blatant curiosity at the tall American. 'This is a friend of mine, Eunice Goodwin,' Megan told him.

'Now I've met two English girls.' Nathan smiled and held out his hand. 'Hi, I'm Nathan Brittles.'

Shaking his hand, Eunice flashed a glance at Megan.

'He's from Kansas,' she explained.

Eunice's eyes widened even more. 'Didn't I see you here last week?'

'You sure did. That's when I met Megan.'

Recalling the other girl's teasing remark, 'Are you eyeing up the talent?' Megan thought – I bet she thinks I'm a right minx! She said hurriedly, 'We'd better go in,' and going before Nathan, led the way upstairs to the gallery. Eunice, who would obviously have liked to follow them, reluctantly went to sit with her parents in their usual box pew.

This time Ben *was* there, sitting not far from Eunice. By his side was his girlfriend, with her expensively dressed parents. Megan stared down at her for a few moments. Not, she thought someone who would stand out in a crowd; her hair was mousy, in fact she was quite ordinary-looking. So it hadn't been her looks that had attracted him. Then with a shrug Megan dismissed him from her mind and despite being acutely conscious of Nathan by her side, tried to concentrate on the service. She enjoyed singing along with Nathan's rich baritone, but as far as the sermon was concerned, she was far too distracted to listen. Suddenly Megan thought about her father. He would have been horrified at the thought of his daughter going to a hotel with a man she hardly knew; full of dire warnings that she'd be 'putting her mortal soul in danger'. Well, she might be inexperienced, but she wasn't stupid; she had no intention of losing her wits by being plied with alcohol.

After what seemed to be endless verses of the last

hymn they were able to leave the gallery, only for Megan to see Eunice trying to attract her attention. Megan swung round only to almost collide with Ben. She saw a flash of startled recognition in his eyes, but he didn't even smile, instead he turned to the girl by his side and taking her arm escorted her out of the church. Eunice, now close behind, pulled a face and whispered, 'See what I mean?' Then once they were all outside, she introduced Nathan to her parents, while Megan stood by his side watching him smile with ease, the slight breeze lifting his brown hair.

Jane Goodwin said, 'You're very welcome here, Mr Brittles.'

'Where in Kansas are you from?' Sam Goodwin asked.

'Wichita. Do you know it?'

Eunice's father shook his head. 'No, I've never been to America, I just wondered. We owe a huge debt of gratitude to your country, young man.'

'Thanks, and for not reminding me that we came in late!'

'Well, you did of course. But I won't hold you personally responsible!'

Nathan gave a grin and explained how his interest in Arnold Bennett's writing had brought him to the Potteries. 'Although,' he said, 'I'm also keen to drive up to Northumberland and to see Hadrian's Wall. We don't have anything like that back home!'

'No, you wouldn't.' Sam laughed. 'Anyway, it's good to have met you, but we must be getting off.' He began to move away, leaving his wife and daughter no choice but to follow.

Nathan turned to Megan. 'Well, honey, I'm starving, I don't know about you.'

'Ravenous,' she said promptly.

He laughed. 'Right – let's head for Burslem and food.'

Although she knew her own southern end of the city, oddly Megan had never been to its mother town. The George was an impressive building and Nathan told her that the original hotel, which Arnold Bennett had referred to as 'The Dragon' in *Clayhanger*, had burned down in 1929 two years before his death, and the present one had been rebuilt on the same site. It seemed funny in a way that someone from another country was telling her facts about her own city. And then Nathan was ushering her through the double glass doors into the vestibule, and pointing out the Powder Room, 'Just in case you'd like to freshen up.'

Megan stared in astonishment at gleaming tiles, high quality fitments and soft fluffy towels. She'd never imagined such luxury existed, at least not in her home town. Then before an elegant mirror she combed her hair, touched up her lipstick and feeling slightly sick with nerves, went back into the richly carpeted reception to find Nathan waiting for her. As she walked towards him he gave her a reassuring smile and after they had checked in their coats, ushered her into a spacious dining room. Among a low buzz of conversation the head waiter led them to small round table near one of the windows, and drew back a chair for Megan to sit before placing a starched white napkin on her lap. She sat upright, put her feet together and hoped she looked more confident than she felt.

Seeing her gaze around at the high ceiling with its deep ornate cornicing, and tall windows framed by damask curtains with fringed tie-backs, Nathan watched her with an inward smile, guessing this was the first time the young English woman had been to a fancy hotel like this. When he opened his leather-covered menu, Megan did the same. She glanced down. Three courses! She'd never eaten three courses in her life! At home – just on Sundays – Ellen used to make a rice pudding or baked egg custard for 'afters', but three courses...

'I'm going to have the beef for my main course,' Nathan said. 'Although I've had your Yorkshire pudding before – hey who ever thought of that one, I mean putting a pudding with meat?'

She laughed. 'Where did you have it?'

'In London, although I can't say I was impressed.'

'Oh, they don't know how to cook Yorkshire pudding down there,' she told him. 'I'm going to have that too.'

'And what would you like to begin with?'

Megan looked again at the choices. What on earth was 'consommé'?

'What are you having?' she said tentatively.

'Consommé.'

'I'll go for that as well.'

Nathan said, 'We'll choose the puddings later.' As the wine waiter approached, he said, 'Would you like some wine with your meal?' and almost spluttered with laughter as he saw the alarm on her face.

Megan shook her head, 'No, thank you.' Even to herself her voice sounded prim and disapproving, and she felt her cheeks flood with colour. He ordered half a bottle of wine for himself and poured her a glass of water from the jug already on the table. So he hadn't 'signed the Pledge' then? Suddenly she realised that although she'd met him at Bethesda, she couldn't assume that meant he was a Methodist – after all, she wasn't. But if not, then why had he returned a second time?

Once their order had been taken, Nathan said, 'Does anyone else in your family work on the same potbank as you, Megan? I've been told this often happens, particularly with the smaller factories.' He grinned, 'You can see I haven't been wasting my time.'

Megan who had been watching his air of assurance as he talked to the waiter, said, 'It happens a lot. For instance, I work for a small family-owned firm and the daughter of someone in the decorating shop has just begun as a lithographer – you know, putting transfers on.'

'Did that happen with you? Did you follow your mother?'

She shook her head. 'Before she got married, Mum worked in a hardware shop – that's where she met my father.'

'They don't go to chapel with you?' Nathan added quickly, 'I'm sorry, that was an impertinent question.'

'I wish they could. Dad died two years ago, and I lost Mum earlier this year.'

Nathan looked at her with sudden sympathy.

'I'm sorry to hear that. But you're not on your own, are you?'

Megan nodded. 'I'm an only child. But I'm managing,' she said brightly. 'I haven't really got much choice.'

Suddenly he put out a hand to cover hers. 'You're a brave kid, do you know that?'

Megan felt the colour rise in her cheeks at the unexpected touch on her skin and looked down at his large-knuckled hand; it looked strong and capable yet somehow gentle as it lay on her own. She felt her breathing quicken and glancing up saw in his eyes something that seemed more than the warmth and concern of a friend ... and then the heady moment was suddenly broken as the waiter arrived with their first course.

Megan felt slightly shaken and tried to turn her attention to the consommé which she discovered was a thin clear soup. She took a tentative sip; it was delicious, with a flavour unlike anything she'd tasted before. Unsure which knife to use, she watched Nathan pick up his smaller one and did the same, taking a curl of butter as he did. Megan began to spread it on one of the warm, crusty bread rolls and then realised that had been the wrong thing to do, because Nathan broke off and buttered only small pieces of his at a time. She filed the detail away in her memory; she wouldn't make *that* mistake again. When the main course arrived, and the waiter offered her one vegetable after another, Megan said, 'yes please,' to everything, and afterwards gazed down in wonder at the amount of food on her plate. There were two generous slices of beef, with roast *and* mashed potatoes, baked parsnips, carrots and brussels and to complete it all, a perfectly risen Yorkshire pudding.

'Now this really does look good,' Nathan said, reaching for the horseradish.

And so they began to eat, while in the background as well as quiet voices, there was the clink of cutlery, and occasional laughter. Megan, the edge of her appetite blunted by the first course ate slowly, wanting to savour every mouthful, to make it last as long as possible. She'd always loved food, had often felt guilty at how much pleasure she took in it. Nathan watched her expression. He'd been amazed to find that even six years after the end of the war, food rationing still existed over here. And as for the low wages paid to women in the pottery industry, even for highly skilled work ... if Megan had to support herself then treats like this would be rare.

Nathan, seeing Megan's absorption, decided not to distract her and remained silent, until eventually he finished, dabbing at his mouth with his napkin. 'Enjoy that?' he said, as Megan put down her knife and fork.

'Oh, yes. Did you?'

'I sure did.'

Megan had been fascinated by the way that Nathan ate, cutting up his food first then replacing his knife before using his fork. She smiled at him, 'And what have you seen over the week?'

'Josiah Wedgwood's factory and Royal Doulton's,' he told her, 'and I had to go to and watch English football, of course. Have you heard of Port Vale?'

'Of course I have.' She smiled at him. 'But most people near me support our other team, Stoke City.'

He grinned. 'I enjoyed it, but give me baseball every time. I've also been to Trentham Gardens which I'm told used to belong to one of your aristocrats, the Duke of Sutherland I think it was. We don't have any of those guys at home, you know.'

'Oh, we often used to have the Queen for tea,' she teased.

A short silence fell between them. Megan couldn't help glancing at Nathan's hand, at the way his fingers curled around the stem of his glass remembering the way she had felt when his skin touched hers...

She looked up to see him watching her, and felt the colour rise in her cheeks. 'I *am* enjoying all this. Thank you so much for inviting me.'

'It's my pleasure.' He leaned forward, 'I mean, look around – can you see any other man with such a delightful companion?'

Megan laughed. The majority of the diners were prosperous older-looking couples, and then suddenly she saw Ben. He was at a table near the wall, his arm carelessly around the back of his girlfriend's chair, while her parents sat opposite. Megan felt hot anger rise within her. What on earth had he been thinking of that day – to come over to her table and flirt? Megan was used to hearing the girls at work say that most men couldn't be trusted, and she was beginning to wonder if they were right.

'Someone you know?' Nathan asked.

She shook her head, 'Only slightly.'

'You have your own language in the Potteries, don't you,' he said suddenly. 'I had a stroll around that Market Hall in Hanley, and I was just having a look at the second-hand books near the entrance, when there was a guy nearby, talking to a woman who seemed to be grumbling about something. And he kept saying this word, marlady. "Marlady wouldna stand for that," he said. Who was he talking about? Is she some local aristocrat or something?'

Megan began laughing. 'He means his wife – it's two words – as in "my lady". It's traditional Potteries' dialect.'

'But you don't speak like that.'

'That's because my father wouldn't allow me to.' She looked mischievously at him. 'But I can if I want to.' She leaned forward and lowering her voice said, 'Anna any on yer any on 'em on yer?' She ran the words together and laughed again at his perplexed expression. 'It's what one man would say to his mates if he wanted a match or a cigarette. It means, "Haven't any of you any of them on you?"'

'You could have fooled me!' Nathan's eyes creased at the corner with amusement as he looked across at the merriment in Megan's eyes. When he'd impulsively asked to see her again, it had been a purely friendly gesture. He always liked to meet local people in the countries he visited. Why, he wondered, hadn't he seen immediately what an attractive girl she was? But then who would have guessed what a swell figure she'd been hiding.

After coffee, they lingered in the hotel, studying the 19th century paintings of the town and region which lined the walls, and then Nathan offered to show her around Burslem. Megan obediently stared up at the 'Golden Angel' on top of the smoke-blackened Town Hall, and then later at the house in Waterloo Road where Arnold Bennett used to live. 'He was actually born above a cafe in Hanley,' she told him. 'My father showed it to me.'

'But he didn't bring you further on to Burslem? It's only up the road.' With a sudden frown Megan realised that he was right. It did seem strange and yet she'd never thought about it before. 'I'll show you the cafe on the way back,' she said. She was beginning to feel cold, and sensing it he tucked her hand into the crook of his arm and as they walked back to the car, drew her even closer.

On the journey back, Nathan drove in silence. He'd enjoyed the day far more than he'd expected and he certainly admired the way that this English girl was managing to make a life for herself without any family support. That took real grit. But his growing feelings for her were ones that had taken him unawares, and ones he hadn't bargained for.

Megan too was quiet, every nerve within her acutely aware of the man beside her. She was finding that she liked – more than liked – everything about him; his broad shoulders, the way he used his hands when he talked, the warmth in his eyes, his considerate manner. She'd never met anyone with such an air of self-assurance, of vitality. And there had been some moments in the hotel...

But the nearer they came to her home, the more uneasy she was becoming. He was bound to expect her to invite him in after he'd treated her to that lovely meal. How could she not do so? And if she didn't invite him then this wonderful day would come to an end even sooner. But after the luxurious surroundings of the hotel, the house was going to seem more cramped and shabby than it normally did and her stomach was already knotting with embarrassment. She wondered what his own home was like and suddenly realised that Nathan had never once mentioned his own home or family or even what he did for a living. He had instead continually asked *her* questions, mainly about the local area and the pottery industry. But then, she reminded herself, don't forget that's what he's really interested in.

Chapter Ten

Nathan had been hoping that Megan would invite him in. Although he'd seen much of the area, he sure would like to see inside one of these little houses. There were so many of them. The main roads linking the towns were lined not only with pot banks but also with rows of terraced houses. The ones in this quiet street might be semi-detached, but they still seemed small with their flat windows and narrow front doors, all painted in the same dark green and he guessed that they were rented rather than privately

81

owned. But it was not just with curiosity about the house that he followed Megan up the short path. This young woman was not only beginning to intrigue him, but his interest in her was accelerating at an alarming rate.

When he stepped inside into what felt like a small box of a hall, he was amused to find that it only took one of his long-legged strides to cross it and enter into a small sitting-room. But then he was absolutely stunned by the scene that met him. As he gazed around in disbelief, Megan hurried to remove a fireguard from before the black grate, and took a poker from the hearth to lift the coals and encourage them to blaze up.

'Please,' she said, straightening up, 'let me take your coat.' Silently, Nathan removed his camel overcoat. He was still standing when she came back into the room, and Megan said awkwardly, 'Do sit down. I'll just go and put the kettle on.'

Nathan lowered himself into one of the arm-chairs with its sagging brown velveteen cushions, thinking – what an absolute dump! As his gaze wandered around the room, he thought he'd never seen anywhere so drab. There was an odd looking mat before the fireplace – surely it was just an off-cut from a larger carpet? Still it did brighten the room a bit, and boy did it need it! So did that meagre bunch of yellow chrysanthe-mums in a cheap glass vase, but neither could disguise the dreariness of the place. And the drapes were terrible; even he could see that and normally he took little interest in such things. But that could be, he thought uneasily, because he'd never had to. His mother was brilliant with soft furnishings. She chose all of his own, even insisting on both summer and winter drapes, saying they dressed the windows suitably for the seasons, and he realised now just how much they gave a sense of richness and comfort to the rooms. These ones hung limply with the narrow frill above gathered on a visible curtain wire and the brown unlined material was of such poor quality that the daylight shone through. If this was all that Megan came home to after a hard day at work, with not a person to greet or welcome her, then the poor girl sure had his sympathy.

Megan came back. 'It shouldn't take long,' she said.

He wondered why she seemed nervous and tried to reassure her. 'It's been a swell day, honey,' he said. 'I can't thank you enough for your company.'

'And I can't thank you enough for such a lovely time.'

'Then we're two happy people.'

She laughed and he was relieved to see her relax a little. She went back to the kitchen and was soon bringing in a tray that she put on the square table. He smiled as he saw the striped knitted cosy on the brown pot, thinking how very English the scene was.

Nathan watched her pour out their tea, amused by the fine line of concentration on her forehead. He had never met anyone like her; she seemed so naive, so lacking in experience. He guessed that she'd led a sheltered life, and that he thought, glancing yet again around the room, was hardly surprising.

'You seem to know an awful lot about me,' Megan was smiling at him, 'but so far, you've told me little about yourself. For instance what sort of work do you do?'

'Hey, you know you're right! Well,' Nathan took a sip of his tea; he was learning that the national beverage had a different taste depending on whether a region's water was hard or soft. This had a pleasurable edge to it. 'What sort of work? Mostly agricultural machinery I guess, it's a kinda family tradition.'

'You mean tractors and things? You must live in a farming area, then.'

He nodded. 'Kansas is a farming state.'

'And what exactly do you do? Are you an engineer?'

He grinned. 'Not me – they keep me away from anything mechanical.' He paused, 'Let's say I'm more into administration.'

'So you work in an office?'

He smiled. 'Yes, I suppose I do.'

'And do you live with your parents?' Megan flushed. 'I'm sorry – I'm asking too many questions.'

'Not at all; you've answered all of mine,' he reassured her. 'I live alone, but very close to them. And before you ask, I have one sister called Helen, who is two years younger than me. So now you have the full picture.' Nathan hesitated then getting up said, 'Do you mind if I use your bathroom?'

Megan stared at him in panic. What on earth did he want to use the bathroom for? Apart from anything else, her underwear and stockings were dangling from the overhead rack!

Nathan saw the consternation on her face and grinned. 'Sorry, I mean your lavatory, er ... toilet?'

'Oh, I see. Yes, of course.' With some trepidation Megan led the way to the kitchen, opened the back door, and indicated another door in the chilly back porch.

'Thanks.'

A few seconds later, Nathan pulled the slightly rusty chain, glanced with disbelief at the squares of newspaper threaded with string and hanging from a hook, and wondered where on earth he was supposed to wash his hands. But when he went back into the kitchen Megan was waiting to offer him a clean, if small and threadbare towel. She nodded towards the kitchen sink. 'I'm afraid this is the only washbasin we've got,' she muttered and hurriedly left.

Nathan ran the tap, washed his hands with a block of harsh yellow soap, and then grim-faced he did something that would have horrified his mother – he abused Megan's hospitality – by peering inside a door that was ajar. It was a larder. Or at least that was obviously its function; the only problem was that apart from a few sparse items on the shelves he was disconcerted, if not altogether surprised to see that it was almost empty.

Megan, who was sitting in a state of nervous tension waiting for him to re-join her, was feeling utterly mortified. It was only now after seeing the Powder Room at the George Hotel, that she realized how cheap looking her own lavatory was. She knew people who worked for Twyfords of course, the sanitary ware company in Hanley – in fact a man down the road did – but she hadn't realised there could be such a difference in something as mundane as a lavatory. And when Nathan came back into the room, it was to see Megan's eyes meet his with a challenge of defiant pride and his own softened; she looked so pretty sitting there in that disturbing sweater, her young face pink with what he guessed was embarrassment. He paused by the bookcase. 'Have you read any of these?' he asked, peering through the glass and raising his eyebrows in surprise at the titles. He'd half expected to find westerns, detective stories or romances.

'All of them,' she said. 'Dad was a great believer in books.'

Nathan noticed that several of Arnold Bennett's novels were there. And glancing around the room thought that this family certainly was a curious combination. 'He worked in a hardware store, you say?'

'Yes.'

Strange, Nathan would have thought that a man with literary tastes like these would have been more ambitious. Maybe it was because they were a Methodist family and believed in Charles Wesley's view – 'the rich man in his palace, the poor man at his gate.' 'You must miss having your parents with you when you go to Bethesda,' he said.

'Oh, they weren't Methodists,' Megan told him, 'and neither am I, really.'

Nathan grinned. 'Well, if it's confession time, I'm not either. We're churchgoers back home. I only went the first time because I was told it was such an interesting building.'

So that explains the wine Megan thought. 'I just wanted a change from the chapel we've always gone to,' she said, and went on to tell him which one.

Nathan gave a silent whistle. He knew of these people, there were chapels like these back home – their views were narrow and strict, almost Puritanical. I hardly think she had much of a childhood, he thought, not with a background like that. Although to be fair, she talked of her parents with affection. But it did explain why she seemed to him so unspoilt. Was it that she was only emerging into the world now she was alone? Was she like a butterfly emerging from its chrysalis? How fascinating was that? His gaze wandered over her face, her lovely eyes, her soft curvy lips and with alarm suddenly realised that he was in danger of falling for this English girl. In a tone more abrupt than he intended he said, 'I shall be sorry to say goodbye, but I'm off to Northumberland tomorrow.'

Megan felt a sickening lurch of dismay, but somehow she managed to keep her voice even. 'Oh yes, I remember you wanted to see Hadrian's Wall.'

Nathan saw the distress in her eyes and mentally cursed. This was a complication he could definitely do without. His only intention had been for them to enjoy spending time together on a friendly, informative basis – he had never expected this to happen to feel an attraction so strong ... and if Megan felt it too... Nathan's breathing quickened...

'Will you be coming this way back – on your way down to London?' Megan's voice wasn't quite steady, every nerve tensed for his answer.

He shook his head. 'No, I need to come down via Norfolk and Suffolk. There are some farming people I've arranged to see. My trip isn't all holiday I'm afraid. But I sure have enjoyed my time here.' He was longing to stretch out a hand to draw her into his arms. Was she aware of how seductive she looked? Nathan doubted it; Megan was virgin territory, he'd stake his reputation on it. I bet she's never even been kissed – the temptation to be the first was almost overwhelming. But the way he was feeling, it wouldn't end with just a kiss and the last thing he wanted to do was to hurt her. Nor did he want to go home with regrets, or even a guilty conscience. For Goddam sake the whole thing was totally impractical, there were thousands of miles between them!

Megan was filled with consternation and despair. He couldn't be going, couldn't be disappearing out of her life? It wasn't that she thought she was losing a potential husband. She hadn't given one thought to her search, not from the first moment that Nathan's car had drawn up this morning. She had just loved every minute she'd spent with him. She couldn't bear the thought that she might never see him again.

Nathan forced himself to rise from his chair. 'Thanks for everything Megan; it's been a real pleasure.'

Megan got up to join him. 'Thank *you*,' she said and her voice shook slightly. 'I hope you enjoy the rest of your stay.'

Nathan gazed down at her for one long moment. How could he just go? How could he leave without ... for one split second he hesitated. Then with an image of Alison waiting for him back home, as he told himself afterwards, common sense prevailed. 'Bye honey,' he said, and bending kissed her fleetingly on the cheek.

Megan felt his lips on her skin and seconds later with the scent of his cologne still lingering she stood before her front door to watch Nathan's car turn the corner and disappear from sight. She just couldn't believe that it had all ended – these magical hours and the joy of sharing them with him. Furiously she brushed away threatening tears. She was used to coping with difficulties but she knew that to try and forget Nathan was going to be the hardest thing she had ever done.

Chapter Eleven

The following morning when Megan let herself out of the house it was raining; a fine rain with moisture that she knew despite her umbrella would ruin her hairstyle but for once she didn't care; the grey skies matched her mood.

Disconsolate after Nathan had left, she had turned to look at her home, trying to imagine how it must have looked to a stranger and she'd felt not only ashamed of its shabbiness but of her own lack of interest in it. After all, what effort had she made since Ellen died, had she even tried to make the small living room her own? Apart from the few fresh flowers and the different rug in front of the hearth – and that was hardly ideal – it was exactly the same as it had been for years. I may not have much money, Megan thought, but surely I've got enough imagination to do something! I could find a remnant of material on the market for instance and make a couple of bright cushion covers. Even if she didn't have a sewing machine, there was no reason why she couldn't sew them by hand. And it might distract her from brooding about Nathan. I've only met three men so far, she thought as she walked through the churchyard; Ben who can't be trusted, John who's courting somebody else, and Nathan, the man she could so easily have loved – would shortly be on the other side of the Atlantic.

When a few minutes later Megan pushed open the heavy door into the decorating shop, the supervisor was still laying fresh newspaper on some of the benches and tables. Megan liked Dora Dawson, a tall, thin woman, with sandy hair scraped back into a bun. All the girls respected her, knowing that when a new pattern was introduced, or a new job came in, she would always fight to obtain a fair piece work rate for them.

She turned as Megan came through the door. 'You're early this morning,' she called, and bent to look under the benches for any signs of mice. The scuttling creatures were a menace in the old building with its uneven wooden floors, and all the decorators protected their colours by covering them with a saucer every night before they went home. A favourite trick with a new girl was to put a dead mouse under hers on the morning of her second day. It had happened to Megan and Audrey when they'd first started, and even now she could remember her jolt of revulsion. She'd managed not to scream but poor Audrey had become hysterical.

Now, almost as though the supervisor had read Megan's thoughts, she said, 'Have you heard from Audrey lately?'

'Yes, she's fine, thank you, Miss Dawson. She still likes Wales, although the last I heard she was looking for a new job. She didn't like it much in that little sweet shop. The woman who owned it was a right misery.'

'There's a lot like that,' Dora said, comfortable in the knowledge that she was popular. Not that she stood for any nonsense, but she reserved her displeasure for the gaffers, not the girls. They only had reason to fear her if their work wasn't of a high enough standard, otherwise she gave them full rein. She glanced at Megan, wondering about this American she'd met. Not that she'd ask her directly but the girls would, and there wasn't much that Dora missed.

She was right, because even before lunchtime, someone shouted, 'What's going on with the Yank, Megan?'

'Is he a good kisser, that's what I want to know?'

'You would, Lizzie. And if he is, are you going to offer your services?'

'Well, it'd make a change, wouldn't it? It ain't the same since Sid had his false teeth!'

91

Megan couldn't help laughing. She called back, 'You won't get the chance Lizzie. He's off back to America.'

'Don't tell us you've let him get away!'

'I've told you, he was just a friend.'

'And we've heard that one afore.'

Jean, next to her, whispered, 'Are you all right with that, love? Him going back, I mean.'

Not to anyone would Megan admit how upset she felt. 'Yes, fine Jean. But we did have a smashing day yesterday. He took me to the George Hotel in Burslem for Sunday dinner.'

'He never did – you lucky devil! What was it like?'

'You'd have loved it Jean.' Megan described the wonderful hotel, the delicious food and the luxury of the Powder Room.

'It sounds out of this world. Are you going to tell the girls about it at break?'

Megan nodded. Nathan had shown her a different face of the Potteries, one of money and good living. And it had been a fascinating revelation.

Jean glanced at her. 'I think you liked him more than you're letting on. Never mind love, it'll soon be Saturday and the Carnival will cheer you up.'

Longton held their annual Carnival in Queen's Park and on Saturday afternoon Megan did her shopping early then at two-o'clock joined throngs of others as they poured through the wide-open iron gates. Everyone loved the Carnival and the crowded atmosphere was already infectious with high spirits. The young Carnival Queen sitting high on her gaily decorated float surrounded by her attendants was waving in delight and then against the background of rousing melodies played by a brass-band, Megan saw Lizzie, her best hat perched on top of her permed hair.

'I like your feather,' Megan said and Lizzie grinned and struck a pose. Then she jerked her head towards her husband, a balding wiry man with a purple-veined nose who was standing before a stall, aiming darts to win a prize. 'Thinks he's a champion – mind you he should be the time he spends down that pub!' Then she gave a squeal of delight as he beckoned her forward to choose between cuddly toys, china dogs, strings of necklaces and bric-a-brac.

Laughing, Megan moved on looking for the hook-a-duck stall hoping to win a goldfish. But her efforts were in vain and after trying her hand on the adjacent hoopla and spending a few coins on the roll-a-penny, she wandered over the tufted grass to where the highlight of the afternoon was taking place. Several troupes of majorettes in their vivid costumes were competing against each other, marching, twisting and twirling while the surrounding crowd watched, enjoying the spectacle. But it was the young girls' finales of acrobatic tableaux that won everyone's gasps of disbelief and admiration, and cheers went up when the winners – a popular choice – were announced over a loudspeaker.

It was when she was waiting in a queue to buy an ice-cream cornet that Megan felt a small tug at her sleeve and glanced down to see little Julie smiling at her, while her mother said that Laddie was growing so fast that he was eating them out of house and home. Afterwards with the sun beating down on her bare arms, Megan waved to Clarice who had her grandchildren with her and began to stroll across the tufted grass. Jean had been right, the Carnival *had* lifted her spirits, but Megan's determination to enjoy the day didn't prevent her thoughts turning yet again to the tall American who had come so unexpectedly into her life and just as swiftly left it. Would he be home yet? She wasn't sure how long it took for a ship to cross the Atlantic.

With determination, Megan pushed all thoughts of Nathan from her mind and during the next few weeks continued her search, going every Sunday full of hope to Bethesda. Occasionally she would spot someone who seemed a likely candidate, only to face disappointment when Eunice told her that he was already 'spoken for', or even married. By now both Clarice and Rita had guessed what she was actually searching for, and confessed that the same thing had been in their minds all along.

'But don't just concentrate on that,' Rita said. 'If you can find someone to go dancing with it will give you a much better chance. What about this Eunice?'

Megan nodded. 'Yes, I'm going to ask her.'

Fifteen-year old Debra had 'got wind' of the master plan, although Clarice swore she hadn't told her. 'But I did mention it to our Avril,' she confessed, 'I should have known better – she never could keep a secret.'

Debra had 'crossed her heart and hoped to die',

and promised Megan not to breathe a word. But the problem was that one Wednesday evening, after giving Megan a cut, shampoo and set, she couldn't talk of anything else.

'I mean, it stands to reason doesn't it? All the best will have been snapped up early – like my Andy. Nab 'em quick, that's my motto, before they go off to do their National Service.'

'But how do you know he's the right one?'

'I just know that's all. Are you all ready for Christmas?' Debra said, and began to laugh. 'I have to ask all the clients that now. At least it makes a change from asking them about their holiday. What I like best is, "have you got anything planned for this weekend?"'

'Gosh, Marlene does give you good training,' Megan said, flinching as Debra unwound a tight roller in her hair. 'And do they tell you? What their plans are, I mean?'

'You'd be surprised,' Debra muttered darkly. 'It's like a confessional in that salon some days.' She patted a minute portion of Vitapointe cream into her palms, smoothed it on to Megan's hair and began to brush it. 'So *are* you all ready for Christmas?'

'I suppose so, more or less. I've written all my cards, anyway.' There had been little effort to mark Christmas in the Cresswell house. As a child, Megan had hung one of Les's old woollen socks at the bottom of her bed, and been thrilled with her apple, orange and small toy stuffed inside. And she'd usually been given a new scarf or woollen mittens that Ellen had secretly knitted. One year, there had been a pair of warm, fleecy lined boots, and even now Megan could remember the joy she'd felt, the pride when she'd first worn them. But there had never been even a tiny tree, or any streamers and balloons. They did have chicken on the day itself followed by Christmas pudding, and when she was old enough, Megan would make a trifle; without sherry of course. But for the Cresswells, it was the religious meaning of Christmas, and the services at chapel that held the most significance. 'Never forget, Megan,' Les would remind her, 'We are celebrating Jesus's birthday; without that there would be no reason for it.'

'Gran says the first Christmas is always the worst,' Debra suddenly said, 'after you've lost someone I mean.'

And Megan knew this would be true; she also knew that she wasn't looking forward to spending such two such emotive days alone.

But Megan's dread of the festive season didn't last long, because when she next went to Bethesda, as always sitting in the gallery so that she could see most of the congregation, Eunice was waiting afterwards.

'I was hoping to catch you, Megan,' she said. 'Have you got any plans for New Year's Eve?'

'Not really, no.'

'Great. Only I wondered if you'd like to come dancing with us. By that I mean me and my cousins, Pete and Brian. I could do with a bit of female support.'

Megan, who had already been to the cinema a couple of times with her, felt a rush of adrenalin. Dancing? That would be heaven. But what on earth could she wear? Her consternation must have shown because Eunice said quickly, 'You don't need to decide now. Have a think about it.'

'I will, and thank you.' As always Sam Goodwin was a hurry to get back to his roast dinner; even now he was already walking ahead. 'Let me know next Sunday,' Eunice called over her shoulder.

And her suggestion dominated Megan's thoughts for the whole of the journey home. She'd never told Eunice which chapel she used to attend, so the other girl would have no idea how startling her invitation had been. But even though she didn't know *how* to dance, Megan was already full of adrenalin and determination. She pushed an image of her father from her mind. He'd had a perfect right to his views, but that didn't mean that she had to go through life simply accepting them. How could she decide whether public dances were sinful if she never went to one to find out? And maybe it would help her to stop thinking about Nathan all the time.

By the time she got off the bus in the windy bus station, there was no doubt in her mind that on New Year's Eve, instead of listening to the wireless and Big Ben's chimes alone, she was going to be out among other people, sharing in their celebrations. And Megan thought with a sense of mischief, her spirits becoming lighter every minute; if I do see some sin, then at least I'll know what it looks like!

And that same afternoon, Clarice came round. 'I want you to come to us for your Christmas

97

dinner,' she said. 'One more won't make much difference, and I'll brook no argument, Megan. It'd spoil my Christmas to think of you sitting on your own on the other side of the wall.'

And Rita, whose back door and porch faced Megan's at the side of their houses, called to her the following Saturday afternoon as they simultaneously went to their dustbins. 'How are you doing, love?' she said, 'I haven't seen you for a bit?'

'I'm fine thanks, Rita.'

'Jack's told me to invite you for your tea on Boxing Day.'

Megan knew that if Jack had issued the invitation, then it was tantamount to an order. As Rita sometimes complained, 'He's never left the blasted army, at least not in his mind. And being made up to a corporal didn't help!'

'That's really kind of him. Thank you Rita, I'd like that very much. I'll look forward to it.'

Later she battled the icy winds to the Market Hall to buy her flowers. It had been an effort to leave the warm fire, but she knew that if she didn't, she would miss their bright faces when she got home from work. But when she arrived Iris, instead of greeting her with a cheery smile was blowing through her chapped hands in their knitted fingerless gloves. 'You'll have to help yourself Megan. I've had it for today; I've got a right cold on me. I'm going to have to pack up and go home.'

She lowered herself on to a stool and looked so wretched that Megan said, 'Let me serve for a bit. I don't know much about flowers but I can always ask you.'

'Would you, love? I'd be that grateful if you could. I think I've got a temperature. I do know I can't stand up another minute.'

And so for the next hour, Megan busied herself on the stall. Standing before it, with bunches of flowers in buckets of water by her feet and stacked in displays behind her, she found herself enjoying their scent, their freshness, even the draught from the door each time someone came into the Market Hall. The customers she served were sometimes hesitant what to choose, sometimes brisk and in a hurry, but all left with a lighter step, carrying their precious blooms with care. What a lovely job, Megan thought, I feel as if I'm not just selling flowers but happiness.

It was almost time to close when a man in his late twenties approached. With a nod to Iris and a curious look at Megan, he studied the stall. 'I'll take those bronze chrysanths this week,' he said, his hand already going to his pocket for some loose change. It was unusual to see a man carrying flowers, and Megan wondered whether they were for his wife or his girlfriend. 'I see you've got yourself an assistant,' he said to Iris.

'She's a customer really, but Megan's a good lass, she offered to help me out,' Iris told him, beginning to cough. 'I'm not so good, I'm afraid.'

'You don't sound it. Can I do anything to help?'

Iris lifted the cuff of her glove and glanced at her watch. 'It'll be time to pack up in a few minutes. You couldn't give Megan a hand, could you? I'm getting worse by the minute.'

'Of course I can.' He and Megan glanced at

99

each other with concern as Iris began to cough again, a deep-seated cough that racked her wiry frame. It took over half an hour to load up her battered van, and eventually, huddled inside a fur collared old coat, she climbed into the driving seat.

'Are you sure you feel well enough to drive?' Megan said.

Iris tucked stray tufts of her hair beneath her grey woollen hat and nodded. 'I learned in the army during the war – it would take more than a cold to faze me, love. And thanks, both of you.' Then she closed the sliding door, revved up the engine, and drew away.

Dark-haired, with a hint of bristle around his chin, her fellow helper smiled, one that lightened his rather ordinary features. 'My name's Terry, by the way.' He bent to pick up his flowers which were propped against the wall, and handed Megan the other bunch. 'Yours, I believe?'

Taking them from him, Megan nodded. They both stood on the pavement hesitating then he gave another quick smile and said, 'Bye.'

And that, Megan thought as later she trudged home, is what they all seem to say.

Chapter Twelve

Once she'd told Eunice that she'd love to go dancing on New Year's Eve, Megan stood before the open door of her narrow wardrobe and desperately slid the few coat hangers along the rail in a futile search for something to wear. The only thing remotely suitable was the seersucker blouse that Shirley had sent, and even then she had nothing to go with it apart from the navy skirt – that was more suitable for an office than a dance. She took out her three summer dresses and held them up. Her favourite was a pink one in waffle cotton but it had a stubborn stain on the front of the skirt, and the others were far too prim and proper. Megan slumped on to the end of the bed, knowing that she hadn't enough time to save up and buy something new. She longed to go, had even asked Debra to teach her some dance steps. Then suddenly the answer came to her – Jean's catalogue! Most of the women at work were customers, paying a small amount each week to enable them to buy something either for themselves, their families, or their homes. Knowing her parents' views on debt, Megan had never dared to join in.

So early on Monday morning, she said quietly, 'Jean, do you think I could borrow your catalogue?'

Jean put down the plate she was painting and

turned to stare at her in surprise. 'Of course you can, love. Flo's just brought it back, so I've got it here with me.' She hesitated then whispered, 'Remember though – the secret is to never commit yourself to a weekly amount you can't afford.'

'I promise. You know,' Megan smiled at her, 'you'll never get rich giving people that advice.'

'Yes, well there are more important issues at stake than my commission.'

'I really admire you, Jean. Not many folk think like that.'

'You don't have to go to church to live a good life, you know. But if you want something, love, you'll have to decide tonight. I'm sending an order in tomorrow and it'll be the last chance before Christmas.'

And so, enjoying the experience more than she'd ever thought possible, that same evening Megan sat until the fire died down, browsing through the Great Universal Store's array of fashions. The choice was overwhelming. Again and again she would be tempted by a dress or a skirt and blouse, but most of all by the illustrations of high-heeled evening sandals. In silver and gold, they entranced her. Megan loved wearing heels, it had been a revelation how much more confident she felt in them. With a writing pad before her, Megan did one sum after another, working out her twenty weekly repayments, rejecting with reluctance the items that were too expensive. Eventually, she made her decision. It was the dress she'd seen and liked first. In shot silk, sleeveless and with a scoop neckline, it shimmered with shades of emerald green. She would have loved a pair of silver sandals, but instead chose ones in navy with a slender heel, knowing that then she would be able to wear them during the summer. Maybe she *was* going into debt but at least she was being practical.

On Christmas morning Megan came down to her empty room, to the few cards with their nativity scenes or robins displayed on the mantelpiece and felt sudden tears rise in her eyes. Normally, Les would have been down first to light the fire before putting his suit on ready for chapel, Ellen would have been cooking bacon, eggs and oatcakes, the table would have already been set with a few presents waiting. How she missed them both. He'd been a strange man her father, sometimes she would catch him watching her, just sitting in his armchair, an unfathomable look on his face. It had made her uneasy at times. And Ellen, with her sweet temper and kindness, it seemed so unfair that she'd had to die so soon. But now there was only one way she could share this Christmas with them. The weather was unusually mild, so later as Megan made her way to Longton Cemetery instead of battling against a wind, or having to be careful not to slip on the pavements, she found herself looking wistfully at other people's houses, seeing windows framed in glittered cotton wool or decorated with paper chains and sometimes even a glimpse of a Christmas tree. A child came towards her riding nervously on a newly painted bike, her father watching proudly from the gate. Megan smiled at her, 'Hello, did Santa bring you that?' The little girl nodded; her face serious with concentration. And there were one or two lone adults on the same journey, carrying holly wreaths festooned with red ribbons as they made their way to remember their loved ones.

As Megan stood before her parents' small grey marble headstone, her thoughts were ones of affection. Her upbringing might have been narrow, but she had been loved and protected, taught by example and in accordance with their beliefs. She glanced up at the overhanging branches of a tree, pleased that they were in such a good spot; beneath shade in the summer and in the winter sheltered from the wind. Eventually, with one last lingering glance and a whispered, 'Happy Christmas,' she turned away and began to walk slowly back to the main gates.

It was as she paused to read the inscription on a stone angel guarding an ancient grave that she saw him. He was carrying an urn of dying flowers, and as she watched, he emptied it on to a compost heap. Drawing near, Megan called, 'Merry Christmas, Terry.'

He turned in surprise and grinned. 'The girl from the flower stall – Megan, isn't it? Merry Christmas.'

She nodded. 'I see you're here for the same reason as me. I've just been to put a wreath on my parents' grave.'

'You've lost both of them? I'm lucky, I've only lost one – my father.'

'Was it recent?' Megan thought he looked more ordinary than ever this morning, and he still looked as if he needed a shave.

He shook his head, 'No, five years ago. And you?'

'Dad died just over two years ago, and Mum earlier this year.'

'That's hard.'

Megan shrugged. 'You manage.'

'No other choice is there?'

She smiled and glancing at her watch began to walk on; her local chapel frowned on latecomers. And later, as she sat in the familiar surroundings, Megan found herself cocooned in the comfort of nostalgia. Since early childhood she'd been brought here every Sunday to worship, and it had felt good to be greeted by so many welcoming smiles from the congregation, with warmth in the eyes of Mrs Eardley and approval in those of Mr Dutton. Megan wasn't of course wearing make-up, and she was still unsure whether her decision not to do so sprang from wisdom or weakness. But then as the carols began, she realised that although the service might be more vibrant at Bethesda, her distraction there meant that she was in danger of losing its true meaning. If she came here a little more often and instead of gazing around for a suitable husband she were to concentrate on prayer, then just possibly her luck might change. She smiled to herself. Now was that a message from her father? Or, having just visited his grave was she being fanciful?

When at half-past twelve Megan went round to Clarice's with a large can of peaches and a tin of home-made mince pies, the preparations for Christmas dinner were already chaotic She was greeted by ten-year old Sheila. 'Mum's started with the baby,' Sheila announced with importance. 'So I brought the twins up to Gran's all by myself!'

'Now then,' Clarice, her face flushed from the heat of the kitchen, bustled forward, 'where's your manners? Come on all of you, wish Megan a happy Christmas.'

'Happy Christmas, Megan,' they chorused.

'Happy Christmas!' She gave them each a small packet of coloured pencils and said, 'I thought Avril wasn't due for another month?'

'She isn't.' Clarice's blue eyes were full of anxiety. 'I do hope she'll be all right. Any other time, I'd be there with her.'

'Of course she will, love,' Tom paused from helping the twins to build a crane out of Meccano and took off his rimless spectacles, 'She always has been afore.'

'It would happen when I'm getting Christmas dinner for everyone!'

Sheila's younger sister Mary, a pudgy eight-year old with mousy hair and pink-framed round spectacles, announced, 'Debra's on the lav.'

'Thanks a bundle,' Debra said coming into the room. 'Very tactful, I must say!'

Megan laughed and offered her a neatly wrapped parcel. 'Merry Christmas, Debra – it's just a little thank you.'

'Go on, open it,' Mary urged.

Debra took the red crepe paper off the parcel, delight spreading across her face when she saw three pairs of nylon stockings. 'Wow! Thanks, Megan.'

'What have you had for Christmas, Megan?' Sheila called. 'I've had a new pencil case, a Rupert annual, a sewing set, and mum made me a selection box – she saved up her sweet coupons.'

Megan felt her face redden. 'Oh, you don't get many presents at my age.'

Clarice paused in the doorway. Damnation! She should have got her something – she'd bet a pound to a penny that girl hadn't had a single one. Annoyed with herself, her voice was sharper than she intended. 'Debra, will you get that table extended and set! And where have your mum and dad got to?' She turned uneasily to Megan, 'They went down to see if there was anything they could do, but it's only ten minutes walk away; they should have been back by now.'

'I've told you to stop worriting,' Tom said.

'But suppose the midwife hasn't come. And she's not going to be too pleased – dragged away from her Christmas dinner!'

'Yes, well babies come when they're ready, they don't wait until it suits other folk.'

Megan smiled. 'Is there anything I can help with?'

'Would you, love? Pauline usually helps me to dish up, and keeps an eye on the Christmas pudding. I'm likely to forget with everything else and let it boil dry.' She hurried into the kitchen with Megan following. The aroma was wonderful, the roast chicken, its skin crisp and golden was resting on a large warm oval plate and a pan of rich gravy thickened with stuffing simmering gently on a gas ring. Megan immediately checked the level of water in the saucepan where a cloth covered basin rested.

'It's all ready.' Harassed, Clarice went to close the window she'd previously opened to let the steam out. 'It'll spoil if they don't come soon.'

But just then the back door opened and Alan, a miner like his father, came in followed by his wife. Pauline was the first to speak. 'God, that midwife. Talk about bossy. She won't let us anywhere near Avril. All I know is there's no baby yet.'

'What about Doug?' Clarice demanded.

'No chance,' Alan said. 'She made it very plain that she'd got no time for husbands.'

Despite being overshadowed with anxiety, the meal was a great success, with much giggling from the children as they pulled crackers and read out the jokes. However even before the table was cleared Clarice was impatient to leave and Megan and Debra tackled the mountain of washing up while the other two women went off to see how the expectant mother fared. And their smiling faces when they later returned with the news that mother and baby boy were doing well was as Clarice said, the icing on the cake. 'She's got to be careful to keep him warm,' she told them. 'At just over five pounds, he isn't classified as premature, though what else they call a month early beats me!'

'What are they calling him?' Megan asked.

'It was going to be Peter, but seeing as he was born on Christmas Day, they're talking about Nicholas.'

Alan, who with Tom had spent the last hour sprawling in an armchair drinking Davenport's beer, said, 'Well, they could always call him Jesus!'

'Dunna be daft,' Tom grinned. 'Mind you, I'm not too sure about Nicholas – it's a bit posh isn't it?'

'I think it's a nice name,' Pauline said. She was a thin woman, whose only resemblance to Debra was the same intense brown eyes.

'They'll call him what they like, no matter what we think,' Clarice said. She was by now looking weary and Megan decided it was time to leave.

When ten minutes later, she inserted the key into her front door, and went back into the empty house, the contrast between its silence and the noise and warmth of the one next door struck into her heart. Megan had been fascinated by the bickering and banter between the young sisters and cousins, had loved their shared humour. And as she removed the fireguard and bent to build up the fire, she thought yet again how much she longed for a family of her own. She straightened up and turned to gaze at the room, trying to imagine what it would look like with one child crayoning on the hearth, another sitting with a jigsaw at the table. All she needed was a husband. And then she remembered her new finery in the wardrobe. Didn't lots of people meet and fall in love at dances? Certainly at least three of the girls at work had. Megan turned back to stare into the mirror. I always used to think of myself as plain, she thought, but I don't feel like that now, not with this new hairstyle and make-up. She definitely needed the added colour; her complexion was so pale against her dark hair. I wish I'd realised it years ago she thought, I wish ... but

109

what was the use in looking back? Megan kept reminding herself of that whenever an image of Nathan crept into her mind. So many times she thought of him, of the fleeting warmth of his hand against her own, of his teasing eyes, his friendliness. How she'd loved being with him, sitting beside him in the car, talking, watching the enthusiasm in his face, his humour. But she knew it was no use wishing or longing for what could never be. Although America might boast that it didn't have a class system, Megan knew of the expression 'from the other side of the tracks', and knew what it meant; so what was that other than a form of snobbery? And because she worked in a factory she had a strong suspicion that was how she'd be viewed.

What I've got to do she determined, is stop dreaming and to look to the future. After all, I suppose I'm a bit like Cinderella really – going to her first ball. And look how it changed *her* life!

Chapter Thirteen

On New Year's Eve, Megan stood before the wardrobe full-length mirror and spent the next few seconds simply staring at her reflection. It was only a matter of months since Ellen had died and yet the girl gazing back at her scarcely resembled the meek, colourless daughter her mother had left behind. And it wasn't only how she looked – and Megan cared not one jot that she was being vain

– it was how she felt; feminine, confident, with silken fabric next to her skin, and a pleasurable swishing sound from the full skirt at her slightest movement. If vanity was indeed a sin then it was a pleasurable one and how could it possibly harm anyone else? Her stomach fluttering with nerves and excitement, eventually the time came to leave but to her dismay it began to rain as soon as she opened the front door. With a chiffon headscarf loosely tied, Megan raised her umbrella and carrying the precious navy sandals in a bag hurried along the pavements lining the main road to the bus station. Fortunately a double-decker was already waiting at her stand and once on board, she swiftly removed the scarf, praying that it hadn't flattened her hair. The seats downstairs were almost full but she managed to spot a vacant one near the back, and sat gingerly in an effort not to crease the green dress.

'Off to the King's Hall?' The auburn-haired girl sitting next to her was drenched in scent. She also had a long, thin umbrella, the spike of which was dangerously close to Megan's nylons.

'Yes, I am. Are you?'

'You bet. I go there all the time. Are you on your own?' She looked hopefully at Megan.

'No, I'm meeting some friends.' Megan shifted her legs slightly to one side away from the umbrella.

'Are you coming back on the late bus?'

'I expect so.'

'Now then, girls, let's have your fares.' The bus conductor stood over them, his hand resting on his ticket machine. With a drooping moustache,

111

and grey hair combed sparsely across his scalp, he grinned down at them. 'I can see some lads are going to be lucky tonight!'

'We hope so,' the girl grinned, giving Megan a friendly nudge as they both took their tickets from his nicotine-stained fingers.

The journey soon over, Megan walked to the large Victorian building of Stoke Town Hall where she could see Eunice already waiting outside. With her were two youths. Megan guessed that they were the cousins, and as they were both fidgeting with impatience Eunice wasted little time on introductions. 'This is Brian and this is Pete,' she said. Megan felt a stab of disappointment. Brian looked about sixteen and when Megan smiled at him blushed scarlet, while Pete, only slightly older with protruding teeth simply nodded. 'Come on then,' he said. 'We haven't got all day.'

Eunice grimaced as she and Megan followed the two boys. 'They're a pair of clots,' she said, 'but it was the only way Dad would let me come.'

Megan smiled, her nerves increasing even more as they queued at the cloakroom to leave their coats and change their shoes. Carrying the silver coloured evening purse that Debra had loaned her, Megan followed Eunice on to the balcony where they joined other people, some sitting at small tables, others like themselves gazing down at the large ballroom below. Megan caught her breath at the sheer glamour of the scene. The ornate ceiling, the stained glass windows, the dancers circling the floor below, the music from the full-sized band on the stage... With shining eyes, she turned to Eunice who smiled and said, 'It's brilliant isn't it? Is this your first time here?'

Megan nodded.

'Where do you usually go, then?'

Megan hesitated then confessed, 'I don't. To be honest, this is the first time I've ever been dancing anywhere.'

'Where on earth have you been living – on the moon? I don't come very often, but at least I've been before. I used to come with Ben.'

Megan gave her a sympathetic glance and in answer to her question said, 'Not quite on the moon. It's just that, well I expect you think of me as a Methodist, but I'm not really.' She told Eunice about the chapel she used to go to. 'It's just that after Mum died, I thought I'd sort of branch out a bit, make up my own mind about things.' Megan had no intention of revealing the real reason why she'd gone to Bethesda.

'I don't blame you! They're very narrow aren't they, your lot – in their views, I mean.'

'Yes,' Megan admitted, 'very well-meaning people though.'

'I like a bit of fun myself,' Eunice grinned. 'To be honest, I'm dying to have a glass of Babycham, but those two twerps down there would be bound to rat on me to my parents.' They both gazed down at the dance floor where Brian and Pete were both standing at the end looking Megan thought, completely gormless.

'I bet they won't find a single girl daft enough to dance with them. Look...' Eunice nudged her and she saw Pete approach a couple of girls, only to be rejected.

Megan was horrified. 'That's awful,' she said. 'It's enough to give him an inferiority complex for life.'

Eunice giggled. 'It won't be the first time, or the last.'

'Well I'll dance with him, if he asks me to,' Megan said.

'We won't dance with anyone unless we go down!' Eunice turned and began to walk carefully down the stairs. 'I haven't got used to these shoes yet, the heels are higher than I'm used to.'

'You look lovely,' Megan said, looking with admiration at Eunice's black taffeta skirt with a white peasant style blouse. And the other girl didn't waste any time, because as soon as the band began to play, *'You are my Honeysuckle,'* she grabbed Megan's hand. 'It's a Barn Dance – come on, we can do this together. I'll take the lead.'

And that was how Megan first found herself on the dance floor. She faltered at first but by watching the couple in front, she soon mastered the routine. Within minutes she was singing along with everyone else, enjoying the catchy tune and nonsense lyrics, loving the way her body responded to the music. And then suddenly the music stopped and the bandleader, rotund and resplendent in a red jacket and black evening trousers, announced over the microphone. 'All right boys and girls – let's make this one progressive.'

Megan looked in panic at Eunice. 'What does that mean?'

'We change partners,' she hissed, 'and I've drawn the short straw. Now I'll have to dance with the women!' She pulled Megan's hand and

114

directed her to the man on her opposite right. He looked even more discomforted than she felt, but obediently held out his hand. Middle-aged with a paunch that bumped against her as they waltzed he just stared straight ahead, and it was with relief that she moved on to her next partner. A slim, gentle-looking man, he held her as if she was delicate china, but when she turned to the next partner, it was to find that he was a sweaty youth whose hand was clammy and she felt anger surge at the thought he might leave a handprint on her lovely dress.

And then when she turned to her next partner, she came face to face with Ben. As she stared at him, he smiled easily and came forward to take her hand. 'Well hello, Megan.'

'You do remember me, then?' Her tone was sharp as they began to move forward. She saw his eyes flicker down to her breasts, and with some satisfaction Megan recalled that at least his girl-friend had little to show in *that* department. What she did have however, was money – or at least the prospect of it.

'How could I forget?' Ben gave her a meaningful look and she realised with contempt that he was nothing but a flirt, the sort the girls called a 'Jack the lad.'

'Quite easily, I would think,' she said airily, and his squeeze on her waist when they waltzed merely annoyed her. He thinks he's God's gift to women she thought, and you Megan Cresswell were so eager for flattery that you nearly fell for it.

But when she and Eunice met up again after

the dance finished, the other girl swiftly showed her envy. 'I saw you dancing with Ben, you lucky thing.'

'You're welcome to him. I wouldn't trust him an inch. Anyway, where's his girlfriend tonight?'

Eunice shrugged. 'I don't know. But you don't know him like I do, Megan. Remember, we went out together for six months.'

'Until he saw a better option – moneywise, I mean! I'd forget him, Eunice.'

'The trouble is – I can't.' Megan saw the glisten of tears in her eyes and was about to answer when as she felt a touch on her shoulder.

It was Terry. 'We meet again.'

She smiled. 'It makes a change from the cemetery!'

'You look fantastic, Megan.' He smiled at her, 'How about a quickstep?'

She took his outstretched hand and hoped she'd be able to follow the steps. But Terry was an enthusiastic rather than an accomplished dancer, and made a few mistakes himself, which gave her even more confidence. The female vocalist was singing, *'I want to be happy...'*, and Megan thought how apt the words were, because everyone in the ballroom seemed to be exactly that, they were all smiling and the atmosphere was wonderful.

'I've never seen you here before,' Terry said.

'It's my first time,' she told him, 'but it won't be my last.'

'That's because you've got a smashing partner.' He clumsily swung her round a corner.

'You could be right.' Not that I'd have a clue

116

Megan thought, seeing that I've never done a quickstep with anyone else. She glanced at him as later they walked off the floor. He was still ordinary-looking even in his navy suit, but at least he'd had a shave. Suddenly she realised that he liked her. It was in his eyes, his manner, the way he was protectively ushering her back to Eunice.

'Can I get you two girls a drink?'

'A Babycham, please,' Eunice darted a fearful look over her shoulder. But there was no sign of her cousins.

Megan hid a smile. 'Could I have a lemon and lime?' she said. Debra had told her that was considered a sophisticated soft drink.

'Of course you can.'

Eunice teased, 'I think you've got an admirer.'

'It's this dress,' Megan said. She was heady with excitement, enthralled by the music, the glamour of the band and the dancers – by the whole experience. Why, oh why, have I been missing all this, she thought? How on earth would anyone fear such a happy experience? I wasn't being protected, I was being deprived! There were even families here, and Megan saw the pride on a father's face as he danced by with his young daughter.

Eunice hissed, 'Look over there!'

Megan turned to see two youths staring at them, and even as they watched one nudged his friend and with an exaggerated swagger they strolled over to the two girls. The one chewing gum, said to Eunice, 'Like to dance?' The other, wearing a shiny blue suit looked at Megan and

117

jerked his head towards the dance floor.

'I'd love to,' she said, 'but someone's gone to get me a drink.'

'Oh, he'll be ages, there's a hell of a queue out there.'

Megan hurriedly put her bag on to the table behind her, and took the hand he held out. The band was playing *'The Tennessee Waltz'*, but her somewhat younger partner soon turned it into a 'smooch'. Held tightly against him as he merely swayed to the music, she was shocked when he rested his cheek on hers, but then found to her astonishment – and some guilt – that although he was a stranger she rather liked the sensation. His skin was smooth, his hair smelt pleasantly of Brylcreem, but when the music ended, he just said, 'Thanks!' and walked away.

Terry's expression was one of annoyance when Megan went back to join him. He handed her the lemon and lime. 'You girls are a right pair,' he said, 'disappearing like that.'

Eunice, looking flushed with exertion came off the floor. 'Thanks,' she said to Terry, taking her Babycham.

Megan watched her friend hesitate then tentatively sip it. 'Watch out,' she whispered, 'here's Brian!' Eunice hurriedly hid the glass behind her and Megan burst out laughing. 'Sorry, I was only kidding.'

And so the evening went on, with Megan dancing exclusively with Terry, while Eunice seemed to hit it off with a young man wearing a sports jacket and flannels. He had Megan thought, rather an odd way of dancing, sort of jigging about, but

Eunice didn't seem to mind and every time Megan saw her, she was laughing. Brian and Pete came over to speak to them a couple of times, but mainly skulked around the perimeter morosely watching everyone else. While Ben seemed to have disappeared.

Then finally the band struck up a drum roll, and the count to midnight began. As soon as the sonorous sound of Big Ben filled the room, there were shouts and exclamations of 'Happy New Year', and Megan found herself swept into Terry's arms. He kissed her resoundingly on the cheek then everyone was hugging everyone else and forming circles to cross arms to sing *'Auld Lang Syne.'* Afterwards a huge net above released coloured balloons which floated down causing much merriment and laughter among the crowd as some began to burst.

'Are you on the last bus?' Terry asked her.

Megan nodded.

'So am I. I'll wait for you outside, and then walk you home.'

The two girls went to collect their coats and change their shoes. 'Terry's on the same late bus as me. He's offered to walk me home.'

'You lucky devil,' Eunice said as she put her coat on. 'I'm stuck with the idiots.'

Megan laughed. 'They're not that bad.'

Later, Terry held her hand as after they left the bus they walked along the pavements away from Longton. It was no longer raining, although the deserted road glistened with moisture beneath the street lamps. An occasional car passed them and other party-goers returning home called out

New Year greetings which they returned. It was Megan thought, the best evening of her life.

Terry told her that he was twenty-four and worked as a fitter at a local engineering firm. Megan glanced sideways at him, at his long nose and slightly receding chin. Nathan's broad shoulders and good looks flashed into her mind, but she knew that there was no point in her wishing for the unattainable. And so when eventually they reached her quiet road, and Terry turned to take her in his arms, she raised her head with both shyness and some curiosity for her first kiss. But his lips were wind-chilled, her own were hesitant and all too soon she was drawing away with a flat feeling of disappointment. However, when he asked to see her again, her answer was swift and positive. And she knew it was the right one. Looks weren't everything and he had been very kind and helpful to Iris. He was also, Megan thought as she let herself into the house, her only prospect – at least so far.

Chapter Fourteen

Their first date was to see *Captain Horatio Hornblower* at the Broadway Cinema in Meir, a ten minute walk away. With its Art Deco style it was a prominent landmark and they climbed the broad steps together and then Megan waited as Terry went to the box-office. She was pleased to see that he'd paid for the best tickets as that meant that they could sit near the front of the balcony. Terry was quiet and companionable during the B film and Pathé News, and when the lights went up for the interval and the usherette in her maroon uniform stood at the front with an illuminated tray, he asked if she'd like an ice cream and went down the stairs to queue for one. Megan watched him. He's definitely not mean, she thought. The girls at work warned her to make sure from the start that he wasn't 'close with his money'. They still had no inkling of her master plan, but it wouldn't take a genius to work out that someone in her lonely situation would be glad to get married.

Once the main feature began, Terry leaned back to put his arm around Megan's shoulders, drawing her closer to him. She sat awkwardly at first but eventually began to relax against the rough tweed of his jacket, although as she gazed up at the screen she couldn't help wishing that he looked more like Gregory Peck. But dutifully she let him kiss her as the film was ending and this time his lips were warm and her own more responsive. When the lights went up they rose for the National Anthem before emerging into the cold night air.

On the way home, Terry told her a story about one of his mates at work. 'Old Dave's a right character. I must tell you this, Megan – it's true, honestly. Well on New Year's Eve, he went for a few drinks at the Dunrobin and took a short cut home through the cemetery. Anyway, a sudden gust of wind whipped his hat off and blew it between the gravestones. It was pitch black wasn't it, and he was scratching around trying to find it when this other guy comes along. Well Dave, daft beggar, rears up from behind a gravestone and shouts, ''ast got a light, mate?' Terry gave a shout of laughter. 'The poor bloke took off like a bat from hell.'

Megan burst out laughing, and tucked her hand more cosily into Terry's arm. A sense of humour, she thought, now that's another good point. During the next few weeks she also soon discovered that he was an ardent Stoke City fan and resigned herself to listening to him talk endlessly about match tactics, stupid decisions by referees, and unfair results. However he wasn't the most romantic suitor and Megan, who was used to hearing the girls at work declare that 'men always try it on,' was beginning to wonder if there was something wrong with her, and felt almost relieved when one night as he kissed her, he slipped his hand inside her coat. Gently he held her breast and she could feel his warmth through her thin blouse. 'When are you going to ask me in?' he murmured. 'Or are you worried about your reputation?'

'You can come in now as long as you behave yourself!'

And he did. Megan liked that about him, that he respected her. But eventually his kisses became more passionate, his hands more searching, and Megan wasn't entirely sure how she was supposed to feel at such times. She liked Terry, liked being part of a couple and quite liked him kissing her, at least most of the time. But surely she thought, I should be longing to see him again, day-dreaming of being in his arms, even of marrying him? Because wasn't Terry the answer to her problems?

Clarice and Rita definitely seemed to think so.

'He's got a steady job, duck,' Clarice said. 'That means money coming in on a regular basis. And if he's still living with his mother, he's probably got a bit in the bank as well.'

The three of them were having a cup of tea and a chat one Saturday afternoon. Tom had gone with Alan to the match and Jack was, as Rita said with a sigh, clearing out his pigeon loft.

'I'm going to meet his mother tomorrow.' Megan hesitated. 'I do like him, but I'm not sure whether...'

'Look love – just be thankful that you've found someone,' Rita told her.

'I admit that Terry's no film star,' Clarice said, 'but just look at our Alan. He was at the back of the class when looks were given out, and yet Pauline thinks the world of him.' Clarice wanted Megan to be happy, to be in love, but one had to be practical. Besides, the girl was beginning to look a bit pinched, and Clarice couldn't help wondering whether she was eating properly. It was only too easy when living alone to snack rather than cook a proper meal. I worry about her, she thought. I worry about her living in this drab place, always anxious about bills, having nobody to share her life with. 'Stick with him,' she advised. 'Anyway, he might grow on you. And it's not as if you don't get on.'

'That's true. We've never had a single argument.'

'That won't last,' Rita said, 'especially if you get married! Isn't that right, Clarice?'

She laughed. 'My old mum used to say that my dad annoyed her so much at times that she could have chopped his head off and kicked it round the room like a football!' She gave a reminiscent smile. 'But they still stayed married for forty-five years.'

Megan decided to change the subject, 'How's little Nicholas?'

Clarice visibly brightened. 'He's a little smasher, gaining weight every week.'

'You're so lucky,' Rita said, 'having a family, I mean.'

Megan and Clarice gazed at her with sympathy. It was well known that Rita and Jack couldn't have children, although they'd kept the reason to themselves.

'I'd have adopted,' she was now saying, 'but Jack was never keen. He said he was blowed if he was going to spend his brass on bringing some-one else's kid up.'

After Rita had left, Megan said, 'I think that's why she's so house proud. She told me once that if she couldn't have a family then at least she was going to have a nice home. Do you remember when she had her tiled fireplace in? She was as proud as punch.'

Clarice nodded. She couldn't imagine life with-out a family – as for her own home, cluttered it might be but it was cosy and comfortable; unlike this dreary place. She glanced curiously at Megan. A lick of paint didn't cost much, and she was surprised the girl hadn't made more effort with it. Maybe, Clarice mused, she's hoping that when she finds herself a husband she'll be able to move. And after all, who could blame her?

Terry's home was a terraced cottage near Queen's Park. Ricardo Street was considered the best street 'on Dresden', with two distinct ends. The 'posh' end consisted of large often detached houses occupied by such superior people as master potters, hospital consultants and solicitors, while the occupants of the more modest end, near the Park Inn on the corner, were mainly pottery workers.

Terry came to meet her, and they walked the short distance up a hill and past the church graveyard before turning right. Megan gazed with envy at the windows of the larger houses; trying to imagine how different life must be in such spacious surroundings. And then as they approached his own home, Terry grinned. 'Mum said I wasn't to bring you along the backs, but to use the front door.'

She laughed. 'You don't normally use it, then?'

He shook his head, 'But I've noticed you do yours.'

'That's because of my dad. He used to say that it was his house so why should he behave like a servant and go round the back!'

'I've never heard that one afore.' He opened a small gate fronting the tiniest patch of garden Megan had ever seen then turned the knob on the front door. It was, she noticed not even locked. They went into a small parlour smelling strongly of lavender furniture polish with the linoleum on the floor so shiny that Megan feared slipping. Crammed with furniture there was a bow-fronted china cabinet against one wall, a heavy sideboard against another, and a small moquette three piece suite before the fireplace. Room to move around was restricted; it was pristine, chilly and obviously rarely used. 'Come on through,' Terry said and ushered her past a steep staircase to an even smaller room, where she was thankful to feel the warmth from a crackling fire in the grate. There was a square table in the middle, and two comfortable, if well-used 'easy chairs'. Sitting in one of them, straight backed, her pepper and salt hair tightly permed was Terry's mother.

'Mum, this is Megan,' Terry said, and when she didn't get up Megan leaned forward and held out her hand.

'I'm pleased to meet you, Mrs Podmore.'

Freda Podmore neither shook Megan's proffered hand nor answered. Instead she said in a sharp voice, 'Put the kettle on then, Terry. You can sit there, Megan.' She pointed to the other chair.

Terry went off to do his mother's bidding, and Freda's glance swept disparagingly over her visitor. 'I hear you live on your own.'

Taken aback by the blunt remark, Megan nodded and explained about her parents.

'There's nobody to keep an eye on what you get up to then?'

Megan stared at her. 'I don't get up to anything, Mrs Podmore.'

'Well, I should hope not if you're seeing my Terry.'

Bewildered, Megan thought that at least one of them should make an effort to be pleasant. She glanced around the spotless room. 'You've a lovely house.'

Freda, almost as stiff as her starched crossover apron, narrowed her eyes. 'Yes, it is. *And* I take care of it.'

Now what was she implying? Surely Terry hadn't complained about her? So what if once when he came Megan had neither dusted nor swept the hearth – it was hardly a hanging offence! But Freda hadn't finished. 'I hear you're religious,' she said. 'I don't hold with it meself. I never go to church, never did.'

'You didn't get married in church, then?' Megan was beginning to wonder why anyone had ever wanted to marry her at all.

'Of course I did,' Freda looked affronted. 'Otherwise folk would think you were living over the brush. But I've never set foot in one since – apart from Ted's funeral.'

'So they do have their uses?'

Freda seemed not to notice Megan's sarcasm. 'I have to accept that. But you should know that our Terry's not a believer either.'

'I do know that, Mrs Podmore.' Megan's reply was terse and she turned with relief as Terry came back into the room. He was carrying two china cups and saucers, and as she saw the pretty pattern, Megan exclaimed, 'That's one of ours!'

'Oh yes,' Freda said, 'You're an enameller, aren't you?'

'Yes. Have you ever worked on a pot bank?'

'I certainly have not!'

127

'Mum used to be in service,' Terry explained.

'I was a lady's maid,' Freda snapped. Then I pity the lady, Megan thought grimly – fancy having that sour face behind you in the mirror.

'But I never had to work at all once I got married,' Freda said with pride. 'Ted didn't believe in women working outside the home and neither does Terry.'

Megan turned to him. 'Don't you think a woman should have the choice, Terry?'

'He thinks like me, that women should obey their husbands.'

Terry didn't say anything; he merely went to fetch a Battenberg cake displayed forlornly on a doily-covered plate. Pulling out one of the chairs from the dining table he slanted it to face Megan, and cut her a small slice.

Megan looked at with dismay. His mother certainly hadn't made much effort with the tea – a shop-bought cake and not a single sandwich?

'And how are you keeping, Mrs Podmore?'

'Not so bad, considering.'

Megan wondered, considering what? She decided not to ask. Any hopes she'd had of marrying into a warm loving family were rapidly evaporating. She looked with suspicion at the colour of her tea and had to repress a grimace when she tasted condensed milk. The next hour was even worse, as no matter how politely Megan phrased her questions or tried to make conversation, Freda would merely answer with an abruptness that was almost rude. Terry tried to help, but there were still several awkward silences. It also seemed odd that not only was

128

Freda wearing a black armband, but she seemed to expect that everyone else should.

'He was a good king, was George VI,' she declared, 'and people should show their respect.'

'She actually cried when she heard,' Terry told Megan. 'But then it was a shock, him dying suddenly like that in his sleep.'

'He was only fifty-six,' Freda said in a sombre tone. She probably goes to the funerals of strangers, Megan thought, and sits at the back of the church feeling noble.

Her relief was heartfelt when she heard Terry eventually say, 'Well, I'll take Megan home, Mum.'

'Don't be late back, will you?' Freda turned to Megan. 'His late nights are only on Fridays and Saturdays, he's got work tomorrow.'

'Don't worry, I'll send him back early,' Megan said, struggling to keep her own tone civil.

As they turned to go, Freda announced, 'I'll come for tea at your house next Sunday, then.'

Megan swung round to stare at her in astonishment, but before she could speak, Terry said, 'Great.'

'Why did you say that?' she demanded once they'd left. 'I decide who comes to my house, not anyone else.'

'I just thought as you'd been to us this week...'

'She doesn't even like me.'

He began to laugh. 'Nonsense, Mum's always like that, it's just her manner.'

'Maybe she should think about changing it!'

He took her arm and turned her towards him. 'Hey, don't be like that.'

'Does she always tell you what to do and speak

129

for you?'

He grinned, 'Most of the time.'

'You still shouldn't stand for it.'

He shrugged. 'I like an easy life.'

Megan glanced sideways at him. If that meant he would be easy to live with, then surely that was a good omen? So why, she wondered, did his attitude fill her with irritation?

Chapter Fifteen

On Tuesday morning Megan woke up with a fiery throat, pain behind her eyes, a runny nose and a temperature. Her dismay was swiftly followed by panic. She couldn't afford to be ill. Every day she was off work was one day's pay lost *and* she'd lose her weekly bonus. Already economising on food, she didn't know what else she could cut down on. Shakily she went downstairs and made herself tea and toast; at least having the grill burning even for a short time meant the kitchen was warmer than in the sitting room. She couldn't face the thought of emptying the ashes and lighting a fire. But the toast hurt her throat, so she had a piece of bread and margarine and went back to bed carrying a stone hot water bottle and feeling so shivery that she had to switch on the rarely used two-bar electric fire. In a haze of wretchedness she struggled through the next two days on cans of soup, hot drinks and aspirin and it wasn't until the third day that she felt well enough to get dressed.

In the chill of the sitting room she laid and lit a fire, then went into the kitchen to clear up the chaos of the previous few days. Despondently washing the congealed dishes, but relieved to find her appetite returning, Megan was wondering whether she could manage to cook when two loud slams on the door knocker made her jump. Hurriedly she dried her hands on a tea towel and seconds later found herself gazing in astonishment at a burly delivery man. A Royal Mail Van was parked outside.

'Here you are, love,' he said, 'all the way from the USA.'

Astonished Megan stared at the large box with its foreign stamps. America? But that could only mean that it must be from Nathan! Joy and excitement rose within her. 'Are you sure it's for me?'

He grinned at her. 'Miss Megan Cresswell?'

'Yes.'

'Then that's what the label says. It's heavy – where do you want it?'

Megan swiftly led the way into the sitting room. 'Anywhere here will be fine. Thank you very much.' He lowered his burden down in the middle of the floor near the dining table, and as she signed the delivery note said, 'I'm glad I've made someone happy.'

'Is it that obvious?'

'Love, that smile will last me all day.'

Once he'd left, Megan went into the room to sit on one of the chairs and to stare at the huge box dominating the hearth. She didn't know whether to open it or wait and savour the delicious antici-pation. But there must be a letter inside! Seconds later she was cutting the string and removing the sealing tape. Gingerly, she opened the top flaps then after removing layers of brown paper saw a cream envelope. Her heart beating so rapidly that she could hardly breathe, Megan went to fetch a knife so that she could neatly slit it open and settling into the armchair, took a deep breath and with suddenly trembling fingers extracted a single sheet of cream notepaper.

When she saw the signature her disappoint-ment was so painful that tears welled into her eyes. Angrily she brushed them away, blaming weakness from her illness. But it still took several seconds before she felt able to gaze down at the letter again and slowly begin to read.

Dear Megan, Nathan has told us how much he enjoyed your friendship while he was in England. He found the Potteries a fascinating area and tells me that you were most informative. He also mentioned that you still have food shortages over there, and asked me to send you this small thank-you gift. As his mother, I am very happy to do so and hope you will find the contents helpful. I also hope that you are keeping in good health, and send you my very best wishes, Elizabeth Jane Brittles.

So Nathan *had* remembered her, and the parcel *was* from him – at least in a way! But oh, how she wished he'd written himself. Slowly Megan leaned forward and removed the top layer of packing to reveal two large boxes of chocolates. Eagerly she turned them over to look at the illu-strations, anticipating the sweetness, the pleasure of the contents, wanting to prolong the moment. Then she put them on the table and delved in again. Wrapped in tissue paper were six pairs of sheer nylon stockings, all in the same shade which meant to her joy that if one laddered, then she would be able to pair it up. One after the other she lifted out the items; coffee, tea, cocoa, tins of peaches and apricots, jars of peanut butter and strawberry jam, cans of cooked ham, turkey breast and corned beef, all packed within straw. There were two tinned beefsteak pies, a fruit cake in a tin and three packets of cookies. Cookies – did that mean cakes or biscuits? Whatever they were, they looked delicious. The brown chenille table cloth was soon crammed, piled high with items.

Nathan had asked his mother to send her all this? It was a treasure trove, and she began to pick items up again one at a time, reading the labels, full of wonderment and gratitude. All this would make such a difference to her life and her budget. Suddenly she couldn't wait to put it all away, to display her booty on the shelves and fifteen minutes later Megan stood back to admire her handiwork. She had never seen the larder so well stocked, just going into it over the next few weeks would be a better tonic than any the doctor could prescribe. And then she thought – never mind baked beans, I'm going to have one of those pies to celebrate! But once it was in the oven, with a saucepan of canned garden peas simmering on the hob, she found she was exhausted, too tired to even clear away the box and remnants of straw. Instead she settled down to re-read the note from Nathan's mother.

'*He enjoyed your friendship*,' then Megan's gaze moved with some dismay to '*you were most informative*.' It made her sound like some sort of guide. Was that the way that Nathan thought of her, merely as a pleasant girl he could talk to about Arnold Bennett and the Potteries. Hadn't she warned herself from the beginning not to read anything else into it? But there had been those magical moments between them; she knew she hadn't been mistaken about those. Or had she? Megan raised her head and stared into the fire at the now leaping flames. Distracted, she remembered that her coal supply was getting short, but then her thoughts returned again to the food parcel and Mrs Brittles' kind words. Megan thought of the tightly-corseted figure of Freda Podmore, with her narrow accusing eyes and her sharp tongue. I can't imagine *her* being so thoughtful, or anything even near it. Now if only Nathan had been here longer, if only ... she gazed again at the thick cream sheet of paper and then with a sigh carefully folded it and put it back in the envelope. Hadn't Ellen used to say that wishing for things didn't necessarily bring them?

'Are you sure you're all right?' Dora Dawson said with concern when the following morning, Megan went back to work. 'You still look a bit peaky.'

'I'm fine thank you, Miss Dawson. It was just a bad cold.'

'Well, I can't deny I'm glad to have you back. We've got a big order in. And there's a collection

going round for Mr Ian's wedding present.'
Megan thought – oh glory, another expense. Not
that she really minded. All the girls thought that
Mr Ian was a real heart throb. Tall and with dark
good looks, the son of the owner was not only
respected but considered a 'right bobby dazzler'.
Not a few of the girls had felt pangs of disappointment when they heard that he was getting
married.

'It'll be some rich girl, you mark my words,'
Lizzie snorted, after she'd taken half-a crown
from her purse.

'Now how do you know that?' Minnie demanded. 'There's nothing of the snob about Mr
Ian.'

'Like mixes with like, always has done.'

'Just because someone's born into money, it
doesn't make them a bad person, you know.' That
contribution came from Jean, and Megan
glanced fondly at her. I don't think she's got a
malicious bone in her body, she thought. But
Jean's expression was pensive and she'd seemed
distracted all through the morning. Megan could
see tension and strain in her face and at first remained quiet, not wanting to intrude. But eventually she whispered, 'Is everything all right,
Jean?'

'Not so bad, love.'

'Is there anything I can do to help – if you've
got a problem, I mean?'

Jean gave a weak smile. 'If only there was.' She
turned and lowering her voice so much that
Megan could only just hear her words, said,
'They've found a lump.'

Megan stared at her. Her own voice almost undetectable, she repeated, 'A lump?'

Jean nodded. 'It's only a small one, on my left...' she moved her hand towards her left breast.

Megan stared at her in horror. 'What are they going to do?'

'I've to go into hospital next week. I haven't told Miss Dawson yet.'

'Oh, Jean ... but surely they'll be able just to remove it – I mean, couldn't it just be a cyst or something?'

Jean shook her head. 'I've already been through that, love.' She looked at Megan and her voice broke, 'They think it could be...'

Megan felt her scalp prick. 'You don't mean...' she faltered, her throat closing, unable to say aloud the dreaded word.

Jean nodded. Seeing tears in her eyes, Megan's heart filled with compassion. Quietly, she said, 'Would you like me to tell the girls and Miss Dawson for you?'

'Would you?'

'Of course I will. And I'll tell Miss Dawson first. Look, are you going out at dinner-time?'

'Yes, I want to go to the chemist's – you know to get a few things to take in with me.'

Megan's tone was gentle. 'I'll tell everyone then and get it over with.' She decided not to mention her good news about the food parcel, it didn't seem appropriate, not now.

'Thank you ... and Megan...'

'Yes?'

'Could you – say a prayer for me?'

Now Megan's own eyes were struggling with

tears. She whispered, 'Of course I will,' and had to look away as Jean bent her head to the petals of the flower she was working on.

Chapter Sixteen

Jean's news had shaken Megan, and still feeling tired after her cold, she was dreading the prospect of Freda's 'visitation' on Sunday. When she got home from chapel she merely opened a can of Heinz tomato soup for her dinner, devoting her energy into making the sitting room so spick and span that even Terry's mother wouldn't be able to find fault. Just let her say one word, Megan thought grimly, just one...

When the eventual knock did come at the door, Freda confronted her resplendent in a velour blue hat firmly anchored with a lethal-looking hatpin. Terry hovered behind her.

Megan forced a tight smile of welcome. 'Please, come in.' She stood aside as Freda stalked into the sitting room. Terry gave Megan a peck on the cheek and followed.

'Let me take your coats,' Megan waited while Freda removed her gloves and fumbled with tight buttons. She kept her hat on. Terry removed his own and gave Megan his raincoat while Freda marched over to sit in one of the armchairs. Terry said, 'Shall I...?' he began to withdraw one of the dining chairs.

Megan nodded. She hung their clothes over the

banister at the bottom of the stairs. In the kitchen everything was ready, with the old wooden tray covered with one of Ellen's embroidered tray cloths and laid with a china tea set. On a cake stand was a fruit cake, which Megan, muttering under her breath with resentment, had baked the day before. As the gas spluttered into life beneath the kettle, Megan went back in and said, 'It's a lovely day, isn't it? I'm glad you didn't have to walk in the rain.'

'I wouldn't call it lovely,' Freda said. 'There's quite a cold wind.'

Megan forced herself to smile. 'I just meant that it was dry.'

But Freda was gazing around her as if, Megan thought, she had a nasty smell up her nose. 'You've still got the old black grate then,' she said. 'We replaced ours with a tiled one two years ago.'

'We were thinking about it just before Dad died, but then afterwards...'

'I remember *him*.'

Megan was astonished. 'You knew my father?'

'Well, I wouldn't say I knew him, not exactly. When Terry told me he worked in that hardware shop in Longton, I guessed immediately who he was. He wasn't what you'd call a barrel of laughs, was he?'

Megan controlled a sharp retort. 'He was a thinking man.'

Freda sniffed. Then she got stiffly up. 'I shall need to avail myself of your facilities.'

More like she wants to nosy round, Megan thought. And her suspicion was confirmed when she later went into the kitchen to make the tea.

Surely the larder door had been closed?

But even Freda couldn't find fault with the china tea service – although Megan didn't tell her it was a 'seconds', and Terry was enthusiastic about the cake. 'I didn't know you were such a smashing cook, Megan.'

'I like a nice bit of sponge meself,' was Freda's only comment, although Megan noticed that when offered an extra slice she took it. 'Of course, some of us have extra help with our rations.'

'What do you mean?'

'Well I couldn't help noticing as I passed that you're very well stocked up – surprisingly so!'

The blatant cheek of the woman! So she *had* looked in the larder. Right, Megan decided, I'll give her something to really get her teeth into. 'Oh that,' she said. 'I had a big food parcel from this American I met just before Christmas. He was over here on a business trip.'

Now it was Terry's turn to stare, 'An American?'

'Yes. He took me for lunch at the George in Burslem.'

Freda's eyes narrowed. 'Did he now? And you say he sent you a food parcel?'

Megan was suddenly hit by a desire to giggle. 'And four pairs of nylon stockings.'

'*Nylons*?' Freda's eyes were now wide with outrage.

Terry was frowning. 'You never mentioned this American to me.'

'I didn't see any need to,' Megan said. 'Anyway, the food parcel only came last week when I was ill.'

'Ill?'

'Yes, I was off work with a nasty cold.'

'You should have let me know.' Terry looked at her with concern.

'How could I? You were decorating your back bedroom, so we hadn't arranged to meet.'

'You're changing the subject,' Freda snapped. 'Whatever would your mother have said? Nylon stockings off a Yank! We all know what that used to mean.'

'Not in every case, Mum,' Terry protested.

'And certainly not in mine,' Megan said. She was struggling to keep her anger under control. 'Nathan was a friend, that's all.' Her voice rose as she asked, 'Would you like another cup of tea, Mrs Podmore?'

Silently, Freda held out her cup. And that was how she remained, silent for at least ten blessed minutes, and then she suddenly said, 'I don't think you should wear them.'

Megan, who had just finished listening to Terry describe the problems he'd had in stripping off the wallpaper, turned to her. 'If you're still on about the nylons, of course I'm going to wear them. Why ever shouldn't I? In any case, it was Nathan's mother who actually sent the parcel, on his behalf. So I can assure you that it was all above board.'

'There you are then, Mum. So that's all right then.'

Megan glared at him, but all Terry did was to grin and surreptitiously wink.

Freda still hadn't finished. As she put down her plate, she said, 'That's an unusually fine silver-backed hairbrush in there.' She jerked her head towards the kitchen.

'You don't miss much, do you?'

'I pride myself on being observant.'

'Well, if you're so interested, you can have a closer look!' Megan's voice was so sharp, that she saw Terry stare at her, but she didn't care. Seemingly oblivious to the angry way in which Megan got up, and then coming back into the room thrust the hairbrush at her, Freda stroked it, turned it over carefully and ran her finger along the beaded edge.

'I'd brought it down to polish.' Megan's tone was curt.

'Yes, I can see you look after it.'

Megan stared at her in astonishment. An actual compliment at last!

'It's beautiful,' Freda said. Then her expression changed to one of suspicion. 'Where did it come from?'

'It belonged to my mother.'

'Do you have the hand mirror as well?'

Megan shook her head.

'Well, there'll be a matching mirror somewhere, you mark my words. As for where it came from – I suppose it could have been an antique shop,' Freda mused, 'but it's odd that there wasn't a mirror with it. Even if the glass had cracked, it would have been replaced. This is real quality, and whose are these initials?' she peered closely at them.

Terry began, 'Mum knows about such things, having...'

'Been a lady's maid ... yes, I'm sure she does.'

141

Irritated, Megan held out her hand for the hair-brush.

'I'd still like to know where your mother got it from,' Freda muttered, handing it back with reluctance.

And I think you should mind your own business! The words almost shot out of her, but instead with a huge effort Megan managed a thin smile. She glanced at her watch, willing the minutes to tick by.

'If women didn't get married because of their future mother-in-law, we'd be a nation of spinsters,' Clarice told Megan. 'In any case you marry the man, not his mother.'

'Take no notice, love,' was Rita's advice. 'I couldn't do a thing right for Jack's mother for the first few years, but she came round eventually.'

During Monday's breakfast break, the girls at work had plenty to say.

'Old Ma Heath was a right cow,' Lizzie said, fingering her new perm which closely resembled a grey scouring pad. 'We made the mistake of renting a house in the next street and if Sid missed a single day in visiting her, she'd give him an earful.'

'You were lucky,' Flo said. 'Mine came to live with us when her husband died. She used to play us off one against the other, and then just to spite me she'd take Jim's side. We had more rows...'

'I hate mine.' That was a flat statement from Enid, who had stopped complaining about her husband's sexual demands; the general opinion was that he was making them elsewhere. They all

142

looked at her with sympathy.

'Did you always?' Megan asked.

Enid nodded. 'I'd think twice, Megan. Marriage is difficult enough without any extra problems.'

'Well,' Jean said, 'I can't really join in this conversation. I've got a good mother-in-law; she's always been very helpful.'

Miss Dawson had told everyone that the best way to help Jean was to behave normally. 'She needs some distraction from the worry,' she said, 'so no outpourings of sympathy, it will only upset her.'

'So that shows they do exist, then,' Minnie said, in a determinedly bright tone. 'Sometimes listening to you lot, I'm glad I stayed single.'

'Well, you were left in a fortunate position, Minnie,' Lizzie said, 'what with your parents owning their own house and leaving you a little nest egg.'

'I know that,' Minnie said sharply. 'But even though I haven't got rent to pay, it's not easy. Why else to you think I'm still working at my age?'

Lizzie grinned, 'Because you'd miss *us*, you daft bat!'

Over the next couple of months, Terry and Megan continued to 'court', as Clarice called it. They went to the pictures and to dances at Longton Town Hall. Terry liked the Cameo ballroom which was above Burton's Tailors in Longton, but Megan found it small. She wanted to go to the well-known ballroom in Trentham Gardens, but Terry refused. 'I'd rather go somewhere more local,' he'd say which as the difference was only about four miles, didn't make much sense to Megan. He also only ever wanted to take her to local cinemas, such as the Alhambra – the one where Megan had encountered the 'pervert' – or the Broadway in Meir, or Empire Cinema in Longton.

'I think he'd be happy if he never travelled more than five miles from home in his life,' Megan complained to Rita. 'He never even goes to an away match.'

'Well, there are worse faults,' was all she'd say.

But Les had been much the same, Megan thought. His flat feet had precluded him from active service during the war and his Air Warden duties hadn't taken him away from home, yet he'd never wanted to go on holiday. 'We don't need to,' he used to say, 'not with Queen's Park only five minutes away. You couldn't find anywhere better, no matter how far you travelled.'

However Ellen and Megan had gone on a couple of bus trips, to Rhyl and to Blackpool. And there had been such a sense of release, of light-heartedness about those hours spent away, that Megan treasured the memories. Maybe, she thought, when the summer comes I might be able to persuade Terry to go to the seaside. Perhaps Llandudno, which Miss Dawson said was 'very select'. But, Megan thought grimly, I'm determined about one thing – if we do go, his mother isn't coming with us!

She and Freda had managed to achieve an uneasy relationship. Freda still made her carping comments, and Megan still struggled not to retaliate. But Freda *was* Terry's mother and

144

Megan consoled herself that although Terry didn't make her heart race, he did make her smile and she had to admit that he was good-natured and thoughtful. He'd even mended her vacuum cleaner.

Iris, now back on her flower stall and fully recovered from pneumonia, was delighted about the relationship. 'You can thank me for bringing you together,' she said one day. 'My two good Samaritans, that's what I call you. You were made for each other.'

Megan wasn't so sure about that. But it was a relief that she now had a potential husband – instinctively she knew that it was only a matter of time before Terry proposed. In fact, she suspected that he was taking it for granted that they would marry. She was brooding on this one Sunday morning as she caught the bus up to Bethesda. Now that Terry was in her life, she usually attended the services at her local chapel, but sometimes she would go to Bethesda; it was a way of keeping in touch with Eunice. With the other girl working on Saturdays, and Megan going out with Terry, there had been little opportunity for them to meet. And for once, Eunice was there without her parents.

'They've gone to my Gran's in Uttoxeter,' she announced. 'She's not well, so they're stopping over.' She laughed, 'You won't believe it but Dad's actually letting me stay on my own. I told him, if Megan can live by herself, surely I can manage it for one night!'

Megan nudged her, and Eunice turned to see Ben behind them, waiting to pass. He nodded to them both, and they watched as he went to meet his girlfriend and her family by their limousine.

'Have you heard of an engagement yet?' Megan whispered.

Eunice shook her head, and it was with dismay that Megan saw the raw longing in her eyes. Again she said, 'Forget him, Eunice, he isn't worth it.'

'You don't know him like I do,' was the other girl's quiet reply.

The following Friday, when Megan got home from work, tired and suffering with period pains, she couldn't face peeling vegetables and cooking a proper dinner. So after she'd placed a fire-lighter in the grate beneath pieces of coal and put a match to it, she decided that instead of saving the oatcakes she'd bought for tomorrow, she'd eat them tonight with cheese on. The rest of the country doesn't know what they're missing she thought as she took them, steaming and covered with bubbling cheese from beneath the grill. And then later as she hugged a hot water bottle, she tried to concentrate, to do some thinking. Because to her shame she'd got into a bit of a mess with money, and Megan was furious with herself. She couldn't blame it on the wages she'd lost when she was ill – the food parcel from America had helped to offset that. She could only blame herself for carelessness when adding up her sums. Maths had never been her strong point.

And so mistakenly thinking she had more spare cash than she actually had, she'd brought Jean's catalogue home again. Tempted by the new summer fashions she'd impulsively ordered several cotton dresses. She loved them all, but knew with guilt that those weekly repayments had eaten so much into her budget that she'd soon be short of coins for the gas and electric meters. At least her hot water was provided by the back-boiler in the grate, so that wasn't a problem. But she needed gas for cooking, and she needed electricity for light. And she didn't dare to economise on coal, not now the weather had turned so cold. There were even blizzards, and her milk was often frozen solid when she took it from her doorstep.

Life wouldn't be such a struggle if she married Terry. Megan stared into the flickering flames of the fire, the prospect playing in her mind. Did she love him? Not in the way love was portrayed in novels and on the cinema screen. But did such love exist in real life? Perhaps everyone had a secret reason for choosing who they married; a man might look for a good cook, someone to make him comfortable; and a woman for a man who offered security – just as she was doing. She knew for a fact that one of the girls at work had got married to escape from a violent father. Megan might have led a sheltered life at home, but working on the pot bank had taught her much about what often 'went on behind closed doors'. She'd heard of children kept short of food, while their fathers drank and smoked or gambled. One woman who worked in the warehouse often tried to disguise a black eye or a bruised arm. Yet there were many happy marriages too. Yet how was she to know that she was making the right judgement?

What if Terry turned out to be a philanderer? Look at the mistake she could have made with Ben! Ellen always maintained that you never knew anyone until you lived with them. But, Megan wondered bleakly, how could you do that unless you married them first?

Chapter Seventeen

The following Saturday, Terry took Megan to watch Stoke City versus Blackpool. 'It's a chance for you to see Stanley Matthews,' he said. 'He's not called the "wizard of dribble" for nothing.'

Megan was quite keen to go, thinking that if she actually saw a game, she might find Terry's endless football anecdotes less boring; she might even understand what 'off side' meant. They had arranged to meet at the bus station and Terry, already there when Megan arrived, was full of impatience. 'We've missed one bus,' he said, 'and kick-off's at a quarter past two!'

'I couldn't come until the buzzer went!' Megan protested, but he was already moving forward as the next bus drew up at the stand.

Once in Stoke, they joined others walking to the Victoria Ground where Megan, impressed by the mounted policemen exercising control, paused to admire the rippling muscles of the powerful horses. Terry however hardly gave them a glance; he was already heading for the Boothen End entrance. They hurried up the steps to one of the turnstiles and once through, he bought meat and potato pies and beakers of Bovril which they carried up yet more steps, and then suddenly Megan stared in astonishment as she gazed down at a massive sea of heads. The noise was deafening, the green grass of the pitch flanked by thousands of supporters standing on the terraces. Most of the men had come straight from work and were wearing caps, many wore football scarves, while others near the front had brought their young sons. Terry threaded his way through to find them a good place and a few minutes later they were biting into the hot savoury filling in its crisp pastry. Sipping her Bovril in the cold air, Megan began to be infected by the excited atmosphere and was soon glancing at her watch with impatience.

Then suddenly the loudspeaker crackled. The announcement that Albert Hobson would be playing at number seven resulted in a surge of disappointed groans. 'What's happened?' Megan said.

Terry's groan had been one of the loudest. 'Stan Matthews isn't playing, he must be injured or something.'

Then ten minutes later there was a roar of acknowledgement as both teams ran on to the pitch. Stoke's strip of red and white was a perfect foil for Blackpool's white shirts and black shorts, and after the toss of a coin, the referee blew his whistle and they were off. Terry soon became so involved in the game that Megan began to wonder if he'd forgotten she was there.

'The goal's the other end, you bloody idiot,' he

kept yelling, always to the same player and Megan, both shocked and surprised at his language, exclaimed in a voice louder than she'd intended, 'Terry, that's not very nice – you'll hurt his feelings!'

There were guffaws of laughter from people around them, but despite the shouting and ear-splitting sound of football rattles much to her surprise she enjoyed the match, and was disappointed when Stoke lost, with Blackpool winning 3-2 after a hat-trick by Alan Brown.

On the way home, Terry was deflated. 'It's only one game,' she said.

'What do you mean, only one game?' He launched into statistics about points and league tables until her brain was spinning.

'You're playing darts tonight, aren't you?'

'Yes, you don't mind do you? I know we usually go out, but I did take you to the match.'

Megan didn't mind at all. A quiet evening in with her library book was something to look forward to. She now called in at Longton Library every Saturday afternoon on her way home from the market. Her first tentative visit to the impressive old building which was named the Sutherland Institute had been a revelation. Outside she had paused, impressed by the carvings above the doors representing local industry – ceramics, coal and steel. Then in the silence and dust motes she'd browsed through the tall shelves, breathing in the smell of polish, astounded by the breadth of literature waiting to be taken home, and full of disbelief that her parents could have deprived her of this wonderful source.

At first she'd found that carrying a bunch of flowers was awkward as she tried to choose her books, but soon the friendly librarian had offered to look after them behind the desk. 'They'll brighten me up,' she said. 'Just don't bring lilies, they give me a headache.'

And later that evening when eventually she put down Nevil Shute's novel, *A Town like Alice*, Megan wondered why it was that her parents had never made any real friends. They were polite to their neighbours, but Megan couldn't recall ever meeting anyone who had known Les and Ellen before their marriage. Ellen's parents had died before Megan was born and she'd been an only child. And why had her father always refused to talk about his? She glanced down at the book on her lap. She was captivated; she loved reading about other countries. Why didn't she try to find one set in America? There might even be a novel in the library that could tell her something about Kansas – if not a novel, then a reference book. At least then, she thought wistfully, I'd have some idea of Nathan's background. She'd heard nothing further from America, although she had written back. Megan went over to the sideboard to browse yet again through her short note. She'd bought a Basildon Bond unlined writing pad in pale blue with matching envelopes and had spent ages trying to compose the right words. She still had the original, having been dissatisfied at first with her handwriting and had copied it out more neatly. Now, sitting back in her chair, she read it once more.

Dear Mrs Brittles

I can't tell you what a wonderful surprise it was to receive your kind parcel. I really am grateful for all the trouble you went to. Everything you sent was chosen so carefully, and it was a joy to unpack such a treasure of foodstuffs. These will help me enormously. Yes, there is still food rationing here, but it is gradually improving, and we are all hopeful of some of the restrictions being lifted soon.

I so enjoyed meeting Nathan and it was lovely of him to remember me in this way. Please do give him my kindest regards,

Again, with much gratitude,

Yours sincerely,

Megan Cresswell

So far Elizabeth Brittles hadn't replied, and Megan didn't expect to hear from her again. After all, she thought, they've made their kind gesture – I expect that will be the end of it. She just had to stop thinking about Nathan, had to stop dwelling on that heart-stopping moment just before he left ... with a sigh Megan put the letter back in the drawer. It was late and time for bed, but at least tomorrow she was going to Bethesda again, which would give her the chance to see Eunice.

When Elizabeth Brittles received Megan's air-mail, her gaze ran over the few lines and then she read it again, this time more slowly.

Ross Brittles, tall and rangy, his handsome face weather beaten from hours spent outdoors, glanced over. 'You seem deep in thought, who is it from?'

152

Elizabeth handed the airmail over to him. 'Sounds a nice girl,' he said. 'Are you going to send her more?'

Elizabeth shook her head. 'I'd like to, but Nathan's not keen.'

Ross filled his pipe with tobacco and pressed it down into the bowl. 'Why do you think that is?'

'I'm not sure.' She was frowning, and he shot her a sharp glance.

'Now then, you know what a fertile imagination you've got!'

'You're right, I'm probably imagining things. Anyway, he's coming over later for dinner.'

Ross grinned, 'After a bit of his mother's cooking? He must know that it's Marcy's day off.'

'She's a very good cook!'

'She's fine, but she hasn't got your magic touch!'

Elizabeth smiled at him. 'You're just biased.'

Later, as his mother gave him the letter, Nathan kept his features carefully controlled. Even as he read the carefully written polite words, he could imagine how Megan would have sat at the square table in that cramped, cheerless room. The whole scene, so much of their time together was still so vivid and the image of her standing bravely on the doorstep as he drove away – he couldn't get it out of his mind. The fact that he didn't seem able to control the memories or the feelings they aroused was infuriating. He was nearing thirty for heaven's sake, he wasn't some callow teenager.

Elizabeth was watching him. 'Are you sure that you don't want me to send more parcels? I'd be very happy to. I'm sure she would welcome them.

153

If comes to either food on the table or a bit of hurt pride, believe me there's no contest.' Elizabeth gazed at him, feeling puzzled. She knew his every expression so well. 'It does seem a shame when...'

Nathan gazed across the room at the graceful woman opposite, her hair in soft silvery waves, her expensive silk blouse framing a perfect row of pearls and shook his head. He knew what was in her mind. He and his sister never talked about their mother's past. It had been the day after Nathan's fourteenth birthday when he and Helen had been summoned to their father's large book-lined den to find him regarding them with both anger and resignation.

'I hear you kids have been pestering your mom again about her father, wanting to know why you've never met him. Now I've told you before, I don't want you asking her questions.' He regarded them steadily in the sun-filled room, his gaze searching first Nathan's obstinate expression and then twelve-year old Helen's troubled one before giving a heavy sigh. 'Okay, you win. I suppose you're old enough to be told the truth.' He ran his fingers through his sun bleached hair. 'You know that your mother was only twelve when your grandmother died, and that there was very little money?'

They both nodded.

'And you know that her Dad was left to bring her up?'

Again they nodded. 'What I'm going to tell you is in strict confidence, and must remain a family matter.' Never a man to waste words, Ross told

154

them, 'Your grandfather had a habit of using his fists. And Elizabeth said that once he even beat her with a leather belt. And that's the reason you don't see him, and the reason why he will never set foot in this house.'

Nathan had waited until he was eighteen. Burning for revenge and confident of his strong physique, he had hired a detective to discover his grandfather's whereabouts. And in a scene for-ever etched on his mind, he had waited with flexed muscles for the bully who had abused his beloved mother. And then in a quiet alley that led to a seedy bar his grandfather had shambled towards him; bent and elderly, his body wasted and frail. Nathan had stared into the vicious face he had dreamed of punching, and with almost superhuman effort managed to keep his clenched fists by his side. He had never mentioned the encounter to anyone.

Nathan looked again at his mother's anxious expression. He could understand her wish to help, but his fervent hope was that if Megan's name was never mentioned, if he went ahead with the life he had planned, then these intrusive memories of their time together would fade. Any-thing else would be crazy. 'I told you,' he said, 'I only met her twice. We've made the gesture and I think that should be the end of it.' Folding the thin paper in half, he handed the letter back.

Ross glanced at him and then at Elizabeth. 'Nathan will have his reasons my love, and I think we should respect them.'

'Yes, of course.' Elizabeth stood up. 'Well, if you guys will excuse me, I think it's time I checked on the pot roast.'

After she'd left the room, the two men sat in silence for a few moments, and Ross's eyes were thoughtful as he smoked his pipe. Then he measured his words. 'Have you seen Alison lately?'

'We went to the theatre last week.'

Ross gave a sigh. 'Nathan, you can't expect her to wait forever, you've got to make a decision, and soon.'

Nathan's voice was low. 'You like her, don't you.'

'We both do, very much indeed. And Helen gets on with her as well. We've known her all her life, and you can't deny that it's an ideal match. Ivy League educated, the daughter of our closest business friends...' Ross gave an exasperated shrug. 'Alison's an attractive girl Nathan and I'll say it again – you can't expect her to wait forever.'

Nathan's proposal one quiet evening was not the most romantic in the world, but Alison seemed blissfully unaware, instead saying, 'I thought you'd never get round to it! I've always known that one day we'd get married, even when you were being horrible to me.'

'When was I ever horrible to you?'

'That time you put a white rat in the pocket of my coat, at Janie Jordan's birthday party. I screamed the place down. You'd have been about twelve at the time.'

He laughed. 'And you still want to marry me?'

Alison gazed up at him, then smiled and kissed his cheek. 'I certainly do.'

Their engagement party was held a fortnight

later at an exclusive Country Club just outside Wichita. The leading citizens of both the city and surrounding county areas were there, and Ross Brittles and Alison's father stood at one side of the room surveying the scene with approval. Alison's mother was moving among the guests greeting and smiling, while Elizabeth sipped her champagne, quietly watching the celebrating young couple. Nathan stood by his fiancée receiving the congratulations of his friends and acquaintances and then alone for a few moments when Alison went to speak to an old school-friend, he turned as a business acquaintance tapped him on the shoulder. 'I hope you know what a lucky man you are.'

'I certainly do, Eddie.' For a fleeting instant the disturbing image of a young English girl gazing at him with her heart in her eyes surfaced, only to be firmly quelled as Alison with her swinging blonde bob, clear skin and splendid smile came back to join him.

As Nathan stretched out an affectionate hand, she said with easy confidence, 'I think we should plan a spring wedding. After all, we have no reason to wait.'

Chapter Eighteen

On Sunday, when Megan, having taken her place in the balcony at Bethesda, leaned over to search for her friend, she saw her immediately. Eunice was wearing the emerald green coat she'd had for Christmas, and sitting beside her father in their usual pew. She glanced up to see Megan, waved and later waited for her outside the chapel, where a few yards away her father was talking to an elderly woman.

Megan went forward smiling, but Eunice was looking uneasily over her shoulder. 'Megan, quickly – tell me, what's your address.'

Startled, Megan told her.

'How do I get there from the bus station?' Her voice was almost a whisper.

Now completely bewildered, Megan explained. 'Will you be in on Tuesday night?'

'Yes, any time after seven would be fine ... but...'

Sam Goodwin, with his usual impatience was already moving away and glancing over at them so Eunice said, 'Sorry, I'll have to go.'

Megan watched her hurry to join him and wondered what all the mystery was.

To her surprise, Megan felt quite nervous about Eunice's first visit. So she made sure the hearth was swept and tidy, pulled forward the vase of flowers and plumped up the cushions. She glanced up at the opaque china bowl hanging on three chains from the ceiling, wondering whether a higher wattage bulb would brighten the room up but after searching in vain to find one, at last she heard the knock at the front door.

Eunice, her expression uncertain, stood beneath an umbrella.

'You found it then,' Megan smiled, 'come on in.' She waited to take her friend's coat and scarf and then gestured to one of the armchairs.

'You didn't mind my coming?'

'Of course not, I'm pleased to see you.'

Eunice hardly bothered to look at the room; instead she sat down and her words came out in a rush. 'Can I talk to you, Megan?'

'Of course you can.' Megan gazed at her with concern; she could now see the strain in her eyes.

'I've just got to talk to *someone*.' Eunice gazed pleadingly at Megan. 'And I thought ... please, will you promise that if I tell you something, you'll keep it to yourself?'

'Yes, I promise.'

Eunice hesitated and in a low voice said, 'It's about Ben.'

I might have known, Megan thought. 'What about him?'

Eunice's lips twisted. 'Do you remember a few weeks ago, when I was at Bethesda on my own, and I was telling you that Mum and Dad were away in Uttoxeter?'

'Yes, I do.'

'Well, Ben heard me.' Eunice looked down at her hands. 'That same night he turned up at the house.'

'He never did!' Megan stared at her. 'The sneaky devil...'

Eunice raised her head. 'It wasn't like that. He said he'd come to realise that I was the one he really loved.' She looked across at Megan, her eyes filling with tears. 'I just couldn't believe that after all these months of missing him and wanting him...'

'So, are you back together?' Megan asked. 'Is that what you wanted to tell me? But I don't understand. Why don't you want anyone to know?'

'We're not back together.' Eunice's voice cracked and she began to fumble for a hanky in her bag as she began to cry, harsh sobs catching in her throat.

Megan hurried across to put an arm around her shoulders. 'Eunice, whatever's the matter? Please...'

'I'm pregnant.' Eunice's voice was muffled through her tears.

Megan drew back. 'You're what? But how on earth ... are you sure?'

'I must be. I'm three weeks over due.' She gazed up at Megan in despair. 'I'm never late – I'm as regular as clockwork.'

Megan didn't know what to say. Slowly she went to slump into her own chair. How could Eunice have been so stupid? Maybe she *was* besotted with Ben, but to go against the teachings of her religion, to take such a risk...

'I'm sorry,' Eunice straightened up, still clutching her now damp hanky. 'Only I didn't know who else to go to.'

'There's no need to be sorry,' Megan said,

straightening up. 'That's what friends are for. But what I'm trying to take in Eunice, is that the minute Ben knew you'd be on your own, he came round and...'

'It wasn't *all* his fault. You know how I feel about him.'

Megan stared at her. 'Hang on a minute. You've just told me that you're not back together. Surely he hasn't gone back to his girlfriend?'

'How do I know? I've hardly seen him since, and never on his own,' Eunice said with bitterness. 'He's still sitting by her in chapel though.'

'So you haven't told him?'

Eunice shook her head. 'It's obvious he doesn't want me.' Her voice was full of pain.

'Do you want him?'

'I love him. Oh, I know what he's like, but I don't care. There'll never be anyone else for me, never!' Eunice twisted the damp hanky in her fingers. She looked across at Megan and hesitated, 'You don't think I should consider...'

Megan frowned, unsure of what she meant, then her eyes widened. 'You don't mean ... you can't possibly mean...'

'It did cross my mind.'

Megan was appalled. 'You can't do *that!* You hear *such stories*... Eunice, apart from the danger it would be taking a human life! You'd never forgive yourself.' Helplessly, Megan stared at the other girl. 'You've got no choice but to tell him, Eunice. You shouldn't have to face this on your own.'

'I just don't know what to do,' Eunice began to cry again.

Megan got up. 'Look, I'm going to make a pot of tea. I think we could both do with one.' In the kitchen, she angrily clattered cups and saucers. She was seething – how dared Ben treat Eunice like this? Oh, he could 'charm the birds from the trees', as people would say, but what was beneath it? Treachery, that's what. Scurrying back to his rich girlfriend the moment he'd got what he wanted! Well, he wasn't going to get away with it. A few minutes later Megan carried in the tray. She put it on the table and looked down at her friend's blotched face and puffy eyes. 'If you want me to, I'll come with you.'

Relief swept over Eunice's face. 'You mean to tell Ben? Oh Megan, would you?'

'Of course I will.' She got up and picking up the poker lifted the coals on the fire. Megan watched them blaze up for a moment then turned. 'We'll go tomorrow night. There's no point in waiting.'

Chapter Nineteen

The two girls had arranged to meet outside Marks & Spencer's in Hanley at half-past seven. Although the weather was now warmer, the evenings were still turning cool, and Eunice was wearing her emerald green coat, matching hair band and black patent court shoes. But as Megan got nearer she could see the shadows beneath her eyes and a pinched look around her mouth. She said with concern, 'Are you okay?'

162

'What do you think?' Eunice said with despondency. 'I still haven't come on, *and* I was sick this morning.'

'Your mum didn't...?'

'No, thank God.'

'There doesn't look much doubt, does there?'

Eunice shook her head, and they began to make their way to the bus stop. Ben lived in Smallthorne a few miles away, but Megan knew little else about him other than that he was a teacher, and that his father had been killed in the war. Glancing at the other girl, she could see in her set expression both anxiety and panic, but Eunice didn't seem inclined to talk; she just stared ahead with compressed lips. With her 'Alice in Wonderland' appearance Megan thought that she was the last person anyone would expect to be in this quandary, after all she hardly looked like a girl to be swept away by passion. But then what did *she* know about passion? It was easy to be virtuous when you'd never been tempted to be anything else. Her own experience of lovemaking was limited to Terry fondling her breasts, and that was only through her clothes. But the sensation, while pleasant enough, had hardly filled her with desire. And maybe it was because he teasingly called her 'a holy Mary' – even though she kept telling him that made her sound like a Catholic – but she'd never once had to 'fight him off', as the girls called it. So maybe he'd never experienced passion either.

Eunice still didn't seem inclined to talk. Instead she spent the journey gazing out of the window and restlessly plucking at her white nylon gloves.

Megan guessed she was rehearsing what she was going to say to Ben.

But when they got off the bus, she said in panic, 'I don't think I can face it. Suppose his mum's there? She's got a weak heart, you know.'

Oh glory, Megan thought – this just gets worse. She caught at her friend's arm. 'Yes you can, you've got no choice. Come on Eunice, steel yourself – there's no going back now, not when we've got this far.'

Eventually, they turned into the tree-lined avenue and then half-way up Eunice indicated a substantial semi-detached house with bay windows. Her steps slowed as they drew near but Megan, now feeling nervous herself, was already opening one of the white wrought-iron gates and standing aside for her to pass. The gate creaked as she closed it. 'You go on,' she said, 'I'll stand back here.'

'Aren't you coming with me?'

'I think it's better if you tell him by yourself. Honestly.' Megan gave her a gentle push. 'Go on,' she said, 'you can't chicken out now.' She glanced around and then went to wait in front of the privet hedge where she would be seen.

Eunice slowly walked the few yards to the front door, then after one anguished glance back at Megan, lifted the knocker and rapped. There was no answer. She drew back.

'Knock again, harder,' Megan called. 'Maybe they're at the back.'

Eunice gave two sharper raps and this time the door opened within seconds. Ben, in shirt sleeves and a fair-isle pullover looked astonished to see

Eunice and when his gaze darted beyond her to Megan, he stepped out and closed the door swiftly behind him.

'Eunice?' Her name was clear on the night air.

'Hello, Ben.' Her voice began to tremble. 'I haven't seen you recently, not since...'

He looked embarrassed. 'I'm sorry. I have been meaning to get in touch but ... well, it's not been easy.'

'Because of *her*, you mean?' Eunice's shoulders stiffened. 'Well you're going to have to forget her – because I'm pregnant, Ben!'

Even from where Megan was standing, she could see his growing horror. 'You can't be!'

'Well, I am.' There was now a sob in her voice. 'I *had* to come and see you. I didn't know what else to do.'

'Are you sure?' His voice was hoarse, strained.

She nodded. 'I'm three weeks late, *and* I've got morning sickness.'

He ran a hand through his hair, and Megan thought she'd never seen any young man look so wretched. 'Have you told anyone else?'

She shook her head, 'Only Megan.'

Ben glanced over to where Megan was standing. 'Yes, I can see you brought her along to back you up! Was that necessary?'

'I was too scared to come on my own.' Eunice gazed pleadingly up at him.

Ben stared down at her, his face contorted with indecision then he said, 'Look, I can't ask you in. I'm going to need time to think about this, Eunice.'

Megan was appalled. Not one word of affection, of reassurance? Surely he could see how upset and worried the girl was? Incensed, she stepped forward. 'Is that all you can say, Ben?'

His expression became stony. 'Forgive me, Megan, but I don't see that this is any of your business.'

'It became my business when Eunice came to me for help.'

Ben glared at her. 'Of course she needs help.' He glanced back at the house and lowered his voice. 'Have I said anything different? I only said that I needed time to think things through. It's a hell of a shock.'

Eunice was saying. 'It's just that I need to know...'

But Ben was restless, impatient. 'Look we can't talk here. I'll meet you tomorrow after work, Eunice. I'll come to the store, I promise.'

'I'm sorry, Ben.' She made a half-hearted movement towards him but he was already turning away, and then he was gone, closing the door firmly behind him.

Eunice remained staring at the oak panelled door, until hearing the creak of the gate as Megan opened it she turned and went to join her. Her face was white, her eyes bright with unshod tears, and a passing woman walking a Yorkshire terrier, turned to look curiously at her. The two girls began to walk back along the narrow pavement then Eunice said, 'It went better than I thought it would.'

'It did?' Megan stared at her with incredulity.

'Oh, I know you think I see Ben through rose-tinted glasses but I don't. I kept having this

166

nightmare that he'd deny it, say it wasn't his. As if I'd ever let anyone else...' Suddenly, the strain of the last few minutes became too much for her and Eunice burst into tears.

Megan tried to comfort her. 'He did promise to be there tomorrow.'

'I know.' Eunice fumbled with the clasp on her handbag and took out crumpled hanky. 'You do think he'll do the decent thing and marry me?'

Megan wasn't so sure. 'Eunice, can I ask you something? I mean, how would you feel about that? Would you have wanted to marry Ben anyway, if this hadn't happened?'

Her answer came swift and definite. 'Of course – it's what I've always dreamed of.'

Megan saw the glint in her eyes, the sudden determined set of her chin, and with a shock into her mind leapt a treacherous thought. Could Eunice have planned all this? She was frightened and anxious now, but that night when Ben had appeared so unexpectedly, had she seen a possible solution, a way of getting him back? Megan felt disloyal for even thinking of it, but after the two girls had parted, with Eunice promising to let her know what happened, the suspicion lingered. I don't suppose I'll ever know the truth, she thought on the way home. But she was sure of one thing – Ben's ambitious courtship of that other girl was over, whatever happened.

The wedding took place four weeks later at Bethesda. Ben, his face pale but resigned, stood at the side of his pregnant bride. In her cream lace wedding dress and veil, Eunice was attended by two nieces; six-year old auburn-haired twins in pale blue satin who stole everyone's hearts. Sam Goodwin, his expression taut, his shoulders rigid, gave his daughter away, while her mother, in a beige costume and coffee coloured tulle hat, tried in vain not to cry. On the other side of the aisle was Ben's mother. She stood alone, small and dignified, quietly dressed in navy, relieved by touches of white. Megan wondered how she was feeling, was she too sharing in the Goodwins' shame? The young couple were to live with her; rented properties were scarce and there was a long waiting list for council houses. As Megan's gaze wandered around the congregation, the atmosphere seemed subdued and she guessed that most of the people there either knew, or suspected the reason behind the wedding.

Megan was there alone. Terry had made the excuse that he didn't know Ben and had only met Eunice twice. Besides he told her, there was a home match on that day. She hadn't minded in the church, but at the reception held in a local hotel when in her new summer dress she stood alone in a corner, Megan felt awkward and conspicuous. The only people she knew were Eunice's cousins, Brian and Pete, who were smirking at a couple of young girls and pulling faces at the little bridesmaids. She's right she thought they *are* a couple of clots. It was only later that she discovered – to her dismay – that she was seated between them at one of the long tables.

Afterwards, before Eunice left for her honeymoon – two days in Blackpool, she made her way over to Megan. Looking pretty in a pale blue costume, she said, 'All's well that ends well, then. Thanks for coming, and for all your help.'

'You're welcome,' Megan said. She hesitated, 'I shall miss you, Eunice, you know – to go out with and things. I do hope you'll be happy.'

Eunice looked over her shoulder to where Ben was saying goodbye to his mother and gave a quiet smile. 'Don't worry – I'll keep him on the straight and narrow.'

Later that evening, restless and too distracted to read, Megan sat in an armchair and thought back over the day's events. To give Ben credit, he'd given no outward sign that he'd been forced into the marriage. And at least she thought, the early wedding would do much to silence any scandal. Eunice wasn't the first girl to get into trouble, and she wouldn't be the last. After all, as Clarice had said, 'not even religion gets in the way of human nature.'

And now Megan couldn't help wondering whether Ben had been telling Eunice the truth that night. *Was* she the one he really loved? Certainly he'd convincingly played the part of a loving bridegroom that afternoon. And whatever Eunice's motives – and Megan still had misgivings – there was no doubt that she was deliriously happy.

Megan, her book lying unread on her lap, stared unseeingly into the distance. Why did that disturb her so much? Was it because *she* wasn't? It was a question that not only unsettled her but one that she was almost afraid to answer.

Chapter Twenty

The following morning, Megan flung out a hand to silence the jangling bell of her alarm clock and lay sleepily content for a few moments before with an inward groan she remembered that it was Sunday. And that meant enduring Terry's mother. Quite how it had happened, Megan wasn't sure, but a rigid routine had become established. One week she would walk up to Freda's to spend a stultifying hour and a half – there was no variation, it was always a Battenberg cake for tea – and then the following Sunday afternoon Freda and Terry would come to her. Today it was her turn to go to them.

But on this particular morning not even that prospect could dampen her spirits as when she opened her eyes she saw bright sunlight seeping beneath the thin bedroom curtains, its rays highlighting patches of dust on the cracked linoleum. She could also hear birdsong and Megan swung her legs on to the small pegged rug at the side of the bed and went barefoot to peer with joy out of the window. Deciding that she wasn't going to waste a moment of this lovely weather, she planned to set off earlier than usual so that she could go up to the park and stroll along the tree-lined paths in blessed solitude. She loved trees, in a strange way she felt calmer when she was near them. If no-one else was about, she liked to go over to one, to lay her hand on a thick gnarled trunk, stroke the roughness of its bark and feel its strength and protection seep into her. I have to spend so much of my life indoors, she thought with regret, either at work or catching up with chores at home. Her own small patch of garden didn't have any trees, just a tiny patch of lawn, a narrow path beneath the clothes line, and a ragged privet hedge. And so after chapel and an early dinner she set out, carrying on up and over the hill, where she turned right and walked beneath the shady trees to the middle gates of Queen's Park. With a cardigan slung over her bare arms and wearing a pair of well-worn sandals, she felt cool and free in the warm sunshine, pausing at the children's paddling pool to watch the excited toddlers splashing and squealing, and smiling at their antics. Then she wandered down a path to the tennis courts where the pavilion door was open. The small square room was empty, but on one court a couple of lithe girls in white tennis dresses were intent on a hard-fought game. Megan watched them for a while. She quite fancied playing tennis, and she and Audrey had once tried to borrow a couple of racquets but without success. I must write to her, Megan suddenly thought. It's been weeks since I got her last letter.

Next she strolled through the rose gardens, past the bowling greens and down to the lakeside. There were several rowing boats already hired, mainly by perspiring youths trying to impress their girlfriends. The Victorian boathouse was busy serving teas and Megan soon found a secluded seat near the lake where she could sit

171

and take in the scene.

For a while she simply enjoyed the peace with sunlight dappling through the trees and watching occasional passersby; a few elderly couples, a man pushing his wife in a wheelchair, giggling teenage girls and parents with skipping children who they warned to stay away from the water.

And it was then that she saw them. The young man was tall with fair hair; good-looking, he wore an open-necked blue shirt while the girl was in a white dress spotted with navy, her dark shoulder-length hair lifting in the breeze that came from the rippling water. They were walking with arms entwined, talking softly and as the girl nuzzled her head against his shoulder, the young man smiled down at her. Their faces were so transparent with love and delight in each other that Megan was entranced. Her gaze followed them and the image of the young lovers lingered in her mind long after they'd passed by. The scene had disturbed her, bringing with it an ache, a sudden longing to share the joy of such a love and she felt tears prick at her eyes, initially of self-pity, followed by an overwhelming feeling of shame.

A few minutes later, as she stared at the dignified swans gliding by some yards away, Megan finally faced up to the unpalatable fact that she didn't like herself very much; at least she didn't like what she was planning to do. To marry a man she didn't love merely to make life easier for herself, to live a lie for the rest of her life. And Megan knew now that she didn't love Terry, that she had never loved him. She had never felt for him even one tenth of how she'd felt, or knew how she could feel about Nathan. Could she live with the guilt that she had cheated a decent man, an unimaginative one maybe, but one who had shown her nothing but kindness? Terry deserved better. And Megan knew that she couldn't let this charade continue any longer. Somehow she must find a way of breaking it off, of explaining to him how she felt in a way that would cause the least hurt. As Megan walked slowly out of the park she couldn't help wondering how deeply Terry did feel about her. It sometimes seemed that they had simply drifted into their 'courtship'. Even when he was holding her in his arms, when he was kissing her, Terry had never once said that he loved her. But then she thought, weren't many men reticent to talk about their feelings? Certainly her father had been like that. Her stomach fluttering with nerves, full of determination she turned into Ricardo Street only to find her steps slowing until she paused outside Terry's home. For one long moment she stared at the small lace curtained window then after a sharp tap on the front door, went inside.

'Hello, it's only me,' she called. Megan was met as ever by the smell of lavender furniture polish and she went through the parlour to the room at the back, where despite the warm weather, both of the windows remained closed. Terry was sprawled in one of the armchairs reading the Sunday People, Freda was knitting. The centre table was set with cups and saucers, with the Battenberg cake in pride of place.

'You're late!' Freda, almost at the end of a row,

completed the last stitch and put down her needles with exasperation.

'Only slightly,' Megan said. 'I went for a walk in the park – it's lovely out there.'

'Go on then, Terry,' Freda snapped, 'she's your guest. At least we can have a cup of tea now.'

He got up and winked at Megan, who gave him a quick smile.

Freda stared at her with suspicion. 'My word, you're dolled up today.'

Megan looked down at her cool turquoise frock. 'It's just a summer dress. It's nice to get out of winter clothes for a change.'

'Is it new?'

'Yes, it is, actually.' Not for anything would Megan tell her that she'd somewhat guiltily ordered it from the catalogue.

Freda snorted. 'You shouldn't have spent your money! Summer clothes are a waste of time – you never get your wear out of them. I'm still wearing the ones I bought before the war.'

And they'll probably last you until the next one if you keep covering them up with those cross-over overalls, Megan thought. The one Freda was wearing today was a blue floral print, and Megan knew exactly where she would have bought it. There was a small haberdashery shop in nearby Carlisle Street owned by a spinster, and there were always some in the window. Megan absolutely refused to wear one. She could understand women protecting their good clothes while they did jobs around the house, but so many kept them on all day, even if they popped out to the corner shop. They must Megan thought, spend so much time washing, starching and ironing the darned things. Megan only ever wore a small waist apron, and she took that off as soon as she sat down to relax. She considered herself to be a person, a human being; not a maid of all work.

Freda was leaning forward, her eyes glinting. 'So, how did the shot-gun wedding go? Don't tell me she had the nerve to wear white!'

'It went very well. And actually she wore cream lace.' Megan's voice was tight. She wished Terry had kept his mouth shut.

'I should think so, as well. I can't be doing with hypocrites, I never could!'

Megan gazed stonily at her, thinking self-righteous prig!

'Were there many up there?'

'The park, you mean? Yes, lots of people.'

'I haven't bothered to go since Ted died. There's not much point on your own.'

'I was on my own, and I enjoyed it.'

Freda ignored her. 'I keep asking Terry to take up bowls. Then I could go with him and sit by the bowling green.'

'I've told you, Mum, it's an old man's game,' Terry said, bringing in the teapot.

'It'd be better for you than drinking in the Dunrobin and playing darts!'

'Did your Dad play bowls?' Megan asked Terry.

'He did not,' Freda snapped. 'He preferred to spend his spare time with me.'

Ever likely he died young, was Megan's silent reaction. She turned her attention to Terry, her stomach already in knots at the prospect of the ordeal before her. How on earth was she going to tell him? As her gaze wandered over his dark hair and now familiar if homely features and he glanced up at her and smiled before slicing the cake, for one split second she wavered. Would she be making a big mistake? But then an image came into her mind of the young lovers in the park and in a low voice she said to him, 'I thought that perhaps later we could both go up to the park; you know, make the most of the good weather?'

'Good idea!' He smiled amiably at her.

'Oh, that's *very* nice,' Freda said, 'leave me on my own then.'

'There's nothing to stop you coming with us, Mum.'

Horrified, Megan held her breath.

'No thanks, I've no desire to be a gooseberry!' Freda's lips tightened. 'And where's my slice of cake, Terry, or have you forgotten I'm here?'

'Now then, Mum, guests first.'

The next stilted fifteen minutes were, to Megan, almost unendurable. Not only was she finding the stuffy room stifling, but her nervousness was increasing with every minute that passed. Eventually she could stand it no longer. She began to get up and looking across to Terry said, 'Shall we...?'

He immediately pushed back his chair and rose. 'We won't be too long, Mum.'

But she didn't answer; instead Freda picked up her needles and began to knit with ferocity, her mouth a thin line of resentment.

Megan turned at the door and gazed at her. In future, whenever she became depressed, whenever problems seemed insurmountable, she would think of this woman and remind herself that things could be so much worse; she could have had Freda Podmore as a mother-in-law. When Terry's mother didn't look up, Megan didn't even bother to say goodbye.

Chapter Twenty-one

'You've what?' Clarice stared at Megan with dismay and astonishment.

'I've finished with him.'

Clarice was bewildered. 'But why, what did he do?'

'He didn't do anything,' Megan said feeling embarrassed. 'I just decided that we weren't right for each other. We'd got nothing in common really.'

Rita's eyes were wide with disbelief. 'And here I'd been counting on a summer wedding. I even had a look at the hats in British Home Stores last Saturday. I'll have to wait for our John now.'

'That was a bit previous!' Clarice gave her an amused glance.

'Well, you have to have something to look forward to.' Rita reached out and took another biscuit. 'These look nice Clarice. Are they Elkes?'

She nodded, still taken aback by Megan's announcement. 'Are you sure you're not making a big mistake?'

'I'm positive,' Megan said. 'It just didn't seem right. Terry deserves better than a wife who doesn't love him.'

'Spoken like a good Christian. But it's my belief,' Clarice said, 'that charity begins at home.'

'Have you thought this through, love?' Rita said with a worried frown.

'It's not that American is it?' Clarice said.

Megan felt the heat rise in her cheeks, 'No of course not.'

The two women exchanged swift and knowing glances. Clarice said slowly, 'You don't want to go on holding a candle for him, love.'

'I agree,' Rita said, reaching out for another biscuit. 'You were ships that pass in the night, that's all. But to change the subject, if you don't mind me asking, how are you managing? I mean that food parcel his mother sent must have been a godsend, but it won't last forever.'

'I'm all right, honestly.'

Clarice noticed that Megan didn't meet their eyes, but all she said was, 'Tom says thanks for the peanuts, by the way.'

'And Jack enjoyed those cookies you sent round.' Rita dusted crumbs from her fingers. 'I just hope you won't regret it, Megan. How did Terry take it?'

Megan's eyes clouded, remembering his shock, his hurt expression. 'Not very well,' she admitted. 'I think he's hoping I'll change my mind, but I won't.' She looked at the two older women, her expression determined. 'I'm quite capable of taking responsibility for myself.'

'That's all very well, love,' Clarice's eyes were now full of concern. 'But principles don't keep food on the table.'

'I've told you, I'm managing.' A few minutes later Megan, wanting to avoid any further questioning said, 'Anyway, I only popped round to tell you. I'd better go – I've got some ironing to do.'

After she'd had left, Clarice said, 'I could swing for that blasted Les. As I've said before, not a penny was that girl left with; no insurance, nothing. And what bit he did leave got used up before Ellen died.'

'He always was a strange man. At least Terry would have been an improvement on him.'

'I know. I worry about that girl, Rita, I really do. Mind you it's her life, and it's her bed he would have shared.'

'You don't think that's it – with her being so religious and everything...' Rita raised her eyebrows.

Clarice shook her head. 'No, I don't think so. It's more likely she's got her head full of romantic dreams.'

'Hadn't we all!' Rita's tone was tinged with bitterness. 'I'd better be off as well. I need to get ready for work tomorrow.'

'Thanks again for this.' Clarice held up a blue knitted pram suit. 'It'll suit little Nicholas a treat.'

'You're welcome. Don't get up, I can see myself out.'

Clarice gazed thoughtfully after her. It wasn't the first time Rita had sounded disillusioned. And who could blame her? Jack had hardly been a bundle of laughs since he was demobbed. But then, who could blame him either? Whatever it was he went through in that prisoner-of-war camp it had changed the man, and he didn't ask for it, did he? That blasted war, she thought. It destroyed so many lives, but there was no doubt it had been necessary. She'd never forget sitting in the Alhambra cinema in a state of shock as the newsreels revealed the full extent of the murder and evil that had taken place, of the millions of Jews who had been exterminated. Clarice may not believe in God or at least in the one that the churches portrayed, but after seeing those shocking, nightmarish scenes she'd come home convinced of the power of the devil.

Megan's thoughts were not of 1945, but of 1952. Her financial situation was much more precarious now than it had been when Ellen died. Megan was brooding on this when the following morning she walked to the pot bank. She still felt guilty about the new summer clothes, but at the time Jean had been due to go into hospital, the catalogue wouldn't be available for a while, and she'd needed something to wear for Eunice's wedding...

I'll survive, Megan thought, it's a case of having to. And after all, she had managed for the past twelve months. But then she hadn't been faced yet with any major expenses and that couldn't last forever. There was the vacuum cleaner for instance. Terry had mended it once, but it was making a very strange noise and the suction was getting weaker all the time. She couldn't expect never to have to repair or replace anything; some of the curtains for instance wouldn't survive another wash. And it wasn't as if she'd been extravagant, all she'd bought was a remnant of material off the market to make cushion covers, and even those she'd sewn by hand. With a sigh she turned under the archway and went up the wooden stairs to the decorating shop where it wasn't until the morning break, that Megan told the girls about Terry.

'Why was that then, Megan?' one woman said as she bit into her cold toast. 'What made you decide?'

Lizzie had a more pointed question. 'Was it because he farted a lot? Sid's terrible for it. When the old dog lets off at the same time, I have to open the back door!'

There were shrieks of laughter, and Megan said, 'No, Lizzie, it wasn't that.'

'Was it that tartar of a mother?'

'Not that, either.'

'Well, what then?'

'Mind your own business,' Minnie snapped. 'Leave the girl alone.'

'Thank you, Minnie.' Megan had decided not to confide her real reason; simply that she didn't love him. Romance is all very well on the cinema screen and love stories but it wasn't real life, was a viewpoint she'd often heard. And yet Megan guessed that when they were young, most of the women had dreamed of it, and some had even found it. One of the lithographers walked home holding hands with her husband when he came to meet her, and they must have been married at least fifteen years.

And that, Megan thought with determination as later she went back to her place on the bench, is the sort of marriage I want to have.

181

But whatever Megan's financial problems, they paled into insignificance when a fortnight later, she went to visit Jean. It had been Miss Dawson's idea.

'You're the one closest to her,' she said with a worried frown. 'I mean, I know she didn't want any visitors while she was in hospital, or just afterwards, and we respected that. But I don't want her to think we've forgotten about her.'

And so the following Saturday afternoon, with a shopping bag filled with offerings from the girls, and Jean's address in her handbag, Megan began the walk up to Meir. She passed the Territorial Army Drill Hall and glancing up at the Broadway Cinema, she saw that it was showing a Western. Terry had loved Westerns; he may not have been the love of her life, but she'd missed him these past weeks. They'd become used to each other, easy friends. Megan wondered whether that had been the problem; maybe they'd merely been friends trying to be lovers, rather than lovers who were also good friends.

Jean lived in a council house in Sandon Road and Megan walked up the slight incline until she came to the right number. She'd never been to Jean's home before, the girls in the decorating shop rarely socialised outside work. They were too busy catching up with their housework and feeding their families to go 'gallivanting' as Lizzie called it. But illness was different.

But Megan still felt apprehensive as she knocked on the front door. Suppose Jean was embarrassed and didn't want to see anyone?

What if her husband objected to a stranger turning up on his doorstep? But when the door opened and a burly man stood there wiping his hands on a tea towel, as soon as she saw his smile she was reassured.

'Yes, love?'

'Hello, I'm Megan Cresswell. I work with Jean. I hope you don't mind my calling but the girls were wondering how she is.'

'She's not so bad. Come on in.' He stood aside so that she could enter the tiny hall and then opened a door, calling, 'You've got a visitor, Jean.'

Megan went into the small square room, and looked across at her friend, who was sitting in an armchair. Jean was not only pale, but she'd lost a considerable amount of weight.

'Megan!' Jean's eyes lit up. 'Oh, this *is* kind of you.'

'It's not far,' Megan smiled, 'and it's lovely outside. How are you Jean?'

'I'm doing all right. Better every day.'

'I hope you don't mind my coming, I know you didn't really want visitors.' Megan tried not to look at the hollow where Jean's breast should have been.

'That was in the early days, love. You've timed it well – this is only the second day I've got dressed.'

Megan reached for the shopping bag. Jean's husband had gone off muttering about putting the kettle on.

'I come bearing gifts,' she smiled. 'The grapes are from Miss Dawson,' she handed over a paper bag of purple grapes. 'Lizzie's sent you some magazines, Minnie's sent you a jar of plum jam,

183

my contribution is the fruit cake...' Megan began to put the items on a small table by Jean's side. 'We all put in a few sweet coupons and got you the Milk Tray, and Flo sent the biscuits.'

Weak tears of gratitude came into Jean's eyes. 'How good they all are. Bill's very partial to plum jam, and I haven't felt up to doing any baking for ages.'

'You're looking well, anyway,' Megan said. Sometimes lies were kinder than the truth.

'I'm better than I was.'

'Mr Ian came down the other day and asked how you were.'

Jean looked pleased, and Megan glanced around. 'Where are the kids?'

'Peter's gone to Scouts, and Bernard's round at a friend's. Everyone's been helping.'

'I've told her,' Bill said, coming back in, 'she's got to take a back seat for a bit. Let her sister look after the old ones for a change.'

'I only went up three times a week.'

'On top of working and looking after two growing lads; you've got to start thinking of yourself a bit more.' Megan saw the concern in his eyes as he looked at his wife. 'She's never been one for putting herself first.'

Megan decided that she liked this bald-headed man with a bulbous nose. Bill worked as a drayman, and looking at his broad shoulders and the bulging muscles on his tanned forearms, she could imagine he would be well suited to it.

'We're all missing you,' she told Jean, and went on to tell her about Terry.

'You know best love,' was all she said. Megan

began to bring her up to date with factory gossip and when Bill returned with two cups of tea, it was to the sound of laughter, and to find Jean with a little more colour in her cheeks.

He looked on approvingly. 'There you are! I told you a bit of company would do you good.' He turned to Megan. 'Shutting herself away she was; as if it's anything to be ashamed of.'

'Everybody isn't like you, Bill,' Jean said quietly. 'You wouldn't believe some of the tales I heard in that hospital. That seemed to be the main worry of most of the women in the ward – how their husbands would feel, what their reaction would be.'

'Well, you've no worries on that score.'

Jean smiled gratefully at him, but ten minutes later, her eyelids were drooping, and Megan said, 'I won't stay too long – I don't want to tire you.'

'Sorry, love,' Jean rallied herself, 'but thanks for coming. And thanks for bringing everyone's catalogue money. Tell them I'll soon be able to take orders again.'

'I will.' Megan got up to leave. 'Bye then, Jean, look after yourself.'

'Bill will make sure I do.' Jean's eyes were already closing.

When he saw Megan out, Bill followed her to the gate. 'She's still not out of the woods,' he said, 'not by a long way. The doctors have done more tests. We're just waiting for the results.'

Megan nodded. 'I'll keep my fingers crossed.'

'She may need a bit more than that love. Thanks for coming.' He gave a heavy sigh and went back inside.

Megan walked slowly down the hill with Bill's last words lingering in her mind. Why was he so worried? Surely taking off Jean's breast had removed the whole growth? Or did he mean, and she could hardly bear to face the thought – that the cancer could have spread to somewhere else?

Chapter Twenty-two

The following afternoon found Megan standing outside and studying her small patch of garden. With the straggly grass and sad looking borders overgrown with weeds, it was a depressing sight. Neither Les nor Ellen had been keen on gardening. Even during the war, when the public was exhorted to 'Dig for Victory' Les had only made a half-hearted attempt. Later he would sometimes attack the grass with a small pair of shears – maintaining that the lawn was too small to warrant the expense of a lawnmower, but the rest was sadly neglected. During a heat wave, Ellen and Megan would occasionally carry out a couple of dining chairs and sit beneath the kitchen window, but with the kitchen drain only feet away, it was hardly the perfect place. The garden had played a very small part in their lives, being mainly used to hang out the washing. But earlier that morning, bored by the droning voice of the visiting preacher, Megan had suddenly realised that there was no reason why *she* couldn't grow her own vegetables – it was bound to be cheaper than buying them. And so now, remembering that Les had once brought home a spade and fork she found them, their handles rough and riddled with woodworm, in a corner behind a clump of lupins. As an experiment, she picked up the spade and tried to dig the soil only to find that the earth was baked too hard. Megan was trying to balance on the spade with both feet to try and force it into the ground, when she was distracted by deafening raps on the door-knocker. The spade wobbled and tipped over. Stumbling, Megan let it clatter on to the concrete slabs of the narrow path, wiped her hands on her old cotton skirt with annoyance and went back into the house.

Opening the front door she found Freda Podmore facing her – bristling Megan thought later like a bantam hen. Without a word of greeting, Terry's mother pushed straight past and marched into the sitting room. 'Do come in!' Megan said.

But as always her sarcasm was lost on Freda who swung round and squaring up to Megan, snapped, 'What do you think you're playing at?'

Megan stared at her. 'I beg your pardon?'

'You know what I mean, young lady. I suppose you think Terry isn't good enough for you, is that it?'

'I'm sorry, Mrs Podmore, I don't think this is any of your business.'

'I'm making it my business!'

'Oh, I see,' Megan said. 'And does Terry know you're here?'

'I don't have to ask *his* permission. If I've got something to say, I say it!'

'All you're doing is causing offence and embarrassment. It's up to me who I go out with, not you!'

'Oh, I see. You've already got another sucker lined up, is that it?'

Megan was appalled. 'What do you mean – sucker?'

'When I think of the money he spent on you!' Freda who had remained standing, now had two red patches of indignation on her sallow cheeks. 'Taking you to the pictures, going dancing...'

'He only spent what he wanted to spend. I never heard him complain.'

'Well, he wouldn't to *you*, would he?'

Megan felt a lurch of shame. 'Are you saying that he has to you?'

'I've got eyes in my head, haven't I?'

You've got a nasty tongue as well! The furious words almost shot out of her and Megan struggled to control her rising temper. 'I don't know what you think you'll achieve by coming up here and throwing insults around,' she said, 'because I've no intention of changing my mind.'

'Change your mind? I don't want you to change your mind. I knew when Terry first brought you home, you were trouble. Leading that lad up the garden path – it's girls like you who give women a bad name.'

'So,' Megan said through gritted teeth, 'if that isn't what you wanted, what have you come for?'

'To let you know how I feel, that's why. When I think of how I made you welcome, how you sat at my table all those Sundays...'

Suddenly Megan couldn't stand the woman's shrill voice a moment longer. She turned away. 'I

188

think you'd better go!'

Freda drew her thin frame up to its full height, the feather in her velour hat quivering with outrage. 'Are you telling me to leave?'

'That's right.' Megan went to the front door and opened it. She stood aside feeling her face burning; anger was almost choking her.

'Of all the damn cheek...!' Freda's lips were tight with affront. 'Well, he's had a lucky escape that's all I can say.'

Megan didn't answer; she simply held the door open wider and averted her face. Without another word Freda, her shoulders ramrod stiff, marched through it. Megan, slamming the door behind her, at last gave way to her feelings by yelling, 'And good riddance!'

But when she went back into the sitting room, she found herself shaken. Terry had spent no more on their courtship than any other man would have done. And she knew he would never have complained about it. But even though she tried to dismiss the ugly scene from her mind, Freda's insinuation still lingered. And Megan's conscience was uneasy. Because in the early days hadn't she gone out with Terry purely because she saw him as a possible meal ticket, someone to give her security?

Slumping into an armchair Megan stared into space. She couldn't believe how calculating she'd been. And not only then, but during those early months after her mother died. She knew now that she'd been blinded by fear, a dread that she wouldn't be able to manage on her own; a belief that finding a husband was her only solution.

Colour rose from her neck as she remembered how blatant she'd been, how she'd spent Sunday after Sunday searching for some unsuspecting young man to entrap. How could she have done it?

Then irritated with herself, Megan got up. She couldn't afford to waste time wallowing in introspection, thinking about things she couldn't change. Instead she went back into the garden and looked helplessly at the spade lying on the ground. She was obviously wasting her time; she needed to wait until the ground was softer, until after they'd had some rain. But she knew that growing her own vegetables was only a small part of her solution and a long-term one. Somehow she needed to find a way of earning more money, and soon – before the situation became even more desperate and she couldn't manage to pay her catalogue debt.

Having made her decision about finding an extra job, Megan couldn't think of anything else. She was thinking about it on Monday morning as she brushed delicate colour into the petals of a rose border on a china plate, and was still wrestling with the problem when she bought a fresh loaf on her way home. Taking on an extra job involved time, and that was something she didn't have. All that was available in the evenings was bar-work and cleaning and she could hardly apply for the first! Since she'd seen respectable people enjoying wine with their meal – including Nathan – Megan might no longer believe that alcohol was the devil's drink, but as a member of the chapel

190

she could hardly take a job as a barmaid. And she hated doing her own cleaning, never mind anyone else's. She tried to think if there was a cafe where she might work as a waitress but any local ones were only open during the day, other than the Milk Bar in Longton. But then she would have to walk home alone in the dark and in all weathers, and to work all day and then in the evening ... what if she became ill? To lose her wages and bonus would defeat the whole object. The thoughts went round and round in her head until later as she grilled some sausages to have with a tin of tomatoes, Megan realised that her only solution was to find a Saturday job. One she could do after she finished work at twelve. And fortunately, she thought she knew the ideal person to approach.

The following Saturday morning passed in an agony of impatience, and as soon as the buzzer sounded Megan called, 'Have a good weekend, everyone. Don't do anything I wouldn't do!' and was almost out of the door before she heard the usual shout of, 'that'll make life boring, then!' She smiled, and then smiled again at the gateman as she passed, but he just lifted one sardonic eyebrow. Honestly she thought – that man's face will split if he ever smiles.

The weather was warm and the sun bright as she came out from beneath the archway and Megan took off her cardigan and folding it put it into her shopping bag. She began to walk into Longton and threaded her way through busy shoppers until nearing the Market Hall she began to rehearse what she was going to say. And there just inside the doors, on her stool sipping a mug of tea sat Iris. With her hunched shoulders, creased face and grey tufted hair Megan thought that she looked rather like a goblin amidst the clusters of flowers. The stall-holder looked up as Megan came towards her. 'A bit early for you, isn't it?'

'Yes, I know.' Megan paused, 'Iris, I haven't come to...'

But Iris interrupted, 'I don't suppose you've made it up with Terry?'

Megan shook her head.

'You don't know when you're well off, girl. I wish I was a bit younger, I can tell you.'

Megan smiled. 'Of course, you're a widow, aren't you?'

'Grass widow, more like! He was a right bugger, was my old man. God knows where he is – not where he belongs, that's for sure.'

'I'm sorry, I didn't know.' Megan realised she knew very little about this woman she'd been buying flowers from all these months.

'No reason why you should.' Iris drained her mug and began to get up. 'So, what'll it be this week? They'll cost you more though, buying this early in the day.'

'I haven't really come to buy. It's just that...'

Iris looked at her with impatience. 'Come on, love, spit it out!'

'I'm looking for an extra job on Saturday afternoons, and I wondered...'

Iris shook her head. 'Sorry Megan. Trade doesn't warrant it. And my nephew comes now and helps me to pack the van. It's a bit of pocket money for him, you see.'

'Yes, of course.' Megan tried to hide her disappointment.

Iris looked at her with concern. 'A bit stuck for cash are you?'

'I just need a bit extra to tide me over – you know what it's like.'

'I've bin there many a time. Look, go round the market and ask at the stalls, there might be somebody who can use you.' Iris frowned. 'The trouble is most people want help all day on a Saturday, not just the afternoon. Still, it's worth a try.'

'Thanks Iris.' Megan began to move away.

'You're not taking any flowers, then?'

'No, I'm sorry, not this week.'

'That's all right, duck. I understand.'

Megan could feel Iris watching her as she walked away and further into the crowded market to walk up and down the aisles trying to spot a likely stall. But most of them didn't seem to need more than one person serving, and the busy ones that did, such as the fruit and vegetable stalls had regular family members on them. Eventually, she decided to take the plunge and to ask at the cheese stall. With his ruddy cheeks and white overall, the man behind it was always cheerful and friendly.

He shook his head, his tone brisk. 'Can't help you, love. No call for it, you see. Now what will it be this week – how about a nice bit of Cheshire to go with your oatcakes?'

She nodded and later moved on to a stall that

sold old fashioned underwear; displaying vests, interlock knickers and folded corsets, with night-dresses and built-up brassieres dangling over-head. A small cluster of customers was building up which she thought was a hopeful sign and she joined the queue, until eventually her turn came. Nervously Megan posed her question to the woman behind the counter.

Plump and harassed, her answer was defensive. 'I can manage on me own, thanks. I've never had any complaints.'

'I'm sorry, I didn't mean...'

'No chance, love.' She turned away raising a pole to lift down a large brassiere. 'Besides,' she added, 'you're too young. I mean, look at the stock – I can't see you wearing one of these!' The brassiere was Megan thought, like a straight-jacket and the cups looked big enough to serve as basins. Then the woman then held up a pink whale-boned corset and began to laugh, 'Or one of these?'

Next Megan tried the man with a long thin nose and prominent eyes who sold wristwatches, belts and braces. He stared at her for moment, then lifted his cap and scratched behind one ear before shaking his head. 'Sorry, it wouldn't be worth me while.'

There were two women on the second-hand bookstall where Megan hastily averted her eyes away from some of the more lurid jackets. One of the women, her fingers stained with nicotine glanced up, 'Yes, duck?'

'I wondered whether you could use any extra help on Saturday afternoons?'

'No, we're all right as we are, aren't we Vera?'

'I'm only looking for a few hours?' Megan was now reduced to pleading.

Vera, older with wispy dark hair streaked with grey looked up from where she was stacking the books in rows. She stared at Megan then said, 'You can sling yer hook, love.' She turned to her colleague. 'If Charlie sees her, he'll be drooling at the mouth. Over my dead body,' she muttered as she bent beneath the stall.

The other woman whispered to Megan, 'That's her husband...'

'Oh, I see...' Megan hurriedly moved away.

Eventually, she gave up, after the swarthy and heavily built man on the leather goods stall said, 'If I needed part-time help, I'd want three days a week, or at least the whole Saturday. You're on a trip to nowhere, young woman.'

So Megan made her away across to the Milk Bar. It was crowded with young people and she opened the door to the familiar strains of Johnnie Ray's voice coming from the Juke Box. A buxom woman with bleached hair piled on top of her head and secured with jewelled combs, had a cross expression as she served a short queue. Megan waited her turn and then with some trepidation asked her question.

'Saturday afternoons?' Megan's hopes rose as the woman glanced around the crowded tables. 'I could certainly do with some help.' But then she shook her head. 'But I know the owner wouldn't wear it; I had a job to get him to pay me enough, I can't see him taking anyone else on.'

So a few minutes later and full of despondency,

Megan began to make her way home. And as she turned into the public library, she knew that it was pointless asking there. Years ago, she and Audrey had fancied being library assistants, until the day they found out that 'O' levels were needed. Megan remembered how she'd asked her father if she could go to night school.

Les had been adamant in his refusal. 'It wouldn't be suitable, a young girl being out in the dark at night. Besides most of the students would probably be men. No,' he told her, 'you're safer at home.' And as Audrey was only allowed to go if Megan did, his decision had denied both girls the chance.

Megan eventually let herself into her silent home. And as she took the greaseproof paper off the small slab of Cheshire cheese she knew that there was only one other option open to her. The one she'd hoped desperately to avoid and which would mean spending even more time inside a stifling factory. Because she couldn't think of any other place where they'd need cleaning done on a Saturday afternoon.

Chapter Twenty-three

'I could have told you that for nothing,' was Clarice's reaction.

'I feel totally demoralised,' Megan said, having now confided in her neighbours. 'It doesn't help your self-confidence to be told you're not even good enough to be a cleaner.'

'Now they didn't say that exactly,' Clarice soothed, 'not from what you told us anyway. They said you hadn't got any experience – which is true.'

'And that I was too young...'

'Well, I've never seen a 20 year old cleaner,' Rita said.

Megan gazed despondently at them both. 'I suppose you're right. I'll have to give up on that idea – I've tried every factory in Longton.'

Rita suggested, 'What about the shop where your Dad worked? Have you tried there?'

'I thought of that. I went in my dinner-hour on Tuesday. But they've already got someone. When I asked about serving in the shop he just said the same as everyone else, that half a day on a Saturday was neither use nor ornament.'

Clarice had an idea of her own and although she was wary of suggesting it, plunged in. 'What about trying to find something on a Sunday?'

'There's nowhere open!' Rita turned to gaze at her with astonishment.

'There's Trentham Gardens.'

'Now that's an idea.' Rita turned with eagerness to Megan, only to see her horrified expression.

'Oh, I couldn't work on a Sunday! Some people won't even hang out their washing on a Sunday, never mind do paid work. It wouldn't be right.'

Clarice gazed at her. She couldn't see anything wrong in it herself. Religion, she thought with scorn, why do people let it rule their lives?

'It's not right to go hungry either, or to worry about paying the bills,' Clarice retorted, and then seeing Megan's mutinous expression, held up a hand in self-defence. 'All right, it was only a thought.'

'I can see Megan's point though,' Rita said. 'I mean, if you're brought up – as most of us were – to think of the Sabbath as a day of rest...' She looked a bit sheepish, 'Even I wouldn't do the washing or clean my windows.'

Neither did Clarice, but only because she didn't want to be the subject of tittle-tattle.

'And I wouldn't be able to go to chapel either,' Megan said shaking her head. 'No, I'll have to try and come up with another answer.'

And then the two older women began to gossip yet again about a woman who lived down the road. 'She still says she only gives that milkman a cup of tea and a bit of toast,' Rita said, 'but I ask you – after seeing that last baby of hers... I mean – if she's going to carry-on, you'd think she'd have more sense than to choose a man with red hair!'

But Megan was only half-listening; her mind was too occupied with her own problems.

It was a week later when she was in the public library, that after several nights of poor sleep and worry Megan's self-control finally slipped. She was standing in the musty silence before a section of books when suddenly the hopelessness of her situation overwhelmed her. Even though in the short-term she might manage to 'get back on her feet', her difficulties seemed to stretch endlessly into the future. Despite her willingness to work there seemed no hope of earning any more money and she felt so helpless that to her horror she found her eyes welling with treacherous tears. Furious with herself, she took down a random book and opened it, pretending to be absorbed in its blurring print while her other hand fished for a hanky in her cardigan pocket.

'Are you all right Megan?' It was a familiar voice that Megan heard every Sunday at chapel. Mrs Eardley was standing at the beginning of the aisle of shelves, clutching a library book. She came hesitantly towards Megan and said in a low voice, 'Whatever is the matter, dear?'

Blindly, Megan shook her head. 'I'm sorry — I'm not usually like this.'

'But what's wrong?' Barbara Eardley turned her gently towards her. 'Come on, bring your book to the desk and we'll go outside where we can talk.'

Hot with embarrassment, Megan had no alternative but to follow. The librarian glanced up as they approached, seeming not to notice Megan's distress; either that or she was too tactful to comment. 'Two of my favourite customers,' she smiled.

'We have different tastes in literature, though,' Barbara was staring in surprise at the title of Megan's book. She frowned, 'I'm more of an Agatha Christie fan myself.'

Megan glanced at the book she'd hastily pulled out. It was 'To the Lighthouse' by Virginia Woolf, an author she'd heard of but had never read.

'Megan usually comes in much later than this,' the librarian said. With a flourish she stamped both of their books, 'And no flowers again? That's two weeks now.'

'We've got some in the garden.' Megan evaded.

Then once outside as they stood in a secluded spot, Barbara in her quiet but determined manner managed to coax Megan to tell her the full story. Megan ended, 'My neighbour suggested I try to find work on a Sunday, but I told her I couldn't do that. Mum and Dad would turn in their graves!'

Barbara gazed thoughtfully at her for one long moment. Then her eyes narrowed. 'Look, Megan. You go on home and have a cup of tea with plenty of sugar in it. I'm not promising anything, but I may possibly have an idea. I'll see you at chapel tomorrow?'

Megan nodded. Even the bus fare it took to go to Bethesda had to be saved at the moment.

'Try not to worry too much and I'll see you then.' She smiled encouragingly, and Megan watched her walk away. Everyone respected Mrs Eardley, but Megan couldn't think how even she could find a solution.

It wasn't until later that evening that she reached out for her new library book. Megan glanced idly down at the blurb on the jacket and then began to read.

The following morning, as she waited outside the chapel, Megan half-expected Mrs Eardley to apologise and to say that on second thoughts her idea hadn't been feasible but instead she said, 'Megan, I'd like to come and see you later. I thought perhaps after the evening service?'

Megan felt awkward knowing that she no longer went to chapel twice on Sundays. But there was no sign of disapproval in Mrs Eardley's eyes as she added, 'Would that be convenient?'

Relieved, Megan said, 'Yes, of course.' Barbara Eardley, an Englishwoman of a certain type – in fact Megan thought, she would fit perfectly into one of her own Agatha Christie novels – was involved in a lot of charitable work. Hopefully she knew someone who needed a cleaner and didn't mind a Saturday afternoon.

As the weather was fine after earlier rain, Megan spent the afternoon tackling the garden. It was harder work than she'd expected, but she managed to dig over quite a stretch of the narrow border. Double-dig, had been the advice in her library book, and she could only guess what that meant, but it was with a sense of achievement that she went back inside to wash and tidy up before her visitor arrived. It was only later, seeing the soreness on her palms caused by the rough-ened handle of the old spade that she realised that she should have worn a pair of gloves. Another lesson she'd learned the hard way!

Megan greeted her visitor with a warm smile. 'That's better,' Barbara said with approval, 'I felt quite worried about you yesterday.'

'I'm sorry about that,' Megan said. 'I'm not usually a tearful person. It just came out of the blue – feeling so low, I mean.'

'There's no need to apologise; tears are nature's release. In any case, it's a strange woman who doesn't cry sometimes.'

Megan smiled at her, thinking yet again what a good Christian woman she was. 'Please do sit down.' She added, 'Your hair looks lovely. Have you just had it done?'

Barbara touched her slightly silvering brown hair. 'Yes, it's a new perm. I'm glad you like it. I go to Marlene's in Chaplin Road.'

'You must know Debra then? Her gran lives next door.'

'I certainly do,' Barbara smiled. 'She's a tonic, that girl.'

'Isn't she just? Would you like a cup of tea?'

'I'd love one.'

It was fifteen minutes later, with Megan thinking she couldn't bear the suspense a moment longer before Barbara began to talk about her idea. And it was now, she told Megan, much more than that. 'Tell me, do you ever go up to Lightwood?'

'I used to quite a lot when I was younger,' Megan said. 'Audrey and I used to walk along Lightwood Road to Rough Close Common.' She smiled reminiscently. 'We used to take a bottle of water and a few jam sandwiches, have a picnic and think it was an adventure.'

'So you'd be familiar with some of the large houses along there?'

Megan nodded and laughed. 'We used to pretend we lived in them and would play-act, holding our heads high and turning into the end of the drives, only to scuttle back out again in case anyone saw us. We were,' she quickly explained, 'only kids at the time.'

Barbara smiled at the image of the two young girls pretending to be 'posh'. 'Well,' she said, 'As it happens, I know someone who lives in one of those houses – she takes an interest in my favourite charity. And when I saw you in the library and realised that you're a reader – and obviously an intelligent one – she immediately came into my mind.'

Now Megan was even more mystified.

'Mrs Bevington hasn't lived there very long – only three years. Her husband was an officer in the Indian Army and they came back to England from India shortly after Partition – you know when we relinquished British rule?'

Megan nodded.

'Apparently they lived in Surrey at first, but the Major couldn't settle. He wanted to come back to his roots in Staffordshire. It's odd you know, but a lot of people who move away hanker to come back. Has Audrey ever said that?'

Megan shook her head. 'Not so far.'

'Sorry, I'm getting off the subject. However, sadly Major Bevington died from a sudden heart attack less than six months after moving here. And his wife – she's a widow now of course – has developed an eye condition. She's finding reading tiring even with her spectacles. And as books have always been her passion, she gets extremely frustrated. So you see,' Barbara explained, 'when you told me of your plight, I thought I'd found the ideal answer for both of you.'

Megan stared at her. Did she mean that this officer's widow needed someone to read to her? I could do that, Megan thought with mounting excitement. And to be paid for it – well it would beat standing on a market stall, or cleaning a grimy factory any day! But would this Mrs Bevington want her? Would she think her good enough, educated enough? 'Have you asked her?'

203

she said. 'After all, she might not be too keen.'

Barbara smiled at her. 'I went to see her last night and told her all about you. She'd like to meet you, so if you could go up to the house next Sunday? I think she's intending a month's trial on either side.'

'Really?' Megan's felt a leap of excitement and then her spirits plummeted. 'But – I'm assuming she'll pay me – that would mean that I'd be working on the Sabbath!'

'I think,' Barbara said, her eyes gently teasing Megan's concerned ones, 'that in this particular instance we could interpret it as a Christian act?'

Megan began to laugh. 'Mrs Eardley, I think you're wonderful.'

'And of course you'll be paid. But I haven't got any details I'm afraid.'

'What time does she want me to go?'

'She thought about two o'clock. Perhaps if you could read to her for an hour, then after a cup of tea, would you mind doing some delicate ironing? You are a good ironer?'

Megan nodded vigorously. 'I quite like ironing.'

'Good. And after that perhaps you could read again to her for another hour? That would give you three hours work.'

'I think it's a miracle.' Megan's mind was buzzing, already doing sums trying to guess the amount per hour that she'd earn.

'One that's a bit more use to you than changing water into wine?'

They both laughed this time, and gazing at the older woman, Megan remembered that even Les had liked Mrs Eardley, while Ellen had always admired the neat way she dressed. But who would have thought that this mainstay of the chapel had such a sense of humour?

Megan was still smiling to herself when she went to bed that night. But before she could settle down to sleep she began to feel apprehensive. Because if Mrs Bevington's husband had been an officer in the Indian Army, that meant that she would have been a Memsahib. And the way some of those women were portrayed – well they seemed to consider that they were superior to the rest of mankind. I hope she's not like that Megan thought as restlessly she sat up and gave the flock pillow another shake, because no matter how much I need this job I've got my pride. Nobody is going to treat *me* like dirt.

Chapter Twenty-four

Megan told no-one of Mrs Eardley's idea, neither Clarice nor Rita or even the girls. After all, suppose this Mrs Bevington disliked her on sight? Megan had little experience of 'toffs,' as Les used to call them. But she did know from her reading that many were excruciating snobs. Although Mr Ian wasn't like that; he treated everyone at the potbank the same whatever their status, and he always had time for a joke. Not like the new under manager whose condescending manner the girls resented.

'I'd thought he might be a fella for you, Megan,'

was Lizzie's opinion, 'but you'd have ter curtsey before you got into bed with that one!'

Well I hope Mrs Bevington doesn't look down on me, Megan thought because I can read as fluently as anyone else. And she wasn't worried about her ironing skills either.

But that didn't mean that her stomach wasn't fluttery when Sunday eventually arrived, and her nervousness increased with every hour. She only realised the extent of it when while she was in the kitchen, a plate slipped through her fingers and crashing on to the red quarry tiled floor broke into several pieces.

'Damn!' The word shot out of her mouth. It was only now that she had the freedom to actually use one Megan realised the release they gave to pent up feelings! Hurriedly, she swept up the shattered fragments. For heaven's sake get control of yourself she thought or you'll be a nervous wreck by the time you get there.

At one o'clock, glad that the weather was fine, Megan put on her freshly laundered turquoise dress and old white sandals that she'd earlier whitened with a sponge and took great care in applying discreet make-up. Her hair, having been washed the night before brushed out sleek and shining, and after checking that she had a clean handkerchief and a comb in her handbag, she took a deep breath, opened the front door and set out.

'Where's Megan going then?' Avril said. She'd wandered over to gaze idly out of the window while Clarice bustled about putting the finishing touches to the dining table.

'I've no idea, why?' Clarice joined her and peered through the net curtain. 'She must have had her dinner early. Don't tell me she's made it up with Terry and is going there!'

'Pity it isn't that American. He was dishy, at least from what I saw of him. You know, I'd never have thought she'd make such an attractive girl,' Avril said. 'When I think what a frump she used to look...' She turned away from the window and went to the mirror over the mantelpiece. Like her mother she tended towards plumpness, but her complexion was clear and unlined and her brown hair as yet showed no sign of grey. She adjusted the chain on the silver locket at her throat and glanced round at her baby son who was sitting propped against the cushions on the sofa. Clarice was holding one of his small fists and gently shaking it. She smiled at his gurgle of delight. 'You'd better get the twins in to wash their hands,' she said. 'And where are Mary and Sheila?'

'The last I saw, they were in your make-up bag!' Avril laughed at her mother's alarmed expression. 'Don't worry, I said they could only look.'

'Yes, and if they're anything like you used to be they won't take a blind bit of notice.'

But Clarice was smiling and Avril glanced at her with affection, musing how life was all chance. Suppose I'd had the bad luck to be brought up in that repressive house next door, she thought? I might have turned out like Megan! Or at least like the girl she used to be. I bet she still doesn't have much fun; what with no booze and all that preaching and primness. Her own childhood had always been full of banter and laughter. 'And so is yours going to be,' she murmured as she lifted Nicholas and sniffed warily at his well-padded bottom. 'Poor Auntie Megan, she hasn't had much of a life so far, has she?'

Megan was walking along the pavement opposite Florence Colliery which Les had once told her was named after the 3rd Duke of Sutherland's eldest daughter. I bet she'd never seen a pit in her life, Megan thought. Accustomed to seeing the blackened faces of the miners, their hob-nailed boots ringing on the pavements as they went home after their shifts, Megan had been glad to hear from Tom that a modernisation scheme was taking place. 'Seven million pounds it's costing,' he told her.

As a child Megan had found it a nightmarish image to think of men toiling unseen in dark tunnels beneath the ground but Tom with his cheerful smile, had told her that the men kept each other's spirits up and he wouldn't want to work anywhere else. 'What he means,' her father had scoffed, 'is that he can earn better money down the pit.' Everything in the world, it seemed to Megan, came down to money.

The walk up the hill to Lightwood became pleasanter the further she climbed. There was little traffic on the road, and the large trees over-shadowing the pavement and the view over the opposite hedges to Cocknage Woods all contributed to a sense of peace and tranquillity. It seemed a different world to the one a couple of miles away with its grimy factories and pottery kilns. The road was long and Megan was beginning to wonder just much further she'd have to go when the right number eventually faced her, displayed on a white post.

The house was at the head of a steep tree-lined drive, situated slightly to the right so that only a glimpse could be seen from the road of its gabled rooftops. Megan remembered it. She and Audrey had thought it mysterious, pretending that spies lived there. Fifth columnists, they'd whispered. The memory made Megan smile, easing her nerves slightly. Glancing at her watch she saw that she was ten minutes early, but decided that could make a good impression. She lifted the latch on one of the double gates and closed it carefully behind her. Mrs Bevington's home was even larger than Megan had imagined, with a sweeping drive before it and a black studded front door screened by a long storm porch. Megan smoothed her hair, and wondered whether she should knock on this outer door, or open it and step inside to the inner one. Warily, she peered through the glass. The porch had a black and white tiled floor, a brown rush door-mat and a blue and white Chinese vase used as an umbrella stand. Seeing that the door bell was on the right hand side of the studded black door, she stepped inside.

She could hear the muffled sound of the bell, but it was a full minute before the door swung open. A woman of medium height, her hair scraped into a bun faced her, her expression unsmiling.

'Hello,' Megan said, 'I'm Megan Cresswell.'

'I know who you are.' Her voice had a Scots burr. 'Come in.'

Megan went into a spacious oak-panelled hall filled with a delicate scent drifting from a vase of red roses on a half-moon side table. She stood uncertainly as the woman closed the door behind her.

'Follow me.' The woman's tone was brusque and when she paused by a graceful door on the left and opened it, all she said was, 'You can wait in here.'

Megan found herself in an airy well-proportioned room with a beamed ceiling and sunlight flooding in from the large leaded windows. The chintz-covered sofa and armchairs with their deep cushions rested on a cream rose-bordered carpet square surrounded by a polished dark oak floor. A mahogany standard lamp stood in one corner, its cream shade edged in a deep pink fringe. Megan glanced around to see well-stocked bookshelves and a carved sideboard on which rested a silver candelabra, a group of ivory elephants, and a patterned china bowl filled with fruit. As she gazed up at the high ceiling with its ornate cornicing, Megan thought it was the most beautiful room she had ever seen. Glancing at her watch she saw that it was exactly two o'clock.

'Good afternoon!' The voice behind her was soft and amused. 'Am I on time?'

With a start, Megan swung round. A tall slim woman, her dark hair in a sleek French pleat and younger than Megan had expected, stood in the doorway. She came forward and held out her hand. 'I'm Celia Bevington. Thank you so much for coming, Megan.'

Fearful that her own hand was warm and sticky after her long walk, Megan hurriedly wiped it on her skirt. 'I was only too pleased to, Mrs Bevington.'

'Do sit down, my dear.'

Megan perched on the edge of the long sofa.

'Did you find the house easily?' Mrs Bevington said, taking one of the armchairs.

Megan nodded. 'Yes, no problem at all.'

'Mrs Eardley did tell me a little about you. Tell me, have you always been fond of books?'

'Yes, ever since I was a child. My father believed that reading was a form of self-education.'

Celia gazed at the young woman before her. She might be nervous and tense, but least she had quite a melodious voice, and so far not a hint of the Potteries dialect. The gardener they'd inherited with the house had such broad speech that sometimes Celia couldn't understand a word he said. There was the area's flat intonation of course, but all would depend on whether this girl could read aloud with meaning and expression – not in Celia's experience, an ability that everyone possessed.

Megan felt that she was in a scene from a film. It was such a lovely room; with the woman before her elegant in her soft green dress with white cuffs on the short sleeves and a gently flared skirt. Megan admired how she sat with her legs gracefully to one side and moved her own to the same position.

'So,' Celia said giving an encouraging smile. 'What are you reading at the moment?'

When Megan told her, Celia raised her eyebrows. 'Virginia Woolf! How are you finding it?'

'Interesting,' Megan said carefully.

Celia smiled at the diplomatic answer. 'She's an enormously intelligent and successful author, but not to my taste I'm afraid.' She saw a flash of relief in Megan's eyes. 'Don't worry, I'll try and find a book that we can both enjoy. There's one here for instance,' she rose and went to the bookshelves. 'I feel ashamed to say that I haven't yet read it. When I was living in India, I had a yearning to read books set in England or America. Perhaps now would be a good time; it would bring back a lot of memories.' She reached to take one out and passing it to Megan said, 'Do say if you've already read it. I want us both to be equally involved in the book we share.'

Megan glanced at the title. It was 'A Passage to India' by E M Forster. She shook her head, 'No, I haven't.'

'Excellent. So if you can make yourself more comfortable – maybe sitting at the end of the sofa nearer to me, shall we begin?'

Megan got up from the sofa and moved further along; this time settling back into the deep cushions. She opened the book leafed through to the first chapter and then pausing glanced across at Celia.

'Don't worry if my eyes are closed,' she said, 'I won't be asleep, just resting them. Perhaps you could read for about an hour, finishing at a suitable place? There's a glass of water by the side in case you need it.'

Megan, her heart beating rapidly, glanced at the

212

small table and nodded. Her mouth felt dry already and she took a small sip of the water, then with a voice that was shaky at first she began, '*Chapter One... Except for the Malabar caves...*'

It was only when she heard the resounding strike of the grandfather clock coming from the hall that Megan realised how long she'd been reading. Apart from nervously glancing up a few times to see Celia either gazing before her or resting her eyes, Megan had been totally absorbed. She continued reading until she reached a break in the narrative then quietly closed the book. For a few moments Celia didn't stir then she opened her eyes and smiled. 'You read that beautifully. How did you like it?'

'Oh, I did – very much.'

Celia turned as she heard a sound in the hall, and seconds later the door opened and Megan watched as the woman who'd first greeted her wheeled in a wooden trolley.

'Thank you, Janet.' Celia waited until she'd left, then leaned forward. 'Janet lives here as my housekeeper. You mustn't mind her dour manner. She's a sweetie really. The Major found her for me. She was married to a Presbyterian minister in the village where his brother lives. There she was up in Scotland and having to move out of the Manse and we were in need of help: so she came down here. It's worked well for both of us, particularly once I was left on my own.' She picked up the teapot and began to pour. 'As my dear, I'm hoping it will for us. Now you enjoy your tea, and do help yourself to a rock cake.'

Megan took the delicate cup and saucer she was

offered, and also one of the tiny cakes. She bit into it carefully, worried about spilling crumbs.

'Sorry, please – take one of these.' Celia passed over a serviette. As she sipped her own tea, she gazed with interest at her young visitor. She was quite nicely dressed if one discounted the shabby sandals. Celia had been surprised and delighted by the intelligent way that Megan had interpreted the prose, at the instinctive pacing of her reading and by how pleasant it had been to listen to her. She was already looking forward to the next instalment and was hoping that Megan's ironing would be of an equally high standard. When Megan finished her tea, Celia rose and smiling down at her said, 'If you'd like to come with me, I'll show you where the ironing room is.'

Megan followed her in disbelief. How could anyone have a room just for ironing! They went up the wide staircase, panelled to the dado and its walls painted cream over a thick embossed wallpaper and she was relieved when Celia indicated a partly open door once they reached the landing. 'In case you need to wash your hands or anything.' She opened another cream painted door into a modest sized airy room where an ironing board was already erected, and on a small table stood a cotton lined rush basket full of clothes. A wooden clothes horse was in one corner, and a supply of coat hangers hung on the curtain rail. 'If there's anything you need, you'll find Janet next door. Please don't hesitate to ask.'

Celia smiled and disappeared downstairs. Megan went along the landing to find a lavatory bowl prettily decorated and even the generously sized sink had matching flowered borders. It was a delight to wash her hands, as the small white towel was so soft it felt almost like velvet.

She was still thinking of the luxury when a few minutes later after switching on the electric iron and after checking the fabric of the clothes in the basket, she turned the setting to low and while she waited for it to heat, went to look out of the window. The garden was extensive, completely private and surrounded by mature trees. The lawns were smooth and neat and the wide herbaceous border imaginatively planted; Megan could see hollyhocks, pink hydrangeas, marigolds, Michaelmas daisies and bordering the path clumps of what she recognised as wild thyme – having been studying the gardening book she'd borrowed from the library. It was lovely and so peaceful.

Then she swiftly turned to concentrate on the ironing which was as Mrs Eardley had said, mainly of delicate things. With some trepidation Megan gingerly tried the iron on the edge of a flimsy fabric and then as she had when reading aloud, began to gain confidence. She pressed several blouses, a cotton dress, silk full slips and waist petticoats edged with lace, a sumptuous oyster satin nightdress, a box-pleated skirt, a knife-edge pleated skirt and several pairs of French knickers. She was folding a pair and thinking that surely they must be draughty to wear when she heard footsteps on the landing. Megan glanced at her watch; she had been ironing for exactly one hour.

As she entered the room, Celia looked at the clothes hanging neatly on the clothes horse and walking over to the coat hangers, examined the blouses and dress. She smiled with approval. 'Well done. Janet, bless her, seems to iron creases in rather than out – unless it's something flat like sheets and tablecloths.'

'It's okay, then? There are a couple of things still...'

'Oh they can wait until next week.' She turned at the door, 'Shall we go and spend some more time in India?'

And just over an hour later, Megan walked home with soaring spirits. In her handbag was an envelope containing two half crowns. All that for spending such an enjoyable afternoon in a beautiful house! She would soon be able to pay off her debts at this rate. And the experience would be repeated not only the following Sunday, but into the foreseeable future, because Mrs Bevington had dismissed the month's trial. And who would have thought that she would be so grateful for one of her father's many rules. Megan hadn't been allowed to talk 'broad pottery,' and any lapse was corrected every time she began to talk in a way her father called 'common'. 'You might hear it at school,' he said, 'and you might even use it in the playground. But you're my daughter and you're to speak properly.' Megan had once heard a neighbour say that the Cresswells thought themselves a 'cut above other people'. She remembered how thrilled she'd been when Nathan had taken her to the George for lunch. Now she was going to experience luxury on a weekly basis. And Mrs Bevington had treated her with both kindness and courtesy.

216

Chapter Twenty-five

Megan wasn't sure whether to mention to the girls about her new job. Pride was one reason – did she really want them to know how much she was struggling for money? But eventually she couldn't resist it and held them spellbound during the morning break as she described how beautiful the house was, and how gracious Mrs Bevington.

'She never paid you all that just for reading out of a book?' Lizzie was flabbergasted, 'Money for old rope, I call it.'

'And doing some ironing,' Minnie put her little finger in her mouth to lift her lower dentures and ease them. 'These damn things aren't half giving me some gip, my gum's that sore...'

'Dab a drop of neat whisky on,' Lizzie advised, 'it'll harden it for you.'

'Oh right I'll try it, I've got some in as it happens...'

'We know – just for medicinal reasons!' One of the girls grinned across at her. 'You can pull the other one, Min.'

'You can all please yourself what you think!' Minnie retorted, 'Anyway Megan I know which house you mean, because our Ivy used to clean there. Mind you it was years ago, and it would be different people then.'

'I think it sounds lovely,' Enid said wistfully.

'And fancy having a flowered lavatory…'

'Hey girls, that's what we'll say in future – we're just off to water the flowers!' Lizzie hooted with laughter.

'A bit more ladylike than what you usually call it!'

The others turned to stare at the speaker and exchanged glances. Avis was new, having been taken on to help with a rush order. She sat in Jean's place at the bench but her caustic tongue hadn't endeared her to anyone. Megan, next to her, had tried to be friendly but to no avail.

'She's just a miserable sod,' was Lizzie's opinion, and the rest of the girls agreed with her.

Then later Miss Dawson, who although she heard much of the talk in the decorating shop rarely joined in, murmured to Megan, 'I'm really pleased that you've got this opportunity, my dear. Try and make the most of it; watch and learn – that's my advice.'

Rita's reaction was to say, 'You jammy devil. Well done love.'

And when Clarice heard she was delighted. 'A right turn up for the books,' she said.

Tom grinned, 'Literally in fact.'

Megan was amazed at how much lighter-hearted she felt. Already she'd calculated that within weeks she would be 'straight' again, and then she was determined to save the money from Mrs Bevington so that she would have a safety net.

And as far as the catalogue was concerned, once she'd paid off what she owed there would be no more impulse buying; in the future she would follow Jean's advice and buy only one item at a time. The following Saturday Megan walked up to Meir to visit her. This time the two boys were at home. As Bill ushered Megan into the room, Peter, a solemn ten-year old glanced up with a shy smile then returned to inserting caps into his toy gun, while twelve-year-old Bernard glanced briefly up from reading the Wizard. Jean was sitting in an armchair, her knitting discarded on her lap. Megan felt alarmed to see how pale and thin she was and glanced over to Bill. His eyes, full of concern met her own. Silently he shook his head.

Jean looked up, pleasure lighting her face at the sight of Megan.

'Hello, Jean. I come bearing gifts again.'

Both the boys looked up with eagerness, and Megan smiled. 'I remembered you two this time.' She took two small slim bars of milk chocolate out of her bag and gave them one each.

'You shouldn't have used your sweet coupons,' Jean protested, but Megan could see that she was pleased.

'And how are you Jean?'

'Coming on,' she said, 'it's just taking longer than I thought it would.'

'What do the doctors say?' Megan settled herself in the opposite armchair.

'Just the same thing – I must get plenty of rest and be patient.'

'It's a good job it's you and not Minnie, then!' Megan was relieved to hear Jean laugh.

'She was born with ants in her pants, that one. How is she? How's everyone? Have we got a full

219

order book?'

As Bill disappeared into the kitchen, Megan brought Jean up to date with all the factory news, and then went on to tell her about Mrs Bevington.

'It sounds a lovely house,' Jean said, 'although I'm not so sure about the ivory elephants on the sideboard. I think it's cruel, killing those poor creatures for their tusks.'

'Tarzan would save them if he could,' Peter said. 'The elephants obey all his commands.'

Bernard snorted in derision. 'He isn't real, you know.'

The younger boy's reaction was to begin firing caps at him. Coming in with a glass of Tizer which he handed to Megan, Bill said, 'Peter, what have I told you about firing that thing in the house. Go outside if you want to play with it.'

With a sulky look at his brother, Peter left the room and Jean said to Bill, 'Megan was telling me about this woman who lives in a posh house up at Lightwood and how she has such beautiful manners. Good breeding shows – I've always said it.'

'A privileged background, you mean,' Bill retorted.

'You can tell he votes Labour can't you?' Jean gave him an exasperated glance.

'So should every working man. Mind you,' he turned to Megan, 'I don't have a closed mind. I went to listen to Hugh Fraser in 1945, when he was standing for the Conservatives.'

Seeing Megan's questioning look, Bill explained, 'He was hoping to get in for this area and held a meeting over at the Broadway Cinema.' His face creased in a reminiscent grin. 'Turned into a "baptism of fire" it did. It wasn't his fault; it was because another Tory candidate had said that all striking miners should be shot. Bloody idiot! Anyway, a crowd of furious miners turned up and it was pandemonium for a while – they even booed the Home Secretary.'

'I think you did *your* share of heckling!' Jean said. 'And wasn't there an American in there taking notes of it all? Now what was his name? I can remember his initials because they were the same as our Jack's...

'Kennedy,' Bill said, 'J.F. Kennedy. But he was only a young chap; a friend of Fraser's I think.'

'My father wasn't interested in politics,' Megan said. 'He didn't even vote.'

Jean was horrified. 'What about your mother?'

Megan shook her head. 'No, I don't think so.'

'Then they were traitors to their class!' The veins on Bill's neck bulged as he became incensed. Ignoring a warning glance from his wife he went on, 'When I think of the sacrifices, aye and lives lost in the struggle to win the right to vote... No, I'm sorry Jean, and I don't mean to upset you lass, but it's folk like that who let the wrong government in.'

Jean said, 'Don't mind him love. Once he gets on his soapbox...'

'He's right, though,' Megan said quietly.

'He very often is.'

Eventually when the time came for her to leave, Bill once again escorted her to the gate. 'You can see how she is,' he said. 'She's got no appetite at

221

all, but the doctors don't tell us anything, not really. All I can do is to make sure she takes it easy.'

'How are you managing – with the house and everything?'

'We get by – my sister helps, and so does Jean's. And my mother, even though she's eighty, isn't past doing a bit of ironing. But thanks for coming, Megan. It's a real tonic for her.' He hesitated, 'I'm not a churchgoer myself, but I wondered if you could say a prayer for her?'

'I always do Bill.' She noticed how he straightened the slump in his shoulders before going back into the house, and sudden tears pricked her eyes. Jean was such a lovely person, all the girls said so. Why should her family have this awful problem? There's so much I don't understand about God's will, Megan thought and her mood was subdued as she slowly began to walk home.

And then fifteen minutes later, she suddenly saw Terry. He was walking on the opposite side of the main road and she watched him for a few moments, thinking that in an odd way he looked almost deflated. She wondered if he was on his way home from the Dunrobin, and had played badly in a darts match. He glanced across and seeing her gave a slight smile, slowed down and hesitated. Megan lifted her hand and waved and he crossed over.

For a moment he stood awkwardly then said, 'Good to see you. How've you been?'

'I'm fine thanks, and you?'

'Not so bad.' His gaze flickered over her. 'You look lovely – I always did like that pink dress.'

'Yes I know, even though it does have a stain on the front.' She smiled at him. That was one thing she'd liked about Terry, he always noticed what she was wearing. 'I've just come from visiting Jean – you know the one who...'

'Oh yes. How is she?'

'Not too good, I'm afraid.'

'I'm sorry to hear that.' Terry shifted from one foot to the other. 'Megan...'

'Yes?'

'I was wondering – is there any chance of your changing your mind – about us?'

Megan looked at his anxious, homely face and felt herself soften. 'I'd like us to stay friends,' she said carefully, 'I really like you Terry, but...'

'That's all ... just friends?' He gazed down at her, his eyes full of hurt.

She nodded. 'I'm sorry.'

'It's all right. At least I know where I stand.'

'It doesn't mean we can't see each other. I mean, if you ever want to go to the pictures? I'd pay for myself of course...'

For one long moment his gaze held hers, and then Terry said quietly, 'I don't think that would be a good idea, but thanks just the same.'

'You'll meet someone else, I'm sure you will.'

He gave a slight shrug. 'Maybe; anyway nice to have seen you...'

'And you.' With some sympathy Megan watched him go, dismayed that he'd been hoping they'd get back together. I feel awful she thought, but it was no good raising his hopes. And now I've seen him again after these weeks apart, I'm even more certain that it would never have worked between us. But she didn't envy him going back to Freda Podmore. In fact Megan thought when later she inserted her key into the lock of her front door, coming home to an empty house has much to recommend it, particularly if the alternative was to be greeted by *her* sour face!

Chapter Twenty-six

When Debra came to cut Megan's hair and heard about her new job, her immediate reaction was to say, 'At least it will get you out.' She stood back to inspect her handiwork. 'Are you sure you wouldn't like it a bit shorter?'

Megan shook her head. 'No, I like it this length. What do you mean – at least it will get me out?'

'Well, according to Gran, you don't go any-where now, not since you finished with Terry.'

'I haven't been to the pictures recently, but that's because I've been saving.'

'You don't go dancing either,' Debra persisted.

'That costs money too, you know. In any case since Eunice got married, I haven't got anyone to go with!'

'Well,' Debra began to collect her scissors and comb from the table. 'It's a pity, that's what Gran says. After you'd come out of your shell and started to enjoy yourself. I'd go dancing with you myself, but I can't really. Not with Andy away doing his National Service.'

Megan smiled at the ludicrous image of herself

standing at the side of the dance floor among Debra and her young friends. And then she frowned. 'Surely he doesn't expect you to stay at home all the time?'

'I still go to the pictures with my friends, but well – dancing, that's different. My Gran says I'm too young to tie myself down, but I know my own mind.' Debra tossed her head as she picked up her shopping bag. 'We're going to get engaged when he's demobbed. I'll be eighteen then.' She gave an impish grin, 'I spend so much time looking at the rings in Simmonds' Jewellers, I'm sure he thinks I'm "casing the joint".'

Megan laughed, 'You've been watching James Cagney too much.' She stood at the door as Debra left; even her walk had a spring in it, a sort of happiness, and Megan thought that this Andy was going to be a lucky young man; life would never be depressing with Debra around.

Two weeks later the whole decorating shop was buzzing with shocking news. As each paintress came through the outside door, she hurried to join the cluster of women at the end of the room. Voices were hushed, expressions ones of alarm and disbelief.

Megan who hadn't seen the local newspaper listened in growing horror as the comments came thick and fast.

'Her husband came home from work and found her lying in a pool of blood in the kitchen,' Enid said wide-eyed. 'Stabbed she was and her jaw smashed.'

'How old was she?' The questions and answers

began to fly around.

'Sixty-two, it said in the *Sentinel*.'

'I've seen that house, *Estoril*. It's a massive place.'

'It had fourteen bedrooms, apparently.'

'And thousands of pounds worth of jewellery is missing.'

'Eh, you're not safe in your own bed,' was Minnie's worried reaction.

'Oh, I think *you* are duck,' Lizzie said, but for once nobody laughed at her quip.

'You'd better warn that Mrs Bevington to be on her guard,' Flo said, 'a wealthy woman like that. If he's killed once, he'll do it again.'

'A right Job's comforter you are,' Lizzie turned as another woman came in through the door and began to take off her coat. 'Hey Lily – your son's in the police force, what does he say about this murder in Barlaston?'

She came across to them. 'He doesn't usually say a lot about work, but he did say they're looking for the gardener. He's gone missing, and he was sacked a few weeks before.'

'That's him then,' Minnie said promptly. 'He wants catching, he does!'

'Talk about stating the bleeding obvious!' But Lizzie cast an anxious glance at the elderly spinster who lived alone.

And that night Megan was extra careful in checking that her doors and windows were secure. And when a sound awoke her in the night she crept to the window and peered uneasily out into the dark, vastly relieved when she saw the shadowy figure of a cat jump on to the top of the fence. But then in the morning she gave herself a talking to. It had taken a long time for her to lose her nervousness at sleeping alone in the house and this murderer would be miles away by now. In any case why would anyone want to break into her home – it was obvious that she didn't have anything worth stealing.

The following Sunday it was only when Megan entered the familiar door into Bethesda and glanced up at the balcony, that she realised how much she'd missed coming. It had been an impulsive decision taken only that morning. She didn't have to worry so much about the bus fare now and it seemed ages since she'd seen Eunice. And to her delight she was there, sharing a pew with Ben and her parents. Megan slipped into the one behind them and leaning forward touched her on the shoulder.

Eunice turned, and it was balm to Megan's soul to see how her friend's face lit up. 'Megan! How lovely... I've missed you.'

'How are you?'

'I'm fine, and you?'

'Great.' Ben turned slightly and nodded, and then the organ struck up and Megan rose with the rest of the congregation as the minister came in. Yet again she enjoyed the excellent sermon but couldn't help glancing around the chapel to see if there were any attractive young men there, although it was now with sceptical amusement rather than desperation. Across the aisle sat the tall sweet-faced young man who Eunice had told her was recovering from tuberculosis. He still looked pale but stronger than before. Megan had liked him from the beginning, he looked sensitive and kind. Then not without some guilt she averted her eyes. The fear of catching TB was ingrained in her – Ellen, with her weak chest had been terrified of catching the disease.

Later, outside the chapel, without Sam Goodwin hurrying her away, Eunice was happy to loiter, eager to tell Megan all about her new life.

'We get on really well, me and Ben's mother,' she said. 'She never interferes or anything.'

'How long are you going to work for?'

'As long as I can; fortunately I'm not very big yet,' Eunice patted her rounded stomach.

'And how's Ben?'

'He's fine.' Eunice lowered her eyes and said quietly, 'You don't need to worry, Megan. He's devoted to me, honestly.'

'And so he should be.' Megan smiled at her with relief. 'I've some news too. I've got another job, just a few hours but I'm really enjoying it.' And the two girls chatted for another ten minutes before Ben emerged from the chapel, telling them that he was going to stand in for the organist the following week.

'You must come and visit us, Megan,' he said, smiling at her. For a split second his eyes held hers and she saw a glimpse of the old flirtatious Ben. Then he took Eunice's hand and they began to move away. As Megan watched them she wondered whether as Clarice had said, that Ben's role as a father really would be the 'making of him.' It may for a while Megan thought, and I do hope so, but I have my doubts as to how long it will last.

It was on Megan's fourth visit soon after the first hour's reading that Celia, who had spent the last few minutes gazing thoughtfully at the young woman opposite, came to a decision.

'Megan,' she said, 'concerning next week; I wondered whether you might like to accept an invitation to Sunday lunch?'

Megan, who had just taken a mouthful of moist gingerbread, stared at her in astonishment.

Celia smiled. 'It's Janet's birthday you see. It would be nice for her to have extra company, and it would give you a chance to get to know each other.' She poured herself another cup of tea and said casually, 'Of course, you may have another commitment.'

Megan hurriedly swallowed her cake. Flustered she said, 'No, I haven't. I'd love to come, thank you.'

'Good.' Celia smiled at her. 'Shall we say twelve-thirty for one?'

Megan was so surprised by the invitation that she found it difficult to concentrate as Celia began to discuss the latest chapter, and it wasn't until later when she went upstairs to begin ironing that she could allow her thoughts to run ahead. The invitation would mean eating in the formal dining-room that she'd glimpsed, and judging by Janet's baking, the food would be brilliant. Megan's mouth watered at the prospect; she couldn't imagine that there would be any penny pinching on cheap cuts of meat in this house. Then suddenly she felt a flash of panic. Conversation would be expected; intelligent conversation, not the sort of chat and gossip she shared with Rita and Clarice. Mrs Bevington was a cultured, well travelled woman. As for the Scots housekeeper, Megan had decided that Janet didn't like her, even resented her coming to the house, because they had barely exchanged half a dozen sentences. Did she know that Mrs Bevington was going to invite Megan on her birthday – would she resent that as well? It was with a worried frown that Megan turned to take out of the basket yet another beautiful blouse, and then as she spread it carefully on the ironing board, she gazed down at it. The material was silky to the touch, the lace hand-made, and it was with a sigh that Megan thought of her own limited choice of clothes. And then she lifted her chin. At least thanks to the catalogue she did have some nice things to wear. And even if Mrs Bevington had seen them all before – Megan always changed and wore her best clothes – what did it matter?

Downstairs, Celia and Janet were facing each other in the drawing room. The two women could not have been more different. Celia in pale blue with a white carnation pinned to the lapel of her cotton dress was sitting gracefully on the sofa. Janet wearing a flowered dirndl skirt, the gathered waist of which did little for her dumpy body, was an awkward figure as she leaned intently forward in an armchair.

'She's coming,' Celia said with complacence.

'Aye, I guessed she would,' Janet said. Her voice was low, her soft burr even more pronounced than usual. 'And much will depend on how it goes.'

'Yes, I know.' Celia gazed at the woman who was not only her housekeeper but had become a close friend. 'Janet, are you're sure that you won't change your mind? It's not too late...'

Janet shook her head. 'I'd like to, but you know why...'

Celia nodded. 'Yes, I do, and you're right of course.'

'I do understand why you're planning to do this. But what you're suggesting...' Janet frowned. 'I'm not at all sure Celia, I'm really not.'

'Neither am I. But at least it will be a challenge, and God knows I need one.' Celia rose from the sofa and turned, spreading her hands in an appealing gesture. 'And it will only be for a short time. If it turns out to be a disaster, I'm sure I'll survive it.'

'Well, as you say, next Sunday will be the deciding factor.' Janet got up to leave and then paused on the threshold. 'It's just the timing that's so unfortunate. On my behalf, I mean.'

'You couldn't help that. And of course I could always cancel...'

'But you don't want to, do you?'

Celia shook her head. 'No. I don't. And I'm hoping I won't have to. Anyway, we'll both observe closely on Sunday and make the final decision then. We must have a coded signal or something.' She laughed, 'It's all quite intriguing, isn't it?'

'I have a feeling that you're enjoying all this.'

Celia smiled. 'How well you know me.'

Janet gave one of her own rare smiles, and then

231

as the grandfather clock in the hall began to strike four said, 'I'd better go and fetch the lassie downstairs. I'll say one thing for her – she's no clock watcher.'

'And that,' Celia said with some satisfaction, 'is a sign of integrity. What I need to discover now is whether despite Megan's working-class roots, she also possesses the necessary social graces.'

Chapter Twenty-seven

A few days later, Megan told Clarice and Rita about the invitation.

'My word, you *are* going up in the world,' Rita said, 'I mean – to be invited as a guest...

'And why shouldn't she be?' Clarice retorted, 'Megan's just as good as anyone else.'

'You know that, and I know it, but those people don't see it the same way. I remember when my mum used to clean at a big house in Trentham Road, she was always given a cup of tea but she never had a bite to eat there, not even a biscuit. There's nobody as tight with their money as the rich.'

'Mrs Bevington isn't like that at all,' Megan said. 'Janet – that's the housekeeper – always wheels a tea trolley into the drawing-room with homemade cakes for us.'

'Blimey.' Rita stared at her. 'You *have* fallen on your feet!'

'It can be tiring you know, reading aloud for

long periods. But I do enjoy it.'

'You like the money as well!' Clarice said. 'Would you like another piece of cake, Rita? Sorry it isn't home-made, but I've had my hands full with Tom being bad.'

'How is he?' Megan lowered her voice, knowing he was upstairs resting.

'He's getting there. But this flu has left him with a terrible cough.'

Rita hesitated a moment then confided, 'Jack's got a cough – a sort of niggling persistent one. I want him to go to the doctor's but he won't.'

They both turned to look at her. 'How long has he had it?' Clarice was frowning.

'It's been a while now. Mind you, he's been having trouble with his breathing for the last couple of years.'

'You want to get on to him Rita. Don't mess about.' Clarice exchanged a worried glance with Megan.

Rita nodded. She knew they were thinking of silicosis, or Potter's rot as some people called it. 'He's worked in the clay end ever since he left school,' she said, 'apart from during the war. And you know what that's like – breathing in all that silica dust can scar the lungs. And of course the years in the prisoner-of-war camp dragged his health down. I'll never forget when he first came home – there wasn't an ounce of flesh on him.'

An image came to Megan of when Jack had first arrived. Hollow-cheeked and gaunt; his dark hair now a greying bristle covering a scabby scalp, she'd hardly recognised him. 'How is he in himself?'

'Not too bad. Mind you he hasn't got much energy left when he gets home from work. But that might be after all he went through.'

'You must be worried,' Clarice said. 'Why haven't you said anything before?'

Rita looked down at her lap, her fingers plucking at her skirt. 'You know what Jack's like. He doesn't like me discussing him.'

Clarice gazed at her. 'Maybe, but you really should get him checked out. Don't take no for an answer, Rita.'

Rita, her concern evident in the shadowing beneath her eyes, gave an exasperated sigh. 'With Jack, that's easier said than done.'

'Cruising down the river,' the girls were singing along with the Skylarks during Workers' Playtime. A sing song brightened their day, and often someone would decide to launch into a popular song and the others would join in. Megan glanced sideways at Avis sitting next to her. She never sang with the rest of them.

When the song ended, Megan once again tried to make friends with her. 'It would be nice wouldn't it? To go cruising on a Sunday afternoon, I mean.'

Avis shrugged. 'It wouldn't appeal to me.' Her tone was terse and she made no effort to continue the conversation.

Megan glanced at her with irritation. How she missed Jean with her gentle humour. And almost as though Miss Dawson had read her thoughts, she came over and said, 'Let me know when you next visit Jean, I've got something for her.'

'I'm thinking of going a week on Saturday.'

Miss Dawson nodded. 'Good, I'll bring it in next week.' She glanced down at Avis whose face was averted. 'Is everything all right, Avis?'

'Yes.' Megan noticed that there was no 'thank you, Miss Dawson'.

Turning to look up at her, Megan saw the supervisor frown and her eyes narrow. Briefly Megan wondered if there was something in Avis's life that made her so sullen, but decided that even if there was – others had their problems but they managed to make an effort.

As it was Friday that meant 'chip day', and this week it was Megan's turn to leave ten minutes earlier at lunchtime to fetch in the girls' orders. She always enjoyed this occasional break in the day's routine, going out into the fresh air to walk to the fish and chip shop with its steamy warmth. And it was immediately on her return carrying the vinegar-smelling parcels that she almost bumped into the stranger. Tall, wearing a suit, with black curly hair and even white teeth, he was laughing at Lizzie who said, 'Hey Megan, have a gander at this one. A bit of an improvement on Arthur isn't he?'

'Thanks very much,' said the tubby grey-haired man as he straightened up. A sales representative, he came each week to supply the liquid gold used in gilding and to collect the rags the gilders used so that the gold residue could be reclaimed. 'You're no oil painting yourself!'

As Lizzie cackled, Megan gave the young man a quick smile and hurried by to the waiting girls. 'Who's that?' she whispered.

'His name's Neil,' Minnie said. 'Arthur's retiring – that's why he's late, he's been introducing his replacement.'

'He's a bit of all right isn't he?' Betty was fairly new and although liked, was considered a bit 'fast' not only because of her bleached hair, but because she wore thick Pan-stick, blue eyeshadow and mascara – even at work.

'Never mind men,' Minnie said tartly. 'Come on dole out those chips before they get cold.'

Sunday eventually arrived, with Megan full of anticipation and not a little apprehensive. As she turned into the gateway and drive leading to the house, and pressed the doorbell she remembered how very nervous she'd been that first time, not even sure whether to step inside the storm porch or not. 'You're very punctual, Megan.' Mrs Bevington gave her a warm smile and led the way into the drawing room. 'Isn't it a lovely day? Now, what can I get you as an aperitif? There's sherry, or perhaps you'd prefer a gin and tonic.'

Feeling somewhat embarrassed Megan said, 'Thank you, but I'm afraid I don't drink alcohol.'

'Don't you?' Celia raised her eyebrows. She couldn't imagine getting through life without a snifter. A drink was in her opinion not only a pleasure but at times an absolute necessity.

Megan felt even more awkward as she tried to explain, 'It's the way I was brought up. You know, going to chapel and everything.'

'Oh I hadn't realised. Although as I know the Methodists are against drink – John Wesley and all that, and so is the Salvation Army, I suppose I

236

should have done. Never mind, would you like a soft drink? We have some tomato juice or orange juice?'

'Orange juice would be lovely.'

'I won't be a moment.' As Celia left the room, Megan looked at the silver tray on the sideboard. With its bottles, decanter, and glasses in readiness, she thought how sophisticated it all looked, and suddenly felt a tinge of regret about her refusal. She'd often read of the custom of having an aperitif, so she knew that it was considered perfectly respectable. And what if there was wine to drink with the meal? Surely just one small glass wouldn't be sinful? Nathan certainly hadn't seemed to think so. But then Megan decided that now was perhaps not the time; it would be awful if she became tipsy and disgraced herself.

Celia returned with a small glass of orange juice. 'Please sit down and make yourself comfortable.'

'It's so kind of you to invite me, Mrs Bevington.'

'It's a pleasure.' Celia smiled at her, and going to the sideboard poured a measure of gin over ice, topped it up with tonic, and then dropped in a slice of lemon. 'Janet likes a dry sherry, but it's not to my taste. Have you never had any alcohol at all?'

Megan shook her head. 'My parents were strictly teetotal, and...'

'Of course, I quite understand. Ah, Janet,' Celia turned as the housekeeper came in. 'Here's our guest.'

Janet was wearing an apron over a straight navy

skirt and a filled white blouse which softened her normal practical, no-nonsense appearance.

Megan looked up at her from the sofa. 'Many happy returns...' She was uncertain whether to use the housekeeper's Christian name which was the only one she knew. Celia had never referred to Janet's surname.

'Thank you.' Janet, glass in hand came to sit beside her on the sofa.

Megan opened the clasp of her handbag and taking out a small parcel, with some shyness handed it to her. 'I hope you like it,' she said.

'Why how kind of you.' Janet gazed with both surprise and pleasure at the gift. 'May I open it now?'

'Of course, but it's not very much...'

Janet untied the white ribbon and opened the blue wrapping paper. Inside was a small square box, its cellophane cover displaying a single white lace-edged handkerchief. She gave an approving nod, 'Now isn't that perfect to pop into the wee bag I've bought for the wedding. My nephew is getting married next month,' she explained, 'and a fine occasion it promises to be. Thank you, Megan, it will be very useful.' She sipped at her sherry and glanced across at Celia who was trying not to look complacent. Janet turned again to Megan. 'We're having grapefruit to begin with, I hope you like it?'

'Thank you, yes.'

'And the pudding is a surprise.'

Celia smiled. 'That's Janet's way of saying that she's tried something new.'

Megan said, 'Am I right in thinking that we're

having lamb? It smells wonderful.'

'We are indeed, with our own vegetables.'

Janet stood up. 'Duty calls. If you'd both like to go along in five minutes?'

After she'd left, Celia said, 'That was very thoughtful of you Megan.'

'I could hardly come to a birthday lunch without a small present.'

'Even so, I'm sure Janet appreciated it.'

Megan was wondering whether it would be too personal for her to say how much she liked Mrs Bevington's cream muslin blouse – the one she had ironed the week before.

Celia was thinking that although Megan's turquoise dress suited her, it was a pity that she'd chosen to wear those same shabby sandals.

Conscious of the gaze upon her, Megan tucked her feet further beneath her and noticing the furtive movement Celia realised with some guilt that the girl was fully aware of how the sandals 'let down' her appearance and embarrassed by them. Surely she didn't only have the one pair? It was a disquieting thought because as far as her plan was concerned, that was one complication that she rather stupidly hadn't considered.

Chapter Twenty-eight

Once Celia had finished her gin and tonic she led the way along the hall and into the beamed ceilinged room that Megan had previously only glimpsed. Overlooking the back garden, its bay window was open to the scent of flowers and a brass fender with green leather seats fronted a dark oak fireplace. Megan gazed with pleasure at the oblong dining table with its white damask cloth and a central arrangement of cream and pink roses. There was a bottle of wine, a jug of iced water and two glasses at each setting. The cutlery was silver with embossed handles.

'Would you like to sit here Megan, on my left?' Celia sat at the head of the table and picking up a glass jug began to pour water. Janet came in with small white porcelain dishes resting on matching plates, smiled at them both, and after taking her own place lowered her head to say Grace. Afterwards Megan murmured, 'Amen'. Celia remained silent.

Watching to see which spoon the others used, Megan carefully inserted her own into the grapefruit desperately hoping that the juice wouldn't spurt up into her face, only to find that beneath its sprinkling of crystallised brown sugar it was segmented and easy to eat. 'This is lovely – I've never had it warm like this before.'

Janet smiled. 'Good, I'm glad you like it.'

'Megan,' Celia said, slowly eating her own grapefruit, 'I believe the pottery industry closes down for its annual holiday soon.'

'Yes, at the beginning of August. It used to be just for Wakes week but now we get a fortnight.'

'And are you going away?'

Megan shook her head. 'No not this year.' There was no need to let them know that she'd never spent a single night away from home.

'Do you know,' Celia said with a frown, 'I have no idea what the word "Wakes" stands for.'

'My father told me once that the word wake means a watch or vigil,' Megan said. 'Apparently a church would hold an all-night one before the annual celebration of its dedication, and also before holy days. So you can see how it became a holiday term.'

'Used mainly in the north, I think,' Janet said. When a few minutes later she got up to collect the used dishes and Megan offered to help, she said, 'Nae lassie, you're a guest.'

Celia began to pour herself and Janet a glass of wine and asked Megan what it was like to work in a pottery factory, listening with fascination as she described the camaraderie of the girls and how they enjoyed a sing song. 'It's hard work though and long hours,' Megan said, 'and it can be very boring sometimes. It all depends which pattern you're working on.'

'Janet and I must go on one of the factory tours – I've heard they're very interesting.' Celia took a sip of her wine, and they both turned as Janet began to bring in serving dishes, a gravy boat and their warm plates. As she began to carve the joint

Megan looked down at the white gold-edged dinner service and thought how unfair it was that the people working to produce such fine china often couldn't afford to own it. Apart from factory seconds sometimes. When Janet removed lids to reveal baby carrots, garden peas and runner beans, and not only roast potatoes but tiny new ones too, Megan longed to pile her plate only to see that the others were taking only small helpings. Then remembering that having seen guests at the George wait until everyone was served before they began to eat, she did the same.

Unseen by her, Celia and Janet exchanged glances.

'An excellent meal as usual, Janet,' Celia commented after a few minutes.

'It's wonderful,' Megan said.

Janet offered her the dish of potatoes. 'Do help yourself, and take more vegetables too.' She took another sip of her wine and must have noticed Megan's sideways glance because she smiled. 'I used to be teetotal just like you, as are many Presbyterians, but Robbie enjoyed his dram of whisky every night, and I don't think I'll go to hell because I have an occasional drink.'

'Well, I'm not going to Heaven unless it's licensed,' was Celia's retort. 'Not that I believe in either of them, as you very well know.'

Megan stared at her. Did that mean that Mrs Bevington was an atheist? It was a good job Les wasn't alive, because if he'd suspected that he would never have allowed her to come to the house. And then she thought, but I wouldn't have let him stop me. Not now, not any more. I've come a long way since those days.

Feeling that she should make an effort at conversation she said to Janet, 'Do you find the Potteries people very different from those in Scotland?'

'To be honest they're friendlier. We Scots tend to be a reserved lot.'

Megan was thinking how different Janet seemed today. It was only her brisk manner that had previously given the wrong impression. Celia was watching Megan, who had finished eating and remembering Nathan's example, was putting her knife and fork together on the plate.

Janet glanced across at Celia who gave a small satisfied smile and said, 'So now we will await this mysterious pudding.'

'I hope you're not disappointed.'

Janet's surprise proved to be an upside-down pudding which she said was an American recipe. Baked in a shallow dish the risen golden sponge was covered with glazed hot golden rings of pineapple. She also brought in a china jug, apologising, 'It's a poor imitation of fresh cream I'm afraid, but with the restrictions it's the best I can manage.'

Megan thought she'd died and gone to Heaven. She ate the sponge very slowly, and almost guiltily accepted a second helping.

Afterwards they drank coffee out of tiny cups, and talked of a new book, *The Diary of Anne Frank*, which had now been translated into English. Janet had ordered a copy from Webberley's book shop in Hanley. 'It sounds as if it's a book everyone should read, particularly the young, just to remind them of what this last war was all about.'

Megan told them of Jack, who had never been the same since his ordeal in the prisoner-of-war camp.

'Where was he?' Celia asked.

'I believe it was Burma.'

'He'll not be the only one,' Janet said quietly. 'Some things you never get over.'

Later and once her kitchen was restored to order, Janet came to join Celia in the drawing room where she was browsing with some difficulty through the Sunday newspapers. Megan, who had completed her first hour of reading aloud, was upstairs ironing.

'Well, how do you think it went?' Janet sat opposite Celia and leaned forward, her expression intent.

'She certainly liked that upside-down pudding. It was superb Janet, you surpassed yourself.'

'And you look like that proverbial cat – the one who swallowed the cream!'

'I do feel quite smug.' Celia's eyes were amused. 'She didn't put a foot wrong, did she?'

'Aye, she did well. I was surprised, relieved too I might add. So am I to take it...?'

Celia nodded. 'I shall go ahead.'

'Good. She's a nice girl Celia. I like her.'

'But there is a sensitive issue – one I hadn't thought of.' Celia told Janet of her new concern.

'Now that will be tricky. She'll have her pride you know.'

'Yes I realise that.' Celia crossed her still

shapely legs. 'I'm going to ask her later before she goes home. Don't worry, Janet, I think I know how to handle it ... remember Daphne?'

Megan paused as she came to the end of a chapter in case Mrs Bevington wanted to make a comment. Sometimes she did, if not she would simply smile and raise her hand for Megan to continue. But today she did neither. Instead she said, 'Thank you Megan, I think we'll leave it there for today. I would like to talk to you about something.'

Megan stared at her with sudden apprehension.

'I have a slight problem,' Celia said. 'Well, not a problem really, just a tiny cloud. Janet and I had planned to take a holiday in Eastbourne – do you know it at all?'

Megan shook her head. 'No, but I've heard of it. It's down south, isn't it?'

'Yes, in Sussex. However Janet's nephew upset all our plans by suddenly announcing that he's getting married in Aberdeen, right in the middle of our holiday. She's devoted to him – she couldn't possibly miss the wedding.' Celia took a cigarette from the silver box on the coffee table, inserted it into her slim holder and flicked on a lighter. She inhaled deeply then said, 'I could of course simply cancel, but I'm reluctant to do that. However the thought of staying in the hotel on my own – a lonely widow sitting at a tiny table for one in the restaurant; being a subject for pitying glances or patronising conversation in one of the lounges...' Celia gave a small shudder. 'That's not my scene at all.'

245

'I can understand that,' Megan said, feeling mystified as to why Mrs Bevington was telling her all this.

'And so Megan, I have decided to invite you to accompany me.' Celia's statement was clear, incisive and she saw Megan's eyes widen with shock and disbelief. 'It is short notice I know, but luckily the date coincides with your Wakes holiday and you did say you hadn't plans of your own. Of course I will take care of all the expenses.'

Stunned, Megan struggled to take it in. Mrs Bevington was offering to take her on holiday? 'Are you sure? I mean that you want *me* to come with you?'

Celia smiled. 'I wouldn't have asked you otherwise. But would you like to? Does the prospect of a fortnight at the seaside appeal?'

Megan couldn't answer; she was trying to deal with the panic sweeping through her. People were bound to dress up in a hotel. How could she possibly go? She thought of the few well-worn clothes hanging in her wardrobe, her one pair of shabby sandals. A whole fortnight! She wouldn't have enough knickers never mind anything else! 'Of course I'd like to come,' she said, 'I'd love to. I still can't believe that you've invited me. But...'

Celia gazed at her, seeing the distress in her eyes. 'What is it that's bothering you?'

Colour rose to Megan's face. 'It's just that... I wouldn't be able to bring enough clothes, not for a fortnight. I could have perhaps managed a week, but...'

Celia gazed at her and smiled. 'You mustn't worry about that. And we certainly can't let it prevent you from coming, not if you feel you'd like to. As it happens I have a niece – I don't think I've ever mentioned her to you. Daphne is clothes mad and completely scatty. When she came to stay last year she left one of her suitcases behind.' Celia laughed, 'Don't look so startled, you wouldn't believe the amount of luggage she brought with her for two weeks. You're both a similar size and she'd think it a lark for you to borrow them – I'm sure you'll find some things in there that you like. And if not, we can think of something else. Really, Megan I think we would get on famously. And if it makes you feel better, you could be a sort of companion. Think of Daphne du Maurier's Rebecca. Although,' Celia began to laugh. 'I can't promise that you'll meet a Mr de Winter.'

Megan couldn't help laughing herself at the thought of pretending to be a lady's companion. Did anyone still have those? Maybe they do she thought; after all wealthy people can afford to pay for anything. Had this been the reason behind the invitation for lunch? Had it been a sort of test to see if she'd be suitable, would have the right table manners?

'Please say yes, Megan. I honestly think you'd enjoy the experience. And you'd be helping me out of a fix.'

Megan gazed at her. It wouldn't be accepting charity ... would it? And even if it meant wearing someone's cast-offs, there was no shame in that. It wouldn't be the first time Megan had worn second-hand clothes. She looked across at the elegant woman before her and knew that she

247

might never get such an opportunity again. 'If you're absolutely sure...'

Celia smiled and waited. 'I'm positive.'

'Then,' Megan said, her eyes shining, excitement rising like a bubble. 'Thank you. My answer is yes, I'd love to come.'

Chapter Twenty-nine

Megan's walk home passed in a blur of euphoria, her mind was in a complete whirl. She clutched the suitcase of Daphne's beautiful clothes – absolutely everything had fitted and she'd gone back downstairs with what Janet laughingly called 'eyes like Christmas trees'. And before she'd left, Mrs Bevington had put an envelope into her hand. 'Please take it, Megan. I did say that I'd pay all expenses and,' her gaze had briefly dropped to Megan's sandals. 'I'm sure there will be other things you need.' Her mind was in such a whirl that suddenly Megan found herself at her front door and couldn't even remember crossing over the road.

The following Friday, there was the usual buzz as the wage packets were given out. Then a few minutes later, Lizzie stood up. 'Okay you lot, Megan's going up to Jean's tomorrow. It's time for another "whip round".'

Megan immediately reached for her purse. Being a married woman Jean hadn't had to pay

the full National Insurance 'stamp', but unfortunately that now meant that she wouldn't get
any sick pay. And every so often they tried to help
out. As Lizzie began to walk along the bench with
a basin, each paintress reached into her purse
and while Lizzie averted her head, put in whatever she could afford. But Avis, with a stony
expression simply carried on shading in the petal
of a rose. With tightened lips, Lizzie moved on.
Later, when she'd counted out the coins and
replaced them with notes, she said to Megan. 'I
know misery guts didn't know Jean. But that's
not the point. We look after our own here.' She
glanced over to Miss Dawson, who had contributed a ten shilling note. 'I think *she* noticed as
well.'

'There's not much she misses,' Megan said.

After she finished work on Saturday morning, it
was with a spring in her step that she set out to
do her holiday shopping. She spent ages in Brass-
ington's shoe shop trying to choose the 'classiest'
pair of sandals, and when she came out carrying
the precious shoebox she was smiling, until
outside on the pavement she came face to face
with Freda Podmore.

With a curt nod, Megan began to walk past her.

'I see you've been spending your money again!'

At the familiar carping voice Megan turned,
and couldn't resist it. 'Well, actually it's someone
else's.'

Freda' s eyebrows shot up.

'Remember me to Terry,' Megan added, already
moving away.

'I'll do no such thing!'

Megan stifled laughter as she carried on to the Market Hall. She bought underwear and nylons, slippers, and to her joy there was enough of Mrs Bevington's money left for a pink waffle cotton dressing gown. There was a frill around the revered collar, a tie waist, and she was thrilled with it. She'd been dreading having to take her old candlewick one. Then before going home she went to the flower stall to see Iris to tell her about the new job and the holiday in Eastbourne. Megan thought she looked thin and tired.

'You make the most of your good fortune, love; you might never get any more.'

'Are you going away?'

She nodded. 'I'm going with my sister to Blackpool. We've been going since we were kids.'

Megan smiled at her. 'I bet you look good in a "Kiss me Quick" hat!'

Iris chortled. 'If I find anyone daft enough to kiss me, I'll make the most of it – never mind a quick peck!'

After changing her library books, Megan was hungry by the time she got home, but after her usual Saturday cheese on oatcakes, she felt revived and ready to walk up to Meir. Bill let her in with only a brief smile, and when Megan went into the sitting room it was to see Jean sitting pale and wan in her armchair. There was no sign of the boys.

'How are you Jean?'

'Not so bad, love.'

Megan reached into her shopping bag and going over put the brown envelope on the coffee table.

Jean looked up at her. 'Oh Megan, they are good. Will you thank them all for me?'

'Of course I will. Look, I've brought you some grapes fresh off the market, and Miss Dawson sent you this.'

Taking off the brown paper, Jean's face brightened as she saw a bottle of Wincarnis Tonic Wine. 'Now that is kind of her. This should do me a power of good, don't you think so Bill?'

'It's very generous of her.'

'Oh, we'll soon have you on your feet.' But Megan's glance went down to Jean's hands and she saw the prominent veins and the thin listless fingers. She knew those hands so well; they'd worked skilfully next to her for years.

'Do you want a cup of tea, Megan?' Bill began to move towards the kitchen.

'No, I won't thanks, Bill. You've got enough to do. Besides I can't stay too long.'

Megan told Jean about Arthur retiring, and his replacement called Neil, who the girls thought was a 'bit of all right'. 'I don't take to him though.'

'And are you still going up to that big house?'

'Yes, do you know – Mrs Bevington treats her housekeeper more like a friend than an employee! Anyway, you'll never believe this...' Megan told her all that had happened.

Jean stared at her in amazement. 'She asked you to go to Eastbourne with her, out of the blue just like that?'

Megan nodded. 'I think that's why she invited me for Sunday lunch. She wanted to see if I knew how to conduct myself; you know whether I ate my peas off my knife! I've got a lot to thank

251

Nathan for, I can tell you.'

'I take it you've never heard anything from him?'

'No, and I don't think I ever will. There's no reason to really.'

'Well,' Jean said, 'I'm really pleased for you. You deserve a stroke of luck.'

That's just like her, Megan thought. Not a hint of envy or self-pity. 'I'll send you a postcard,' she promised, 'and bring the kids a stick of rock.'

'It's going to be the nearest they'll get to the seaside this year, that's for sure.'

Later when she left, Bill pulled the front door to behind them and said in a low voice, 'I can't see her ever coming back, love. Can you let Miss Dawson know...'

Early on Wakes Saturday with the windows fastened, the back door locked and her milk cancelled and feeling slightly sick with nerves, Megan waited by the front window. Then at last she saw the taxi turning the corner and fifteen minutes later it drew up outside Stoke Railway Station. The entrance was crowded with families; children clutching buckets and spades, elderly couples struggling with their luggage, even two young men with bicycles, and once inside with Megan beside her, Celia in a lightweight blue tweed suit stood slightly apart from the throng. Whether it was her supremely confident air or the sight of her expensive crocodile luggage, Megan wasn't sure, but within minutes a porter was approaching, and soon they were through the barrier to wait on their platform which

252

although busy, was quiet compared with the one opposite which was packed with holidaymakers.

'Where on earth are they all going to?' Celia asked.

'Rhyl or possibly Llandudno and Colwyn Bay; but lots will be going to Blackpool. People look forward to this fortnight all year.'

They gazed across the dividing tracks, smiling at the excited children, and then ten minutes later the impending arrival of the London train was being announced and the heavy locomotive pulled into the station surrounded by a cloud of steam, its powerful engine hissing as it slowly drew to a halt. Almost immediately the same cheerful porter re-appeared, coming forward to open the door to an empty First Class carriage and lifted in their luggage before storing it on the overhead rack. Celia's generous tip was ready in her gloved hand and taking it with a delighted grin he touched his cap and was gone. Megan stood hovering unsure which seat to take until Celia chose the forward one. 'I hope you don't mind sitting with your back to the engine.'

'This is fine,' Megan told her and sat opposite by the window, impressed by the monogrammed antimacassars on the backs of the seats and the scenic pictures displayed above. First Class travel looked very different from the other carriages she'd seen then guards went along the train slamming carriage doors, and after a piercing whistle the train began to move and to pick up speed. Celia watched as Megan peered with eagerness out of the window at local landmarks until at last she sat back with a sigh of pleasure and glancing across saw the older woman's amused gaze. 'My first time,' she confessed.

Celia was incredulous. 'You mean you've never been on a train before?'

Megan decided to be completely honest. 'I've never been away on holiday before.'

Slowly Celia shook her head in disbelief. 'I find that astonishing. I'm sorry, I didn't mean...'

'It's all right. Mum and I did have a couple of day trips though, but it was cheaper to go on the bus.'

'Oh, I see. Then in that case, I feel quite proud that I'm giving you this opportunity.'

'I can't tell you how grateful I am. I'm really looking forward to it.'

Celia smiled. 'Good, so that's out of the way. Now after all the effort of getting this far, I intend to sit quietly and relax. I find travelling to be an excellent time for getting one's thoughts in order.'

And so Megan became absorbed in watching the passing scenery, listening to the rhythmic beat of the wheels and reflecting on everyone's amazement when she'd told them her news. But after a while her early start caught up with her and relieved to see that Mrs Bevington had leaned back and closed her eyes, Megan gave in to her own drowsiness. But inevitably they were joined later by other passengers, two well-dressed women who began to gossip the moment they entered the carriage. All conducted in piercing voices that sounded, to use one of Rita's expressions, as if they had 'plums in their mouths'. Eventually they arrived at Euston, with its noise and crowds, but again within minutes Celia was sweeping through the station accompanied by a porter. Megan wondered whether it was her poise, expensive clothes or her blithe expectation of personal service that brought them such results. She had been looking forward to seeing the capital and on the journey to Victoria was so busy staring out of the black London taxi at all the buildings and shops and craning her neck not to miss a single landmark, that she was unaware of Celia watching her, a quiet smile playing around her mouth. So far, so good, Celia thought. The girl hasn't been a chatterbox, and it's rather refreshing to see her reactions, her interest in everything.

It wasn't until they were halfway to Eastbourne and alone, that she began to talk to Megan of the coming holiday. 'We have to think of appearances,' she said. 'We don't want to risk any confusion, any misunderstanding. Other guests are bound to wonder what our relationship is when they realise that we're not mother and daughter and that I'm not your aunt.' She smiled across at Megan, 'And I think our little private joke about your being my companion ought to be just between ourselves, don't you agree?'

'Yes, but of course I expect to...'

'Be helpful? You always are, Megan. I suggest that we merely state the truth. That the friend I'd planned to come with had to cancel at the last minute, and as you live near me and have never been to Eastbourne, you stepped into the breach.'

'That sounds perfect.'

'Good. And we can hardly spend the next two

weeks with you calling me Mrs Bevington all the time. So, I think it should be Celia.'

Megan felt flustered. 'Are you sure you won't mind?'

Celia laughed. 'I'm not royalty you know.'

At last they arrived at their destination, and they came out into the warm sunshine and the plaintive cries of seagulls to find a taxi waiting. Celia, glancing at Megan's eager expression told the driver to take the route along the seafront.

It was so long since Megan had seen the sea... And then she was lost for words as she gazed out of the window at the impressive Victorian pier, the formal flowerbeds along the promenade, the circular band stand and the many elegant hotels. There wasn't an amusement arcade or a souvenir shop in sight and she learned afterwards that the town was one planned 'by gentlemen for gentlemen', and that the 7th Duke of Devonshire who was a principal landowner, had stipulated that there were to be no shops built on the seafront. Then as they passed an expanse of green open space, the taxi indicated right and Celia was pointing out a fluttering flag with the name 'Hydro Hotel'.

Megan straightened the Peter Pan collar of her white blouse and leaned forward eagerly. Once at the top of the hill, they turned a corner and seconds later were drawing up outside an entrance displaying a gleaming brass nameplate and flanked by a profusion of hydrangeas. As a liveried porter came out to meet them and took their luggage from the boot she was painfully conscious of the contrast between Minnie's scratched cardboard suitcase and Daphne's pigskin one. But his expression was impassive as he led the way, and with nervous anticipation Megan followed Celia up a short flight of marble steps and through gleaming revolving doors.

Chapter Thirty

Later that evening Megan stood at the far end of the sweeping lawn and gazing at the horizon listened to the distant swishing sound of the waves on the shingle beach below while soft music drifted across the grass. Could all this truly be happening to her? She glanced down at her borrowed blue cocktail dress, at the way the bodice clung to her breasts, outlined her slim waist and flared into a full skirt. When earlier, nervous and self-conscious, she'd descended the broad carpeted staircase Megan had felt embarrassed about the amount of bare flesh it revealed, but the glances of admiration as she and Celia went into the cocktail bar had reassured her, and now she was loving the sensation of the soft warm breeze on her bare shoulders. She turned and looked at the pretty southern facade of the hotel, with its ornamental balconies directly facing the sea, feeling as if she was in a scene from a film. Her delight in her surroundings gave her confidence and she felt poised and feminine as she began to walk back across the lawn, past the tennis court and to the long veranda above beds of geraniums, alyssum and marigolds where Celia was sitting, a cigarette in her elegant holder. She smiled as Megan came near. 'Lovely view, isn't it?'

'Perfect. I really am grateful, Celia...'

Celia held up a hand. 'Now that's the last time... I'm delighted to have you with me, Megan.' She hesitated, 'By the way, my son and his wife are coming tomorrow.'

Megan looked at her in surprise. 'You mean to stay in the hotel?'

'Perish the thought!' Celia grimaced. 'Not because of James, I hasten to say. No, as they live not too far away, they're coming to join me for Sunday lunch.'

'Would you like me to make myself scarce?' Megan said, 'I can always go and explore.'

'That's very sensitive of you.' Celia gave a tiny yawn. 'I know there's dancing tonight, but I think I'm only fit for bed after the journey.'

Megan, thinking of her small but cosy bedroom agreed. Dinner in the elegant restaurant with its crystal chandeliers had been wonderful, but even she was tired after such a long day.

Early the following morning Megan opened her bedroom door and peered cautiously along the corridor. Feeling rather daring in her dressing-gown and slippers she hurried along to the lavatory and carefully locked the door behind her. Safely back in her room she washed at the small sink, marvelling at the luxury of having hot and cold water in a bedroom, and then gazed thoughtfully at the bed. Last night she'd found that someone had been in and not only turned down the covers, but laid her nightdress neatly on the coverlet. Just as if she was incapable of doing it for herself. But surely she would be expected to make her own bed? Once she was satisfied with its neatness and delighted to see that the weather promised to be warm and sunny, Megan tried to decide what to wear. Twenty minutes later after hanging outside her door the label saying that her room was ready for making up – whatever that meant – she walked along to the area where the narrow corridor widened and tapped lightly on Celia's bedroom door.

It was opened almost immediately. 'Come in Megan, I won't be long.'

Megan went into a spacious sitting area. Celia's room was a double one with a private bathroom and large windows overlooking the sea. Apparently it had been her husband's favourite. 'Giles valued his privacy,' Celia explained. 'I know it's rather indulgent just for me, but I was feeling nostalgic when I booked it. Now we'll be able to come up here for our reading sessions; after all you can hardly read aloud to me in public.' She laughed, 'Certainly not in the library – we'd soon have the old colonels scowling at us.'

'It's lovely,' Megan said, and then seeing that Celia's bed was still unmade moved forward to straighten it.

'There's no need to do that,' Celia said. 'The maid will only undo all your work and make it again.'

'Oh, I see.' Megan turned to her. 'But I do want to help, and you wouldn't let me unpack for you.'

Celia smiled at her. 'I'm not helpless you know. Besides I rather like unpacking and putting my things away in a hotel room. It reminds me of playing house as a child.'

Megan laughed. 'I know what you mean.'

'Did you sleep well? I must say you look very smart in that linen skirt. Cream suits you.'

'Thank you. Yes I slept very well, did you?'

'Perfectly.' Celia picked up her handbag and began to lead the way out of the room. 'I think you'll enjoy your breakfast. They're famous here for their bacon and sausage.'

Megan's eyes widened. She'd never had bacon and sausage at the same time. She thought again of the delicious four-course meal the night before. Taking Celia's advice that after travelling one should choose something light, Megan had ordered Dover sole. Even now she could remember its delicate flavour. And she had been astonished when Celia had told her that many of the guests dining alone were probably permanent residents.

Later, they relaxed in the 'long lounge' as Celia called it with their Sunday papers; Celia simply browsing through the headlines; the smaller print she found too tiring. Megan was revelling in such relaxation. No guilt that she should be catching up with housework, no worries about the next meal; her mind was not even wrestling with budgets and problems. She glanced at the oil paintings adorning the walls, resolving later to read the small gilt name plates below and studied the one opposite the damask sofa where they were sitting. It portrayed a woman with protruding pale eyes, her dark hair piled high, ringlets cascading to white shoulders, her voluptuous breasts rising from a blue silken gown. She remembered seeing a similar portrait in a book on art that she'd once borrowed from the library.

'She looks rather supercilious, don't you think?' Celia murmured.

'She looks rich!'

Celia gave a low laugh. 'I've no doubt that she was.' She glanced at her *Times*. 'Good heavens, I see here that they've introduced colour television in America. It's just a beginning – a one-hour programme, but I suspect that may be how the future lies.'

'I've only ever seen television once,' Megan told her. 'That was in Lewis's department store in Hanley.'

'It's certainly the coming thing. I've been prevaricating but when we get back I think I'll look into buying a set.'

The mention of America brought with it an image of Nathan, but realizing that Celia was asking her a question, Megan tore her mind away. 'Have you any plans,' Celia was saying, 'for today I mean?'

Megan said with some awkwardness. 'I thought I'd try and attend a service somewhere.'

'God doesn't give you a Sunday off? Not even on holiday?'

'Oh, I don't have to. It's just that...'

'I'm only teasing.' Celia smiled at her. 'I'm sure they'll help you at reception. Don't forget to hand in your room key. Whereas I,' she began to return to her newspaper, 'shall simply await my

261

visitors; if I know James, they'll be here at least an half an hour before the due time.'

Megan found that that she wasn't the only guest with such an enquiry. At the reception desk a middle-aged couple stood asking for directions to the nearest Catholic Church and as Megan listened she realised that this was an ideal chance to satisfy her curiosity. So many times she had walked past St Gregory's in Longton and wondered what a Catholic mass was like. Here she was unknown; there was nobody to see her, no-one to criticise. Pushing from her mind the thought of how outraged her father would be, Megan followed the couple out of the hotel, and for the next fifteen minutes walked discreetly behind them along tree-lined roads. The church was called Our Lady of Ransom, situated on a corner and built of stone with an impressive tower and adjoining side chapels. But as Megan drew near to join the worshippers it was to see that any woman not wearing a hat was covering her head as she entered; sometimes with a square of black lace, or at least a headscarf. As she hesitated, two young girls came near, one clutching her head and wailing that she'd forgotten her mantilla. 'You'd forget your head if it was loose,' said the other, 'we'll just have to sit at the back.'

Megan followed them, planning to do the same and when she saw them both genuflect she rather clumsily did the same before taking her place just inside a pew on the left. With sun pouring in through the stained glass windows and beautifully arranged flowers on the altar, the church was full of colour and warmth contrasting sharply with the plain austere interior of her chapel at home. Candles were flickering before a side altar on which stood a statue of Mary, her serene face framed by a soft blue robe. And on the opposite side another small altar, again with lighted candles on a small stand; this time before a statue of Christ on whose chest seemed to be a bleeding heart. Megan frowned – she wasn't sure that she liked that one. And then to the sound of organ music the priest walked to the main altar, tall and dignified in richly coloured vestments and attended by six altar boys.

Megan had known that a Catholic mass was said in Latin and had expected not to understand the priest's words or the altar boys' responses. But she was surprised to find that congregation also replied in Latin, many reading from a black prayer book. At first she found the service rather bewildering but she sat, knelt and rose when everyone else did, enjoying the music and joining in the hymns. The sermon was in English and mainly explained the day's gospel, and later to the sound of soft organ music and the scent of incense she watched the procession of men, women and children move slowly down the aisle to kneel at the altar rails to receive communion. Megan would have liked to join them, but unsure of the rules remained thoughtfully in her seat. Moved by the atmosphere of reverence and devotion, she was finding the whole experience deeply spiritual, and wondered why her father had been so scathing of Catholics and what he used to call their idolatry. Megan looked again at the statues and the elaborate crucifix – if such images helped people to feel closer to God, then how could they possibly be wrong? And when on leaving she saw that people were dipping their fingers into a font of water just inside the door and then crossing themselves, on impulse she did the same.

Half an hour later, she was standing before the sea taking slow deep breaths, her lungs filling with clean fresh air, her lips tasting its saltiness. She gazed down at the beach, at the striped deck-chairs, at the distant swimmers, at the small squealing children safe at the edge as they paddled and jumped over the trickling waves. The sky was blue, although there were a few threatening clouds, but at the moment there was sunshine and she turned to look at the promenade – long, level and inviting. With a heady sense of freedom and the eager stride of youth Megan set out towards the distant pier.

'James and I are rather concerned about you being here on your own, Celia.' Verity's voice had a clarity that gave an edge to her words. 'I mean, if you'd wanted a change of scene you could have come to stay with us.'

They were all sitting on the veranda and Celia gazed at her daughter-in-law who was wearing a pale green dress and jacket, her slim legs in sheer nylons, her slender feet in white heeled sandals. With her red-gold hair and green eyes, Celia couldn't deny that the young woman was attractive but why did she always manage to be so irritating?

'That's very kind of you, Verity, but I felt that I

needed some sea air. In any case, I'm not on my own.'

'But you told us that Janet had to go to a wedding in Scotland.'

'Yes, that's true. So I brought another friend with me instead.'

'Who was that then, Mother? Anyone I know?' James, his legs stretched before him was surreptitiously watching two young women playing singles.

'I don't think so. She lives nearby.'

He removed his pipe. 'I thought you said you had little to do with the neighbours.'

'Not as close as that. Actually, she's someone who comes to read to me every Sunday. She irons for me as well.' Celia waited. She rather enjoyed baiting Verity.

Verity's finely plucked eyebrows rose. 'You mean that you pay her?'

'That's right.'

'But if she needs to earn money in that way, then how can she afford to…'

'Stay here? She can't. I invited her as my guest.'

'You mean that you're paying for both of you?' Verity swung round to James. 'Did you hear that? Aren't you concerned that your mother's being taken advantage of?'

'She's hardly going to allow that.' But the inference was enough to distract James from admiring a brunette on the court, and he turned to look enquiringly at his mother.

'Thank you for that vote of confidence, James. If you must know, Megan is a perfectly nice girl. She had no idea that I was going to invite her.'

'Did you say girl?' Verity's expression was one of astonishment. 'I was imagining a middle-aged widow. Exactly how old *is* she?'

'I'm not sure. I would imagine she's about twenty or twenty-one.'

James was now leaning forward, his eyes intent. 'And would you mind telling us how long you've known her?'

Celia gave an inward sigh of exasperation although she knew that James was only being protective. 'Not long – possibly a couple of months.'

Verity and James exchanged glances. 'Let me get this straight,' James said slowly. 'A girl comes to help you in the house and the next thing is that you invite her for an all expenses-paid luxury holiday? Really mother, have you taken leave of your senses. What do you know about her?'

'I know that she wasn't born with a silver spoon in her mouth. And she has to work hard to support herself. I also happen to think that she has integrity.'

'But what can you possibly have in common?'

Celia hid an exasperated sigh. Only Verity could ask such a crass question! 'Well, a love of literature for a start.'

James however was still probing. 'You say she has to support herself? What about her family?'

Celia shook her head. 'She hasn't any. First she lost her father, and then her mother died last year.'

'And they didn't leave her provided for?'

'The working classes,' Celia said drily, 'don't earn enough to leave inheritances and trust funds.'

266

'And what exactly does this Megan do?' Verity said.

Celia paused for a second. 'She works in a pottery factory.'

Verity's pencilled eyebrows almost collided with her hairline. 'But I thought you said she liked books!'

'There are such things as public libraries, Verity. And unless the government has recently passed a law, reading isn't confined to a certain social class.'

Verity's eyes narrowed. 'But whatever were you thinking of to bring a factory girl *here?* It's hardly fair on the other guests, Celia.'

Behind them Megan was standing appalled on the edge of the veranda. Shaken, she backed into an adjacent small lounge, empty except for an elderly man gently snoring in a winged leather armchair. But she could still hear every word.

'And why would that be, Verity?' Celia's tone was deceptively mild.

'She won't know how to behave for one thing, and you are doing her no favours at all, you know. Bringing her to a hotel like this, exposing her to a different way of life. It only unsettles these people.'

'You were quite happy for my housekeeper to come,' Celia countered. 'And she also works for me.'

'That's a totally different situation. Janet is a woman of breeding, one who was married to a minister.'

Celia gazed at her son's choice of wife wondering yet again why on earth he'd married her. He'd

267

been a delightful small boy, he was now a successful stockbroker, but as for his judgement of the
fair sex … and she hadn't missed his preoccu-
pation with those girls on the tennis court either.

'Well,' she said briskly, 'you'll both meet her
next Sunday, because I intend to ask her to join
us for lunch. You can regard it as part of your
education Verity. But I shall expect you to treat
her with respect.'

'Come on,' James objected, 'I don't think you
can fault Verity on her good manners.'

'I wouldn't dream of it,' Celia said drily. 'Now
you did say that you didn't want to stay for tea.
They will be serving it soon.'

'No, I think we'll make a move.' James turned
to his wife. 'Are you ready, darling?'

'Yes, of course. No don't come with us Celia –
you could lose your comfortable chair. We'll look
forward to seeing you next Sunday, then.'

Megan on hearing the sound of movement
swiftly withdrew further as James, taller than
she'd expected and with a thin dark moustache
strolled by. Verity followed – expensively dressed
and with an air of easy arrogance that made
Megan's burning resentment turn almost to
hatred. She moved forward to watch them leave,
James with a protective hand beneath Verity's
elbow as they went out through the glass
revolving doors. Megan was seething; she should
have confronted the flaming snob, not just stood
there in meek silence! But to do so would have
upset and embarrassed Celia and Megan would
never do that. And then reaction set in and her
eyes began to sting with tears of humiliation as a

sickening thought struck her. Would other people think the same if they knew of her background – that her presence in the hotel was 'hardly fair on the other guests?'

Not even the prospect of afternoon tea and cakes could tempt her to stay. How could she just walk on to the veranda and join Celia as if nothing had happened? With a choking sensation, Megan almost ran up the staircase to her room. It had been such a lovely day; she'd been feeling so happy, so confident.

Chapter Thirty-one

The following morning although apparently immersed in *The Times*, Celia was feeling uneasy. Last night at dinner and again at breakfast she'd sensed a difference in Megan. There was tension there in her face, wariness in her eyes.

'Megan, is everything all right?'

'Yes fine, thank you.'

'It's just that you seem ... a little on edge.'

'No, I'm fine, honestly.'

'Good. I do want you to enjoy our stay, Megan. I know all this,' Celia waved a hand around the spacious lounge, 'is very different to what you're used to, but...'

'Oh no, I love it here.'

Celia gazed at her. 'If there is anything troubling you, I'd much rather you told me.'

For one split second Megan wavered; but she

knew that Celia must never know the truth. Megan *was* feeling on edge; she was desperate for some reassurance, anything to stop those hateful words from endlessly circling in her mind.

'It's that...' she began, 'well everyone here is so ... oh, I don't know – educated and professional. I don't suppose there's anyone else like me – just someone who works in a factory.'

Celia froze. Could Megan possibly have over-heard Verity? Appalled at the thought Celia glanced swiftly at the young woman by her side. No, she couldn't have done. Megan had mis-judged the time and returned so late to the hotel that she'd even missed afternoon tea.

Celia frowned. 'Let me tell you something, Megan. There will be several guests who even if they don't consider themselves working class, their fathers or grandfathers probably were. And in any case, when we do begin to socialise more, it's entirely up to you what you tell them about yourself. Certainly I have to say that you fit in beautifully, if that's what's bothering you.'

'Only because of the clothes you let me borrow,' Megan said.

'They help of course, but you have to take some credit yourself. You're a lovely girl with your own dignity, Megan. Don't ever forget that.'

'And it doesn't matter that I speak with – well you know – a Potteries accent?'

'But you don't at all,' Celia said with surprise. 'Oh, there's the Midlands intonation in your voice, but your grammar is correct and that's the important thing. Mind you, I'm not saying that there won't be any snobs here, I'm afraid they exist everywhere unfortunately. The best thing is to ignore them. And sometimes in a social situation it can be wise not to be too specific. If you're asked a direct question, then that's different Megan. But otherwise, there's no harm in being economical with the truth if that makes you feel more comfortable.'

Megan hesitated. 'What sort of job did you do? Before you were married, I mean?'

'I've never done anything very useful, I'm afraid. My father was what people called "something in the City." He would go up to London each day, leaving my mother and myself in leafy Surrey.' Celia smiled, 'It was rather a privileged existence I suppose. After boarding school, I simply came home to accompany my mother on her shopping trips, play tennis and go to parties and dances – the usual things a girl of my set did in those days. It was just after the First World War when those young men who returned were desperate to try and put its horror behind them.' She paused, her eyes shadowing, 'Not that they managed to, of course.' She folded her newspaper. 'It's time for our constitutional I think. Which way shall we walk today?'

Megan considered. 'Could we go to the right towards Beachy Head? I haven't been that way yet.'

'Excuse me – I was wondering whether you'd like to make up a foursome.'

It was a few days later and Megan, who had been watching a singles match on the tennis court, glanced up to see a girl slightly younger

271

than herself smiling down. 'Only I've noticed you like to watch and if you haven't got a partner...'

Megan, sitting alone on the veranda said with some embarrassment, 'That's really kind of you, but I'm afraid I don't play.'

'What, not at all?' The girl sat in the chair opposite. 'Gosh!'

'I do love to watch, but ... it's just something I've never done.'

'Well, we can soon put that right. I'm Angela by the way and you're...'

'Megan.'

'Well, if you'd like to try, I'd be glad to have a knock-up with you.' Angela, leaning forward lowered her voice. 'We could always choose a time when there is hardly anyone about if you're worried about showing yourself up – probably when they're all titivating before dinner.'

Megan laughed, instinctively liking the slim blonde with her good-humoured freckled face. 'But I'd need a racquet...'

'You can borrow mine – I'll use my mother's. And don't worry about whites either; if it's just a knock up we can both wear a cotton skirt. What do you think?'

Angela's enthusiasm was infectious and Megan didn't hesitate. 'I'd love to, thanks.'

Later Celia stood at her bedroom window, watching the two girls on the tennis court below. As Angela had forecast, the gardens were almost deserted, and Celia smiled as she saw Megan fumble with a backhand shot. But although new to the game, she was already developing a half-decent serve and seemed to have a good eye for the ball. Now why Celia thought turning away, couldn't James have provided her with a daughter-in-law more like Megan? Someone she could become close to, could laugh with, could indulge. Verity had been spoiled all her life – what could Celia offer? And yet she had always longed for a daughter. Even now, after all these years, the sad memory of her tiny two-day old baby who had lost her fight for life had the poignancy to bring tears.

The following day, they both walked down the hill and past the splendid Grand Hotel. Celia told Megan that she and her husband had once spent a wonderful weekend there, but that he later preferred the view from the Hydro where he could put his binoculars to better use. They were heading for the town, but after a while Celia took Megan to explore the narrow side streets with their small boutiques, second-hand bookshops and art galleries. And it was then, as they were browsing before the window of an antique shop that Megan saw it. There, nestling on a bed of blue velvet was a silver, oval hand mirror.

Celia heard her sharp intake of breath. 'What have you seen? Something you like?'

Megan pointed. 'It's that silver hand mirror – it matches a hairbrush I've got.'

'Have you?' Celia peered closely. 'Are you sure?'

'I'm positive.'

'How very intriguing; shall we go in?' Celia suggested. She opened the door to the sound of a tinkling bell, and with Megan following they went inside. The shop was small and cramped, every corner displaying its treasures. Brass carriage clocks, silver cutlery, pocket watches, collectable dolls, and objets d'art jostled for space, the walls were crowded with framed prints and paintings while small tables displayed antique jewellery and porcelain. At the back of the shop was an old shabby desk where an elderly man sat, half-moon glasses on his beaky nose, his grey hair sparsely scraped across his scalp.

Celia went towards him. 'Good morning. You have a silver hand mirror in the window...'

He gave her a thin smile, got up stiffly and shuffled on carpet slippers to unlock the wooden shutter and reach into the window. Holding out the mirror still nestling on the blue velvet cloth, his keen eyes swept over Celia to appraise whether she was a prospective buyer. She looked down at the way the silver gleamed, at the intricate decoration and silently handed it to Megan.

'Yes, it's exactly the same, even to the initials.' Perplexed, Megan ran a forefinger along the beading and turned to the dealer. 'Are they the initials of the maker?'

'No, they're personal. This will have been specially commissioned.'

Megan glanced in trepidation at the amount written on a small white ticket. As she'd expected, the cost was far beyond her means, and with a stab of disappointment, she handed the mirror back to him. 'Thank you, but it's a little expensive for me, I'm afraid.'

'Sorry, I can't let it go for any less.'

Celia said quietly, 'Do you know its provenance?'

Megan watched as the old man scratched

behind his ear. 'I should have a note of it some-where; it only came in a couple of weeks ago. I'm a bit behind with my records I'm afraid.' He went back to his cluttered desk and began to search through bills and receipts.

'What does "provenance" mean?' Megan whis-pered to Celia.

'Its history, where it came from.'

'Ah, here it is.' He came back to them with a slip of paper in his hand. 'It's on this list here, among some items my brother bought at a house auction up in Staffordshire.'

Staffordshire! They both stared at him, then Celia said decisively, 'Wrap it up, we'll take it. You'll accept a cheque?' She was already opening her handbag and going to the desk to pay.

The same afternoon having enjoyed their lunch, Celia and Megan relaxed in Celia's room. With a small coffee table between them, they sat on gold velveteen chairs, while Megan read from *A Passage to India*. They were now more than halfway through and she was finding both the story and the background fascinating. It was with reluct-ance that she eventually closed the book because there was, she'd discovered, a limit on how long she could read aloud, not only because her throat became hoarse, but her concentration began to flag.

'The culture is so different,' she said to Celia. 'It must have taken a lot of courage to go and live out there.'

'I didn't really have any choice,' Celia admitted. 'A woman doesn't only marry a man she marries his way of life. And to be honest at twenty-one it all seemed rather an adventure. I thought myself so sophisticated, so mature, but I wasn't at all prepared. Not for the heat, the smells and certainly not for the maimed beggars in the streets. And then there were the Memsahibs.' She gave a self-deprecating laugh. 'I don't know what they made of me, I'm afraid I've never been one to conform to social conventions. And at first I was dreadfully homesick. But it's such a beautiful country, if one of contrasts. I wouldn't have missed the experience for the world.'

'I'd love to travel,' Megan said. 'I've only ever met one foreigner, although I don't suppose an American is a foreigner really, not like someone who speaks a different language.'

Celia looked at her in surprise. 'You met an American?'

Megan nodded and told her about Nathan, how he'd taken her to the George Hotel in Burslem and about the hamper his mother had sent.

Now this Celia thought, explains a lot. If Megan hadn't had that experience and learned from it, would she have passed the Sunday lunch test? If not, then she might not be sitting here. How small happenings in our life have far reaching effects, she mused. And from the soft, almost luminous look in her eyes as Megan had talked of this American, Celia guessed that the fleeting acquaintance had meant far more to her than it seemed to have done to him.

She smiled. 'Now – could I possibly see your hairbrush? I'm dying to see the two items side by side.'

'Yes of course.' While Megan went along to her room and picking up the brush, hurriedly began to try with a comb to remove every last trace of hair, Celia waited with impatience for her to return. It was all such an odd coincidence. Celia might not believe in vicars, priests and church services, but she did believe in fate. Minutes later she was examining the silver-backed hairbrush closely. Then she picked up the hand mirror and compared them, turning each one over and tracing the decoration. 'You're right,' she said slowly, 'they're an exact pair.' She peered at the tiny scrolled initials. E.F. 'Now I wonder who that could be?'

'I've no idea,' Megan said.

'It looks to me as though the mirror has hardly been used at all, and the hairbrush very little.'

'It belonged to my mother but as far as I know she never used it. I rarely do either. I just brought it with me as a sort of special treat.'

Celia looked thoughtful. 'You know, I think this mirror has been kept shut away in a drawer, possibly in tissue paper, at least most of the time.'

Megan looked at it again. 'I see what you mean.'

'To come back to the hairbrush – do you know how it came into your mother's possession?'

Megan shook her head. 'She just said that it had sentimental value, and she was saving it for me for when I came of age. But I'm sure she came by it honestly.'

'Now Megan, whatever made you think that I thought differently?'

Megan felt heat rise in her cheeks. 'Freda Podmore certainly implied it. She seemed to think there was some sort of mystery.'

'And who is Freda Podmore?'

Megan began to tell her about Terry's mother, and her indignation and resentment rising, she described her as pinch-faced and ramrod straight, her colourful account causing Celia to crumple with laughter. 'Oh, do tell me more. The woman sounds such a buttoned-up horror!'

And then Megan began to laugh as well as she related her cold welcome in Freda's home and the everlasting Battenberg cake.

Celia wiped her eyes. 'Oh, Megan I am glad you've come.'

'So am I.' And *that* Megan thought, is one in the eye for the venomous Verity!

Chapter Thirty-two

The following morning dawned with grey skies and a steady downpour. So after they had browsed through the day's news, it was light relief to see Angela strolling towards them. 'Isn't it a filthy morning?'

'Awful.' Megan introduced her to Celia and then turned as a tall, fair-haired young man joined them.

'This is my brother Rupert,' Angela said, 'he's just arrived. And please ignore his stupid outfit – he seems to think it's funny to resemble a bear annual!'

Megan couldn't help laughing as she saw his

278

yellow-checked trousers. An older version of his sister, he grinned at her and then drew up a chair with alacrity when Celia offered coffee.

'Terrific, I could do with the caffeine, having just driven down from Gloucestershire.'

'He's been overseeing the harvest, or so he says. Not that he does any real work!' Angela said.

'You're from a farming family then?' Celia glanced up as a waiter approached.

'Yes, we have a few acres.' Rupert leaned to whisper to Megan. 'Will they bring biscuits?' She smiled and nodded.

After giving her order, Celia looked thoughtfully at his silk cravat and hand-made shoes then turned to smile at Megan's new friend. 'And what do you do, Angela?'

'Lazes about,' Rupert said.

'No I don't! Why does no-one take my music seriously? You'll be singing a different tune when I have my first violin recital.'

'What about you, Megan,' Rupert said. 'How do you keep your nose to the grindstone?'

She felt a sudden lurch in her stomach. 'I'm a paintress.'

'What a lovely word for a lady painter,' Angela leaned forward with interest. 'What sort of subjects?'

Megan remembered Celia's advice. 'I paint flowers.'

'Do you prefer water colours or oils?'

Megan thought of her workbench spread with newspaper and of her jar of turpentine. Her colours were oil-based, weren't they? 'Oils,' she said, and with warm cheeks darted a quick glance at Celia, but she was looking relaxed and non-committal.

'I saw you at breakfast Angela, with your parents,' Celia said. 'Don't tell me that they've gone out in this weather?'

'Oh yes. Father's dragged mother off to Battle Abbey would you believe. He'd planned it for today, and says that no Englishman lets a drop of rain change his plans. Fortunately, I had to wait and welcome Rupert.'

'Yes, I do need a nursemaid!'

After they'd enjoyed their coffee and Rupert had demolished most of the biscuits, Angela got up. 'Come on brother, let's go and see if your room's ready.' She turned to Megan. 'Are you both coming to the Gala Dance tonight? If so, do join our table, that would be lovely wouldn't it Rupe?'

'It would be a beacon of light at the end of the day.'

Angela laughed. 'Oh, stop practising your charm, nobody's impressed!'

Celia watched them go. 'What nice young people. I think you handled that very well, Megan. And you were not the only one who was economical with the truth.'

Perplexed, Megan said, 'What do you mean?'

'Just that I don't think you should take his reference to a 'few acres' too seriously. I don't think Rupert gets up at the crack of dawn to do the milking. Or to spread manure or whatever it is they spread on fields. He just isn't the type.'

'Oh, I see. At least I think I do.'

Celia smiled. 'I did have mixed feelings about

this Gala Dance, but now with new people to meet, I think I might enjoy it – even if I will feel like one of those matrons in a Jane Austen novel.'

'A chaperone sitting at the side, you mean?' Megan laughed, 'I'm a bit old for a chaperone, Celia. I'm looking forward to it, I love dancing.'

The rain continued all day and in the afternoon after their reading session, Celia retired for a nap, while Megan went back to her room to write the postcards she'd bought the previous day. For Jean, she'd chosen several views of Eastbourne, for Clarice and Rita a traditional seaside one, with a rosy-cheeked large-bottomed lady and small henpecked husband. For Eunice she had chosen a scene with children playing on the beach.

Megan would have liked to have sent a picture of the hotel to Miss Dawson, but she was what the girls called, 'a very private person', and Megan didn't know her address. The supervisor had drawn Megan aside just before the factory closed down for the Wakes fortnight to say, 'Megan, fortune does seem to be shining on you, and there is nobody more pleased than I am. I think in everyone's life there's a "golden time." Sometimes it's only a few days, weeks or months. An era you will always remember.' Her eyes had clouded, and Megan remembered the girls saying that Miss Dawson's fiancé had been killed in the war. 'So promise me that you'll make the most of this holiday. And I don't just mean by enjoying it; this is a real opportunity for you.'

'Watch and learn,' Megan said and smiled. 'I

281

remember – just as you told me once before. I will, Miss Dawson.'

But she did send a card with a picture of the hotel on the front to Audrey in Wales.

'*Dear Audrey,*

This is where I'm staying – I still can't believe it. Having a lovely time and am going to a Gala Dance tonight. Have just met someone called Rupert!! Can you imagine anyone being called that in Longton? Raining today, but who cares. How's the postman? Love Megan xx'

She smiled to herself at the last line. Audrey had confided that she had a 'pash' on the post-man in their village, and Megan had urged her to invest in a pair of court shoes. '*You'll be amazed,*' she'd written, '*how different you'll feel wearing heels. He'll look at you with new eyes. And new shoes will do wonders for your confidence. My life changed from the moment I bought my first pair from the Co-op in Hanley. I can't believe we only ever wore those old-fashioned sensible ones.*' It would be great if Audrey did find a husband, but as an image came to Megan of her friend's homely looks and constant battle with her weight, she knew that only a perceptive man would take the time to find out what a lovely person she was.

Later when they went down for tea they could see Angela and Rupert sitting with their parents, and Celia gave a friendly wave, while Megan smiled at Angela. Rupert had his back to her but later as she and Celia sat at a small round table some distance away, Megan saw him glance over his shoulder, twist around and when his gaze met hers he gave a swift smile.

While they were enjoying their almond tarts Celia began to look thoughtful, and then said, 'The question is what are we going to do about this little mystery – about the mirror I mean? There must be a reason why it became separated from the hairbrush.' She slowly stirred a lump of sugar into her tea, and then looked up with a delighted smile. 'I know – I rather fancy playing Miss Marple. When we get back would you like me to do a bit of sleuthing? After all, you're working so I have more time – of course only if that's what you want – to probe further?'

'I'd love to know who the original owner was. Are you sure you don't mind?'

'Megan, when you get to my time of life, anything that's a novelty or a challenge is more than welcome.' Celia smiled at her. 'In fact I shall look forward to it.' She picked up the hand mirror. 'I'll hold on to this for now, but actually I bought it for you – it would be a crying shame for you not to have it.' Celia held up a hand as she saw that Megan was about to protest. 'Please, no arguments. I'm finding that there is a lot of truth in the old saying that "it is more blessed to give than to receive".'

'I'll never be able to repay you for all you've done for me,' Megan said. She was feeling somewhat embarrassed. Strangely it wasn't easy to always be on the receiving end in a friendship; her use of that word startled her. But it was true – during these past few days, spent almost exclusively in each other's company, she *had* come to feel that Celia was a friend.

'You've already brought a breath of fresh air

283

into the house. And I think I needed that.' Celia smiled at her. 'Somehow youth has a golden quality that we lose as we get older.'

'I think I know what you mean – even at my age,' Megan said. 'For instance, Clarice who lives next door to me has a granddaughter called Debra...'

Celia chuckled as Megan described the irrepressible young girl with her sense of fun and sublime confidence. 'I must make a note of this hair salon and pay it a visit,' she said.

'It's not a very posh one...'

But Celia refused to be deterred. 'Well they do say that variety is the spice of life.'

Later Megan enjoyed the luxury of deep scented water in a capacious Victorian bath. Gazing at the high ceiling, and glossy black and white tiled floor she thought yet again how very different it was from her own cramped bathroom with its cheap wallpaper and rusty stains on the enamel beneath the old and pitted chrome taps. These taps were huge and gleaming and – absolute bliss – her enormous fluffy towel was draped over a warm radiator. She lay there in a hazy daydream until she heard someone try the knob on the locked door and with reluctance realised that another guest was waiting.

When later she opened the wardrobe to search for something to wear it was only a token gesture because she knew exactly what her choice would be. It might have thin shoulder straps and a daring neckline, but that first evening she'd felt so feminine wearing it, so confident. Taking out the blue cocktail dress she held it against her, imagining how the full skirt with its silk lining would swish and swirl. She loved that sensation. Would she be dancing with Rupert? Megan smiled to herself, remembering that swift backward smile.

Chapter Thirty-three

Later that evening, as the strains of music drifted through to the lounge, Megan waited with growing impatience as Celia lingered with a cigarette after her coffee. When eventually they did enter the ballroom it was to see Angela raising a hand to beckon them over. She had obviously inherited her freckles from her mother, whose sun kissed complexion made her look younger than her years. Her father, a taciturn man whose voice was clipped as his thin moustache shook Celia's hand, smiled at Megan, enquired what they would both like to drink and sent Rupert off to the bar.

Angela, looking slightly bored and wearing a red dress with a halter-neck looked up at Megan, patted the seat next to her and murmured, 'I haven't seen anyone dishy yet.'

Megan glanced around at the men in the ballroom; most of whom were middle aged and with their wives. There were a couple of younger ones standing together who were already glancing over in their direction. But one was only about eighteen, and the other was as round as he was tall. 'I see what you mean.'

'It's all right for you – don't think I haven't seen you and Rupert making sheep's eyes at each other!'

'I've hardly spoken to him,' Megan protested annoyed to feel herself blushing.

'I can't see what all the girls see in him. But then I know his disgusting habits.'

'And whose disgusting habits would those be, may I ask?' Rupert, back with their drinks held a full glass perilously over his sister's head.

Celia laughed, turning to his mother. 'What a handful these two must have been!'

'They still are.' She smiled. 'Angela tells me that you're both from Staffordshire.'

'Yes. Megan stepped in to fill the breach when my original companion had to cancel her holiday.' Celia glanced sideways at the woman by her side whose tinted hair and smooth complexion owed much to an expensive beauty parlour. 'You're farmers, I believe.'

Felicity Penrose laughed. 'Not in the literal sense of the word. But we do have farms, yes. And you?'

Mentally noting the plural word, Celia replied, 'My husband was Indian Army but I was widowed two years ago.'

'Oh, I'm sorry to hear that. You must find a chance to talk to Charles. He's a military history buff.'

Just then the band struck up with a foxtrot and with alacrity Rupert got up, took Angela's hand and gave it a tug. 'Come on, trouble.'

Megan had been sitting in a flutter of anticipation and with slight disappointment began to look around the room. She decided that some of the older women would have been wiser to cover up their plump or sagging flesh, and the amount of jewellery they wore only seemed to accentuate it. But she knew that in reality she was resenting their comfortable lives, comparing them to those of people like Minnie and Lizzie, of Jean and even Miss Dawson. How hard they worked; were still working.

While Celia talked with Felicity and Charles, Megan concentrated on watching Rupert and Angela. Even on the dance floor they were fooling around and trying fancy steps. Rupert may look about thirty she thought, but he acted much younger. And then ten minutes later she was being held in his arms and as the band played a quickstep and he looked down at her there was no more teasing in his eyes, instead they were warm and appreciative. 'I love that dress,' he murmured. 'God, I'm glad you're here to relieve the boredom. I mean look around you. What is a red-blooded male supposed to do in such company?'

'I don't know – I've never been one.'

He laughed and drew her closer.

Over the evening Celia apart from dancing dutifully around the floor with Charles, did indeed feel like a middle-aged and sidelined matron. But although Rupert repeatedly chose Megan as his partner, Felicity gave the couple scant attention as she gaily related stories of their social round, and described earlier visits to Wimbledon and Henley.

When eventually Rupert remembered his social

duties and invited Celia to dance, she said, 'I'm glad that Megan has made friends with you and your sister. It's so much more interesting for her than being with me all the time.'

'She's a smashing girl. So you wouldn't mind if I take her out tomorrow?'

'Of course I wouldn't. Where were you thinking of?'

'Has she been up to Beachy Head yet? We could go for a brisk walk – blow the old cobwebs away and all that?'

'Actually no,' Celia said. 'We've walked along in that direction but...'

'Brilliant!' He smiled down at her, a lazy relaxed smile, and Celia doubted whether Megan had ever met anyone like him. Not even the American she talked of could have been like Rupert. He was a typical product of an English public school; with an air of self-assurance and easy charm. It was a certain aura they had; her husband Giles had possessed it and it was damned attractive. Ever likely Megan had succumbed, Celia thought. She was looking almost beautiful, happiness bringing a sparkle to her eyes and a glow to her cheeks.

Megan was indeed happy. It was not only that Rupert was an experienced partner, it was the intimate and exciting way that he held her, his thumb occasionally caressing her palm, his fingers stroking her bare back. Any conversation between them however was frivolous, their laughter frequent, and it was only later just before she drifted off to sleep that she realised that she knew little more about him, or he about her, than when they'd first met.

Unfortunately, the following morning dawned with grey skies and the threat of yet more rain. Megan, with Rupert and Angela beside her, stared out of the window without much optimism. 'No English person worth their salt lets the weather interfere with their plans,' Rupert said.

'Maybe a sensible person does!' Angela was distinctly gloomy, having complained to Megan earlier that the dance had been a damp squib as far as she was concerned.

'I've got a plastic mac,' Megan said, 'and I don't mind rain. It's good for the complexion.'

'And what am I supposed to do?' Angela complained.

'Go and spend your allowance in the shops. You don't usually find that a hardship.' Rupert glanced across the room to where his parents were talking to another couple. 'Although I'm sure father's got something planned. I can't see him sitting around here all day.'

Angela pulled a face. 'They're going to Alfriston to see some sort of Priest's House and then to have lunch. I'm hardly going to find a holiday romance there.'

'Do I detect the green eye?' Rupert glanced at Megan and winked.

'No,' she said, 'just sympathy for poor Megan being landed with you. And that's only because there isn't any opposition.'

But Megan who had sped upstairs to get ready, certainly didn't feel in need for anyone's sympathy and her eyes lit up when several minutes later she saw Rupert's red MG sports car. As he opened the top she tried to settle herself elegantly into the low-slung leather passenger seat, then thankful she'd brought a headscarf hurriedly tied it under her chin as he switched on the ignition and roared away. The journey was short but exhilarating, the wind whipping her cheeks as Rupert drove at what seemed to her an alarming speed along the narrow roads. She glanced aside at him, admiring his long fingers on the steering wheel. In a white polo neck and brown leather jacket, his skin lightly tanned and his hair tousled he was she realised, the perfect image of a hero portrayed on the jacket of a romantic novel. Then within minutes he was parking the car, and then he took her hand as they made their way to the wide open spaces of Beachy Head. With the ease of youth they covered the ground, Megan – used to walking to work – having no difficulty in keeping up with Rupert's long strides. To her it was wonderful just to be in the fresh air, with extensive views of the English Channel and green expanses of grass; the feeling of space and freedom feeding her spirit which was so confined for much of the year. The lowering sky became a challenge to them both, something to be defied, and they carried on walking well away from the cliff edge. 'Damn this weather,' he called against the increasing wind. 'The forecast is pretty poor as well.'

But Megan wasn't worrying about the future because Rupert suddenly reached out for her waist, drew her towards him and kissed her full on the mouth. Startled, she kissed him back, the taste of his cool lips lingering as he drew away laughing. 'Ready, steady ... go!' he shouted. Gripping her hand he began to run and exhilarated Megan raced along with him along with him until he drew to a halt, and they both had to stop for breath. She was the first to feel the first heavy drops of rain. Looking up she saw the darkening clouds. 'Here it comes!'

'Best foot forward,' Rupert said swiftly and turning they began to race back.

'I'm *"Singing in the rain"*,' Megan's voice was lost in the wind but she persisted, while Rupert laughed at her. 'You're crazy!' But she didn't care. This wasn't like hurrying in rain to work, this was an adventure. She was like Thomas Hardy's Tess battling against the elements, but it was tough going and eventually her breath was raw in her chest and her legs began to lose their strength. When she stumbled, Rupert put his arm around her shoulders which slowed them down and by the time they reached the car they were both absolutely drenched. 'It's a good job you put the hood up,' Megan gasped as she sat in the passenger seat and removed her sodden head-scarf.

'I'd have been an idiot not to,' Rupert said, running a hand through his wet hair. He leaned back. 'God, I'm exhausted, how about you?'

'Shattered,' she said, thinking what a fright she must look. She glanced at him and began to laugh, 'I enjoyed it though.'

He leaned over and lightly kissed her, rain from his hair dripping down onto her face. 'You're a good sport, Megan. Come on, let's get back. I think we deserve a brandy after all this.'

Celia was at Reception buying postcards when they arrived. She turned to stare at the two bedraggled figures coming through the revolving door. 'Good heavens,' she said. 'You'd better go and have a hot bath, Megan.'

'I thought a brandy might be in order,' Rupert said. They were both holding their wet macs and he looked down at them with dismay. 'What are we supposed to do with these?'

'Allow me, sir.' One of the porters came forward and held out his hand for the offending garments. 'I'll take them for you. You can collect them once they're dry.'

'Thanks,' Rupert put a hand in his pocket, and passed over a coin. 'Now then, about this brandy...'

Megan moved away. 'Not for me, if you don't mind. I'll take Celia's advice and go and have a bath. I think there's just about time before lunch.'

Celia turned to Rupert. 'I'm happy to join you,' she offered. 'I'm always ready for a gin and tonic. And I hate drinking on my own.'

'Fine – I'll just pop up and get into some dry clothes.'

Celia ordered a Remy Martin for Rupert, and taking a sip of her own drink waited for him at a small table in the cocktail bar. The young man intrigued her; so far she hadn't seen the slightest hint of a serious side to his nature. While Megan ... but then there seemed to have been hardly any gaiety in her life, and perhaps Rupert was just the tonic she needed. But she hoped that the girl wasn't going to take either him or any romantic overtures seriously, because in her opinion…

'Here I am, fit for company,' Rupert said. He sat opposite, his skin fresh from the rain, his hair still damp. Celia was appalled to feel a frisson of attraction. She might be lonely at times, might miss the warmth and passion of her marriage bed – Giles had been a lusty lover – but for God's sake, she hoped she wasn't becoming one of those pathetic older women who lusted after young flesh.

'Disappointing, isn't it,' Rupert commented, 'the weather I mean.'

'According to the Head Porter, it's going to be the same all week. But you're only on a fleeting visit aren't you?'

He nodded. 'Yes. Father does like one of us to be around during August. Although to be honest my presence is completely superfluous. I just ride around the farms and try to cheer everyone up.'

'Is that what you do?' she said casually, 'help your father with the estate?'

Rupert took an appreciate sip of his brandy. 'Yes, I suppose so. Not hands-on I'm afraid, but I'm a wizard with the accounts, that sort of thing.' He smiled at her, 'Your Megan is quite a girl. You should have seen her up there; she wasn't a bit fazed by inclement conditions.'

Celia laughed. 'No, she might have been wet, but she looked glowing when she came in.'

'Pity I'm not here longer,' Rupert said, 'But now that the weather's really set in, I'd better get back.'

'Would you care to join us for lunch?'

'Thanks for the offer, but I've fixed up to meet

an old friend from Oxford. He's only a few miles along the coast.'

And then their conversation turned to literature and they were discussing the latest Hemingway when Megan now warm and recovered from her soaking came over. 'I'm ravenous,' she announced. 'It must be all that exercise.'

'We'd better go in then.' Celia smiled at her. 'I invited Rupert to join us but he's off to meet a friend.'

Megan felt a pang of disappointment. 'Maybe we'll see you later?'

'Possibly, although I think we're dining out tonight.' His smile was charming and easy, as they watched him go Celia murmured, 'It looks as though he'll be leaving earlier than planned, at least that's what he told me.'

Chapter Thirty-four

Rupert left the following morning. His farewell kiss was careless and it seemed to Megan, final. 'I shall think of you every time I get caught in a downpour,' he grinned. She tried to hide her stab of hurt, knowing it was unrealistic. But she had no illusions; within a few weeks' time he wouldn't even recall her name. Their time together may have been short, but she'd loved every exhilarating minute. And it could never have been more than a fleeting holiday romance; how could a privileged young man like Rupert understand her very different way of life? But she knew that she would always remember him.

The rest of the Penrose family stayed on until Saturday morning. 'I'm glad we booked for only one week,' Angela said as she came to say good-bye.

Megan was sitting on the sheltered veranda, determined not to let the damp atmosphere deprive her of sea air. 'Apparently the weather's the same over most of the country,' she said. 'Anyway, have a safe journey and thanks for the tennis lesson.'

'It was a pleasure. It's been lovely to meet you.' Angela bent and kissed Megan's cheek and seconds later she was gone.

The rest of the day passed quietly. Celia and Megan had lunch together then afterwards Megan continued to read *A Passage to India*. When she closed the book, neither she nor Celia spoke for several moments each immersed in their own impressions and moved by the powerful story. Then after a few moments Megan said, 'I almost don't want it to end. It's been a symbol somehow of how much my life has changed. I'll always remember how nervous I was that first time, terrified that you wouldn't like the way I read, or that my voice would irritate you. I needed – and wanted – the job so much.'

'Were things so very desperate?'

Megan nodded, remembering her strained finances, her terror of not being able to get out of debt. 'You saved my bacon – almost literally.'

'Well, I'm glad I'm some use in this world.' Celia stifled a yawn. 'Oh dear, I think I'm in need of a rest.'

'I'm going to wrap up and go for a walk.'

As Megan paused to open the door, Celia said, 'Have you remembered that we have guests for lunch tomorrow?'

As if I could ever forget, Megan thought! A few minutes later, waterproofed and wearing a head-scarf, she walked past the convent opposite and made her way down the hill. The rain lessened as she walked along the broad promenade below the Wish Tower. Celia had explained to her that it was a Martello tower, built for defence and that during the War it had been armed with gun placements and constantly manned. There were still a few reminders of the bomb damage that Eastbourne had suffered and Megan found it difficult to imagine the peaceful resort being under threat, but of course during those terrible years so had the rest of the country. And as far as she was concerned tomorrow was a threat, be-cause she was going to have to face the venomous Verity. Even now she could hear that clear supercilious voice with its cutting words. Megan could just imagine the scene at lunchtime. Celia would be restrained and try to smooth any social unease, James polite and mildly interested while Verity would be ... Megan searched for the right word – poisonous! She probably thinks that I'll talk with my mouth full and put bread in my soup, Megan thought bitterly. So why don't I give her what she wants? Not bad table manners of course, but if she's expecting me to be a cross between Lizzie (bless her) and Gracie Fields in *'Love on the Dole'*, why don't I play up to her?

Glancing over her shoulder to check that there was nobody else around – only a few hardy souls had faced the bad weather – Megan paused and leaned over the rail gazing out at the grey sea. She thought back to the decorating shop, at the way that everyone laughed and occasionally winced at the blunt earthiness of Lizzie's humour. Megan may not have been allowed to use the 'broad Pottery' dialect at home, but she'd heard enough spoken in the playground and on the potbank to be able to use it. Should she? Would she dare to? With a delicious anticipation of Verity's shocked expression before her Megan, recalling some of Lizzie's more choice phrases began to smile and then laugh. And by the time she arrived back at the hotel, she was word perfect.

At breakfast the following morning, Megan told Celia that she intended to change when she got back from church. 'I'm bound to get creased up with this damp weather,' she explained.

'Why not wear the pale blue cotton?' It was a deceptively simple dress that Daphne had bought from a local dressmaker in Surrey. For Megan to wear a label that Verity was familiar with would only invite a sarcastic comment.

Megan went again to Our Lady of Ransom knowing that there was an earlier mass which would enable her to be back in time for Celia's visitors. This time she remained in her pew as the rest of the congregation filed out, and then she made her way rather self-consciously to one of the side altars and paused before the stand of candles.

There was a small box with a slot in the top and she opened her bag, took sixpence from her purse and hesitated. Would that be enough? She glanced over her shoulder, but there was only one other person in the church, an elderly woman whose eyes were closed, fingers threaded with rosary beads as her lips moved silently in prayer. Megan inserted the coin in the box, picked up a slim white candle and as she had seen others, touched the wick to one of the already lit ones before pushing it firmly into a vacant holder. Then she stepped back, looked at the statue of Mary with its serene face and after a moment's pause, Megan bowed her head and whispered her concerns for Jean and for Jean's family. Later as beneath her umbrella she walked back to the hotel, she knew that Les would have accused her of praying to an idol, a false image, but as one of the girls in the decorating shop who was a Catholic had explained, they didn't pray *to* a statue, it was simply an icon to help them to focus. 'We pray to Mary to intercede for us,' Teresa had said. 'After all, everyone listens to their mother!'

Celia was fortifying herself with a gin and tonic in the bar when Megan joined her. 'I got you an orange juice. That dress was the perfect choice, you look lovely.' She glanced at her watch. 'They should be here soon, James is always early.'

'I suppose stockbrokers have to be organised,' Megan said. She was familiar with the Financial Times as its large pink sheets often lined her bench. Old broadsheet newspapers were considered very useful. And although it was cluttered with ware either waiting for her to decorate, or patterns she'd completed, sometimes she'd try to make sense of the columns of figures, usually without success. 'He must be very clever.'

'He is, at least in some ways. Anyway, here they are.'

Megan stood up as the couple approached. Looking at ease in a blazer and flannels, James smiled at Megan and leaned forward to kiss his mother. 'What on earth have you done to the weather?'

'I know. And the forecast is mixed for next week.'

'Hello, Celia.' Verity pecked at her cheek. 'Well, what can you expect if you holiday in England? You'd have been better going to the South of France.'

'May I introduce you to both to Megan?'

Verity's gaze raked over her. She gave a slight nod. 'Hello.' James held out his hand. 'It's good to meet you, Megan.'

She took his firm grasp and smiled. 'And you too.'

'Right, I see you're both fine for drinks.' He turned to Verity, 'What would you like, darling?'

'I'll have a gin and tonic – as usual!' There was a note of exasperation in her voice, and as he went off to the bar she said, 'I don't know why he bothers to ask.'

'He was always a stickler for good manners,' Celia murmured. 'Blame his father.'

Verity studied Megan's blue dress with a slight frown then said, 'And how do you like Eastbourne?'

'I do, very much.'

There was a short silence then Celia said, 'How was the journey?'

Verity, now seated, crossed her slim legs. 'It was fine. Whatever have you done with yourself all week?'

'Oh, I've managed to occupy myself. And Megan and I are enjoying *A Passage to India*. As you can imagine, it brings back lots of memories. What has it been like where you are?'

'Pretty much the same, I'm afraid.' Verity glanced up as James came back with their drinks and a small bowl of peanuts. Megan, watching, thought that her gaze held annoyance and wondered whether the couple had been arguing.

James settled himself in his chair and turned to his mother. 'Have you heard from Janet?'

'Yes, I've had a letter. The wedding wasn't until yesterday, but before then she was having a great time, catching up with relatives and old friends.'

'Such a pity she couldn't come,' Verity murmured.

'Yes. I was lucky that Megan could join me.'

'I was the lucky one,' Megan said.

'Indeed.' It was a simple word but Verity managed to imbue it with a wealth of meaning.

Megan tightened her lips. With regret she'd realised that however much she might long to parody Verity's snobbish expectation of a 'factory girl', what would she actually achieve? Megan doubted that Verity would even know it was an act. And it would be a humiliating 'slap in the face' for Celia. Both Verity and James would be swift to question her judgment; she would be the one to suffer any repercussions. But Megan now had a different plan. She intended to beat Verity at her own game. And so, noting the exquisite poise of the other girl, she straightened her own spine and shoulders, lifted her chin, and in an almost perfect imitation of Verity's condescending tone said, 'Did you always live in the southern counties, Verity?'

She looked startled. 'Yes. I was born in Maidenhead.'

'James and Verity met at a ball at Sandhurst,' Celia said, 'Verity's cousin is an officer there.'

'Have you ever been to a ball, Megan?' Verity's pale blue eyes held a glint of malice.

Megan spoke decisively. 'Not an actual ball. But we do have the Duke of Sutherland's estate in Trentham which is near to where I live. The ballroom is a great favourite of mine.'

Verity stared at her. 'The Duke of Sutherland's estate...'

'Yes,' Megan said, 'Most of the famous big bands come to play there. And the gardens are beautiful. Many people only view the Potteries as an industrial area, as indeed it is. But the city is actually set amongst beautiful scenery.'

Celia was gazing at her in growing admiration. She could hardly believe that this was the nervous, gauche young woman she'd met only a couple of months ago. She tried to turn the conversation in another direction. 'How are your parents?' she said. 'Well, I hope? And James tells me that your father has taken Silk?'

Verity launched into an account of her father's ambition to become a judge. After a while

301

Megan, who hadn't known what 'taking Silk' meant, realised with a shock that Verity's father was now a QC. Suddenly Megan's carefully bolstered self-confidence began to waver. How could she sit here and think she was the equal of the daughter of an important man like that? It was ludicrous! Her mother would have said that she was 'getting above herself', and perhaps she was right. But the memory of Verity's insults the previous week soon spurred Megan to regain her resolve. There would be barbs to come, she had no doubt of it, and her plan was her only defence.

A few minutes later, they were all seated in the restaurant. Megan sat opposite Celia, with James on her right and Verity on her left. 'Celia tells me that you work as a paintress in a factory,' she said. 'Tell me, is that terribly hard work?'

I wonder if she learned that patronising tone in a previous life, Megan wondered. Perhaps she used to make charitable visits to the workhouse. She paused for moment. 'Creating beauty is never easy, but if you're blessed with a talent, then I think you should use it.'

'Have you always been artistic?' James said.

She smiled at him, remembering how as a child she'd sat at Clarice's table painting paper doilies. 'Yes, I suppose I have.'

'And what exactly are these things of beauty that you create?' Verity drawled.

'I'm sure you possess some fine china?' Megan raised her eyebrows in exactly the same patronising way, 'Perhaps a floral tea set or a pretty vase? Well I paint the lovely, quite delicate patterns.'

'You must have a gift,' James said, as the waiter

placed a bowl of cream of asparagus soup before him. Megan, who had also ordered soup, waited until they had all been served, then conscious of Verity's gaze upon her, broke her roll, glanced up and slowly and deliberately used her soup spoon correctly. She was full of adrenalin, knowing that she had won the first round. But later, when succulent slices of roast beef and a small and fluffy Yorkshire pudding were placed before her, her pleasure must have been apparent because Verity gave a malicious smile. 'I see you enjoy the food here.' She picked daintily at her own. 'I would imagine that cuisine of this standard must be quite a treat for you.'

'I do enjoy the meals here at the Hydro,' Megan said, 'but you know Verity – we in the Midlands don't live totally on fish and chips and tripe.'

'I certainly don't,' Celia tried to ease the tension. 'Not with Janet's cooking.'

After a few minutes, noticing that the waiter had removed Megan's wine glass, Verity attacked from a different angle. 'Don't you like wine Megan or,' a tiny smile played around her lips, 'is it that you're not used to it?'

Megan gazed steadily at her. 'I never touch alcohol.'

'Is that for religious reasons or...?'

'Religious, I suppose. I was brought up that way.'

'And you've never fallen by the wayside?'

Megan put a small amount of horseradish on the beef she'd just cut, and wished Verity would stop firing questions at her so that she could enjoy it. 'Not yet.'

'So did you go to church this morning?'

'But of course,' Celia said. 'Megan puts us all to shame.'

'Not you, mother,' James grinned at her. 'We all know your views.'

'I had enough of piety at boarding school.' Celia took a sip of her wine and glanced with irritation at Verity as she continued to probe.

'And which church did you go to, Megan?'

What is this Megan thought, the Spanish Inquisition? 'Actually I went to the Roman Catholic church,' she began.

With triumph Verity turned to Celia. 'Now that's one piece of information you *didn't* tell us!'

'I hardly thought it was relevant Verity dear,' Celia said trying to keep her voice calm. 'You make it sound as if Megan has leprosy or something. Besides she's actually a chapelgoer. As she would have told you, if she hadn't been interrupted.'

'Then why...?'

'I was just interested,' Megan explained. She turned to James, 'It was so different from what I'm used to. I found it,' she hesitated and then decided to be truthful, 'a rather spiritual experience.'

James smiled at her. 'Good for you.' He turned to Celia, 'What you didn't tell us was how attractive and intelligent Megan is.' His gaze lingered briefly on Megan's lips and throat. 'I'm not surprised that you invited her to replace Janet.'

Celia's eyes narrowed, remembering his distraction the previous Sunday as he'd watched the two girls on the tennis court. James might be her son but she could recognise when a man was ripe for an affair. Celia studied Verity who with tightened lips and narrowed eyes was pressing her napkin to her mouth. Were things not as they should be in the bedroom department? Certainly there was no sign of a pregnancy yet even though they had been married for three years.

But Celia now had the measure of the lunch and drew on her incomparable social skills. The remainder of the meal passed if not in complete harmony, at least in an imitation of it. It was later, when they had taken coffee in the lounge, and Megan thought she was safe that she made her second mistake. She needed to go the Powder Room and unfortunately her timing coincided with the very moment that James made the decision to leave. Megan came out of her cubicle to find Verity waiting for her, her eyes gleaming with triumph. There was nobody else present. Megan silently moved past her to the vanity unit.

'You may have fooled my mother-on-law, but you don't fool me for a minute.'

Megan slowly washed and dried her hands, then turned to face her. 'And what is that supposed to mean?'

'"An intelligent girl" indeed – it shows how blind men can be. Although you're cunning, I'll grant you that. What do you think Celia is – your Fairy Godmother?' Verity's voice was like splinters of ice.

'And what,' Megan said quietly, 'makes you think that you have the right to say such things?'

'I'm part of her family, that's why.'

'Not the best part, in my opinion!' Megan had

reached the limit of her patience. Now that there was no Celia present to embarrass, she didn't care who Verity was, she wasn't getting away with any more of her unpleasantness. 'I don't have to explain myself to you, Verity. I may be a "factory girl", as you so patronisingly described me. You may well look surprised – I heard you! But do you know how another "factory girl", one I work with would describe *you?* She'd say you were "a stuck-up smart-arse". And I'd say that you're a snob of the worst kind – ignorant of anything outside your privileged existence!'

Determined to have had the last word, Megan opened the door so violently that she almost collided with a woman entering. Her face was burning with anger. Worried that Celia would guess that there had been a scene, Megan was relieved to find James was alone. 'My mother's gone upstairs,' he explained. 'She has a slight headache.'

Megan tried to keep her voice steady. 'I'll say goodbye too, James. It's been lovely to meet you.'

'And you too, Megan.' He smiled and leaning forward kissed her cheek at the very moment that Verity, her expression furious, walked towards them.

Chapter Thirty-five

That same evening Celia was rather quiet and Megan, who was beginning to feel guilty about her outburst – although heaven knew she'd been provoked – was rapidly becoming anxious. Had Verity complained to James? Had he 'phoned his mother? I've probably ruined everything, Megan thought with misery; Verity was right – she *is* part of Celia's family, and families protect their own. After all that Celia's done for me, I had no right to...

Just then Celia looked across at her. 'Megan I feel so embarrassed. When Verity followed you to the Powder Room I knew that if you came back upset, I'd completely lose patience with her. I'm afraid that for the sake of family harmony, I invented a headache.' She frowned. 'I hate to say such a thing, but my daughter-in-law can be an awful snob.'

Megan hesitated. 'Don't worry Celia, I think she met her match.'

'You were alone in there – the two of you?'

'I'm afraid so.'

'Then whatever passed between you is your business, not mine!' Celia let out a sigh. 'I can't defend her. Megan, I must be the worst mother-in-law in the world.'

Megan laughed. 'Not you, Celia. You should hear some of the tales I have.'

'Oh, please tell me. I could do with some light relief!'

And during the second week Celia listened to more snippets of Megan's background. She smiled at Rita's complaints about Jack's pigeons, warmed to tales of Clarice's kindness, and laughed at the story about the dead mice left on the work bench.

One morning they went down to the bandstand and sat in deckchairs enjoying the spectacle of a military band in dress uniform. There was a sense of camaraderie among the holidaymakers as they made the most of spells of weak sunshine interspersed with sheltering beneath umbrellas and enjoyed the rousing marches and light music. It was, as Celia said, a traditional English scene and one to be cherished. And then Friday came, and their thoughts turned to the journey home, with Celia saying how much she was looking forward to hearing all of Janet's news.

'Would you like me to come on Sunday or...?'

Celia shook her head. 'You'll have lots to see to at home, and you'll be tired after the journey back. We'll leave it to the following weekend if that's all right with you?'

'Yes, of course. I can't believe it's our last day.' Megan looked wistfully around the lounge. 'I shall really miss all this.'

'The most important thing is that you've enjoyed it.'

'Much more than enjoyed, it's been absolute heaven.'

Megan, seated in the back of the taxi as it made

its way from Stoke Station, found herself gazing out of the window as they travelled along the A50 through Fenton and Longton, as though for the first time. After the gentle scenery of Sussex, the familiar landscape had never seemed so industrial, so forbidding. She thought of Beachy Head with its space and wonderful views, of the beauty of the Georgian buildings in Eastbourne, of the wide roads and the sea, and felt that she couldn't bear it that the dream, the fantasy, had ended.

And that feeling intensified a hundred-fold when the taxi turned into her road and she bade farewell to Celia. Megan looked at the small house she had lived in since birth and slowly went up the path to open the door. She stepped inside to be met by stale air and an eerie sense of emptiness. On the doormat forlornly lay a couple of postcards and what looked like an electricity bill. With an inward sigh, Megan put down her case, picked up a bottle of sterilised milk from the doorstep and even before taking it through to the kitchen, went into the sitting-room to open the windows. As soon as she turned round, the walls seemed to close in on her – had it always been so small, so cramped? She told herself that it was only because of the stark contrast to the spacious rooms she'd become used to, but to her dismay she could now recognise how cheap and even ugly the furniture was, and those curtains... As a beam of sunlight revealed the greying patches of flaking plaster on the ceiling, Megan felt ashamed. Months ago she had intended to brighten up this room and she'd still done nothing about it, apart from making those cushion covers. Instead she'd been more interested in buying clothes. But now she knew that she could never be satisfied with things as they were, as they had been, not any more.

Meanwhile Celia was thoughtful as the taxi drew away. It was difficult to reconcile the exquisite silver-backed hairbrush and mirror with a background like Megan's. Did that small drab house hold a secret? She was becoming more and more intrigued.

On Monday morning, Megan hurried beneath the archway and just as the time-clock ticked towards eight o'clock, with relief she inserted her card. She had slept through her alarm, having found it impossible to get off to sleep until the early hours. Then at the bottom of the wooden steps she had to pause to avoid a young mould runner who was balancing a plank laden with clay teapots on his shoulder, ready to be dried and then fired in a kiln.

'Mornin', Megan,' Minnie called as Megan went into the decorating shop.

'You sound chipper this morning!' No-one knew exactly how old Minnie was. But as a spinster who lived alone, her part-time job and the company of the other girls was, as she told them, her life-line. And there was no doubt that she was a skilled worker.

'Aye, I am.' She lowered her voice to a whisper. 'I had a win on the gee-gees on Saturday. Me accumulator came up. I won twenty quid!' Minnie was one of the ones who passed her bets to a man in the slip house; her nickname was 'Oxo'. The practice of collecting bets to be taken to a bookie's runner was common in most of the local firms. Minnie studied the racing papers with a passion, and at the lunch-break could often be seen marking out suitable races and runners. Her lined face split in a wide grin. 'I'm treating meself to a new bed and eiderdown.'

'Good for you!'

And Minnie was so full of her good fortune that later Lizzie snapped, 'Give it a rest, Min. Honestly can't a woman have a bit of peace first thing? All this rabbiting, it's enough to give you a headache.'

'What's up, Lizzie? It's not like you to be so crabby.' Minnie glanced at her in surprise.

'I'm not getting me sleep, that's why. There's some dog across the backs, who barks on and off all night. I reckon the poor thing's tied up outside.'

'It's cruel that,' Enid said, and then as she saw Miss Dawson looking across at them, hurriedly put on her overall.

But the main talk in the decorating shop was not only of the disappointing holiday weather, but of the catastrophic floods at Lynmouth where after torrential rain the river Lyn had burst its banks.

'It says here,' Minnie was reading from the Daily Mirror, 'that they've already had 12 deaths and a lot of people are still missing. There'll be a lot more dead – you mark my words.'

'You just never know in this life, do you?' another woman said.

'I heard on the news that they're without any

gas or electricity,' Lizzie said, 'I mean can you imagine it? And water ruins everything; just think what even a bit of damp smells like.'

'Yes, we should count our blessings,' Minnie said. 'We may breathe in smoke and dust all the time, but at least we're dry.' She looked critically at her piece of cold toast. 'Look at this, all burnt around the edges.'

'It's good for your stomach, charcoal,' Betty told her. 'The vet at the PDSA told mum to give our dog charcoal biscuits.'

'Thanks very much for that advice,' Minnie retorted, 'the next time I bark I'll let you know.'

Lizzie, draining her mug of tea said, 'Come on then, Megan, tell us all about this holiday of yours?'

'It was brilliant.' Megan looked at their expectant faces. 'Honestly, you wouldn't believe how the other half live.'

'Yes, but did yer meet a millionaire?' was Lizzie's question.

Megan almost told them about Rupert and his yellow-checked trousers, knowing they would find the tale hilarious, but then felt ashamed. He didn't deserve to be made fun of. 'That's for me to know and you to find out.'

'That means you didn't,' Lizzie said promptly. 'But go on, what was it like?'

'Absolutely wonderful, and the food...!' Megan had a rapt audience and they all got up with reluctance when the break ended.

As they went back to the bench Lizzie whispered, 'Has she said anything about a new paintress?'

'Miss Dawson? Not a word.'

Lizzie glanced at the empty place next to Megan's chair. 'Well, I hope that misery guts Avis hasn't been taken on permanently. I was praying we'd seen the last of her.'

'If I know Miss Dawson, I think we will have.'

And Megan was right, because the woman who eventually took Jean's place was what Lizzie called, 'a different kettle of fish altogether.'

Hilda was in her fifties, an experienced paintress who used to work at the nearby Blue Bell Pottery, and with her sense of humour and friendly nature settled in immediately, and when only a few days after she'd joined them she promised to knit a fair-isle pullover for one of Jean's boys, her acceptance was assured.

During the following week however, Megan found herself constantly teased.

'He was giving you the glad eye again,' Lizzie called once Neil, the new sales representative had left.

'No more than he was you,' Megan said, and everyone laughed.

'He'd have to be blind as a bat or barmy to fancy me,' Lizzie cackled, 'Even my old man has a job to these days.'

'That must be a relief,' muttered Enid, whose errant husband had begun to pester her again on a nightly basis.

'Seriously though, I bet he'll ask you out,' Betty said. 'Are you going to go?'

The following Friday, Lizzie couldn't resist it. Within minutes of Neil arriving to deliver the liquid gold and to collect the rags, she shouted,

'Where are you taking our Megan then, is it the pictures or dancing?'

He gave a cheeky grin and as he left called along the bench, 'I'll meet you outside the Empire Cinema, Megan. Tomorrow night at seven o-clock!'

'I could murder you, Lizzie!' Megan hissed.

'He's a cocky devil, isn't he?' Minnie commented.

'Well he needn't expect me to come running,' Megan said. 'He's not my type. He probably wouldn't turn up anyway.'

Debra told Megan that Celia's promised visit to the hair salon had been an unqualified success. 'Doesn't she talk nice,' she said as she trimmed Megan's hair. 'Course, I only shampooed her – it was Marlene who set her up.'

Megan tried without success to imagine the elegant Celia beneath a hooded dryer, the rollers in her hair covered with a pink net. 'Was she pleased?'

'She seemed to be, she gave us both a good tip anyway.' Debra went on to prattle about her boyfriend, and the airmail letters she got from Germany. 'I love it when the airmail letter comes with "S.W.A.L.K"', on the envelope.'

'What does that mean?'

Debra stared at her with amazement. 'You know, sealed with a loving kiss. Honestly Megan I sometimes wonder what world you live in!'

'I've never had your advantage,' Megan pointed out, lowering her head so that Debra could trim around her nape. 'No young man has ever written to me from abroad.'

'Not even that American? Mum said he was quite dishy, even if he did wear glasses.'

Megan laughed. 'They suited him actually. But no, Debra, he's never written to me.'

Debra stood back and looked critically at her. 'Maybe you should have shown a bit of cleavage. But I suppose you'd never do that, not with being religious and everything.'

Megan smiled to herself, remembering the blue cocktail dress.

Coming round to the front to check her handiwork, Debra gazed wistfully at Megan's firm and full breasts. 'I wish I was more like you. I'm only a 32A.'

'You've got time to develop yet.'

'I'm not bothered for myself, it's for Gordon. I shan't have my hair like this when he gets back either,' Debra said, tossing her ponytail. 'I may even have a perm.'

'But you've got lovely hair. I think a perm would make you look older.'

'That's the whole idea!'

Later Megan watched her click down the street in high heels and was about the close the door when Rita came out of her own and began to dust her front window sill. 'Honestly,' she said, 'just look at these smuts, I only did this a few days ago.'

'One of the penalties of living around here,' Megan said with a guilty look at her own less than pristine one. 'Debra's just been and she says Clarice is feeling much better. It was just her luck to come back from Rhyl with a bad chest. Talking of which, how's Jack's cough?'

Rita lowered her voice. 'I've persuaded him at long last. He's promised to go to the doctor's one night this week.' She glanced at Megan. 'By the way, our John's coming for his tea on Saturday after the match. Why not pop round?' Rita laughed at Megan's startled expression. 'Don't be daft – we both know he's spoken for. I just thought it would be nice – a bit of young company for him.'

John's expression lit up when Megan came into the room. 'This is a turn up for the books. Auntie Rita didn't tell me *you* were coming.'

'Well, if I save up my coupons and do a fair bit of baking, I like enough mouths to feed,' Rita told them. 'You sit there Megan, while I call Jack.'

'Just like last time,' John grinned.

He looked exactly the same, Megan thought; fresh-faced and open, a thoroughly decent young man. She was a lucky girl, this fiancée of his. 'How are things with you?' she asked.

'Fine thanks. Frances has gone off to visit her cousin in Chester; bridesmaid stuff and all that.'

'Oh, when's the wedding then?'

'Not until Easter, but she likes to get things organized ahead. And you?'

'Fine too.' She leaned towards him. 'I can't stop too long because I'm going to the pictures later. I want to see *"The Quiet Man"*. It's on at the Empire.

'Hey, mind if I come with you? I was wondering what to do later.' He gave a sheepish shrug. 'I'm at a bit of a loose end with Frances away.'

'Of course not, that would be brilliant!'

Rita beamed with approval at their plan, and even Jack admitted that he'd heard it was a good film. It was only when she and John walked along Commerce Street that Megan saw Neil waiting by the steps into the cinema. Her hand went to her mouth. 'I'd forgotten all about *him!* I think he's waiting for me. Not that I ever agreed to meet him.'

'Leave it to me,' John said. 'I know his type.' Tucking her hand into the crook of his elbow, he swept her silently past an astounded Neil.

'Wow,' Megan said, 'I didn't know you could be so masterful!'

The film was wonderful, with both of them laughing at the Irish humour while Megan thrilled to the turbulent romance portrayed by John Wayne and Maureen O'Hara. Afterwards John offered to walk her home. 'Never let it be said that I'm not a gentleman.'

'No-one could ever say that, John.' Megan smiled at him and as they walked along the quiet roads, he told her that he liked working in the pottery industry, and that his father and grandfather had worked at Wedgwood's, one as a thrower and the other as a cooper. 'I've worked hard to get this far,' he said, 'I was determined to get a white collar job, though. I know that round here people say "it's not what you know, but who you know", but I intend to make sales manager one day.'

Megan glanced at him. His face was determined, confident, and she said quietly, 'Then I hope you do.'

They chatted easily the rest of the way, and when Megan invited him for a cup of cocoa, John accepted and then smiled down at her as they approached her gate. 'Do you remember how Auntie Rita tried to throw us together that time?'

'I certainly remember her ploy of sending us to the shop to fetch cigarettes.'

It was then as beneath the lamplight she laughed up at him, that the car drew to a halt a short distance away. But as John followed her up the path, Megan was too busy finding her front door keys to even give it a second glance.

Chapter Thirty-six

Sitting in the quiet car in the narrow road, Nathan cursed himself for being a romantic fool. Slowly he turned off the ignition and stared at the modest house, the now closed front door. Had he expected that Megan's life would remain as it was? That she would be in that dingy room, lonely and waiting for him to arrive like a medieval knight on a white charger? He closed his eyes for a moment, unwilling to admit the depth of disappointment he felt. And yet he had no right to feel even that. After all, it had been his own decision to put Megan out of his mind, to try to regard the whole incident merely as a fleeting attraction. He had fought so hard against his desire to see this English girl again; even now he felt ashamed that he'd prevented his mother

318

from sending her further food parcels.

As he sat motionless in the car watching a grey-haired man walk his dog along to what was obviously its favourite lamp post, Nathan thought of the last time he had seen Alison. When she had confronted him one evening over dinner, it had come as no surprise. She was no fool. His constant excuses about fixing a date for the wedding were beginning to sound hollow even to his own ears.

'Nathan...' She had taken a sip of her white wine, her grey eyes considering him over the rim. 'Don't you think it's time you were truthful with me.'

He gazed at the girl he considered his best friend. 'Alison ... I don't know how to explain...'

'That you've got cold feet about marrying me? Try it...' Her voice was quiet.

'You know how fond I am of you...'

'And I am of you.'

Nathan seized on her words. 'But don't you see Alison, that's just the trouble – we're fond of each other. Okay,' he admitted, 'more than fond. But is it enough?' He appealed to her. 'Don't you ever find yourself wondering whether our relationship is more about family and background, rather than a man and a woman being madly in love?'

'Why Nathan Brittles, I didn't know you were such a romantic!' But there was a flush staining her cheeks, and Nathan knew he'd hit the right button. 'Don't you think that sort of feeling exists only in books and films?'

Nathan shook his head. 'No, I think it's real enough.'

319

'And you don't think we have it.' Alison took another sip of her wine and they waited as the waiter brought their main course. She looked down at the rib-eye steak and salad and slowly picked up her fork. 'Okay, let's say you're right. I still think we have enough between us to make our marriage work.'

'I think that could be true but I also think that you deserve more.'

'Nathan, why do I have this feeling that there's something you're not telling me?'

Meeting her frank gaze, he took a deep breath. 'Well if you really want to know I met this girl in England last year – just for a couple of days, that's all.' He held up a hand. 'Nothing went on between us, I swear.'

'And yet you still think about her?'

Nathan nodded.

Alison slowly put down her fork. 'In that case Nathan, don't you think you'd better get your ass over there and sort yourself out?' She took off her engagement ring. 'I shall put this back in its box until you've made up your mind.'

'Alison I...'

Her eyes held his. 'At least I know what's been going on in your head. It's a relief in a way. We'll tell everyone we just need space, time to reflect on things. That it's a mutual decision, that sort of thing.'

'You've actually broken off your engagement?' Elizabeth said in bewilderment, 'but aren't you in love with Alison? I'm sure she loves you.'

'I'm not,' Nathan's voice was quiet, 'one

hundred percent sure that she does. She's fond of me, she loves the idea of a wedding, and being part of this family but...'

'Spit it out, Nathan.' Ross waved an impatient hand. 'The situation is embarrassing for both families.'

Into the silence Elizabeth said, 'Has this got anything to do with that English girl you met, the one we sent the food parcel to?'

'Megan.' It was a relief to Nathan to be able to say her name aloud. He gazed at his mother and spread out his hands. 'I can't seem to get her out of my mind. She was such a brave kid and...'

Ross Brittles spoke slowly. 'Are you trying to tell us that even though you proposed to Alison, you have some sort of feelings for this girl?'

Nathan shrugged helplessly. 'No ... yes, hell I don't know. I suppose I must have. We had such a brief time together but...'

Ross and Elizabeth exchanged glances. Ross drummed his fingers on his large desk. 'Apart from the fact that in my opinion you were a fool, I think you'd better go on the Europe trip instead of me and finally make up your mind. It's a bit short notice, but the arrangements can be changed.' He frowned. 'And if and when you do see this Megan again, I want you to promise us one thing. That you'll be careful how much you tell her. Remember Nathan that just as all rich folk aren't grasping and selfish, not all poor people are non-materialistic.'

Nathan was already feeling the adrenalin rush through his veins. 'I'm a pretty good judge of character, Dad.'

Elizabeth expressed her own concern. 'You tell me this girl has no education. What if you brought her over here? Remember I was working as a waitress when I first met your father, and the social scene wasn't easy for me, particularly in the beginning.'

'You managed, and you've been happy.'

'I've been very lucky. Your father is a marvellous man.'

Nathan grinned. 'So is his son.' And then his expression became serious. 'Don't worry – I'll probably come home with my heart intact.'

'And be able to give it to Alison? That's what we're all hoping.'

But now as he sat in the quiet car, Nathan could only think that it was damn good luck that he'd this crazy idea to take an early detour along Megan's road. What if he'd carried out his plan to surprise her the following morning, to try and recreate their last meeting by taking her to the Bethesda chapel and for Sunday lunch at the George Hotel? For all he knew she could even be married to that guy; after all, it was late and they had gone together into the house. And even if she wasn't married but involved with someone, was it fair of him to turn up on her doorstep? She had obviously built a life for herself – did he have any right to complicate it, to cause her possible heart-break? He'd been selfish once before, he had no intention of being so again.

I was probably fooling myself anyway Nathan thought grimly as he began to draw away, picking up speed as he drove along the almost deserted roads. I'll check in to the hotel just for tonight and then move on. After all, even if Megan and I had met again, how do I know that the magic would still have been there? He pushed away the glimpse of her beneath the street lamp – she had looked so lovely ... at least now he could relegate her to the past which would sure be a relief to everyone back home.

Chapter Thirty-seven

At break, Megan told her workmates what had happened on Saturday night outside the Empire.

'You mean he was stood there waiting for you, and you turned up with another fella!' Lizzie hooted with laughter.

Megan swiftly explained, 'John's only a friend. I felt a bit awful about it, actually.' Then she began to laugh, 'You should have seen Neil's face!'

'It serves him right!' Minnie said tartly.

When lunchtime approached on Friday morning, Megan pleaded with the girls not to say anything, and breathed a sigh of relief when Neil came into a quiet decorating shop with everyone's head bent silently to their work. Out of the corner of her eye Megan saw him glance once along the bench towards her then he shrugged, collected the gold rags and left. 'I reckon you did him a good turn,' Flo said afterwards. 'He needed bringing down a peg.'

Earlier that week Celia, impatient to delve into the mystery of the silver hand mirror, was feeling somewhat frustrated.

'You could always just go and see Barbara Eardley,' Janet pointed out.

'No. I want to be more subtle than that. I think she's likely to reveal more about Megan's father in a casual conversation after the committee meeting. It's only a couple of days now.'

'You're keen on this particular charity, aren't you, the children's one?'

'Yes, we achieve a lot. And after all I have the time to spare and I have been very lucky in my own life.'

Janet checked her knitting pattern and began a new row. 'Aye, a little luck goes a long way, you've only got to see what a difference it's made to Megan.'

Celia waited until the grandfather clock in the hall had finished striking. 'You and I, although we've become such good friends, we've never mentioned the possibility of marrying again. Do you ever think about it?'

'There'll no be a man anywhere fit to take my Robbie's place,' Janet told her. 'Is this to do with what you told me last night, about that young Rupert?'

'I should never have had that third glass of wine and told you! It made me think, that's all. To feel like that, even though it was only for an instant...'

Janet put down her needles. 'If we're being honest, I have to confess that sort of feeling never meant much to me. I could never under-stand why people get themselves in such blather

324

about it all.'

Celia struggled to suppress a smile. 'Well,' she said, 'it's unlikely that I'll meet another Giles, so we'll probably still be sitting here like this in another twenty years.'

'Suits me,' Janet said, while Celia began to leaf again through her glossy magazine. But her thoughts were elsewhere. When she'd phoned James the previous evening about some share investments, she'd sensed tension in his voice. Although she might dislike his wife, she had no desire to see her son's marriage break down, bringing with it the inevitable shame and unpleasantness of a divorce. And Verity wasn't the type to go quietly, or without enormous expense. Celia sighed. Once a mother, always a mother, she thought, and suddenly thought of the tiny form and blue eyes of the baby daughter she had lost.

The Committee meeting was one of co-operation and good humour and Celia was smiling as she came out of the double doors. 'Oh good, tea and biscuits,' she said to Barbara, who was already lifting the teapot. 'They do look after us very well here.'

Barbara smiled at her. 'I'm so glad to see you,' she said, 'I did catch sight of Megan on Sunday, but didn't have a chance to talk. How did the holiday go?'

'It was excellent. Megan has grown so much in confidence.' Celia led the way to a table. 'She absorbs knowledge and new experiences like a sponge.'

'I'm so pleased. I used to feel sorry for her with that father of hers...' Barbara's voice tailed off.

'Now he's a man I would like to hear more about,' Celia said. 'Megan does mention odd things now and then. He sounds rather a repressive sort.'

'He was certainly that.'

'I just feel that it would help me to understand her better, if I had some idea of her childhood, her background.'

'Les and Ellen Cresswell were staunch members of our congregation,' Barbara said, 'but in any religious gathering or denomination, there are always those who take teachings and concepts to the extreme. Les regarded any form of pleasure, such as dancing, theatres or the cinema as instruments of the devil. It was almost as if he was afraid of temptation.'

'So they weren't part of your teaching, in the chapel you go to?'

Barbara shook her head. 'I admit that some of the older ones may have held similar views. We do tend to live our lives quietly, we don't drink for instance, but otherwise we're a happy congregation. I have,' she added quietly, 'gained much comfort and support there, especially since my husband died. Please don't misunderstand me, they were loving parents, and I'm sure they thought they were doing the right thing. But there's no doubt that Megan was brainwashed from birth. I don't think she was even allowed to make friends, apart from a girl called Audrey who she met at chapel.'

'I find it surprising that Megan knows nothing

of his family,' Celia said, 'or even of his life before his marriage.'

'That sounds like Les. He was always secretive.'

Saturday was a good drying day, so Megan hand-washed Daphne's clothes in Lux soapflakes, and hung the blue cocktail dress outside her wardrobe for dry-cleaning. She was going to miss wearing such lovely things. The hotel now seemed almost a fantasy in this sparsely furnished bedroom. There was no pretty eiderdown, no tasselled curtains or warm carpet beneath her bare feet, no cosy bedside lamp, just curtains so thin that the light came through and only that drab brown candlewick bedspread. Mum must, she thought, have had the word 'serviceable' engraved on her heart.

On Sunday afternoon when Megan arrived carrying the suitcase, Janet stared at her in astonishment. 'What's all this? Don't tell me you're running away from home?'

Megan laughed. 'No, I've brought Daphne's clothes back, all except one that is.'

'Oh, I see.' Janet stood aside to let Megan pass. 'She's in the drawing room.' She leaned forward and whispered, 'James and Verity are here.'

Appalled, Megan twisted round to face her. How could she walk into that beautiful room knowing that the last thing she'd called Celia's daughter-in-law was a 'a smart arse?' 'We'd better hide the suitcase then.'

Janet picked it up. 'Leave that to me.'

Anxious to escape, Megan was already moving towards the stairs. 'I'll go and start the ironing.'

'You can't just disappear,' Janet reproved, 'they will have heard the doorbell!' She went to open the door leaving Megan no choice but to go in.

As she entered the room, James immediately stood up and came towards her holding out his hand, his eyes warmly welcoming. 'Megan, it's good to see you again.'

She smiled up at him. 'And you, James.'

Verity merely gave a slight nod.

'I won't disturb you, Celia,' Megan said, 'I'll go and do the ironing, and see you later.'

'Thank you,' Celia added, 'By the way, I have a new book for us.'

'What sort of book do you like to read, Megan?' The edge to Verity's voice was like a razor blade.

'An intelligent one,' Megan told her, and saw Celia's lips twitch.

Upstairs, as she waited for the iron to heat, Megan wondered why James and Verity had made the long journey to so soon after seeing Celia in Eastbourne.

Downstairs Celia was also wondering about the visit and eventually asked the question hovering on her lips. 'It's lovely to see you both but is there a particular reason...?'

Verity glanced at James and then said, 'Yes there is, Celia. James was going to ring you about it, but I wanted to make my suggestion face-to-face, so to speak. It's just that he's been invited to go over to New York to spend two months on Wall Street...'

Celia interrupted, 'Really? That's wonderful James, such an excellent opportunity for you.'

'Thanks, I'm looking forward to it.'

Celia turned to her daughter-in-law. 'So sorry Verity ... you were saying...?'

Verity smiled sweetly at her. 'To be honest, I'm not at all keen on rattling around in that big house on my own, certainly not for that length of time. I'm sure you can understand how I feel?'

'You're not going with him?'

'According to James,' Verity glanced across at him and her lips tightened. 'That's not an option.'

'Oh, I see.'

'So I thought,' Verity went on, 'that it would be rather a good idea for me to spend one month with my parents and one month here with you.' She paused and gave a tinkling laugh. 'That's if you'll have me of course.'

Horrified, Celia with a supreme effort managed, 'Verity, you know you're always welcome.'

'So that wouldn't cause you a problem?'

Celia glanced wildly at James, but he was staring ahead, his expression carefully blank. This is all part of a plan, Celia suddenly thought. He wants to get away, I was right – this marriage *is* in trouble. She glanced sharply at Verity, but could only see in her face a hard determination. Or was this anything to do with Megan? Was Verity still seething from the scene – and Celia had no doubt that there had been a scene – in the Powder Room? Was she hoping that her presence here would give her a chance for revenge? Celia tried to calm her nerves, to regain her equilibrium. Perhaps she was being too harsh. Verity could simply be telling the truth, maybe she really didn't want to spend the next two months alone.

Celia forced herself to sound enthusiastic. 'No, of course not, I was just wondering whether you might not become bored.'

'I'm sure I'll find enough to occupy myself. For instance, I could read to you as Megan does. At least then you wouldn't have to pay someone.'

Celia drew a deep breath and tried to control her swift anger. 'That's a very kind suggestion, Verity, and of course during the week I shall welcome it. But I can hardly cancel my arrangement with Megan on Sundays, after all she does have to work for a living and support herself.'

'Oh,' Verity waved a dismissive hand. 'She can always come and do a few jobs for Janet instead, in the kitchen or something. You and I can begin the new book together when I come.'

The girl's arrogance left Celia almost speechless. 'That's hardly practical, I mean...' She turned to James. 'When are you actually planning to go?'

'They want me there by the end of next week.'

Dismayed, Celia looked at Verity. 'But surely you'll wish to visit your parents first?'

She shook her head. 'They're away in Madeira. So I thought I'd drive up next Sunday, and we can begin the new book then. Of course, if you prefer, I could begin reading it to you today before we leave.' She turned to James, 'You wouldn't mind, would you darling?'

'I don't think that will be necessary.' Celia was beginning to feel helpless, manipulated. And James was no help at all; instead he seemed to finding his fingernails a subject of fascination. She drew a deep breath, 'Do you have any preference as to which room you would like?'

'Oh, the one James and I usually have will be fine.' Verity yawned. 'Gosh, I'm feeling rather tired. Maybe we shouldn't be too late making a start back. We can't stay as James has to be in the office early tomorrow.'

'It really is a lightning visit.'

'I'm afraid so. I'll just go and powder my nose.'

When she heard the footsteps on the stairs, Megan thought they were Janet's but her smile faded when Verity opened the door to the ironing room. She walked in and without a word went over to examine the neatly pressed items hanging on the clothes horse. 'Not bad,' she said, 'I think I'll be able to trust you with my things.'

'Sorry?'

Verity swung round and raised her perfectly arched eyebrows. 'I'm coming to stay here for a month, beginning next weekend. So you won't be required to read to Celia, instead you'll be helping Janet in the kitchen. However, I do like to change my clothes frequently so I'm sure you won't find yourself idle.'

Verity swept out of the room leaving Megan speechless. She picked up the iron and stared at it. She'd never singed anything ... yet!

Chapter Thirty-eight

Janet too was less than enthusiastic about Verity's visit, although she tried not to show it. She and Celia were relaxing in the sitting-room, waiting for Megan to join them after finishing the ironing. 'If the lass won't be reading to you today, I'll have to think of something else she can do.'

'I do feel awkward about this,' Celia said.

'Don't worry. I'll not be asking her to scrub floors.'

Celia laughed. 'I was thinking. You know the clothes Megan borrowed? I'm inclined to ask Daphne if she can keep them.'

Janet's expression was one of horror. 'You can't do that!'

'Why ever not, she's got far more clothes than she needs. I can easily ring and ask her.'

Janet gazed at her. 'Think of it rationally,' she advised. 'Megan's worn the clothes and laundered them. Isn't she going to feel that Daphne doesn't want to wear them after she has?'

'Good heavens,' Celia was astonished. 'I never thought of that.'

'Why not offer her one thing? Something she was especially fond of.'

And later as she walked home, Megan's annoyance, her anger about what she saw as Verity's interference, was tempered by delight. The blue cocktail dress no longer needed to be dry-cleaned, it was hers to keep. 'I've just spoken to Daphne on the phone and it was her suggestion,' Celia said. 'She'd be delighted for you to have it.'

And although Megan had missed their reading session, she'd quite enjoyed 'doing out' the larder; she'd not only discovered new spices but Janet had given her a few tips on how to use them.

One of Celia's irritations – and there were several, about Verity's lengthy visit, was that her presence would interfere with the enquiries about the mirror.

'You could begin today,' Janet pointed out over breakfast. She poured them both more coffee from the silver pot. 'Do what you can over the phone while you can't be overheard.'

'That's true.'

And so Celia spent the following hour telephoning local auctioneers, and eventually to her profound relief discovered that during the week in question, there had been only one major house auction in Staffordshire.

In triumph she went to find Janet. 'What a stroke of luck. If there had been several, it would have been much more difficult.'

'So what's your next step?'

'Ours, you mean. I thought you might want to take part. You could be my Dr Watson.'

Janet laughed. 'I thought you were Miss Marple!'

'I think Sherlock Holmes is a much more fascinating character. Did you know that he smoked opium?' She laughed as she saw Janet's disapproving expression. 'You needn't look so

333

worried – I'm not going to get into character! I thought we'd take the mirror to the Auctioneer's offices in Hanley and see what we can find out. And why wait? As you say, we need to make the most of our limited time.' Celia paused, 'I tell you what, let's put our hats on and have lunch in Huntbach's afterwards.'

And so later in the morning Celia led the way into the sanctum of the auctioneers, where it proclaimed that they specialised in antiques, collectables, fine art, household and general goods.

'Have you an appointment?'

'No, I'm afraid not. My name is Mrs Bevington – I phoned earlier this morning about the recent auction at Blaisden House, near Biddulph.'

Janet smiled to herself as she saw the young receptionist react to Celia's confident approach and perfect vowels. 'Oh, yes. I remember. I'll see if Mr Marsden can see you.'

Through an open glass door, Celia watched the girl approach a tall, middle aged man behind a desk and as she finished speaking, saw him glance past her into the outer office. He gave a nod, and the girl returned. 'Would you come this way, please?'

Tall and well built with silvering temples, he rose as they approached and Celia held out a slim gloved hand. 'Mr Marsden. Thank you so much for seeing us.'

He gave an easy professional smile. 'Please do take a seat. How can I be of assistance?'

Celia opened her large handbag and took out the tissue-wrapped mirror. 'I recently bought this mirror in Eastbourne,' she explained, 'and I'm very keen to find its provenance. The owner of the antique shop told me that his brother had bought it at a house auction here in Staffordshire and according to the date, it would appear to be Blaisden House. I believe you handled the sale.'

'Indeed we did. May I see the mirror?'

Celia passed it over to him and watched as he silently examined it, running his finger over the engraved initials. 'The initial F would be for Frayne, the surname of the family who owned Blaisden House. I would imagine that this belonged to one of their daughters.' He handed the mirror back to her. 'May I ask your interest in it?'

'A friend of mine has the matching silver-backed hairbrush. Would you know whether the daughters are still alive?'

He shook his head. 'I'm afraid not. The reason the house was sold was because the only remaining relatives, some distant cousins, live abroad; South Africa I believe.'

Robert Marsden smiled across the desk at them both, but his gaze lingered on Celia. Conscious that they were taking up his valuable time, she asked her final question. 'I wonder, do you know of anyone who perhaps used to work at the house, not just recently but many years ago?'

He thought for a moment. 'Could you leave that with me? I'll need to make a few phone calls.'

'That would be wonderful, thank you.' Celia wrote her number on the small white pad he pushed forward.

Janet hid a smile wondering whether the auctioneer would have been quite so helpful if she'd been the one asking the questions.

A few days later, Megan and Rita went round to visit Clarice. It had been some time since the three of them had been together and as it was a fine evening, they sat outside to catch up with each other's news.

'Have you heard anything about Jack?' was Clarice's first question.

Rita shook her head. 'No, we're still waiting for the results of the x-ray.'

'You don't think it could be his pigeons, do you?' Megan said. 'I read somewhere that they can cause chest problems.'

'We wondered about that. But apparently it isn't that they can cause chest problems, just that they can aggravate them. I've told him, if he has got silicosis, those birds will have to go. I'll brook no argument about it.'

'Poor Jack, that would be a shame,' Clarice said.

'For him it might.' Rita stubbed out her cigarette on the ashtray on her lap. 'As for me, perhaps then I'd be able to get a bit more conversation out of him.'

They both glanced at her, and in an effort to change the subject, Megan said, 'And how are things with you Clarice? Is young Sheila looking forward to going to the High School?'

'She certainly is. Avril took her to buy her school uniform last week, you wouldn't believe how much it cost!'

'She deserved to pass the scholarship,' Megan said. 'She always was a bright little girl. I'm glad they're giving her the chance.'

'Isn't it about time you got a new beau,

Megan?' Rita said, turning to her. 'There must be *some* nice fellas out there.'

Clarice shot Megan a sympathetic glance. 'Maybe she just doesn't fancy them, Rita.'

'You mean she expects too much. You don't want to let your head be turned by that fancy hotel, Megan.'

'I think I'm more sensible than to let that happen.'

'It's that American,' Clarice said quietly. 'You've never really got him out of your system, have you? Look love, he's gone, accept it.'

Megan stared out over the small garden, kept neat by Tom, with a miniscule lawn and vegetable patch at the end. Clarice still had a sheet on the clothes line and Megan, watching it billow gently in the breeze was thoughtful. Clarice, dear perceptive Clarice, was probably right. Megan closed her eyes for a moment, remembering that incredible moment when she'd thought that Nathan was about to kiss her. And she could still remember the scent of his aftershave, the brief touch of his skin on her own. She had never felt that yearning since, certainly not with Terry, nor with Rupert. But Nathan was thousands of miles away...

Chapter Thirty-nine

When the phone call came Celia was in the garden. But all thoughts of whether to choose cream or crimson roses for the hall table disappeared when Janet told her that it was the auctioneer on the line.

'Good morning, Mr Marsden.' A moment passed as Celia listened. 'So this Mrs Finney definitely worked at Blaisden House? When she was younger? And you have the address?' She scribbled on a notepad on the hall table. 'I can't thank you enough for being so helpful.'

'I thought he'd soon be back in touch,' Janet said with a slight smile, 'What did he say?'

'That this woman was the cook there. Come on, let's find a map.'

But a few minutes later, after they'd decided that Biddulph didn't look too difficult to find Janet said, 'Much as I'd like to come, I think it should be only you and Megan. It will be quite enough to have two strangers arriving on her doorstep, never mind three.'

'Oh, Janet...'

'Never mind, one has to be sensible, anyway I'm sure I'll hear all about it.' She frowned, 'As for when you should go, how about tomorrow? Remember you'll have Verity here on Sunday.'

Celia frowned. 'Megan works on Saturday mornings. Still I suppose the afternoon would be all right. I'll pop down later and put a note through her door.' She gazed thoughtfully down again at the address – Rose Cottage. Would this Mrs Finney recognise the mirror?

As soon as she joined Celia in the car Megan said, 'I don't smell of turps, do I?'

Celia wrinkled her nose. 'You reek of it.' Then she laughed, 'Of course not, why should you?'

'I wore these clothes for work this morning and didn't have time to change. At least I put something decent on.' As she listened to Celia's description of the visit to auctioneer's office and his later phone call, Megan felt a fluttering of nerves. Who knew what they might learn that afternoon? Freda Podmore hadn't bothered to disguise her suspicions. But then she saw the worst in everyone. Besides, Megan refused to believe that her father with his strict morals could ever do anything even remotely dishonest. There had to be a perfectly simple explanation.

When they approached Biddulph, lying in a valley about five miles away from Burslem, they decided to look at Blaisden House and a few minutes later, parked outside impressive entrance gates they found themselves gazing down a long tree-lined drive leading to a graceful manor house. Half covered in ivy with Georgian pillars before a well-proportioned front door it represented, Celia thought, the best of traditional country architecture. 'Now that,' she said to Megan, 'is a house I would like to live in.'

While I, Megan thought with a wry smile as they drove back into the centre of Biddulph – a small town with coal mining as its main industry – would probably have been one of the scullery maids!

After following Celia's habit of asking someone for directions, 'Maps were never my strong point,' she told Megan, they found Rose Cottage – halfway down a small lane, with a glorious cottage garden while the porch really did have roses growing around it. 'Idyllic,' Celia murmured, and Megan too was enchanted. The cottage was one of a terraced row of four, and after they went through a small green gate and passed between hydrangea bushes, Celia tapped lightly on the front door.

It opened to frame a small plump woman, her white hair neatly braided in two coils on each side of her head. Her expression was one of irritation, and as her hands were dusted with flour, Megan guessed that they had disturbed her baking. 'Yes?'

'Mrs Finney?'

'Yes?'

Celia smiled at her. 'I can see that you're busy, and we're sorry to bother you. We've been told that you used to work at Blaisden House?'

'I did, but it's a long time ago.' Her forehead creased in a frown.

'I wondered – could we possibly talk to you about your time there? We would try not to take up too much of your day. My name is Celia Bevington, and this is Megan Cresswell.'

At the mention of Megan's name, Mrs Finney's expression changed. Visibly startled, her gaze darted to Megan. She hesitated. 'You'd better come in.' They followed her into a small room, its tiny windows set deep into the wall and although dim after the brightness outside it was cosily furnished. Told to make themselves comfortable Megan and Celia sat next to each other on a two-seater tapestry settee leaving the matching armchair vacant for Mrs Finney. 'I'm afraid you'll have to wait a second,' she muttered, 'while I finish off in the kitchen.'

As soon as she came back to join them Celia said, 'What a lovely home you have.'

'Thank you.' She folded her arms over her floral pinafore. 'I've lived here nigh on fifty years.'

Celia smiled at her. 'And are you the gardener?'

'I am now I've lost my husband. I read in a poem once, that you're nearer to God in a garden than anywhere else on earth, and I think there's a lot of truth in that.' But her attention was wandering, her gaze flickering yet again to Megan. 'So, how can I help you?'

Celia related how the auctioneer had given them Mrs Finney's details as someone who might be able to solve a small mystery.

'I remember him,' she said, 'a tall, good-looking chap. I went along to the sale meself, and bought that vase over there.' She turned to look at an exquisite china vase. 'It's Minton, and used to stand in the hall. Mind you, I had to dip into me savings to afford it.'

'It's lovely. Sometimes you can't put a price on beauty,' Celia said. 'Now,' she took the tissue-wrapped hand mirror out of her bag and offered it. 'This is what we've come to see you about. We found it in an antique shop in Eastbourne and were told that it came from the Blaisden House sale.'

Mrs Finney took off the tissue paper and looked down at the mirror. For one long moment she remained silent, her forefinger slowly tracing the initials. 'This was Miss Elvina's.'

'We've only just found out who the initials belonged to,' Megan said. 'I always wondered.' She opened her own handbag and took out the hairbrush. 'Because you see this was always in our house. I couldn't believe it when we found the matching mirror.'

Mrs Finney held out a hand that began to tremble as she stared down at the silver-backed hairbrush. 'After all these years... I did hear right then – your name *is* Cresswell?'

'Yes, Megan Cresswell.'

'And your father was...?'

'Les Cresswell.' Megan caught her breath. 'You mean you knew him?'

'Oh yes,' Mrs Finney said. 'I knew him.' She was still looking at the hairbrush then she raised her head and said, 'Megan, do you mind telling me how old you are?'

'Not at all – I'm twenty, well almost twenty-one really. But how did you know my father?'

'The Cresswells lived in the end cottage, Les was their only child. His parents, God bless their souls, lie in the churchyard not ten minutes walk away.'

Megan stared at her in astonishment. Her father had lived in one of these cottages, her grandparents too? 'I didn't even know he came from Biddulph,' she said, 'He would never talk about his early life.'

'I suppose I can understand that,' Mrs Finney said slowly, 'after what happened an' all. He'd want to turn over a new leaf, start again.' She looked at the hairbrush again and then at the mirror. 'I don't know love, whether it's right to tell you about all this.'

Megan stared at her in dismay. 'Please,' she said. 'I know my father gave it to my mother, but she never used it and I always thought that was strange. All she would say was that she was keeping it for *me*, for my twenty-first birthday, only she... I'm afraid she died last year.'

'I'm sorry to hear that.' Mrs Finney's expression was one of compassion. She hesitated, 'Is your father still alive?'

Megan shook her head. 'We lost him two years ago.'

'That *is* sad news.' She became reflective, 'but then it does make a difference...' She gave them back the mirror and hairbrush and got out of the chair with some difficulty. 'I'll just check on the oven. I'm sorry – I didn't ask if you'd come far?'

'From the Longton area,' Celia said.

'You'll be ready for a cup of tea, then.'

The cottage was so small that it was impossible for Celia and Megan to talk without being overheard so instead they exchanged an anxious glance and waited in silence. Megan spent the time looking around, trying to imagine her grandparents living in a similar cottage, her father as a small boy. Had he perhaps visited this one, been in this actual room? Mrs Finney seemed as though she would be a kindly neighbour ... and

343

then she was bringing in a tray with tea accompanied by two warm scones with a tiny dish of creamy butter and one of strawberry jam.

'All right love,' she said to Megan. 'I've come to a decision. Perhaps you do have the right to know. But before I begin, there's something upstairs that I think you ought to see.' She moved towards the steep staircase. 'It might take me a bit to find – so if you don't mind helping yourselves...'

Megan's rising excitement was tempered with apprehension. Why had Mrs Finney wanted to know how old she was? And why had she waited to find out whether her parents were dead before deciding to confide in them? It could only mean that she had wanted to protect her ... but from what?

Chapter Forty

For Megan the waiting was agonising. After all the years of ignorance, of wondering why her father was so secretive about his early life, could it be that she was now going to discover why? Impatiently she glanced once again up at the ceiling, and then at last she heard Mrs Finney slowly descend the stairs. 'I could have sworn this was in the bottom drawer,' she said, a bit short of breath. 'But never mind I found it eventually.' She put a faded dog-eared brown envelope down on the seat of the armchair and bent to remove the tray.

344

'The scones were delicious, thank you so much,' Celia said with a grateful smile.

Returning from the kitchen Mrs Finney picked up the envelope and settling down said, 'It's a long time since I've looked at these.' She removed three photographs and after glancing down handed one to Megan. 'That's Miss Elvina. I was told once the name meant "friend of the elves", and my word it certainly suited her!'

Megan gazed down at the elfin face. Pretty with dark riotous curls, Elvina was smiling happily at the camera, one hand shading her eyes from the sun. 'What a lovely girl.'

'She was about seventeen there. And this is her older sister, Miss Esme. They may look alike, but in nature they were as different as chalk and cheese.'

Megan looked at the solemn expression, at the way that Esme stood with squared shoulders. 'I see what you mean.' She passed both photos over to Celia.

And then Mrs Finney looked down for one long moment at the remaining photo. 'I don't know where or how this one was taken, but I think there's someone you'll recognise.'

Megan took it from her and then caught her breath at the image of her father laughing down at the upturned face of Elvina, one arm around her waist, the other fingering a lock of her hair. It was definitely him; although he looked younger and more carefree than on his later wedding photograph there was no mistaking the features she knew so well. Megan stared at it in shock. She had never imagined for one minute ... she examined it again, searching her father's expression, seeing the intimacy of the pose, and then almost reluctant to relinquish it, she held the photo out to Celia.

'It was Miss Esme who gave me that photo,' Mrs Finney said, 'I was supposed to pass it on to Les, but by then he'd...' She broke off, 'Sorry, I'm running ahead of myself.'

Celia silently returned the photo to Megan who said, 'How old was he when this was taken?'

'Not much older than you, about twenty-two I think and of course devoted to the chapel. But Miss Elvina saw something in him she wanted and that young madam was determined to have it. She always was a bit wild; they even expelled her from boarding school. Only this time she got more than she bargained for. When Mr and Mrs Frayne found out she was pregnant...'

Megan shocked intake of breath was so audible that Mrs Finney gave her a sympathetic glance. 'Sorry, love, but you did want to know. That's why I was loath to tell you at first.' She went on, 'We weren't supposed to know of course, but one of the maids heard whispers, then the house was terrible for weeks, what with rows and atmospheres. These things always get about. There was no question of them getting married; Miss Elvina must have known that the Fraynes would never have accepted a shop assistant as a son-in-law. It's a source of wonder to me how they got together in the first place.'

Megan was staring at her in horror and disbelief. Her father, the self-righteous man who had brought her up had fathered another child out of wedlock?

But Mrs Finney was continuing, 'They told everyone that she'd gone to study art in Europe, but the letters that came for Miss Esme had a Devon postmark.' She gazed at them both with sad eyes. 'The Lord's ways are hard to understand. Why that poor lass and that baby had to be lost is beyond me.' She gazed sadly at them. 'But that's what happened. When her time came and she went into labour, it turned out to be twins and nobody had guessed. Anyway something must have gone wrong; I don't know all the details. But I do know that Miss Esme was devastated, weeping in her room for days she was. Of course when he found out, Les blamed himself. He said it was God's wrath, his judgment on their wrongdoing. I never saw a lad so disturbed.'

Megan felt stunned. How could her father have borne such suffering? And that happy young girl in the photograph, to die so soon after it was taken. 'You said "that baby",' she said in a whisper. 'Was it just one twin who died?'

'Aye lass, it was.'

'And what happened to the other baby, the one who lived?'

There was a short silence.

'I'm looking at her love.'

Megan felt the blood drain from her face and Mrs Finney said swiftly, 'I'll get you a tot of brandy.' As she went to a cupboard in the dresser, Celia put out a hand to steady Megan. 'My dear, you've had a shock. Take several deep breaths, and do take the brandy, it will help.'

Megan's obeyed, fighting the shakiness that

threatened to overwhelm her. Then she picked up the photo again, her eyes filling with tears as she gazed down at the dark-haired girl who had died giving birth to her. This was her mother, her real mother? Then Ellen...?

But Mrs Finney was handing her a tiny gold-rimmed glass of brandy and as Megan took a small tentative sip, she continued, 'The Fraynes washed their hands of the whole affair. After the funeral, every trace of Miss Elvina was removed, all her clothes, her possessions, everything.' She looked at Megan, 'It was Miss Esme who found out where you'd gone, what arrangements had been made. She had to do it in secret of course. Mind you, a tragedy like that can't be hushed up, although the Fraynes tried hard enough. When Les's boss found out, he sacked him. Soon after that he moved away; I never did know where.'

Glancing with concern at Megan's strained face, Celia said, 'Would you know how Megan's father came to have the hairbrush?'

'Now that I can tell you, because I was the one who put it into his hand. Miss Esme came into the kitchen one day and told me that she'd hidden the mirror away but she wanted me to give the hairbrush to Les as a keepsake.' She shook her head. 'I remember when he took it – he looked as if he had the world on his shoulders.' She paused for a moment, 'You can keep the photo with your father in it love; I'd have sent it to him but I didn't know where he'd gone.'

'He worked in a hardware store in Longton. That's where he met my mother.'

'Oh, I see. I know that he wrote to Miss Esme,

348

just the once. Not that she told me where he was
– saying that he was married and wanted to bring
you up himself.'

'And that's when he found out where I'd been
sent?'

'Not until she'd been to visit the couple who
took you in. But she wasn't very impressed; said
you looked like a little frightened waif.'

'And so...'

'To put it bluntly love, she paid them off. Her
grandmother had left her a legacy and she used
some of that. Then she wrote back to Les, gave
him the address and a note of authority to collect
you.'

Megan tried to imagine the emotional scene, of
her father seeing her for the first time. Would
Ellen have gone with him? 'But what about my
other grandparents, did they reject me as well?'

'They had Les late in life and had gone to their
rest long before all this happened. I suppose you
could say it was a blessing in a way.'

'Esme sounds like a very resourceful young
woman,' Celia said. 'Would it be possible to meet
her?'

Megan's spirits lifted, she owed this unknown
aunt so much, and then she saw the answer in
Mrs Finney's eyes. 'It's too late isn't it? You're
going to tell me that's why she never got in touch.'

'Yes, you're right love. I'm afraid she died
shortly after Les adopted you,' she paused at
Megan's sharp intake of breath. 'Yes, he did it all
legal, she told me so herself. She was never very
strong you see, not since childhood, and she took
it very hard, the way her parents treated Elvina.

One day her heart just gave out.'

Celia was frowning. 'I take it that she never married?'

Mrs Finney shook her head. 'That's why Blaisden House was sold, there was only a distant cousin who lives in South Africa and he didn't want it.' She fell silent and Celia began move, feeling that it was time they left.

'Thank you so much, Mrs Finney. I'm sorry we've taken up so much of your time.'

'That's all right.' She looked across at Megan. 'Don't take it too badly love. The truth's better out than in. Any road, I'm glad things turned out right for you, and Les made a life for himself.'

As they stood by the front door Megan turned and on an impulse bent to kiss Mrs Finney's cheek. 'Thank you, you've been so kind.' Then she added, said, 'Can you tell me exactly where it was that my grandparents lived?'

'Just along there – the end cottage.' Megan stared at it, trying to imagine what it must have been like for Les to grow up in such a small peaceful lane. Mrs Finney also gave them directions to the churchyard and when later they found the modest and neglected gravestone of Ernest and Lily Cresswell, Megan made a vain attempt to brush moss away from the stone's rim. She wondered where her real mother was buried, and what of her twin sister? As she turned away Megan had to brush tears from her eyes as she thought, I don't suppose I'll ever know if she even had a name.

Celia, sensing that Megan needed silence, concentrated on the route home. Beside her, Megan was struggling with her chaotic thoughts, and then opening her bag she gazed again at the image of the laughing young man and the privileged young girl. What crime had they committed except to be in love? Megan had no doubt that the tragedy had eaten away at her father's soul, that his self-blame had made him into the rigid-thinking and repressive man he later became. This discovery explained so much. Why Les had always refused to go on holiday, or indeed to go anywhere. He had been fearful of meeting someone who knew of his past, of what he would have thought of as his 'sin', and instead had built a wall of narrow living around his family. And Ellen, bless her, it was so typical of her view of Christian duty to take on somebody else's child. Megan looked at the road they had so recently driven along and turning to Celia said in bewilderment. 'I can't believe that my whole life has changed in a matter of hours. I feel...'

'Stunned, I should think.' Celia glanced at her. 'Can you remember anything of the other people, the ones who took you as a baby?'

Megan shook her head. 'I was only two when we moved to Longton; we were in lodgings in Fenton before that. At least that's what I was always told.'

'So as far as anyone else was concerned...'

'Exactly – and I want it to stay that way.'

'It's your private family business, Megan, nothing to do with anyone else.'

'You didn't mention the mirror to Mrs Eardley?'

Celia shook her head. 'The only person I've

discussed it with is Janet. If you remember, she came with me to the auctioneer's office.'

Megan thought for a moment. 'I don't mind Janet knowing; having been a minister's wife she must be used to discretion – but absolutely no-one else.' All she wanted to do, all she longed to do, was to curl up in an armchair and to shed the tears she was trying to hold back. To find out that Ellen, who had shown her nothing but love and kindness, was not her real mother filled her with heartbreak. And as for her father, how could he have been so judgmental of others, have so little sympathy with human weakness when ... and then she felt an unexpected wistfulness. He must have loved Elvina so much. What was the saying, 'it is better to have loved and lost, than never to have loved at all'? And Les had found love twice. Perhaps not with the same passion that he'd felt for Elvina, but he had loved Ellen in a quiet, loyal way, Megan was sure of that.

And then Megan suddenly remembered Mrs Finney's initial description of Elvira, *she was always a bit wild*. Could Les have feared that as her daughter Megan would be the same?

Chapter Forty-one

On Sunday morning, Megan decided to go up to Bethesda. Her feelings were still too raw to be surrounded in her own chapel by a congregation who had known her father. Les hadn't been

352

liked, but he had earned their respect. And she would keep his secret, his and Ellen's, even as far as Clarice and Rita were concerned. Megan wondered whether her own respect was any less for him, but in a strange way, instead she felt an added warmth and affection. Her reaction to the scandalous revelation may have been one of shock, but Megan's overriding emotion was one of sadness, wishing that her father had trusted his own family more, had shared his burden of guilt and unhappiness. Surely it could only have brought them all closer together? She had spent a disturbed and emotional night, hardly able to sleep, her thoughts full of memories of Ellen, of how she had always sat up with Megan through childhood illness, of her rare but precious cuddles. I was so lucky, Megan thought, so very lucky.

Her other reason for going to Bethesda was that she wanted to see Eunice. Since marrying Ben, her friend had naturally been drawn into his family life, and was full of excitement becoming a mother, longing to finish work, and could talk of nothing else but Ben, knitting patterns, and baby names. Celia and Janet were friends, very special ones, and of course there were always the girls at work, but only Eunice was her own age; besides they had shared so much.

When Megan turned into Bethesda Street, it was almost deserted. But Ben was there, talking intently to his previous girlfriend, the one with the wealthy parents. She was gazing up at him, her face pale even in the distance and as Megan watched she saw her put a pleading hand on his arm. Megan tried not to feel a stab of alarm, telling herself that she must be imagining things. Surely even Ben, while his wife was pregnant wouldn't stoop so low as to get involved with someone else? And after all, even if she was his ex-girlfriend they had a perfect right to talk to each other. Just then Ben turned to glance over his shoulder and seeing Megan he bent to say something to the girl, who left him and hurried into the chapel. He came to meet Megan, an easy smile on his lips. 'So if it isn't the holiday girl! Thanks for the postcard. You had a good time then?'

'It was brilliant. Where's Eunice, I was hoping to see her?'

'Feeling a bit dickey this morning – nothing to worry about – something about the baby "turning", at least that's what Mum said.'

Megan knew that Eunice was now finding her pregnancy difficult, and had confided that she was dreading the actual birth. 'Oh, remember me to her won't you?'

'Of course I will.'

With an image in her mind of her friend's rapidly swelling stomach, as Megan watched him go she couldn't help some misgivings. She also could hardly believe now how naive she used to be. Was it really only a year ago?

In the afternoon, Megan set out with some frustration to walk up to Lightwood. She would have liked to talk further with Celia about the previous afternoon, but Verity's presence was going to make that impossible. Megan was in no mood for sparring with that madam. And, she thought with some bitterness, I can just imagine what *she'd* think if she found out that I was a ... the word still had the power to hurt.

When Janet opened the door, she said that their visitor had arrived just before lunch, and was even now reading to Celia. 'Are you going to pop in and say hello?'

Megan shook her head. 'I'll start on the ironing. What would you like me to do afterwards?'

'There's one job I'm finding it difficult to get down to these days – it's the oven – you wouldn't like to tackle that?'

If there was one job that Megan detested... She forced a smile, 'Of course I will.'

Janet lowered her voice. 'And we can have a wee chat about what happened yesterday. Celia was that worried about you when she came home.'

'It was an awful shock.' Megan's voice was equally low.

'Now lassie, you've nothing to feel ashamed about. You're not the first to be born on the wrong side of the blanket, and you won't be the last.' Janet smiled reassuringly at her, and watched as Megan went slowly up the staircase. How could those people have cut their grand-daughter so completely out of their lives? Never even to see the child. It was incomprehensible. She and Celia had decided that Megan's illegitimacy and lack of inclusion in the will would preclude her from inheriting even a small part of the Frayne estate. Although Janet doubted that the girl would be interested anyway, to discover the harsh rejection by her mother's family must

355

have been a severe blow.

In the drawing-room Celia was discovering that her Sunday afternoon experience of listening to Megan's melodious voice bore no comparison to the ordeal of sitting through an hour of Verity's piercing vowels.

'Thank you,' she said with relief, when at last the book was laid aside.

'It's a bit heavy going don't you think?' Verity stifled a yawn.

'You don't find it interesting?'

'Not yet, perhaps it will liven up a bit.'

Celia looked at the book lying on the coffee table. It was one she had chosen with Megan in mind, thinking that she'd enjoy being introduced to Trollope.

'What sort of thing do you usually like to read? I mean, if you're not keen on this one, we could easily get another. There's an excellent bookshop in Hanley, I'm sure Webberley's would have something you'd like.'

'I don't suppose there any decent clothes shops there?' Verity's tone was dismissive.

Celia gave a tight smile. 'Oh I think you'll be surprised.' She leaned back in her chair feeling exhausted with the strain of suppressing her irritation. And this was the first day, what on earth was she going to feel like after a whole month? 'Maybe you'd like to go up and get settled into your room now? And then I'll ask Janet to bring in tea. I think she's made some gingerbread which is always a treat.'

As Verity neared the door Celia added, 'I heard Megan arrive, but I'd rather you didn't disturb her; she has more ironing to do than usual.'

Hearing the light footsteps on the stairs Megan guessed they belonged to Verity and tensed but to her relief after a tiny pause outside the room, they moved on.

Later, when she went downstairs to tackle Janet's oven, Megan was relieved to find that her fear of losing her temper with Verity was unfounded.

'I tapped on the door and peeped in to see if she was all right,' Celia said as she joined them in the kitchen, 'but she's fallen asleep. It was of course, a very long drive for her.' Her lips twitched as she saw Megan's carefully guarded expression, while Janet kept her thoughts to herself.

Chapter Forty-two

It was on Wednesday morning that the girls heard. Less than an hour after they had begun their day's work, Miss Dawson took up a position in the centre of the decorating shop and said in a voice that was clear and yet full of tension. 'Could I have everyone's attention, please?'

She waited until they were all facing her and when Megan saw the grave expression on the supervisor's face a slow dread began to creep up from her stomach.

Dora's normally decisive voice was strained. 'I'm sorry to have to tell you all that I've just received bad news. I'm afraid Jean, our friend and

357

colleague, has passed away.' After the shocked and dismayed gasps had subsided she told them, 'Apparently she died quite peacefully yesterday afternoon, and her husband was with her. I understand that the funeral details will be given later in the Sentinel. Meanwhile, if we could all include her in our prayers...' Visibly affected, she turned away, leaving a stunned silence behind her.

Megan was fighting tears. The older woman had taught her so much, not only of the skill of enamelling, but also about common sense and loyalty. On Megan's first nervous day in the decorating shop, it had been Jean who reassured her that as she was painting on glazed ware, she could easily wipe off any mistakes. 'If you look along the bench,' she'd said, 'you'll see that all the girls have a rag and turps by them. And even the most experienced have to use one sometimes.' Megan thought of Jean's home, of her two sons, of the warm affection in that small family. What an emptiness her death would leave.

Minnie said at break. 'You were the last one to see her, Megan. How was she then?'

'I thought she looked very tired,' Megan was still feeling shaken. 'I went up to take her a box of fudge and some Eastbourne rock for the boys. You know Jean, she puts a brave face on, but I could tell even then that she was struggling.'

'However will Bill cope?' Flo said, dabbing at her eyes with a fraying hanky. 'And those two little lads...'

'He'll have no choice.' Megan thought of the muscular man whose strong build belied his gentle nature. 'But this will devastate him, he was devoted to her.'

'And she to him,' Minnie said. 'Why is it that couples like that...' her voice trailed off.

'I'd intended to go and see her last weekend,' Megan said later to Miss Dawson. 'I feel awful now.'

'Megan, there's always regrets and feelings of guilt when someone dies. You couldn't have known the end would come so quickly. I suppose you'll be going to the funeral?'

Megan nodded even though it was unlikely that she'd get paid for the time she took off work. But what was money when friendship was involved?

'The coast's clear,' Janet said when Megan arrived on Sunday afternoon, 'Why not nip in and have a word with Celia – she could do with a bit of light relief.'

'Well, I don't think I'll cheer her up,' Megan said, 'I've had some bad news.'

'Oh dear, you'd better tell us all about it.' Janet led the way into the drawing-room, where Celia was trying to repair her frayed nerves by doing some embroidery.

'Here's Megan, but she's just told me that she's had some bad news.'

Celia put down her sewing and leaned forward with concern as Megan sat opposite them both and in a low voice told them about Jean. 'I suppose it was obvious really,' she said, 'every time I went she seemed weaker, but it's still come as a shock.'

'I'm afraid it always does,' Celia said. 'Now why should a good woman like that be taken away, leaving a bereft young family? It just doesn't make sense. But then so much of life mystifies me; it's one reason why I'm a non-believer.' She turned to Janet, 'Didn't your Robbie ever question such things?'

'He'd be a poor human being if he didn't,' Janet said. 'We all do. But he used to say that there was a greater plan of life than we could understand, and it was a test of our humility to accept it.'

'And how are you Megan,' Celia looked at her with concern. 'After our visit to Biddulph, I mean. It's the first chance I've had to ask and well – you've been on my mind?'

'Mine too,' Janet said.

Megan looked at them. 'You're really are so kind, I'm always saying it! I'm coming to terms with it all, I haven't much choice really.' She hesitated and said with some embarrassment, 'I'm just glad that nobody else knows about it.'

'Just remember, that you're the same lovely girl you were before. It doesn't change anything.'

But Megan noticed that Celia's normally serene expression seemed somewhat strained. 'And how are you Celia?'

'I'm fine,' she said then admitted, 'perhaps missing our quiet way of life a little.'

'It must make a difference, having someone to stay for a whole month. Where is Verity, by the way?'

'Gone for a walk – quite a new experience for her I think,' Celia said drily. 'I sometimes think she's welded to that car of hers.'

Janet explained, 'Verity's a bit miffed because she hasn't had a phone call from America yet.'

'But it must be dreadfully expensive...' Megan said. 'Perhaps James is thinking of the cost.'

'Whatever the reason,' Celia said, remembering Verity's thunderous expression and sulkiness all morning, 'let's just say that she isn't taking it very well.' Then she frowned. 'You know Jean's husband is going to find it very difficult to look after those two young boys on his own. I was wondering if there's anything we can do to help.'

'How about if I do some extra baking,' Janet suggested. 'On a regular basis, I mean. I've never known a man – not to mention two laddies – who wouldn't welcome that.'

Celia said, 'What an excellent idea! I've got a small wicker basket with a cover stored somewhere in the loft – that would be perfect.'

'And I could take it to them when I leave here on Sundays.' Megan was astonished at their generosity. After all neither of them had known Jean, and they certainly didn't know Bill and the boys.

'Then I shall insist on driving you,' Celia said.

Suddenly there came the sound of the front door opening and seconds later Verity came into the room. She gave Megan a sharp glance and completely ignored her. Megan said pointedly, 'Hello Verity.'

She gave a curt nod, and flopped into an armchair. 'It's quite a hill, that one. You certainly need a car to live up here.'

Megan got up. 'I'd better go and start the ironing.'

'By the way,' Celia called as Megan reached the door. 'You can ignore the small basket. Those are

Verity's things and, naturally she will be looking after her own clothes.'

Megan took one look at Verity's outraged expression and escaped. As she ran up the wide stairs laughter bubbled inside her. Bless you Celia, she thought, you're an angel!

Chapter Forty-three

On finishing the ironing, Megan went down to the kitchen and after helping Janet make tomato chutney she sealed the last of the warm jars, stuck on a label and glanced at the clock. 'That was good timing. Will you say goodbye to Celia for me?'

'Beating a hasty retreat? Of course I will.' Janet nodded to the small white envelope on the dresser. 'She popped in earlier and left your money.'

The late afternoon was still warm and sunny, a welcome respite from the previous cooler weather as autumn drifted in, and as Megan strolled along the pavement beneath the shade of the trees she thought how quiet everywhere seemed; it was a typical Sunday teatime scene. It was only when she turned the corner that she saw the tall man in the distance. He was standing before a parked black car, and with a raised camera taking photographs. Idly curious she put up a hand to shade her eyes against the sun, and then her breath caught in her throat. It couldn't be ... it couldn't possibly be ... it was Nathan! With disbelief and joy sweeping through her Megan quickened her step to a run in panic as she saw him sling the camera into the car and get into the driving seat. He was leaving! He was going to pull away! She ran faster ... suppose he'd already called at her house? And even if he hadn't and was now on his way there, he'd find it empty and leave! Frantic, Megan stepped into the road and waved furiously. He hadn't seen her – the car was gaining speed. In desperation she ran faster her feet in their sandals pounding the pavement ... and then suddenly she had to stop and clutch at her side. The stitch was agonising, but it wasn't pain but frustration that brought tears to her eyes. She was going to miss him...

A few days earlier, Nathan's feelings had been mixed about his mother's transatlantic phone call. 'Oh good Nathan, you're still in Scotland. I thought you might have checked out. Dad and I were wondering – have you been to Stoke-on-Trent yet?'

He was guarded in his answer. 'Not really.'

'Only your Uncle Joe's been to visit and amazingly he was stationed there during the war. He wants you to take a photo for him. I've got the address here...'

He drew forward a page of the hotel's headed notepaper. 'Okay, go ahead.'

'It's Lightwood Road, Longton.'

Nathan's hand stilled.

'The servicemen gave it the name Pittsburgh House so I'm not sure if it's still called that, but someone will know. Is that something you can do?'

Nathan stared down at the now scribbled words. 'Sure Mom. No problem.'

'I'm surprised you still haven't seen Megan...'

He hesitated, 'I'll tell you all about that when I get back.'

'All right son. You take care now.'

Nathan replaced the receiver in his hotel bed-room. So Uncle Joe had been stationed in the Potteries? He'd never mentioned it, but then he lived so far away that they rarely saw him. And this place was in Longton? Now wasn't that the oddest thing? But his mother had been right, she had just caught him. Although he'd enjoyed see-ing Edinburgh castle and the picturesque glens and lochs of Scotland, he was due to sail from Southampton in a couple of days, and his case was already open ready to be packed. And now he'd have to make this detour. Fate sure could play some strange tricks.

Nathan cruised slowly along, peering at the names of the houses, and found that a large resi-dential home set back from the road was indeed called Pittsburgh House. He grinned – it was good to think that these folk had kept the name their American visitors had used. As Nathan got out of the hot car into the bright afternoon sun-shine he glanced up the deserted road and tried to imagine Uncle Joe with his hearty laugh and freckled face in uniform striding along these sidewalks, or pavements as they called them over here. Clicking the shutter, Nathan used up the remainder of his roll of film, put the camera back in its case and tossed it on to the passenger seat.

Climbing into the cramped space before the wheel, he squinted into the sun to check the road, swung round the car and began to draw away. But as he gained speed, his mind returned yet again to the niggling doubts that had plagued him during the long drive down from Scotland. Suppose he'd been a tad hasty? What if Megan *wasn't* married? That guy could just as easily have been a date or a boyfriend. But then if he did call and she *was* married would her new husband welcome some stranger turning up on the doorstep? And what if she was still free and single, did he really want to complicate his life? Hang it all, his home, his family and friends were all on the other side of the Atlantic. Why was he even considering an action that could only complicate his life? And yet the lingering memories of this girl had not only interfered with his life for almost a year, hadn't he come over to try and lay her ghost to rest? If he could be sure that the attraction was no longer there, then wouldn't that be a sort of freedom? As the car neared the point of decision, Nathan's jaw tensed, and with one swift glance in his rear mirror he swerved to take the right hand turn.

This time as he drew up outside the houses slumbering in the afternoon heat, there was no nudging of net curtains. The only sign of life came from a ginger cat lazily grooming itself in front of a gate. He switched off the ignition and got out of the car. It took only two long strides to cross the narrow pavement, two more to reach the front door and he smoothed his hands on his pants before giving a sharp rap on the door, and waited. There was no reply. He stood back and glanced up at the bedroom window. The wave of jealousy that swept through him at the thought that she might be up there with her husband was hot, searing and totally unexpected. Nathan swallowed hard. He waited a few seconds then knocked again, louder this time with the sound echoing through an obviously empty house. He frowned then walked down the side path to the back; the small patch of garden was deserted.

Walking slowly back he stood for a few moments and then gave a resigned shrug. At least he'd given fate its chance ... and after quietly closing the gate behind him, went to the car. It was then that he heard a distant sound behind him; a girl's voice – high, desperate. Nathan swung round to see Megan, her dark hair dishevelled, limping along the pavement. As she saw that he'd heard her, seen her, she slowed down with one hand clutching at her side. Nathan's long stride took him to her in seconds. 'Honey, what's wrong?'

'A stitch,' she was struggling for breath. 'I've been running to try and catch you... I saw you from up the hill, taking photos...'

'You saw me...? You've run all that way?'

As Nathan's gaze flashed to her left hand, Megan nodded, pushing her hair back from her perspiring forehead. 'I must look an awful mess. I can't believe you're here. I was so scared of missing you.'

Side by side they began to walk slowly back to the house with Nathan saying, 'Is it easing?'

Megan nodded. 'Yes, thank goodness.' Once

they were in the house she turned to him. 'Can you give me a minute to freshen up? I won't be long.'

Still breathless she escaped upstairs to take off her now creased and limp pink dress. Feeling so excited that she almost felt shaky she glanced in the mirror and was horrified. Megan hurried into the bathroom to splash her beetroot face with cold water, then back in the bedroom she put on clean underwear and a cool short-sleeved white blouse and navy and white spotted skirt, hurriedly brushed out her hair and put on a light touch of lipstick. Hopefully, her colour would soon return to normal ... and then suddenly none of that mattered ... just to know that Nathan was waiting for her downstairs... What if he'd left and hadn't come back? She couldn't have borne it.

Nathan, one hand in a pocket jingling his car keys, was looking around the sitting room. It still seemed incredibly small and dreary, although there were a couple of bright cushion covers and half-made curtains draped across the table. But when Megan returned looking delectably pretty, everything else went out of his mind. He had to remind himself that just because she wasn't wearing a wedding or engagement ring, that didn't mean that she was single and heart free. There was still that guy she'd been with ... but he mustn't run ahead. Okay, his heart had catapulted on seeing her but... 'Feel better now?'

Megan nodded, unable to take her eyes off him. 'Can I get you a cup of tea?'

What Nathan would have liked was a cold beer straight from the refrigerator. But there was little chance of that. 'You wouldn't have a cold drink?'

'Yes of course.'

Glad of a long drink herself, Megan came back with two brimming glasses of dandelion and burdock and they sat opposite each other. They both took a couple of sips, and Nathan said, 'This is a bit like the sarsaparilla we drink back home.'

'Are you over here on business again?'

'I'm supposed to be.' He grinned at her, 'Only I played truant and went to have a look at Scotland.'

'Did you see the Loch Ness monster?' Megan began to smile.

'Sure did, but he took one look at me and beat a hasty retreat.'

She laughed. 'Why were you taking the photographs?'

Nathan told her about Pittsburgh House. 'It's something isn't it? That Uncle Joe was stationed just up the road from you?'

'It's unbelievable. I wonder if he met any local people. I might know some of them.'

'I'll get Mom to ask him.' Nathan drained his glass. 'And what's been happening in your life since we last met?'

Megan thought immediately of Mrs Finney's revelation then hurriedly pushed it from her mind. Instead she said, 'Quite a lot actually.'

He felt a sudden lurch of his stomach. Here it comes, he thought. You should have listened to your Goddamn brain and driven straight past.

'For one thing,' Megan said, 'I had this lovely surprise parcel from America. Nathan, that was a Godsend, I can't thank you enough.'

'That's okay honey, it was a pleasure. In any case, it was Mom who did all the work.'

'Well, do thank her again for me.'

Nathan looked at her and suddenly couldn't wait any longer. To hell with this chit-chat he thought, I need to know. He twisted the empty glass round in his fingers. 'I did wonder whether you might be married or engaged or something.' He glanced across at her. 'I wasn't sure whether some English guy would give me the cold shoulder...'

Megan began to laugh. 'No, you needn't worry about that. There was someone...'

'Was that recently?'

'No, it was in the spring.'

Then who, Nathan wondered, was that guy I saw? But he didn't have any right to probe. 'And how's the world of the china factory?'

'Fine, although...' she told him about Jean.

'Gee, that's tough luck, I'm sorry honey.' There was something different about her – he couldn't quite put his finger on it. And then he realised that it was poise. Gone was the hesitant, gauche girl he remembered. Was this something to do with her statement that 'quite a lot had happened?' Nathan frowned, beginning to feel uncomfortable. This all seemed a bit stilted; they needed to be in a different setting, one where they could relax. 'Megan, how are you fixed for coming out for dinner?'

'What now – on a Sunday evening? I can't think of anywhere...'

'We could eat at the George; it would be just like old times.' He grinned at her. 'I'm sure they'll

369

feed us. I booked in for a night before going down to Southampton. What do you think?'

Megan gazed at him in delight. 'I'd love to. But,' she warned him, 'I'd have to change.'

'You look okay to me...'

'Ah, but you're a man...'

Nathan watched her run up the stairs. It was astonishing. She was so full of confidence. And yet that slight shyness, that vulnerability was still there. Now what he wondered had brought about the transformation? Had it been the boyfriend she'd mentioned? Had he taken her places, brought new experiences into her life? And he was again startled by a stab of jealousy. And yet when he'd once seen Alison having dinner with a stranger – who later turned out to be an old friend – he'd only felt a mild curiosity.

Megan was rifling through her wardrobe. How she would have loved Nathan to see her in the blue cocktail dress, but that could be over-dressing, something Celia had warned her about. So instead Megan, only wishing that she had the clothes she'd borrowed for Eastbourne to choose from, took out a blouse she'd bought from the catalogue. It was white, pretty with sheer sleeves, and new. The skirt she was wearing – was it too casual? Swiftly she put them together, slipped into her navy court shoes and looked in the full length mirror. Yes, add Ellen's single strand of pearls and she'd be fine. And even she could see the glow in her eyes. Then her glance went down to Elvina's hairbrush and mirror lying side by side on the dressing table. Had her mother truly loved her father? Had she felt this excitement before she went to meet him? And yet the ending for her had been so sad...

It was only then that the significance of Nathan's words hit her. He'd said that he was on his way to Southampton, that he was staying at the George for one night. Only one night and then he was going to Southampton? But wasn't that where the liners left from?

Chapter Forty-four

The following morning Celia was in her garden, standing beneath the shade of an apple tree and trying to understand her gardener's explanation of why he hadn't been the previous day.

With his gnarled hands resting on an old garden spade he told her, 'It was ar youth. He were took bad.'

Celia looked at him with sympathy. 'Your son?'

'No – me brother!' He looked pityingly at her. Celia was sure he thought she was what people locally referred to 'as a bit short of a shilling.'

'Oh, I see. And he was ill?'

'That's right. So I couldna come you see, cos somebody had to look after him. And his missus, well they gerralong all right but she's about as much use as half a farthin.'

'Well, I hope he soon feels better. Who's looking after him now?'

'His missus is, she's pulled herself together,' he turned away to his digging muttering, 'I never saw such a useless woman.'

Celia continued to wander, enjoying the solitude and the sounds of birdsong, only to sigh with exasperation as she heard Verity's clear voice calling, 'Ah, there you are, I wondered where you'd disappeared to.'

'I was just looking around for some flowers for the house,' Celia said.

'Let me choose.' Verity's gaze was already sweeping the herbaceous border for likely blooms. 'Are there gloves?'

'Sorry, I tore a hole in them only last week.'

Celia said, 'Just a minute, let me introduce you to Bert.'

His only response was a disdainful glance and a muttered, ''ow do!'

Verity raised an eyebrow and Celia wondered whether the ridiculous girl was waiting for him to touch his forelock!

But peace only reigned for ten minutes because Janet, preparing vegetables for lunch, glanced out of the kitchen window to see Verity remonstrate with the gardener. As the sound of their voices heightened, she went into the hall and called, 'Celia, you'd better come. I think she's upsetting Bert.'

With a muttered exclamation, Celia left the letter she was writing and hurried outside. Verity was standing with her hands on her hips while Bert was gripping his spade. The partly-filled trug lay between them on the lawn.

'Is there a problem?' Celia said.

Verity swung round. 'Your gardener refuses to cut the flowers I've told him to.'

'It ain't my job to pick flowers for the 'ouse!'

'Well he can't expect me to ruin *my* hands!' Verity showed Celia a scratch on the back of one.

'Missus 'ere pays me to dig the garden, not to pansy about picking flowers,' Bert said. 'She does that 'erself.'

'If I, as a guest, ask you to do something to help me, then you should do it!' Verity's voice was icy.

Bert chewed on his lip then gave Verity a long, disparaging look. 'Are yer stoppin' long?'

Celia's lips twitched, but to show some sign of support to her daughter-in-law said, 'It's my fault Bert. I ruined my gloves last week and threw them away. But don't worry about it, I'll nip out in the car and buy some new ones. You carry on with what you were doing.'

'I'd dismiss him if he worked for me,' Verity snapped as they walked away.

'Would you?' Celia kept her tone mild.

'Certainly, I did the same with mine not long ago.'

'Did you have much difficulty finding another?'

Verity shrugged. 'I'm still trying. But then when one has high standards…'

Celia swallowed hard and decided that it was going to take rather a long time to find the right gloves. She might even decide to go for a drive.

Megan was glancing at her watch. Not a word had she said to any of the girls; Nathan's reappearance in her life was too precious to expose it to any sort of teasing. Last night, being with him across an intimate table, talking and laughing with every nerve increasingly aware of the

373

growing attraction between them; she'd felt more alive than at any time in her life.

All the way home in the car she had been almost feverish with anticipation. She had no doubts that Nathan found her attractive, it had been in his eyes, in his smile, in the fleeting moments his fingers had brushed against her own. And then Nathan had refused her invitation to come in. 'I'm bushed honey,' he said. 'Let's call it a night.'

Megan's euphoria had shattered. Was that it? Was he going to say goodbye and disappear again?

'But I could see you tomorrow.'

The words were a ray of sunshine. Then with dismay, she exclaimed, 'I'm working.'

'They must let you out to eat – say at lunchtime?'

'But I thought you were leaving, going to Southampton?'

'A few hours won't make that much difference. What do you say?' Nathan was desperate to give himself leeway, some time to think, and to think with his mind, not with...

'Of course, but I don't know where...' Megan suddenly thought of the Dorothy Cafe in Longton. It was somewhere she'd never been to as Ellen had considered it a bit 'pricey'. Not wanting him to be waiting conspicuously outside the potbank, she gave him directions.

'Sure thing,' he said.

Megan had hesitated, half waiting for him to kiss her, which he did – on her cheek – leaving her to toss and turn all night, wondering why he had turned away from her expectant lips. For an

374

evening like that, full of romance and promise – to end with a light kiss on the cheek? Why?

And in the cold light of day, Megan had felt a dread rise within her. Was she fooling herself, mistaken? Could it be that Nathan was engaged? Or even married?

Nathan didn't wait for Megan outside the Dorothy Cafe. With his collar turned up against a chill breeze, he was leaning against the ancient wall of a church across the road from the factory. To be so close and yet to have to waste his limited time was frustrating in the extreme. But at least soon now she would come out from beneath that archway and he wanted to watch her. To be un-observed, to try to see her – as it were – from a distance. He had to try and figure out just what it was about this ordinary girl from the Potteries that was tying his heart and mind into knots.

Last night as she'd turned so enticingly towards him, he had almost weakened; it had taken every remnant of his self control not to draw her close, to hold her in his arms, to kiss her in the way that he longed to. But that would mean crossing a line. And he wasn't ready for that.

Earlier, sitting opposite Megan, he'd been entranced. Watching the different expressions flitting across her face, he could only marvel how struggle and sacrifice had honed her character. Appalled at first to discover that she'd had to take an extra job to make ends meet, when she'd explained about Celia, and then Eastbourne, he'd been at first surprised and then fascinated by the affection in Megan's voice. Here was the reason for her transformation. It hadn't been another man but this woman who had introduced Megan to a different, a more sophisticated way of life. No longer fazed by the dining room at the George, her easy confidence had at first amused and then captivated him.

Nathan knew that he was already half-way in love with her. And he suspected that she felt the same way about him. But did he want to risk raising her hopes only to leave behind a broken heart? If he did cross that tantalising line, and with every fibre of his being he wanted to – then his fear was that Megan might get hurt. He kept reminding himself that she not only lived on the other side of the world, he hardly knew her. Not in the way that he knew Alison, whose family background was so similar to his own. Heck he could even remember her in pigtails. Whereas Megan – he studied the industrial landscape with its bottle kilns and smoke-blackened factories. How these people remained healthy baffled him. He thought of the clean air, the sub-tropical climate at home. There a man had the best of both worlds; space to breathe, the outdoor life and with the cultured city of Wichita within easy reach.

He glanced at his watch, surely it was time? And then he could hear the sound of a buzzer and seconds later a trickle of workers began to emerge from beneath the archway. Nathan straightened up to wait with increasing impatience and suddenly there she was. Megan didn't see him, didn't even glance across to the church, but instead began to walk down the hill, eagerness in every step, her head held high... Goddam it, what was it about her that...

He went swiftly out of the churchyard, only to have to wait for a red double-decker bus to pass before he could cross the road. It only took seconds to catch up with her, and her eyes lit up. 'Nathan! Where did you spring from?'

'I was just having a nosey around your churchyard. Had a good morning?'

'Not too bad. We've just had a collection for a wreath for Jean. The funeral's on Wednesday morning.'

'Will you go?'

She nodded. 'Yes. A couple of the girls are going as well. The others can't afford to lose their pay – well, I can't really, but some things are more important than money.'

Nathan glanced down at her. It sure was a strange world. He'd just been lucky he guessed, because he'd never had to worry where the next dollar was coming from.

The Dorothy Cafe was situated above a cake shop, just before the railway station and across from the Town Hall, and Nathan declared it was 'real cute'. Megan suspected that was because of the trim waitresses in their black uniforms and white frilly aprons. Soon they were seated at a small table, but even when their food arrived, somehow Megan couldn't seem to relax. Even her appetite was lacking, Nathan's impending departure hanging over her like a black cloud. Eventually and with some desperation she said, 'Do you come to England every year?'

He shook his head. 'This trip was a bit of a last

377

minute one.'

'It was lucky that you'd saved your holidays then, so that you could see Scotland.'

'Sort of,' he said quietly.

'I'd like to go to Scotland.' Megan knew she was talking much too fast. 'I want to have one of those Scottish collies one day. I love the Lassie films.'

'Hey that's my plan – to have one of those.'

'I'd like a girl dog.' She smiled across at him. 'Yes, I know the right name is a bitch, but people use that as an insult. So I prefer girl.'

He laughed and then his gaze held hers. 'Have I ever told you how delightful you are?'

Her breath caught in her throat. 'No, you haven't.' Megan smiled at him but the question was burning in her. Should she ask him? She would never rest until she found out. She tried to keep her tone light. 'I remember you asking me about my love life, but you haven't told me anything about yours? What was the question they used to ask the GIs during the war – is there a girl back home?'

As an image of Alison came into Nathan's mind, of her honesty and patience, he knew he couldn't lie. And why should he? 'In a way I suppose there is,' he said quietly.

The words were like a blow. Then what was he doing with her? Paying her compliments, making her feel … her mind shied away from a horrifying image of Ben. Megan said in a tight voice, 'And is it serious?'

He hesitated, 'Honey, the answer is yes and no. I've known Alison since we were kids and well to

378

be honest, we sorta drifted into an engagement. But when it came to planning the wedding ... let's just say that we both agreed to give ourselves some time for reflection.'

'So you mean,' Megan's fingers played with her teaspoon, 'that you're not engaged now?' She raised her head and her eyes searched his, seeking the truth, desperately hoping for the right answer.

He shook his head. 'No honey, I'm not.'

'But it's still a possibility – with you and Alison, I mean?' She was torturing herself, she knew she was. The thought of him being in a relationship with this unknown girl...

Nathan ran his hand through his hair. He didn't reply. How could he? But he did know that the unexplored relationship with this English girl could haunt him for the rest of his life. It had already caused problems back home, it would always hover as a 'what might have been'. And what of Megan, whose feelings were even now shining in her unguarded eyes. What they needed, what they desperately needed was a chance to spend time together, to discover each other. Abruptly he removed his hand from hers. 'Come on,' he said, and getting up put a hand in his pocket and flung a pound note on to the table.

'That's too much,' Megan gasped as hurriedly she joined him.

'Who cares?' They clattered down the stairs, with Megan calling, 'Where are we going?'

'You tell me. But you're not going back to work.'

'I can't,' she gasped. 'I can't just take time off like that!'

'I don't see why not? You could be feeling ill or something...'

'But...'

He swung round to face her as they went out into the street. 'One afternoon; that's what I'm asking you for – one afternoon. Will you give me that ... please?'

Megan tensed. Then silently she nodded.

'Where can we go to have some time together? Somewhere we could walk, talk...'

'The Park,' she said swiftly. 'It's in Dresden, about ten minutes away.'

'Okay.' Nathan grabbed her hand and she had to hurry to keep up with his long urgent strides. It was only when they were in the car and heading out of Longton that a delicious image came into her mind – there were some very secluded spots in the park...

Chapter Forty-five

'Where's Megan got to? Did anyone see her clock in?'

'Not me, Lizzie,' Betty said. 'But then I was nearly late meself.'

'She's more than just late!'

Minnie said nothing. But her discretion was wasted, because when Enid came back from the WC, she said, 'Hey, one of the lithographers says she saw Megan in town. She was with a tall bloke wearing glasses.'

'She never did!' Flo turned to the others. 'Did anyone here see her?'

Minnie leaned forward and put a finger to her lips. 'Sssh...' She jerked her head at Miss Dawson, who was discussing a new pattern with one of the under managers. But as soon as they'd left, Flo urged, 'Come on, Min. What's going on?'

'All right then. I think it was that Yank.'

'What Yank?' Hilda said.

'It was before your time,' Flo told her. 'Megan met an American last year. But Minnie, how do you know it was him?'

''Cos I saw them,' Minnie said. 'I was keeping quiet for Megan's sake. I reckon she's crogged off for the afternoon.'

'What, Megan?' Lizzie exclaimed, 'never on this earth! Anyway, what makes you think it was him?'

'Yer can always tell – they wear different clothes. Ever so smart he was, in a grey gabardine suit. He had lovely broad shoulders.'

Enid, sitting next to her sighed with envy. 'I wondered why she was a bit dressed up this morning; I noticed it when she was putting her overall on. Now why can't I meet someone like that?'

'I'd get rid of that useless lump you're married to first!' Lizzie leaned back and stretched. 'God, my back aches today.'

'Oh yes, and what have you bin up to?' Flo began to chuckle.

'Chance would be a fine thing. I've told yer, it's a thing of the past since Sid had his false teeth. He takes 'em out as soon as he gets into bed. Says his gums are sore. And he won't talk without 'em in,

381

or smile either. What with that and his gnashers grinning at me from that glass ... it's hardly romance is it? Still,' she said, having cast a furtive glance over her shoulder to make sure the supervisor hadn't returned. 'As far as Megan's concerned, I'm glad for her. It's about time she misbehaved herself. If you don't do it when you're young, you never will.'

'Let's just hope she doesn't regret it,' Minnie muttered.

Queen's Park was exactly how Nathan had imagined an English park to be; neatly laid out flowerbeds, winding paths, benches to rest, a paddling pool and lake, a children's playground. The previous cool wind had eased and there were now blue patches of sky. 'I love it here,' Megan said as they strolled along hand in hand.

He drew her aside to let an elderly couple pass by. The woman's gait was slow and awkward, her legs bowed beneath her turquoise crimplene pleated skirt. Her husband, who was carrying a small bowls bag, grinned at them. 'How do! It's a bit better now.'

'It sure is,' Nathan said, always amused how the weather was a constant topic of conversation over here.

'Hey Rene, here's a Yank.' He gave a roguish grin. 'Got any gum, chum?'

'Take no notice of him, love,' his wife said. 'You have a nice afternoon.'

When they'd gone by, Megan twisted round to Nathan. 'Come to think of it, I've never seen you chewing gum. I thought all Americans did it, that's why they've got such white teeth.'

She burst out laughing as Nathan stretched his mouth in a wide smile. 'Mom brought us up never to chew in company,' he said, 'but okay I hold my hands up. I've got some in the car. Do you want me to leave you some?'

'Yes please, it's still rationed here.' But how she wished he hadn't used the dreaded word 'leave'. By now they had circled most of the perimeter of the park and were beginning to approach a quieter, tree-lined and eventually deserted area. And suddenly they weren't talking, their steps were slowing and she stared ahead, tense, waiting, hoping.

'Megan?' His voice was so quiet she could hardly hear him. She turned to meet his eyes, warm and caring and then like a homing pigeon she at last went into his arms. His lips came down to hers in their first tentative, wondering kiss, and then as they kissed again and again, their mouths clinging, searching, she felt herself melt in such a delicious way that that she never wanted the moment to end. But the sound of footsteps forced them to draw apart and Nathan held on to Megan's hand as a man in uniform with a peaked cap walked by. 'The park-keeper,' she whispered.

Nathan's expression was taut. He hadn't intended that to happen. It was the first time in his life that he'd allowed himself to be ruled by his emotions, and it shook him. Hadn't he meant these hours to be a sort of testing time, a way of finding out what they had in common? And then the moment they were alone... He glanced down at her, seeing Megan's flushed and happy face.

What the hell was he doing with this girl? She didn't deserve to be treated lightly, as if he was just a guy fooling around with a girl. Fooling around? He was kidding himself. With her pliant body against his own, even for that short time, he'd felt that he could conquer the world. As they began to walk slowly on, he stared into the distance, knowing that time was against them. If he was to make any sort of decision, it needed to be very soon.

Megan was in a whirl of mixed emotions. Held in Nathan's arms, she had been in heaven. Now her throat was tight with unshed tears. To know that he was leaving her, that within a few hours he would be thousands of miles away… She was staring down at the narrow path when to her horror she heard a familiar strident voice.

'I see you've got yourself another sucker!'

Freda Podmore, in a grey buttoned-up coat and sturdy lace-up shoes stood before them, blocking their way. Her glance swept derisively over them both. 'Don't think I haven't been watching you two, canoodling.' She turned to Nathan. 'As for you, I don't know who you are but I warn you, you're asking for trouble with this one.'

Stunned Megan could only stare at her. Anger surged through her, this wretched woman – of all the people to meet... 'And what exactly do you mean by that? And what has my business got to do with you anyway?'

Nathan was appalled by both the verbal attack and by Megan's furious defence. Who the hell was this unpleasant woman?

'She's a strumpet, that's what she is.' Freda's

lips folded into a thin line. 'Even when she was coming to my house, accepting my hospitality, she was cheating on my son.'

Horrified, Megan's resentment, her bottled up hatred, burst from her. 'Oh, change the record can't you? How dare you say such things? You're a bitch, do you know that ... an absolute bitch!'

Freda turned to Nathan. 'She thought I was born yesterday – claiming those nylons and all that food was sent by somebody's mother. We all know what nylons off a Yank means! I said she was a strumpet then, and I'll say it again.'

Nathan froze. His swift glance took in Megan's stricken face and taking her arm he drew her slightly back then moving forward he towered above the small wiry older woman. 'Say that again.' His voice was low, the three words spoken slowly to disguise his American accent.

Triumphant, Freda said, 'I'm only trying to warn you. Took nylons off a Yank she did, glory knows what else she took off for him. And then she had the nerve to lead my Terry up the garden path.'

'I don't know who you are,' his voice was as hard as ice, 'but I can easily find out. I'm sure there's a law in this country against defamation of character, there certainly is in America.'

'I'm only telling the truth!' But Freda's voice was less certain, her eyes darting between Megan and Nathan.

'No you're not. You're lying. And I should know, because as I think you've just guessed, I'm the Yank you're referring to. So, I think you owe this young lady an apology, don't you?'

385

'I'm not apologizing to *her!*'

Nathan turned to Megan. 'Who is this Terry?'

Megan's voice was tight, her throat closing against threatening tears. This could spoil everything! For Nathan to be a witness to such a dreadful scene – and the things she'd just said, calling an older woman a 'bitch'! Whatever must he think of her ... she managed to say, 'Terry Podmore – he was my boyfriend at one time. She's his mother.'

'Then Mrs Podmore, I can only thank God you're not mine! Now if you'll kindly move aside?' He took Megan's hand, feeling it trembling inside his own and Freda, shooting a venomous look at both of them, was forced to move out of their way. But that didn't prevent Megan from seeing the look of satisfaction on her face.

'I'm sorry about that.' Megan's voice was tight.

'It was a lousy thing to happen. What's wrong with the woman?'

'She's never forgiven me for what she calls "dumping" her son. It was months ago as well.' Her voice shook on the last words. Nathan glanced at her. His curiosity was biting – so there *had* been someone else. But now wasn't the time, and as they walked along in silence he realized with a jolt that the ugly encounter had served to crystallize his thoughts.

Turning to Megan he said, 'Is there anywhere we can sit and talk?'

Her voice wasn't steady. 'If we turn round and go back to the bottom lake, there are some secluded seats near to the boathouse.' Had Freda's accusation, her use of the word 'strumpet', sown

386

doubt in his mind? And Nathan still didn't know that she was illegitimate... Megan felt sick with nerves as they circled the lake and then she saw that her favourite seat – slightly recessed and sheltered by a stone wall – was unoccupied. But within seconds of their taking it, Nathan's arm was encircling her and he drew her close. With his lips on her hair he said, 'Megan, do you think you could put up with me for a bit longer?'

She raised her head to gaze up at him. 'How do you mean?'

'What if I stay on for ... let's say another couple of weeks.' He twisted round to face her. 'We need time sweetheart, time to get to know each other.'

'But can you do that? What about your boss, your work? Oh what a pity you weren't able to come and see me before you went up to Scotland.'

Nathan grimaced. 'But I did in a way.'

Megan was bewildered. 'I don't understand.'

He told of her of the night he'd sat in the car in the quiet street. How he'd seen her illuminated beneath the lamp post, laughing up at another guy. 'And when I saw him follow you into the house, well you can guess what I thought...'

'That would only have been John! He's just a sort of friend... Oh, Nathan...'

'I'm a lousy idiot aren't I?'

'Yes, you are!'

'Is this our first row?'

She began to laugh and Nathan leaned forward and kissed her gently on the lips. 'So it's a deal? I stay on for a couple of weeks?'

'If you're sure that you can.' Megan was becoming anxious. 'I wouldn't want you to lose your job.'

Nathan hesitated – he hated concealing things from her. 'You don't need to worry about me, honey. But it would drive me insane to kick my heels all day while you have to work. Can't you take the same time off?'

She stared at him in utter consternation. 'You mean two whole weeks?' How could she do that? Even if the firm allowed her to, she'd lose her wages.

Nathan saw her alarmed expression and said quickly, 'Okay it would be without pay, but don't you worry about that, honey. I'll cover it.'

'I'm not sure,' she began, 'I don't know whether they would...'

'But you *will* ask?'

'But...'

He leaned forward and taking her hand held it firmly in his own. 'Please sweetheart, just do it. Okay?'

Megan had expected questions the following morning, but not to find that her secret was already public knowledge. The moment she stepped into the decorating shop, Betty called, 'I hope he was worth it!'

'Keep yer voice down,' Minnie hissed, glancing hurriedly over her shoulder.

'It's all right, she's just gone out.' Betty glanced at Megan and raised her eyebrows. 'All dressed up again, I see. And we know why that is.'

'You were seen love, by one of the lithographers,' Minnie told her. 'Go on, I'm guessing it was that Yank. Am I right?'

Megan nodded, and seeing the colour rise in her cheeks, Lizzie chortled. 'The girl's in love.'

'Leave her alone,' Minnie snapped. 'You're only jealous.'

'Well, I certainly am,' Enid said as she joined them. 'I suppose he's rich as well.'

Megan shook her head. 'I don't think so.'

'Even so, I bet he's got a few bob more than us,' Betty said.

'You'd have a bit more yourself if you didn't buy so much from that Avon catalogue,' Lizzie snapped. The girls exchanged glances.

'People have different priorities,' Flo said, 'Betty likes to look nice, don't you love?'

'Oh take no notice of me,' Lizzie muttered. 'I got out of the bed the wrong side.'

Megan went to sit at the bench, every nerve alive for the sound of Miss Dawson returning. And when she did, within minutes she came over. 'And what happened to you yesterday afternoon?'

Megan turned to look up at her. 'Can I have a word, Miss Dawson?'

Straight-backed, the supervisor led the way to a quiet corner. Megan explained about Nathan. 'I'm sorry, Miss Dawson, I've never done anything like that before.'

Dora was unsmiling. 'Just this once we'll say no more about it. You'll lose an afternoon's pay and your bonus, though.'

Megan nodded, her hands were clammy with nerves and she wiped them on her overall. 'How do I go about applying for two weeks' unpaid leave?'

Dora drew a sharp intake of breath. 'Two weeks? Is this to spend time with him?'

'He's cancelling his sailing. We want to give ourselves a chance to get to know each other.' Megan suddenly saw a fleeting sadness in the supervisor's eyes and remembered that her fiancé had been killed in the war. She must have known moments like this, when time was limited, precious...

But when Dora spoke it was to be brisk. 'You'll need to put a request in writing, giving the reason, to the Departmental Head. If you haven't any paper with you, I'll let you have some.'

'Oh, thank you, please if you could. How long will it take? To get an answer, I mean?'

Dora's expression softened as she saw the anxiety in Megan's eyes. 'If you write it now, I'll take it in myself and tell him it's urgent.'

'Do you think I have a chance?'

'Well, it's not up to me, but orders have steadied down a bit, so you might be lucky.'

Megan went back to take her place at the bench, and Hilda whispered, 'Everything all right, love?'

She nodded. 'I'm going to ask for some time off.' And within minutes, Miss Dawson was calling her name. She gave Megan a sheet of paper, an envelope and handed her a Conway Stuart fountain pen. 'Don't press too hard or you'll damage the nib!'

The wait was agonising. The girls all had their own opinions.

'I reckon it all depends on the mood he's in,' Betty said. 'He can be a right mardy devil at times. What will you do, if the answer's "no"?'

'I'll take it anyway.'

There was a shocked silence then Lizzie said, 'Well, you'd soon get another job. Any of us could walk off here at lunchtime and find another one the same afternoon. I mean, there's loads of potbanks in Longton.'

'It wouldn't be the same though, not without you lot. I've been here since I left school.'

'Well, let's hope it won't come to that,' Minnie said. 'And I hope your American will see you right – about your lost wages I mean.'

'He's already offered but...'

'A bit tricky that, taking money off a fella,' Lizzie advised. 'It can make them think they've got rights – if you know what I mean.'

Megan bent her head to her work, uncomfortably aware of the truth in Lizzie's words. And the agonising wait continued, until at last just before the buzzer went at lunchtime, Miss Dawson came over to the bench. She touched Megan on the shoulder. 'It's all right. He says that you can take unpaid leave for the rest of this week and the following one.'

And, as Hilda later told the others, Megan couldn't have looked more delighted than if she'd won the football pools.

Chapter Forty-six

Early that same evening they went to look at the North Stafford Hotel in Stoke, where Nathan said it would make sense for him to transfer to. 'Why waste time in travelling, when we have so little of it.'

'I wish I could ask you to stay with me, but can you imagine the scandal? I'd never be able to hold my head up again.'

Nathan said, 'If they have a free table, I'll book us in for dinner.'

'We can't keep eating out,' Megan protested. 'We had dinner at the George again last night. It must be costing you a fortune.'

'I'll let you know when I'm down to my last dollar. And don't forget, I'll cover any wages you lose.'

Megan's lips set in a stubborn line. 'It wouldn't feel right, taking money from you.'

'But honey, you took the time off at my request.'

'Maybe I did, but you're paying for everything else, our meals, the petrol, and you've got the hotel as well.'

Nathan glanced at her. Was there anything about this lovely girl he didn't like?

Later, after dinner Nathan reserved a room for the rest of his stay, they drove home along the quiet rain drenched roads. As they drew up outside Megan's house, he glanced at the lamp shining outside, remembering the time he thought he'd lost her forever. What a fool he had been. But once inside Megan's half-hearted offer of cocoa was ignored. Their need was to be in each other's arms, with kisses and caresses that gradually grew ever more passionate, more urgent. Nathan's lips moved down to her throat, to the soft swell of her breasts, his hand gently beginning to exploring beneath her skirt until his fingers were stroking the soft skin between her suspenders, delighting in her response. But with a groan Nathan suddenly pulled away. 'Sweetheart I want you so much, it would be so easy … but it isn't going to happen, honey. I'm not saying that you would…'

Megan's cheeks flamed. So now she knew what love really was, the delicious sensations that lovemaking could arouse, the longing to be part of someone else. Would she have given in? Risked becoming pregnant as Eunice had? Her hand was shaking as she tidied her clothes and when Nathan eventually left, her last thought before drifting into a contented sleep, was that whatever this was leading to, whatever happened in the future, no-one could ever take that delicious knowledge away from her.

Jean's funeral was held the following morning at Holy Trinity Church in Meir, and despite Megan's protests, Nathan insisted on driving Megan to the church.

'It's hardly the best way to spend your extra time here.'

'Honey, just as long as I'm spending it with you.'

As they left the car Megan could see Flo and Minnie waiting outside the porch and said, 'Oh there's the other two girls.'

Nathan stared in disbelief at the two women standing alone and letting other people pass by. One seemed pretty ancient to him, and the other was fifty if she was a day.

Seeing his confusion Megan explained, 'We're all called "girls" at work, no matter what age we are.'

'Oh, I see.' He grinned, 'For a minute there I thought I was hallucinating. Sorry, honey, I shouldn't be joking, not on a serious occasion like this.'

Slowly they walked towards them and Megan introduced Nathan to her wide-eyed but subdued colleagues. Both were wearing dark clothes and hats, while Megan was in the grey Courtelle dress that she'd worn for both of her parents' funerals and a black angora beret. Then they joined the trickle of mourners entering the rapidly filling-up small church, and took their places in a pew near the back. When within minutes they were joined by a dark-suited slightly built man who glanced along the row and gave a nod of recognition, Megan whispered to Nathan, 'He's from management.'

And then the funeral procession arrived. To see the two white faced young boys walking with their father behind the coffin was heartbreaking. Bill had one hand on each of their shoulders, while his own were rigid, his neck stiff. And that was how he remained throughout the service. His self-controlled dignity tore at Megan's heart. The vicar spoke movingly and with sincerity about Jean, the hymns were the 23rd Psalm, and 'Abide with Me', and then it was all over, and within minutes Jean's family, some with downcast eyes, others staring tearfully straight ahead, were following the coffin as it was brought out of the church. Megan, watching them with unutterable sadness felt the warmth and comfort of Nathan gently taking her hand. She gave him a grateful smile and then they were joining the rest of the congregation and going out into the welcome fresh air, the surrounding trees a vital symbol of life and renewal.

Flo and Minnie stood awkwardly for a moment then Flo asked, 'Are you going to the cemetery?'

Megan shook her head. 'No, I thought just the church – how about you?'

'We're the same.'

'I'd better go and have a word with Bill.' Megan left Nathan with the two women and walked slowly over to where Jean's husband was standing with the boys among a small cluster of mourners, waiting for several moments until at last he was free. He turned to her and now that she could see him closely, Megan was shocked to see the ravages that grief had wrought. He looks she thought, ten years older. 'I'm so sorry, Bill,' she said. 'You know how much I thought of Jean. Tell me, would it be all right to come and see you in a couple of weeks?'

'Yes, of course.' His voice was weary. 'Thank you for coming Megan, and the others.' Megan looked down at the two silent boys, and tried to give them an encouraging smile. They had done so well, but how would it affect them when they saw their mother's coffin was being lowered into the ground? I'm glad I'm not going she thought, blinking away sudden tears. I don't think I could bear it.

Meanwhile Nathan was good-naturedly fending off questions from Minnie. 'You weren't over here in the war then?'

He shook his head. 'No ma'am.'

'And how do you like the Potteries?' Flo asked in her best speaking voice.

'It's a great little place. Full of history and,' he lowered his voice, 'the girls are smashing.'

They both laughed. 'I can see why Megan's fallen for *you!*' Minnie said.

Flo nudged her. 'Minnie...'

'Well he must know she has, why else would she take time off without pay?'

Nathan hid a smile. 'She won't lose out by it, I promise.'

Minnie's sharp gaze swept over him. 'Good lad,' she said and as Megan came back and the funeral cars began to move away she said, 'We'll be off now love.'

'Shall I offer them a lift?' Nathan murmured as the two women began to move away.

Megan shook her head. 'No, they can walk to the factory from here and they'll be glad of the fresh air.'

'That poor guy,' Nathan said, as he unlocked the car door and came round to open the passenger door for her.

Megan nodded. 'He's made of stern stuff is Bill, he'll manage somehow, but it won't be easy.'

She told him of Janet's offer to bake for the bereaved family. 'I thought it was really kind of her, she doesn't even know them.'

Back at the house, and changed into a summer dress, Megan picked up the letter from Audrey that had arrived just as they'd been leaving for the funeral. She held it up. 'Do you mind?'

Nathan was settled in an armchair preparing to read a copy of the *Times* that he'd brought with him from the hotel, 'Of course not. Who's it from?'

'Audrey. You know – she used to be my closest friend and lives in Wales.'

Megan flopped into the opposite armchair and slit the envelope. A few minutes later, Nathan glanced up to see her smiling. 'Listen to this,' she said, *'It worked! The new shoes, I mean. I made sure I was wearing them and hovering about – you know what I mean, when the post was due. The very next week he asked me out – to go to a concert by a male voice choir. We got on really well, his name's Dai, and I'm on cloud nine.'* Megan laughed then explained, 'Dai is their postman and Audrey's fancied him for ages. I told her to invest in a pair of court shoes – you know, with a high heel? It certainly worked for me!'

Nathan put down his paper. 'How do you mean?'

Megan felt a bit sheepish. 'You wouldn't believe what I used to look like, Nathan. It was only after mum died that I began to come out of my shell.'

'When I first met you, I thought you were like a butterfly emerging from a chrysalis,' Nathan

397

said with a grin.

'Was it that obvious? Anyway, it was only then that I bought my first pair of heeled shoes and well – my whole life changed.'

He raised his eyebrows. 'You were wearing shoes with a heel when I met you in Bethesda. I remember thinking what slim ankles you had.'

'That was the second time I wore them.'

'And what happened the first time?'

She laughed. 'I was flirted with, believe it or not for the first time. Actually it was Ben, the one who got Eunice into trouble.' Megan hesitated, 'I worry about her sometimes. Even though she knows he's got an eye for the girls, she's crazy about him. But I don't trust him.' She paused then said softly, 'Not like I trust you – especially after last night.'

Chapter Forty-seven

The following evening Tom, sitting in his armchair and trying to have a quiet smoke was complaining that Clarice was driving him nuts. Once more she was peering out of the window. 'Drat, the car's left and I missed it – again!' She swung round to him. 'There's definitely something going on. That was the same black car as in the last couple of days.'

'Cease your fretting woman and make the cocoa.' Tom yawned. 'And stop being so nosy, it's a wonder you haven't put a glass to the wall.'

Clarice gave him what was for her the nearest to 'a dirty look'. It was one thing for her to peep out from behind the curtain, but to suggest that she'd eavesdrop...

The following morning she listened in vain for the sound of Megan's front door closing. So the girl hadn't gone to work! By half-past nine, Clarice couldn't wait any longer. Megan greeted her with a smile. 'I wondered when you'd be coming round.'

Clarice stepping inside said, 'What on earth's going on? You're obviously not ill. And whose is that car I've seen?'

Megan led the way into the sitting-room and turned to smile at her. 'You'd better sit down. You won't believe what I'm going to tell you.'

Later on Tom had hardly recovered from his shift at the pit, before Clarice confronted him. 'Don't make any arrangements for tomorrow night,' she said, 'pub or no pub. We're entertaining.'

He lowered his pipe. 'Entertaining who?'

She told him about Nathan. 'The girl's that crazy about him that she's taken almost two weeks off work. There's nobody else to keep an eye out for her Tom, so we'd better see what sort of man he is. I've asked Rita and Jack round as well. Just a few beers and I'll make some sandwiches, that sort of thing.'

He frowned. 'I thought we'd got the twins for the night.'

'That's why I picked tomorrow. You can tell a lot about a man by what he's like with kids, and it won't seem so formal. I think we ought to do this Tom, I feel a bit responsible for her in a way.'

He nodded. 'Yes, you're right. Did Rita say whether Jack's heard anything about his chest?'

She nodded. 'There's no sign of silicosis, thank God. But he has got a weakness there and the doctor's advised him against keeping pigeons.'

'That'll please Rita.'

'If he takes any notice, that is.'

'Jack may be many things, anti-social being one of them, but he's no fool, Clarice. If that's what the doctor says, believe me he'll take notice.'

That same evening Celia was waiting for her transatlantic call to come through. Verity had gone to bed, muttering about reading a 'light' novel and as the only telephone was in the hall, Celia was hoping that Verity's room, situated as it was at the far end of the landing would prove to be sufficiently sound-proof. Impatiently she hovered by the receiver and snatched it up at the first ring.

'James?'

'Hello Mum, is anything wrong?'

'No, everything's fine, and with you?'

'Terrific.' His voice was light, confident.

'So you like New York.'

'It's a wonderful city, so fast-paced.'

Celia drew a deep breath. 'James, I don't want to interfere but don't you think you should be saying that to your wife?'

She could almost hear the silence on the line. 'Is she making an issue of it?'

'Well naturally she's wondering why she hasn't heard from you.'

His voice was evasive. 'It's just been so busy, Mum. I promise I'll call her tomorrow.'

A minute later, Celia replaced the receiver thoughtfully. It was obvious that her son was hiding something. And the initial adrenalin in his voice – was that simply due to New York, or ... she felt a dread in the pit of her stomach. Yet would she really be surprised if James met someone else? As Celia switched off the hall light and began to climb the stairs, she wondered yet again how one guest's presence could so disrupt the tranquillity of the house. But when that guest was Verity ... for example it was obvious that she found their afternoon reading sessions tedious; she read in such a bored tone that the hour had become excruciating for both of them.

Megan and Nathan spent the following day walking in Dovedale. The ancient limestone gorge with its steep wooded hills of rock and gurgling stream was the perfect backdrop for them to stroll, sometimes holding hands, at others with their arms entwined. Nathan was relieved to be able to breathe in clean fresh air; Megan was content because she was with him. They had lunch at the nearby Izaak Walton hotel with its many original features. The fact that it had been converted from a 17th century farmhouse and named after the famous author of the Compleat Angler fascinated Nathan. And of course they found more than one secluded spot when close in each other's arms, they entered their own world. It was Megan told Nathan, a 'shining day.'

And they talked. Or at least Megan realised

afterwards, she talked. She found it so easy to confide in him, to let the words pour out of her, about her childhood, the silver-backed hairbrush and the visit to Mrs Finney. Hardly daring to look at him, she found the courage to confess that she was illegitimate. 'So you see,' she said, 'I'm not really respectable.'

Nathan caught at her hand. 'Honey, that's a crazy thing to say. Didn't you tell me that you were legally adopted? And by your real father as well. Heck, what else could he have done for you, but to give you his name?'

Megan felt relief flood through her. So he didn't mind? 'I hadn't thought of it like that.' She undid the clasp on her handbag and taking out a small envelope, showed him the snap of Elvina. 'I've begun to carry it with me.'

Nathan gazed down it, his lips twisting with compassion. 'I can see where you get your looks from.'

'It all explained so much,' Megan said. 'I never did look anything like my mother, or who I thought *was* my mother. I can understand now why Dad was so strict, so protective. I don't think he realised that he was draining the spirit out of me. He was just trying to shield me from the world.'

'He sounds like a man with a deep conscience which is never an easy thing to live with. But what about your mother, did she go along with all this?'

'Mum tended to defer to his wishes in everything. Is your mother like that?'

Nathan thought of Elizabeth with her quiet but

402

strong personality, and shook his head. 'Nope, I guess not. I think she and my father are sort of equal partners.'

'Tell me about your sister. What does she look like for instance?'

'Helen? I guess she's quite attractive. Brown hair – not as dark as yours, and our eyes are the same colour. But she's petite like Mom, not tall and rangy like me.'

'And are you *sure* they didn't mind? When you phoned and told them you were staying on longer?'

'No. Like I told you, they could see the sense in it.' He gazed down at her and when she smiled up at him, paused as they reached an old tree by the side of the narrow and now deserted path. Nathan leaned back against the rough bark of the thick trunk and drew her towards him. As Megan snuggled into him she felt his lips on her hair, on her forehead and he murmured, 'We've done lots of talking honey, but I'm dying to kiss you, so while we have the chance...'

By seven-thirty that evening, Clarice's household was organised like a military operation. The twins were issued with comics and told to sit quietly on the floor, Tom had at last found his collar studs and presented himself for inspection, while the refreshments were under covered plates, the glasses polished and paper napkins ready folded.

'Men are the best judges of other men,' Clarice told him, 'and two heads are better than one. That's why I'm glad that Jack's coming. To be honest, I wasn't sure he would.'

But as Rita told Tom when they arrived, Jack had 'a lot of time' for Megan. 'He thinks she's coped really well since she was left on her own.'

Nathan of course was well aware of the reason behind the invitation. Megan had told him how supportive her neighbours were, and he'd hooted with laughter when at last she admitted that she'd deliberately sought him out that first time in Bethesda. 'I can't believe I ever did it,' she confessed. 'I must have been crazy, thinking I had to find a husband just to exist.' She smiled at him, wondering how it was possible to feel so at ease with another person. 'And then I went to a dance with Eunice and met Terry. We went out together for a few months and then...' She described to him the young couple she'd seen in the park one Sunday afternoon. 'They were so in love, Nathan, so happy. It made me realize how unfair I was being, not only to myself but also to Terry. He deserved a girl who could love him like that, and I knew I never could. That's when I finished with him.'

'And his mother never forgave you! Wow, she was a battle-axe if ever I met one.'

'I pity whoever ends up as her daughter-in-law.' But Megan's tone was bitter, and Nathan guessed that the scene in the park hadn't been the only ugly one between them. And then promptly on time they presented themselves at the front door of the 'joined on' house like Megan's. It was the twins who broke the ice. Nathan had just accepted a beer from Tom, inwardly grimacing when he felt the temperature of the glass, when

404

one of the youngsters on being told that the visitor came from Kansas in America, piped up, 'Do you know Dorothy?'

Nathan began to laugh. 'Well, let me think. Would that be the Dorothy who has a little dog called Toto? Who was in the Wizard of Oz?'

'Yes!' Both children's faces lit up.

'I should think I do. I bet you don't know the song, *"Somewhere over the Rainbow"*.'

They both scrambled up to give a proud if not altogether tuneful rendition, whereupon Nathan lifted the flap on his jacket pocket. 'Now I wonder if anything is hiding inside here.' He grinned as two small hands discovered a couple of Hershey chocolate bars.

Clarice glanced at him with approval. 'I've heard of those,' she said, 'but I've never actually seen one before.'

'Knowing your rationing, I brought a few with me.'

'Can we eat them now? Please...'

'Do they always speak in unison?' Nathan said as Clarice smiled and nodded.

'A lot of the time, but we're hoping they'll grow out of it.' She looked at the tall American. He had such an engaging grin she could certainly see why Megan had fallen for him.

'So, what's it like where you live, Nathan?' Rita was looking smart in a red twinset and pearls. 'Different from around here, I'll bet.'

He laughed. 'It certainly is. Kansas is real cowboy country.'

'I hear you're in tractors and things,' Jack said, sitting stiffly on one of the dining chairs. 'Is that what brings you over here?'

Nathan nodded. 'That's right. We're always on the lookout to improve our export trade. You also export a lot – china from the Potteries is world-famous.'

Jack nodded. 'There's about 80,000 people employed in the pottery industry or at least that's what I heard.'

Nathan blew a low whistle. 'Say that's some number.'

'And what did you do in the war?' Jack asked.

'Came in late,' Tom said promptly, only to be shot a severe glance by Clarice.

'Don't worry, we're used to it,' Nathan told her with a grin. 'I was out in the Pacific, Jack, on reconnaissance mainly.'

Megan gave a teasing glance at Tom. 'The last time Nathan was here, he went to watch Port Vale. He said how good they were.'

As she'd anticipated Tom exploded. 'If you wanted to see real football you should have gone to watch Stoke City. In fact there's a match on Saturday if you want to come. We're playing Manchester United.'

'Tom!' Clarice was exasperated. 'He's only got a few days with Megan; he hardly wants to spend it watching eleven men kick a ball around.'

'Say, Manchester United is a pretty famous club. In other circumstances I'd enjoy seeing that game but...'

Megan suddenly had a thought. 'Why don't you go? It would give me a chance to go up and see Celia and explain about Sunday.'

Nathan gave her a grin. 'Okay then Tom. Shall

I come and pick you up?'

'I didn't tell you it was an away match – but you could take us down to Stoke Railway Station.'

'Hey, that would be even better. You can get a real taste of a country travelling by rail.'

And as Clarice got up to go into the kitchen, Megan looked around the small cosy room and felt a glow of content. It was wonderful to see Nathan so relaxed with her friends. Sometimes she felt she would burst with happiness. What had Miss Dawson referred to – a golden time? She had been talking then about Megan's holiday in Eastbourne but this period she was spending with Nathan was even more than that, it was a gilded one and she was fiercely determined not to spoil a single second of it by wondering about the future. If she got her heart broken then she would just have to cope with it.

Chapter Forty-eight

It was Janet who opened the door on Saturday afternoon. With a surprised but pleased expression she stood aside for Megan to come into the hall. 'What a shame Celia isn't here – she's taken Verity to Stafford.'

'Oh, what a shame, I've got such a lot to tell you both.'

'And it's all good judging by that glow in your eyes. Are you going to tell me who put it there?'

Megan began to laugh. 'Is it that obvious?'

'You'd have to be a blind biddy not to see it.'

'It's Nathan.' Megan's smile was, as Janet later told Celia, enough to light up a room. 'He's back over here.'

'The American you told us about?'

Megan nodded. 'So I was wondering, do you think I could work this afternoon instead of to-morrow?'

'I don't see why not. I was going to ask you to clean and defrost the refrigerator. That can be done just as easily today, and I can soon sort out the ironing.' With a delighted smile Janet was already heading for the kitchen. 'I'll come and sit with you a wee while and then you can tell me everything. And here I was thinking it was going to be a boring afternoon.'

It was half an hour later when Celia and Verity, both laden with shopping bags, returned. As they flopped into armchairs in the drawing room, Janet told them of Megan's presence and Celia could see by her attempted signals with her bushy eyebrows that she had news. 'Verity,' Celia said, 'why not treat yourself to a hot bath before we have tea and scones. You could use some of that new bath essence we bought.'

'What a good idea, I do feel rather tempted. I always find shopping for clothes so exhausting.' Languidly, she got up and headed for the door. 'A good session though, wasn't it?'

'You certainly found some nice things.' Then as soon as Verity had disappeared, Celia said, 'Well Janet? Don't keep me in suspense. Why is Megan here today instead of tomorrow?'

'Celia – the lassie's head over heels in love.'

Now it was Celia's finely arched eyebrows that shot up.

'You remember her telling us about that American?'

'You mean Nathan?'

Janet nodded. 'He's back.'

Celia listened spellbound to the whole story. 'You mean she's taken time off without pay? But she can't afford to do that! I can't believe it. She must be besotted.'

'You'd only need one look at her to know that.'

'Oh Janet, what are we going to do? We don't know what sort of a man he is? Suppose he's not to be trusted.'

'That's what I'm worried about. She's too fine a girl to be taken advantage of.'

'We must meet him.' Celia's tone was decisive. 'I shall give a dinner party next week and invite them both. Now then, let me think who else. Barbara Eardley would be a good choice. She has Megan's best interests at heart and she's got a shrewd head on her.'

'You can hardly sit the poor man down with a table full of women,' Janet protested. 'Remember there'll be Verity as well.' Janet kept her tone casual. 'Why not invite that auctioneer chappie? It could be a sort of thank you for all his help.'

'Now that *is* an idea.' Celia brightened. 'And we could invite Barbara's minister too; after all he's known Megan since childhood. So let me see,' she counted on her fingers, 'that's you and I and Verity, then Megan and Nathan, Barbara and the minister, Mr Marsden and his wife...'

'Maybe he's not married,' Janet said hopefully.

Celia began to laugh. 'You don't give up, do you?'

'I liked him.'

'I'm sure his wife does as well! Now what do you think? Shall we say next Thursday? We don't want to leave it too long.'

Janet nodded, but then glancing at Celia saw her frown. 'What is it?'

'It's an awful thing to say, but it's Verity. I just hope she behaves – as far as Megan is concerned. As we've said, she seems to have her knife into the girl. I just don't understand it.'

But within minutes, they both had even more cause to be bewildered.

'That girl is a thief!' Verity burst into the room and confronted them both, one hand holding out an amber pendant on a fine gold chain.

'What on earth do you mean?'

But Megan was close on Verity's heels, her face flushed with anger. 'She's lying!'

'Just a minute, both of you...' Celia rose from her armchair, while Janet hovered in the doorway. 'What on earth do you mean, Verity?'

'I caught her red-handed. There she was – in the ironing room – actually holding it in her hand. A minute later and it would have been in her pocket.' Her expression was one of triumph.

Celia looked at Megan's stricken face and then at a loss glanced wildly across at Janet, whose own face was grim. 'And where did you leave this pendant Verity?'

'On my dressing table – I wore it yesterday.'

Megan burst out. 'I never go into Verity's room. In any case, I would never steal anything – ever.

The pendant was mixed up with the ironing.'

'That's a paltry excuse,' Verity snapped. 'You don't even do my ironing.'

Celia knew this was true.

Megan was furious. 'But...'

In distress, Celia forced the question, 'Megan – did you have the pendant in your hand?'

'Yes, but I was only admiring it. Honestly Celia, it was caught up in a blouse. The chain is so fine that I had to untangle it.' Megan was struggling to control tears of hurt and injustice. As if she would ever...

'Again,' Verity said with a sneer, 'a likely story.'

Celia held up a hand. 'I think we all know your view.'

Megan's throat closed in panic. This couldn't be happening ... for her to be accused of *stealing*...

Nonplussed, Celia turned to Verity. 'I hope you know Verity, that this is a very serious accusation.'

Verity's glittering gaze swept over Megan. 'I think we should call the police!'

Megan gasped – the police? 'But I haven't done anything!' She appealed in horror to Celia and Janet, 'You can't possibly believe her.'

Janet stepped forward. 'I don't for one.'

Celia turned to Verity. 'There has to be some explanation...'

'Oh I see,' Verity's lips tightened. 'You're more inclined to take *her* word against that of your own daughter-in-law!'

Celia felt as if she was in the middle of a nightmare, and then Janet suddenly said. 'It's Saturday!'

They all turned to stare at her.

'Don't you see? I usually put ready the clothes to be ironed ready for Megan on Sundays. Verity, didn't you put aside a blouse ready to press it? The pink one with the dolman sleeves?'

'Yes, but...'

Janet's face flooded with relief. 'That's the answer. With Megan coming today, I was put out of my usual routine. I must have put it in with Megan's ironing by mistake.'

Verity's eyes narrowed. 'That doesn't explain what she was doing with my pendant.'

'I told you,' Megan burst out. 'The chain was caught up in it, in the collar. I admit that it was in my hand when Verity came in, but I'd no intention of taking it.'

'May I see the pendant, Verity?' Celia held out her hand and examined it. 'See, the clasp is broken. It must have attached itself to the blouse when you took it off and you didn't notice.'

'Let me see...' Verity almost snatched it from her.

'I think you owe Megan an apology, don't you?' Verity's face was like granite and when she remained silent, Celia's voice was razor sharp. 'Verity...'

With fury and ill-grace, Verity snapped, 'All right ... I apologise.'

'Good,' Celia said. 'So that's an end to it. I'm very sorry Megan, that you should have been subjected to such unpleasantness.'

Megan went back up the broad staircase, and on seeing again the pink blouse thought, thank God I never got around to ironing the damn thing. I wouldn't cross the road for that spiteful cat, never mind iron her clothes. On an impulse she flung the blouse violently into a corner of the room.

'Did that relieve your feelings?' Janet stood in the doorway.

'She's lucky I didn't rip it apart,' Megan muttered, then said, 'Sorry Janet, I didn't really mean that.'

'I wouldn't have blamed you if you had. She's not an easy one, that girl.'

'I just can't work out why she hates me so much.'

'It's no use asking me how her mind works. I doubt though that it's you in particular. It's more what you represent.'

'How do you mean?' Seeing Janet hesitate, Megan said, 'Sorry, I'm not asking you to be disloyal; I know it's difficult for you to discuss Verity with me.'

'Just forget about the whole thing,' Janet advised. 'I'm sure you've more important things on your mind. Are you spending the evening with Nathan?'

Megan smiled at her. 'Yes I am. And Janet ... thanks for sticking up for me.'

Downstairs, Celia was appalled that such a scene should have occurred in her home. And suddenly her patience, long worn thin, snapped. She went to sit opposite Verity, who was sulkily flicking through the pages of *Country Life*. 'Do you mind telling me what all that was about?'

'How do you mean?'

413

'I would be most interested to know Verity, what exactly it is that you have against Megan?' She held up a hand, 'No, my dear please don't try to deny it. It's been apparent from the first moment.'

'It's a free country, isn't it? Surely one can like or dislike whoever one chooses.'

'That is of course true. But at times your behaviour towards her is intolerable.'

Verity shrugged her shoulders. 'I'm sorry if you feel that.' She put down her magazine. 'To be honest Celia, you do seem to have taken on the role of protector towards that girl. I would remind you that your son should be your priority.'

Celia felt a jolt. 'Are you questioning my role as a mother?'

'No, of course I'm not. But one can't help wondering about your motive in all this. Sometimes I think you see Megan as a replacement for the daughter you lost.'

Celia became very quiet. 'I don't think I've ever told you about that.'

Verity's tone was bitter. 'You don't confide in me about anything, we don't seem to have that sort of relationship. It was James who told me.'

Celia was taken aback. Not because her son had talked about her loss, Verity *was* his wife. But it had never occurred to her that despite her best efforts, the coolness she felt towards her daughter-in-law might have been sensed. Was it possible that Verity's dislike of Megan was based not just on snobbishness but also on jealousy? Celia recalled that Verity had never seemed close to her own mother. The daughter of globe-trotting parents and sent away to boarding school at a very early age – there wouldn't have been much opportunity for a close-knit family life. Have I been mistaken, she thought. Is Verity more sensitive, does she have more depth than I'd thought? After gazing helplessly at the slim, expensively dressed girl, her face set in discontented lines, Celia could only say, 'Then perhaps my dear, we should both make an effort to become closer.'

Tom and Nathan returned from Manchester in good spirits despite the fact that Stoke lost the match with two goals scored against them. Tom, being a seasoned supporter was philosophical about it.

Clarice was more interested in his opinion of Nathan. 'He's a decent bloke,' Tom told her. 'Mind you, he wasn't giving anything away, so it's no use you asking me anything else.' He rubbed his hands together. 'Now then love, what's for tea, I'm right clemmed.'

And on the other side of the wall, a hungry Nathan wondering the same thing, found himself despatched to the nearest fish and chip shop while Megan warmed plates, put out salt and vinegar and cut several rounds of bread and thinly applied butter. 'You can now regard yourself as a fully-fledged tourist,' she told him, when with satisfaction he finished the meal. 'We British are famous for our fish and chips.'

Nathan grinned and leaned back to enjoying his cup of tea. 'So, what do we do tomorrow? A nostalgia trip – Bethesda followed by lunch at the George?'

Megan smiled. 'Perfect.'

'And I thought that as we're over that way, perhaps you'd like to carry on to Biddulph. Visit your grandparents' grave – take some flowers or something. And you could show me Blaisden House.'

Megan's face lit up. 'Could we? Oh, but flowers … there'll be nowhere open.'

Nathan nodded across to where Megan's modest vase was almost overflowing with the bouquet he'd bought her the day before. 'Why not take those?'

'You wouldn't mind?'

He smiled and shook his head. 'Sweetheart, I'd buy you a florist's shop if you wanted one.'

They returned to find Celia's hand-delivered invitation waiting, saying there was no need to reply unless they couldn't accept.

Megan read it out with delight. 'I'm dying for you to meet them.'

'Say that sounds great. I'm being checked out again, I guess! Hey is this a formal thing, do I have to wear a tux?'

Megan laughed. 'You mean a dinner jacket? I shouldn't think so, otherwise Celia would have said.'

The next few days seemed to fly past, with the Dorothy Cafe becoming their 'special place'. At lunchtime it offered a four course meal and Megan was intrigued to discover that local businessmen often had their own regular tables. And later in the afternoon dishes on the menu included gammon and egg and Welsh rarebit, or they could choose afternoon tea with such treats as chocolate éclairs and custard tarts. Megan wanted to cook for them at home, saying that it would be cheaper, but Nathan just grinned at her. 'Honey, I haven't stayed in England to wait while you slave over a hot stove. Besides this is our vacation.'

On Wednesday, she took him over to the Market Hall and introduced him to Iris, whose creased face split into a broad smile when Nathan bought a lavish selection of her most expensive blooms. 'Yer lucky devil,' she whispered as they left. 'Make the most of this one, love.'

When later an excited Debra arrived to give Megan her monthly cut, shampoo and set, she exclaimed with disappointment, 'Oh, he's not here.'

Megan laughed. 'I hardly want him to see me with my hair in rollers. He's gone to get changed.'

'It's so romantic!' Debra breathed. 'Just like on the films.'

'And a lot of it is due to you,' Megan told her. 'Can you remember when you came that first time? When my hair was parted in the middle?'

'And you wore those awful slides!' Debra giggled. 'You were a right frump.'

'Thanks a lot. And how's your love life, everything still okay?'

'Smashing,' Debra said. 'He's hoping to get leave soon.' She paused, comb in hand. 'But what's going to happen with you and Nathan? When he goes back, I mean?'

Megan took a long time to answer. Then she said quietly, 'If only I knew.'

Chapter Forty-nine

Celia glanced over to the sofa where Verity was flicking through a magazine. 'You've remembered that we have people coming tonight.' Her voice was careless, but every word had been rehearsed.

'I'd forgotten, you did fleetingly mention it. How many will there be?'

'Just a few people I owe a favour to. Barbara Eardley is a fellow member of my children's committee and a stalwart member of a local chapel in Longton. She will be bringing her minister. There's an auctioneer who has been helpful to me and...' Celia paused. Janet glanced across at her but kept her expression bland.

Verity put down her magazine. 'I can't say that it sounds very stimulating. Sorry Celia, I know what these duty dinner parties can be like.'

'Of course you don't have to be present. I was thinking about that old school friend of yours in Sandbach. Didn't you say you were hoping to meet up with her? This might be a good opportunity, after all you're due to go home at the weekend.'

Verity considered. 'Maybe I could wangle an overnight stay. It's a bit short notice but...' She glanced at her watch, rose from the sofa and went into the hall. The cadence of her voice, rising and falling followed by laughter drifted into the drawing room, and Janet whispered to Celia, 'Fingers crossed!'

Seconds later Verity returned. 'All fixed,' she said airily, 'her husband's away on business too.' She added with some bitterness, 'But I expect *he* phones on a regular basis!'

'He probably isn't in New York,' Celia pointed out.

'Maybe not, but it isn't as if we're paupers!'

Celia said smoothly, 'It will be good for you to have a chance to talk over old times.'

'We're going out for dinner, so I'll change and then pack a bag. You know, I'm quite looking forward to it!'

Celia watched her leave. She knew that she'd blatantly manipulated the girl; not one of her finer moments but it didn't trouble her conscience in the slightest.

Megan and Nathan were the first to arrive, a deliberate ploy by Celia. After being favourably impressed by Nathan's firm handshake, direct gaze and exquisite flowers she sipped her gin and tonic and thoughtfully watched as he answered a question from Janet.

'Yes, I'll be home in plenty of time for Thanksgiving, my mother would never forgive me if I missed that.'

'My Robbie went to New England once.' Janet turned to Celia. 'I never did tell you that. He liked it fine and said people in Boston were very cultured.'

'That would describe them perfectly.' Nathan smiled at them both. 'We have our own share of culture in Wichita though, which is only a few miles away from where I live.'

'You've been to London of course?' Celia said.

'Yes, several times. I had thought of taking Megan there for the weekend – all on the level – but she seems to think that would paint her as a scarlet woman.'

Celia laughed. She glanced over at Megan, who was looking elegant in a pretty white blouse with sheer sleeves and plain pencil skirt. Around her neck was a row of pearls with matching earrings, but her true beauty was in the happiness that shone out of her. Oh my dear, Celia thought, a sudden lump in her throat, how wonderful that this has happened to you. She looked again at Nathan. The young American was undoubtedly attractive, and his tall broad physique gave an impression of strength, steadiness. But Celia thought, as Nathan was talking to Janet that he didn't seem to fit the picture of an office worker, even one who travelled for his firm. His shoes were too good, they could even be bespoke. His jacket was expertly cut, his shirt of excellent quality, his tie of silk. And when one considered that he was staying at the North Stafford Hotel ... or was it merely that Americans were paid higher salaries?

Nathan found himself liking instinctively the woman he thought of as Megan's fairy-god-mother. Elizabeth, he mused with an inward smile, would describe her as the epitome of an English gentlewoman. Janet on the other hand seemed a true Scot, practical and sensible and typical he suddenly thought, of the many pioneers who had helped to open up the West.

And then Barbara and her minister – who proved to be a thin bespectacled man who looked as if he would benefit from a decent meal – arrived. Several minutes later, amid the bustle of introductions and drinks, the door bell pealed again. Janet didn't move, instead she shot a glance at Celia, who with an amused smile excused herself to the minister and went out into the hall.

'I'm so glad you could come.'

Robert Marsden, in a well-cut camel overcoat gave her a warm smile. 'It was a very welcome invitation.'

'A little short notice, I'm afraid but...'

His intelligent eyes above his greying moustache met her own. 'Celia, I was glad to have an excuse to see you again.'

A few seconds later with him by her side, she introduced him to everyone and soon the drawing room was buzzing with the low sound of conversation. Barbara, politely listening to the minister and Janet discussing congregation numbers, watched a glowing Megan at the side of Nathan and couldn't help remembering the anxious girl she'd found in tears in Longton library. She felt a stab of pride – what an inspired idea it had been to bring Celia into her life.

Later seeing that Janet was beginning to leave the room, Megan went over to her. 'Is there anything I can do to help?'

'I *could* do with a wee hand, if you don't mind.'

'Of course I don't.' Megan threw an apologetic smile at Nathan who was talking to Robert, and after following the housekeeper into the kitchen whispered, 'It was such a relief to find that Verity isn't here.'

Janet handed her a small white apron and gave a quiet smile. 'I can imagine.' She checked on the vegetables, and then seeing Megan's expectant expression murmured back, 'It's early yet, but Nathan seems a fine young man to me.'

Megan's face lit up. Then glancing around she said, 'What would you like me to do?'

'Could you put the plates to warm? We're having melon for the first course, so that's already on the table. And if you could get the ice bucket and take in two bottles of white wine from the fridge. I've already opened the red.' She turned and said in a low voice, 'What do you think of Robert? He's a widower, his wife died three years ago.'

'He seems really nice.' Megan began to laugh. 'Don't tell me that you're matchmaking?'

'And why not – Celia's a very attractive woman.'

'I shall take a lot more notice of him then.'

It was when Megan emerged from the dining room that she saw the flashing lights in the drive. To her utter dismay within seconds the front door opened and Verity stalked in. She brushed past Megan without a word and went into the drawing-room where Megan heard Celia say in astonishment, 'Why Verity, whatever's happened?'

'The car broke down just outside Newcastle and I had to wait ages for the AA. Even then the wretched man couldn't fix it; all he could offer was a tow, so I thought I'd better come back here.' Her glance swept the cluster of people and then her eyes glittered as she saw the tall

American. In a black cocktail dress with a plunging back, Verity gave him the sole benefit of her brilliant smile.

'I'd better introduce you to everyone,' Celia said evenly, and minutes later explained, 'Nathan is over from America on business.'

'Now this does promise to be an interesting evening,' Verity almost purred. 'You must sit next to me at dinner and tell me all about the States.'

'Verity's husband is over in New York,' Celia explained and then turned to Robert. 'May I get you another drink?'

'Thank you.' Leaving Verity to talk to Nathan, Robert followed her to the sideboard. 'I'm so pleased that I was able to help in that little matter of Blaisden House.'

'I would appreciate your discretion though.'

He smiled at her. 'Of course, and what a lovely home you have.'

Janet had received the news of Verity's arrival with a heavy sigh. 'Now isn't that typical? At least we weren't at table.' She was already taking another melon from the refrigerator. 'Hopefully there should be enough of everything.'

'Would you like me to set the extra place?'

'Would you? And then could you tell Celia that I'll need another five minutes.'

Megan glanced through the open door of the drawing room as she went past. Just as she'd expected, Verity was monopolising Nathan, smiling up at him, her slender body tilted almost provocatively towards his. I should have warned him about her, she thought suddenly, who knows what poison she's pouring into his ears. And I'd better take off this apron otherwise that madam will be treating me like a servant all night. But it was too late. She had only just relayed Janet's message when Verity's imperious tone reached her. 'I'll have another gin and tonic, please Megan.'

Megan saw a flash of consternation in Celia's eyes and gave her a reassuring smile. Silently, she took the glass from Verity's red-tipped languid hand and went over to the sideboard. It was then that Verity, her clear voice and its perfect vowels carrying throughout the room explained to Nathan, 'Megan is a local factory girl, a sort of protégé of my mother-in-law.'

There was a stunned silence. Megan sensed Celia move forward, but Nathan was even swifter. His American accent more pronounced in a voice tight with anger he said, 'That's the difference between your country and mine, Verity. In the States we have respect for someone who works for a living.'

Verity hesitated for a split second, then recovered herself and said lightly, 'How very quaint.'

The clink of ice as it was dropped into Verity's glass was the only sound in the stunned silence, and Megan added a slice of lemon and then walked over to her. 'I hope this is all right for your high standards,' she said, 'I did wash my hands before I came.'

Verity's eyes narrowed then she gave a tinkling laugh. 'What a droll sense of humour.' Taking the glass from Megan's outstretched hand she said, 'Doesn't Janet need you in the kitchen?'

'I shouldn't think so.' Megan paused. 'Actually

Verity, I happen to be here as a guest.'

Verity stared at her then frowned. 'You're a guest? Celia didn't mention it.' As she saw Megan move to Nathan's side where he held out a hand to take hers, Verity's eyes widened in horror. 'You can't mean that you two are...'

'Here together?' Megan's voice was cool and dismissive. 'Yes, of course. Life really is full of surprises isn't it? And it is so rude to make personal remarks, Verity. I thought you would have been taught that at finishing school.'

Celia came over and turned to both of the girls. 'May I remind you that you're both guests in my house?'

Later that evening as they drove home, Nathan said, 'That Verity dame is a right bitch, honey. Don't let her get to you.'

'I felt awful when Celia said that – about being guests in her house, but at least it made Verity refrain from any more digs and spiteful remarks.'

'She sure thinks people should know their place. What sort of guy is her husband?'

'James? He's not like her at all; in fact he's rather nice.'

'With a mother like Celia he would be. And as for Janet, she sure can cook. That apple pie was terrific.

'And was I was approved of?' Nathan turned and grinned at her. 'I saw a few people whisper when they said goodbye.'

Megan laughed. 'You know you were.' The distance was so short that already they were turning into her road. 'Are you tired? It's pretty late, so if you just want to drop me off...'

He turned to her and said in low voice, 'Are *you?* Tired, I mean.'

She thought of the flimsy blouse she was wearing, how easily it would slip down from her shoulders. She murmured as the car drew to a halt beneath the lamplight, 'I'm sure I could be tempted to stay awake for a while longer.'

Chapter Fifty

It was on Saturday that Megan accepted defeat. She knew that she could no longer ignore the future; it was looming ahead and approaching at an alarming speed. On Monday she would be returning to work and the following day Nathan would depart for Southampton. Those were the stark realities. The emptiness his leaving would bring was beginning to haunt her. She loved him so much, had never known that to be with one special person could bring such happiness. But as yet Nathan had never once said that he loved her. Had he discovered that these two weeks had been sufficient to 'get her out of his system'? She was sure that his parents were hoping so, and that he would be able to return to a life with Alison. After all, she was someone they had always known, a girl from their own background. Megan went to the front window, wondering whether she would often stand here in the weeks and months after he'd gone, remembering; even fruitlessly hoping to see his car turn the corner.

And then her spirits began to lift as she saw him draw up outside. It was one of those rare cloudless October days, and when he came in he brought its freshness with him. 'Morning, sweetheart, it's a great day out there. How about we go visit our favourite park?'

They decided to walk and as they passed Chaplin Road, Megan told him that the famous Reginald Mitchell who had designed the legendary Spitfire had grown up nearby. 'He went to Queensberry Road School as I did,' she said. 'Of course that was before my time.'

'Hey, is that a fact? That was a fantastic plane, an incredible design – it changed the outcome of the war. Wow, honey, I never realised he was born in your Dresden.'

'He wasn't actually born here, I think that was near Talke on other side of the city, but this is where he grew up.'

'So he would have known this park then?'

'I'm sure he would.' She smiled up at him as they went through the large gates and began to enjoy the autumn sunshine as they strolled, smiling at the squirrels as they darted among the trees. The shouts from teams of young boys playing football created a different atmosphere from their previous visit, and as they drew aside more than once to let children run by, Megan glanced up and saw Nathan frown.

'It's much busier with it being the weekend,' she explained. 'Does it bother you?'

He shook his head. 'Heck no, it's great to see kids having fun. But today, well...' They were heading towards what Megan thought of as 'their bench', but there was already a young woman there with a toddler in a pushchair and a small boy before her feeding the ducks. 'Damn. Sorry honey, but there's something I want to talk about, and I'd hoped...'

There was a note in his voice that made Megan's heart give a sudden lurch. Was this was going to be the time? Her whole life, all of her future hinged on what Nathan was going to tell her. Every instinct told her that they were meant to be together, that they were soul mates. Or was she being naive, too trusting? Her throat closed with panic. Could he be about to tell her that while it had been wonderful, their time together had served its purpose? Say reassuringly that she would go on to meet someone else; that he would never forget her but... And yet as she answered him, her voice was calm. 'I do know of a quiet place.'

Her tension grew to an almost unbearable level until at last they were going up an incline to a narrow deserted path. 'There's a bench further along,' she said, and led him to it. 'Not many people come up here because the colliery trucks run along the back. I used to come up here and read.'

Nathan took her hand in his and she felt a painful lump in her throat; the touch of his firm palm had become as familiar as her own. How would she bear it if...?

And then he raised it and touched each finger with his lips. 'Sweetheart, you know, don't you, that I'm in love with you.'

She felt such overwhelming relief, such bliss. She gazed up at him and said, 'I love you too. I feel as if we belong together.' And then they were in each other's arms with their kisses deepening, the only sound the gentle breeze rustling the trees. He smiled down at her, his eyes full of tenderness. 'But Megan, before I say anything else, I haven't been entirely truthful with you.'

She stared at him. 'How do you mean?'

'Do you remember last year when you asked me what I did for a living? I said that I was in administration and you assumed that I worked in an office?'

'But you do work in an office – don't you?'

'I do *have* an office, rather a large one, but that's not quite the same thing. And do you remember that I kept telling you not to worry about my taking time off?'

'Yes, of course.'

'I didn't have any reason to honey. I work for my father.'

'You mean it's a family firm? But why not say so?'

'You were just so cute worrying about my spending my money that I just let it run on.'

'You mean to sort of tease me?'

He smiled at her. 'It's a bit more than that. Dad started off with just one company making agricultural machinery, and then as time went on he expanded with others. We own several now.' Stunned, Megan could only gaze at him as he went on, 'So my darling, I thought you ought to know before ... oh heck, we both know that I'm going to ask you to marry me.'

She had never known such happiness could exist. She didn't care that marrying him meant living in America, she would go anywhere in the world if it meant she could be with Nathan. As for his revelation about his background she suddenly took a sharp intake of breath, her eyes widening in shock. 'You didn't trust me, did you? That's the real reason. You thought I might be more interested in your money than in you!'

'Honey, no...' Nathan was horrified. 'If it was just left to me I would never have concealed anything from you. But I'd made this promise to my parents – they wanted me to be careful...'

'Why, because they knew that I work in a factory?'

'Of course not; come on sweetheart, you know it happens. That a girl will marry a guy for the luxury she'll have.' He ran his fingers through his hair. 'I know it's a surprise, but I didn't expect you to react like this.'

Megan couldn't believe that her euphoria had so swiftly changed to anger. 'It's because I can't bear to think that you didn't trust me.'

'But I did, I do,' he protested. 'Otherwise I wouldn't have told you, at least not until after I'd proposed. I didn't need that proof, that reassurance. Megan, don't you know how much I admire you – your courage, your strength of character? I love the bones off you, honey.'

Megan sat gazing at him. It was true, if he had proposed to her first and then told her the truth, wouldn't she have been even more convinced that he didn't trust her? Her sudden anger began to evaporate only to be followed by a stab of guilt. She'd tried so hard to suppress the name, even the unknown image. She said slowly, 'And what about Alison? I feel awful...'

'There's no need to feel that at all, honey. She knew I was coming over here to meet you again.'

'She did?'

Nathan nodded. 'She's a great girl and I'm hoping you'll eventually become friends.' He put out a hand to cover her own trying to reassure her. 'And now that I know what love really is ... even if you'd turned me down, I wouldn't have gone ahead and married her. She deserves better than a husband living a lie.'

'But what about your parents – they'll blame me!'

He shook his head. 'Of course they won't. I talked to them before I came over, so it won't be the greatest surprise. I know they'll love you, just as I do. As for your working in a factory, will it make you feel any better if I tell you that they met when my mother served Dad pancakes in a diner?'

She stared at him in amazement.

He grinned. 'It's the gospel truth.' He leaned forward to kiss her. 'You know what your problem is – you worry too much.' And then his voice was gentle as he said, 'Come with me, honey, we need to do this properly.'

Megan followed him back along the path and down the incline, until they reached the same spot where they had first kissed. Nathan turned to face her. 'Remember?' he murmured. 'I thought I would ask you here, where it all really began. Before then sure there was an attraction, but as soon as I held you in my arms I knew that I couldn't just leave and go back to the States. Megan, you're the love of my life,' his voice became intense, 'You might think I'm crazy after such a short time, but please say you'll marry me.'

'If you're crazy then I am too.' Leaning up she gently kissed him and said, 'Yes, a thousand times yes.'

Chapter Fifty-one

The engagement ring was chosen in the exclusive Pidduck's Jewellers in Hanley. Nathan's request had immediately brought the manager in his black jacket and pinstriped trousers to attend to them. After shaking his hand, Nathan drew him aside and murmured a few words and then Megan was ushered to sit on a gilt chair before a showcase while the manager bustled away and then placed before her a velvet tray with a small selection of exquisite diamond rings.

She still couldn't believe that all this was happening, that she and Nathan in a matter of only two weeks could have reached this certainty, this belief in their future together. She knew that everyone else would as Nathan said, think that they were crazy. Yet she had no doubts. And she knew that he was equally confident. It had been fate that had brought him to Bethesda, fate that had taken her there on that one particular Sunday morning.

'Is there one that you particularly like?' Nathan's voice was low and encouraging and she glanced up to meet his reassuring smile. She instinctively knew that the rings before her, their stones sparkling in the afternoon light were ones that most girls could only dream of. Drawn to one, with one large square cut diamond and surrounded by smaller stones, she hesitated ... the tiny tag portrayed only a serial number...

Nathan was smiling to himself as he watched her anxious expression, guessing what was in her mind. Bless the girl, she still hadn't really understood.

'What a lovely surprise!' Celia welcomed them into the hall with a warm smile and led the way into the drawing room, where Megan turned towards her with a glowing face and held out her left hand to display the beautiful diamond solitaire on her third finger.

Celia was stunned. Then recovering herself, she went to kiss Megan on the cheek and to shake Nathan's hand. 'Congratulations! I can't believe it, when did all this happen?'

'This morning,' Megan said. 'Isn't it beautiful? I can't stop looking at it.'

Celia gazed at the ring and seeing the sparkling clarity of the stone knew that she had been right about the young American's background. 'It's a wonderful choice. But just a minute, I must go and call Janet...'

Within seconds Janet had joined them, her face wreathed in smiles. 'I couldn't be happier for you, lassie.' Megan went to show her the ring and after it had been duly admired, Janet said, 'You make a fine couple and,' she turned to Nathan, 'you are a very lucky young man.'

He put an arm around Megan's shoulders. 'I know that.'

Celia wasn't sure exactly how she felt about it. She was thrilled for Megan, for both of them, but after only two weeks? Whirlwind courtships had been frequent during the war, but that had been because people had seized happiness while they could. I should have foreseen this she thought. It was obvious the other night how much in love they were – but the other side of the Atlantic? I'm going to lose her Celia thought and it was only then that she realised just how much Megan, sitting opposite and holding hands with her fiancé, had become part of her life.

'I know you're going to think it's all a bit rushed,' Megan said, 'but we know we're doing the right thing.'

'By the time Megan is able to join me and with the residency restrictions once she arrives, it will be quite a few months before we can actually get married,' Nathan said. 'So don't worry, if she changes her mind and decides I'm a monster, she'll have plenty of time to back out.'

Megan laughed. 'I don't think there's much danger of that.'

Nathan hesitated, 'We were wondering, whether either of you have any plans for tonight?'

Celia shook her head. 'No, just a quiet evening with the wireless.'

'We'd intended to go dancing at this Trentham ballroom I've heard so much about. But now, we'd sure love you and Janet to join us for dinner instead at the George in Burslem. That place has become kinda special to us.'

'And I'm going to wear the blue cocktail dress,' Megan announced, her face glowing with happiness, 'and I might even have a glass of champagne. It's been a wonderful day and we can't think of anyone we'd rather share it with.'

Celia felt a lump in her throat, and then glancing across at Janet saw her smile with pleasure. 'I think,' she said softly, 'that I can speak for both of us when I say there is nothing we'd like more.'

Early on Sunday morning, still full of adrenalin from the previous day, Megan knocked first on Clarice's front door and then on Rita's. 'I wondered if you could pop round for a minute – say in about half an hour?'

Clarice was clutching a tea towel. 'Yes I can love.' As she turned away she said over her shoulder, 'Did I see in the Sentinel that your friend Eunice had a little boy?'

Megan nodded. 'Yes I saw it too; the baby must have come early. I'll see you later then.'

The two neighbours arrived together, and once in the sitting room waited expectantly. 'So,' Rita said, 'what's all this in aid of.'

Megan had hidden her left hand behind her back, but now she held it out.

'Well, I'll go to the foot of our stairs!' Clarice said. 'You haven't wasted much time.'

'It's a bit too quick if you ask me.' Rita leaned forward. 'Let's have a closer look at that ring. Glory, he must be worth a bob or two.'

'Yes,' Megan said quietly, 'I think he is.'

'It's beautiful, really beautiful, and I'm thrilled for you,' Clarice said. 'That night he came round we could see you were made for each other,' she hesitated, 'but…'

'I know what you're thinking. But there was no sense in waiting; he's leaving for America in a couple of days.'

Clarice gazed keenly at the girl she'd seen grow up. 'You are sure, aren't you love?'

'Yes, I am.'

'Then,' Clarice said. 'I'm really happy for you. We all liked him, didn't we Rita?'

Megan said, 'He wants me to follow him to America and for the wedding to be over there.'

'What, immediately?' Clarice glanced at her with alarm.

'Yes or at least as soon as possible.'

They both stared at her in shocked silence, then Rita said, 'I'll have to forgo a new hat then!'

Megan laughed and then gazed at them both. 'I'll never forget all you've done for me. After all, you were the ones who gave me the push I needed. If it hadn't been for that, none of this would have happened.'

'I've always held that one thing leads to another,' Clarice said, but she found herself fighting tears. This was wonderful news, of course it was, but even so her voice shook slightly as she said, 'We're going to miss you, lass.'

'I'll miss you too, both of you.'

In Lightwood, Celia was preparing, with heart-felt relief, to bid farewell to her house-guest. She only hoped that James appreciated the supreme effort she had made on his behalf. Although judging by Verity's raised voice in the hall last night and her dash upstairs after the phone call to New York, Celia's fears about their marriage hadn't been imagined ones.

Verity came into the drawing room. 'Well, I'm all packed,' she said. 'My mother's expecting me for lunch, so I'd better make a start.'

'I'm so glad your parents had a good break in Madeira.'

'I'd just to thank you Celia, for your hospitality.'

'It's been a pleasure.' Celia moved forward and tried to convey warmth in her polite kiss. 'Have you said goodbye to Janet?'

'Not yet, but I will. She's a funny old stick isn't she? But I still think you're lucky to have found such excellent paid help. Still, I suppose it's because of her background.'

Celia winced. Paid help? Janet was so much more than that. 'Background is crucial as far as you're concerned, isn't it?'

'But of course.' Verity's tone was one of surprise. 'You can always tell good breeding. Isn't it everything?'

Celia gave up. She had tried, and she didn't like to accept defeat, she was almost beginning to hope that there *was* to be a divorce. She could survive a scandal. But it was becoming increasingly difficult to pretend, even to her son, that she could ever become fond of his wife.

Chapter Fifty-two

Sunday afternoon was spent discussing their plans. Nathan stared at Megan who was sitting opposite him in one of the darned uncomfortable armchairs. 'Honey, it's crazy for you to be shut away in a factory on our last day together. Wait until Tuesday, when I've left for Southampton.'

'But I'm due back tomorrow – I gave my word. They were good enough to let me have the time off, Nathan. I don't like to let people down.'

'But it's only one extra day and surely you'll be handing in your notice anyway?'

She stared at him in astonishment. 'I hadn't even thought about it, not yet.'

'But you'll have lots to do, to arrange, before you can follow me. There's your passport, then you'll have to go to London and apply to the American Embassy for the correct visa. All of your personal stuff to sort out, clearing this house, that sort of thing. And to be honest there's no need for you to carry on working, not any more.'

Megan looked at the small sitting-room which held so many memories, finding it difficult to believe that she would be leaving it forever. Then she turned to him. 'I still think I should go in to work.'

Seeing the determined set of her chin, with a sigh Nathan capitulated. 'Okay, if you insist. We'll just have to meet at lunchtime. But before I go maybe you could tell me the name of your nearest bank, because I'll need to arrange an account for you.'

Megan made to protest but he said, 'Honey, will you forget that pride of yours? Just think about it. You'll have to leave work in order to make all the arrangements. And you'll still have rent to pay, and other bills. Of course I should take care of things.'

Megan stared at him. 'I suppose I've become so used to managing on my own, struggling on my own – and I have coped you know...'

He smiled at her. 'Back home we'd call you a tough cookie. But you've got me now sweet-heart.'

The decorating shop was struck into silence, but only briefly.

'Yer never...'

'Do you mean you'll be going to live in America? But you've only known him five minutes!'

'I hope you know what you're doing, love.'

'You're bloody mad, girl,' Lizzie said, 'traipsing half-way across the world. There's no knowing what you'll find when you get there.'

There was lot of head-shaking and it wasn't until break that Megan could try to reassure everyone, explaining that she'd spoken to Nathan's parents on the phone, and remembering the warmth in Elizabeth's voice, she said, 'They're lovely people honestly; you don't have to worry – everything's above board. And,' she paused, 'I didn't want to wear it at the bench but...' she unfastened a fine chain around her neck on which she'd threaded the engagement ring.

'Flaming Nora, he's definitely on the level then. And he must be a millionaire!' Flo said. 'We're all delighted for you aren't we girls?' There was a chorus of agreement mixed with a few envious glances.

'And if it doesn't work out and you have to come back,' Minnie said, 'there's always my spare room you could use until you got yourself sorted out.'

'Thank you Min, I'll remember that.' Megan gazed at them all with affection. 'You know, I'm going to miss you lot.'

Afterwards she went over to an expectant Miss Dawson. 'I've never seen such a fine ring,' she said when shown it. 'And I think you're sensible enough to know what you're doing; although I wouldn't say that to everyone after two weeks. I'm really pleased for you.'

'One thing I plan to do when I get there is to see if I can send food parcels to Bill, the boys would love that.' Megan hesitated, 'Miss Dawson, do you think I'd be able to paint a personal plate? I'd rather like to take one with me to show Nathan and his family. I'd put my name on the back so it couldn't ever be sold.'

'Well, I'd have to clear it with the decorating manager,' Dora began, then she nodded, 'I'm sure he'll allow it, and as you've been with us a long time he'll probably let you have a gold signature.'

'Thank you,' Megan smiled gratefully at her. 'I just hope I can cope over there. There will be so much to learn, to get used to.'

Dora smiled at her. 'The fact that you're English will count for a lot. You'll be absolutely fine.' As Megan went back to her bench, Dora gazed after her. What she was doing was a huge undertaking but all credit due to her; she'd taken advantage of every opportunity. When she remembered the quiet and mousy girl who had first joined them – she'd always liked Megan, but who would have ever have imagined...

Chapter Fifty-three

It was a long and frustrating wait and because of the legalities involved, almost three months before Megan was able to leave for America. The week before she left, she said her last goodbyes, going up to visit Eunice who, with her adorable baby son in her arms, was still claiming a part in the romance. 'I was with you when you first saw him, remember? We wish you every happiness don't we, Ben?'

Ben looked across at Megan and at the expensive ring on her finger. 'You've certainly come up smelling of roses,' he said and she could hear envy, even bitterness in his voice. She looked around at the small front room with its inevitable baby clutter. Living with someone else, no matter how kind, wasn't an ideal beginning to married life.

And then at last, with all the emotional farewells over she found herself among other excited passengers at the rail of the Queen Mary, waving to the crowds on the quayside, where she could just make out Celia and Janet with the tall figure of Robert Marsden behind them. She thought of the last passionate hours that she and Nathan had spent together; to their joy in each other, their longing to be able to fully express their love. Their separation had seemed endless. As for his final airmail – she almost knew it by heart.

My darling girl, I've missed you so much. I'll be waiting when you dock in New York, where we'll stay for a few days before flying on to Kansas City. Everyone here is sure looking forward to meeting you – Mom has even bought new drapes for your bedroom while you're staying there. As you know, I won't be far from you. Helen is already looking at bridesmaid's dresses and Mom is full of plans. It's wonderful news that Celia and Janet are planning to be with you on the actual day. We are going to be so very happy, honey. Thank you for giving up so much to be with me, for leaving your friends and the Potteries. Meanwhile, every time you hear the Irving Berlin song, 'Always', then think of me, I can't wait to see you again...

She remembered the snapshot he'd sent her of the beautiful house, surrounded by trees; sprawling and spacious with a veranda running along its length. She still couldn't believe that this was going to be her home. Yet Megan knew that once the voyage was over, there would not only be new horizons and a new life – she would be able to join the man she loved.

442

And then with a low deep rumble and sense of vibration beneath her feet there came the deafening sound of the ship's horn and at long last it slowly began to move.

The publishers hope that this book has given you enjoyable reading. Large Print Books are especially designed to be as easy to see and hold as possible. If you wish a complete list of our books please ask at your local library or write directly to:

Magna Large Print Books
Magna House, Long Preston,
Skipton, North Yorkshire.
BD23 4ND

This Large Print Book for the partially sighted, who cannot read normal print, is published under the auspices of

THE ULVERSCROFT FOUNDATION